To Vivienne
Best v-
Paul
Happy Reading! 😊
Dec' 2023

Colour is my day long obsession, Joy
and Torment......

Claude Monet

'Art of Revenge'

by

Paul Graeme

A big shout out to family and friends for your support, help and encouragement with this book you know who you are – Thank you all

'Art of Revenge'
Chapter One
Blood Red

'Quinacridone and pyrrolidone co-precipitated'

Deep dark bluish red

Ross Campbell slumped down onto the chair, his face drained of life. Pale and distraught he placed his one and only real possession in front of him on the café table, a Nikon 35mm roll film camera from the early 1980's. Now, in the digital age it is viewed as 'old technology' but in its day was 'state of the art'. Originally 'cool' and ergonomic with chrome and black livery. Ross held his 'Nikki' in high esteem and had always treat it like a favourite son, but today it was covered in blood-stained fingerprints, and resembled more of a murder weapon than a means for capturing the ever-present tragedies of life as 'art'. Just like Ross, the camera had taken its knocks over the years, its lettering and name were fading, its body worn smooth and revealing the base metal in places, antique shops now call this wear 'patina', in reality it was just loved and used and most importantly still did its job. A good and faithful friend, bought new, its cost had represented a sizeable chunk of his student grant but now it was worth a fraction of what he had paid for it originally. He'd spent his morning trawling through the backstreets of the capital as he often did. Photographing the 'real London' as he saw it, capturing its 'rawness' and giving a visual voice to the lost and struggling souls that slept rough or drank their bleak existences into oblivion. Ross sat trance like and stared at his hands, he held them palm up in front of him, almost in a religious gesture asking for help or forgiveness. They were covered in dried blood, it wasn't his! Sitting motionless he was unaware as Val, the owner of the café came and stood beside him and stared at the blood, 'My God Ross what have you done? Are you hurt?' she said. He turned to Val and just shook his head, 'it's as good as murder', Ross muttered. Val immediately sat down and held one of his outstretched hands, it was ice cold, like death itself. 'What have you done? Just tell me Ross, please just tell me, it's OK' she said with a warmth in her voice, 'you can tell me'. 'I found him' said Ross, 'Who? Who did you find' asked Val, after what seemed like an eternity Ross eventually spoke, 'one of the rough sleepers' he stared again at the congealed blood, 'Poor bastard, must have fallen when he was drunk, smashed his head open, he might even have been attacked, I don't know what happened, but he was dead Val, I tried to help him, but he was dead, dead'. Ross shook his head in despair, 'It's almost legalised murder,

4

people having to sleep rough night after night and this fucking government doesn't give a damn'. Val breathed a huge sigh of relief as she said, 'my God, Ross, I thought you had done something bad', 'no, no, I just wanted to help him that's all, that's all I've ever done, tried to help,' said Ross. Val tightened her grip on his hand, which now began to warm with her touch. 'Go and get cleaned up', she said, now rubbing his arm and as she stood up smiled and in a warm comforting almost motherly tone repeated 'go and get cleaned up, I'll be back'. Ross stood in the café toilets and washed a 'strangers' troubled life from his skin and watched the lifeless crimson water spiral in the bowl and then disappear away down the sink, never to be seen again. He stared at his face in the mirror and shook his head disconsolately as he thought about life and its unfairness. Despair was now rapidly being replaced by anger, he took a deep breath and slammed the side of his fist against the wall, the despair that had consumed his soul seemed to escape from his body along with his breath. He splashed water over his face and then rubbed his wet hands through his uncombed hair. His normal composure began to return, he had witnessed scenes of human despair before, but this morning's experience had angered and unsettled him. After a few moments he returned to his table to find a cup of coffee waiting for him, Val he thought, 'you're a good sort', without friends what did you have, what did anyone have. On the empty table opposite, lay a discarded local newspaper which he rescued and brought to his table. Ross hadn't read a newspaper in years, he despised the media, the right-wing voice of the Tories' but he felt desperate and needed a distraction, anything, just to occupy his mind. He glanced at the headings 'West Ham in dramatic comeback', he sighed bloody 'sport' who gives a damn he thought, nothing but overpaid wannabee celebrity sportsmen. His eyes glanced through the items for sale section, but there was a problem, as usual he didn't have any money, keep going he thought, lifting his now half empty cup of lukewarm coffee that had left a perfect circular stain on the table. He was just about to take a sip, as sipping normally spun out the coffee and his day, when a heading caught his eye and without warning re-ignited his earlier despair and anger. He read, '*It used to be called graffiti now its contemporary street art*', Ross read on, '*Yet another work by the 'unknown' artist whose nom-deplume is the only clue to his or her identity,* nom-deplume Ross laughed to himself, it's a 'tag' man, a 'tag' he repeated in his head, the street artists signature. The 'papers' can't even get that right he thought or was it their way of de-sensitising the subject for their liberally minded middle-class reader, making it socially acceptable and appealingly 'arty'. Ross read on, he knew that some street artists were making money out of the current art establishment trend for what they described as 'gritty street realism'. The article described yet another piece of street art that had been enclosed behind Perspex to protect it from vandals. Don't they get it, that's exactly what it is, a protest, an act of anarchy, someone saying 'I don't give a damn, this is what I think, this is me, I'm no politician, I'm just like you, this is my voice, my protest'. Ross saw the establishment manipulation of street art as hegemony of the worst possible kind, it diluted real voices and feelings. It even made 'urban art' seem almost respectable and like a raging storm at sea, it created huge destructive waves that rounded off and dispersed the jagged stones of anarchy, stones that could and should stick in the throat of authority, choking them, which in turn released their grip and control of society. The article continued *'this current body of work by the now famous but unknown artist, unknown that is apart from his street nom-deplume SPOOKZ could be worth as much as two hundred and fifty thousand pounds, if it could be safely removed and then sold at one of the major auction houses'*. Ross had to re-read the last sentence again, he couldn't believe it, 'SPOOKZ, SPOOKZ, SPOOKZ' he kept repeating the name in his head, as if to convince himself this was real. He couldn't believe it, he knew the identity of this so called 'unknown artist', he should do, they had been, 'been', being very much in the past tense, close friends for nearly nineteen years, but things had changed dramatically towards the end of their friendship. Ross's almost forgotten hatred of the 'unknown artist' was like a smouldering fire doused with the petrol of painful memories, it now exploded, flared, and roared out of control. Ross saw him as the enemy, now just another establishment lackey that pretended he still cared about people and real issues, but he was now just some cheap 'art whore' who would do anything for money. This current media frenzy just reinforced his bitterness, perhaps there was also a touch of jealousy, but it wasn't to do with money, no, this was personal, very personal. Inside Ross there was a growing anger that was morphing into a 'target', an overriding aim to strike back at 'the unknown artist' his former one-time friend and fellow street artist John Noble. Maybe the press would pay handsomely for his story, 'Mysterious Street artist unmasked' but Ross had never been that interested in money, thirty plus years as a street artist, defacing buildings, living in squats, said it all. 'No' this wasn't about money, he wanted revenge, anonymous revenge, if possible, but he didn't really care, he was incensed and this thought of revenge was now like a drug rush to him, a major driving force and purpose in his life that had been missing for some time. Ross was by nature compulsive, proactive, the anarchist's hedonist, but he realised this needed planning, like a military operation, a major bombing campaign would be required? Ross laughed at his own street terminology, 'Bombing' meant a major defacement of buildings with street art over a wide area, but he knew the 'press' would describe such a demonstration, as an unlawful and mindless act of graffiti and vandalism spread across a respectable neighbourhood. Ross thought perhaps such an indiscriminate campaign wouldn't suit his plans' he needed a slow burn, wanted to be the irritant in the shell of conformity 'the beginnings of a Pearl of destruction' that would grow and become a large and substantial headache. 'Yes', he thought, that was it he needed to be more like a drone, identifying a specific target and taking decisive and focused actions. Ross thought that Dylan Thomas had it just right when he penned 'rage, rage, against the closing of the light', rage, is the fuse that ignites the deepest emotions, and he now wanted to fight. 'Penny for them', a quiet voice muttered, it shook Ross out of his almost catatonic state of inner thought. It was Val Benson, the owner of the Pink Flamingo café in which Ross was currently sitting, 'how are we now' she said, 'OK, OK, and thanks for, well you know...' replied Ross. Val just nodded, she could see he felt better and was more like his usual self. 'I was miles away' said Ross, 'so I gathered, I could see you were engrossed in that paper you were reading, I could almost hear the cogs clicking in that little brain of yours' said Val. 'Little that's about the size of it, but once they start whirring – well there's no stopping them and anyway you need something to focus your ambitions and desires upon,' replied Ross. 'Desires! Now that sounds interesting, new girlfriend perhaps? Replied Val. 'New! It's been that long, I don't even think you could say I have an old one' said Ross now raising a brief smile. He continued 'No, it'll be a little more important than that, perhaps I'll tell you all about it one day, just before it hits the tabloids eh', Ross smiled again as he said, 'only joking', although he knew deep inside, he probably wasn't. Val was a good sort, Ross had known her for some five years, she was something of a surrogate mum for him, well that's how he thought about her. She wasn't a great deal older than Ross maybe ten years at most, he didn't know for sure, she could be his age, he wasn't very good at telling peoples ages but always got a shock when he found out, sometimes thinking 'my God' they look older than that and they're actually younger than me! How old does that make me look? Val was tall, slim, and rather elegant even in her blue nylon char lady 'chic' over-coat, with tied back long greying hair now recently complemented with the addition of a broad pink coloured streak, specially chosen to celebrate the café's recent change of name and exterior 'colour'. The 'Pink Flamingo' surprised and confused many people who always for some reason assumed it was some sort of new trendy lefty café probably frequented by the LGBT community amongst others, much to Val's bewilderment. However, Val always saw the funny side of people's presumptions, especially when she had changed the name of the café on a whim to celebrate her sixty fifth birthday, from the original name of 'Benson's Milk Bar', which had been a family-owned dynasty for the provision of sandwiches, drinks and more importantly gossip for over one hundred years. After re-branding the cafe, Val was immediately approached by an LGBT magazine and some of the local papers who offered her some free advertising which she gratefully accepted but never let on about the real reason for the café's change of name, which when she looked back was probably quite silly but had put it down to the eccentricity of her impending old age. However, the papers interest had served her well and business was still good despite the competition from the major high street cafes that had opened up nearby. Maybe her success was her enduring charm but realistically she knew it was more likely that you could still get a Bacon sarnie and a cuppa in the Pink Flamingo for under three pounds. 'So come on Ross, spill the beans, what's it all about, I could do with a bit of excitement?' 'Oh, nothing much', he replied guardedly, 'just the start of a new adventure', 'does that mean I won't have to give you free meals in future, because your always skint', replied Val. For the first time that day Ross laughed, 'I'm afraid this venture like most of my life's endeavours isn't' a money maker, it's more of quest, yeah, a quest, that sounds good Val, Ross's quest'. He liked the idea of a quest, very Arthurian, but only this one wouldn't be very gentlemanly, no, he saw himself very much as the Black Knight in the proceedings. 'Well Val, I'm going to push off before you ask me to give you a hand with the washing up' said Ross, 'You wash up, yeah like when you have ever done anything remotely domestic', she sarcastically replied. 'Can't help your nature, I'm an anarchist, always have been and always will be'. 'Yeah, whatever' replied Val shaking her head in total disbelief, 'but you still like a free cup of coffee you anarchists, go on then push off and cause some mischief elsewhere and I'll just tidy up after you shall I' said Val laughing. Ross collected up his array of belongings, his newfound buoyant mood subsided slightly when he looked at his blood-stained camera, but he now felt empowered and grabbed his camera, lighter, tobacco and the all-important newspaper that had acted as a catalyst for his newfound determination and resolve. Ross stepped out of the door and Val watched him walk away, she liked Ross and thought he reminded her of her late brothers somewhat wayward son, at heart a 'good sort' but unfortunately the possessor of an unpredictable and at times destructive nature. She didn't know a lot about Ross's background, knew he came from a little village somewhere in Scotland and that'd he'd left there in his late teens. Just like most people's neighbours you knew the face and name, you passed verbal pleasantries on a daily basis, but their real stories were always hidden behind closed doors, sometimes physical but usually psychological ones. Val turned the sun faded café sign to closed, switched off the dim yellow lights that had shone across the ageing Formica topped tables, that were described by one of her young professional customers as 'bang on trend', she laughed to herself, and half wished she was also 'bang on trend'. As the pale orange sky of winter gradually disappeared into the night in a small East London borough situated in what the estate agents now called an 'up and coming area', their euphemism for 'an area where people without money were being squeezed out and the young professional with money was moving in'. Across town in W1 'up West' the spotlights shone brightly in one of Mayfair's newest contemporary galleries. Named 'Contemptuous', it proudly displayed the latest offering of works by 'SPOOKZ', the media's favourite 'unknown street artist'. The gallery had polished wooden floors and the ubiquitous white painted walls. The exhibition was being orchestrated by the owner Dave Hemmings, of medium height and stocky build, dressed in a grey suit and white open necked shirt, in his early fifties, dubbed contemptuously and somewhat jealously by his rivals as the 'Arthur Daley' of the burgeoning contemporary art scene. Dave stood holding what appeared to be one of the free glasses of vintage champagne on offer to his assembled guests, who attended the opening of this 'new vision' by 'SPOOKZ'. Dave was actually drinking lemonade, it wasn't that he didn't drink alcohol but he was like the best Las Vegas gamblers, who pretended to be drinking alcohol to lull their fellow players into maybe having a drink or two and thus dulling their senses just enough to make them vulnerable to a killer hand of, even, very average cards, or in the case of his clients paying well over the odds for nothing more than media hyped art. Dave was savvy and extremely sharp, a man of the streets and he knew people and what their expectations were. A one-time second-hand car salesman but as Dave was always quick to point out to his detractors, they were Bentleys and Astons he used to sell. Now he had turned his sales expertise and guile to the mysterious but highly profitable world of contemporary 'street' inspired art, something he didn't really rate, a world of incomprehensible and wordy artist statements with their pointless epithets of 'de-construction, symbiosis, parallel shifting paradigms'. It was all 'bollocks' to him but the supposedly 'art aware, socially minded left-wing middle-class trendies' that attended his gallery bought into it all, they thought if ordinary 'working-class' people didn't rate something then it must be 'real art'. Dave considered himself to be more of a Monet man, Waterlilies that kind of 'thing', now that was real art to him. Dave was talking to a well-dressed couple in their mid-thirties, his typical 'punters', that's how he viewed them, everyone was a punter in his world of wheeling and dealing, at one time he sold cars now it was art, he didn't see a difference, knowing he could sell 'anything'. Dave happily and convincingly 'smoozed' about the street art on show and threw in all the 'happening phrases' socialism, inequality, deprivation, political angst, in fact all the topics that seemed 'on trend' in the contemporary art world and the media, especially the media. It attracted the socially conscious well heeled, who could at least convince themselves they were doing a little something to promote awareness of these 'social' issues but the fact that not a single artwork was priced at under twenty thousand pounds would probably gain an ironic smile from even the most 'light weight' of socialists. Dave was a firm believer in the mantra that 'bull shit baffled brains' and he could convince anyone that not only was this great 'street art' but it genuinely was a sound investment as prices for these works of art had soared recently and there seemed an inexhaustible appetite for more of the same. Dave spouted forth his little spiel and on finishing said to the couple, 'well, I'll leave you to take it all in and if you want any further help, just ask Simon our resident contemporary art guru'. He then pointed to a sagacious looking silver haired man, dressed in a quality but somewhat tired 1980's blue blazer complete with gold buttons, oversized lapels, and a light dusting of dandruff. Simon was a 'jaded has-been' an ex-fleet street hack who had reported on the art scene for over thirty years and had become tired of its falseness, he had suffered the indignity 'as he saw it' of having to describe Tracey Emin's un-made bed as 'art'. This betrayal of his true feelings combined with the gossip that surrounded his sacking for sexism in the workplace while under the influence of alcohol made him very much Dave's sort of bloke and an ideal employee. Dave had him on the Conservatives favourite kind of employment contract, the 'zero hours money spinner' for the employer of course. To Dave that was cash in hand jargon and as long as Simon could impress the punters with his undoubted knowledge of the current art scene, he was a definite asset. Dave excused himself and made his way to his own personal office which sat behind a rather grand looking six panelled mahogany door complete with a 'Private' sign written in 'Times Roman' antique gold lettering with the obligatory black shadows to emphasise the importance of its occupants. The door opened into a sumptuous interior 'ala Gentleman's club' which Dave referred to jokingly as his 'man-hogany' cave. As he entered the office he saw John Noble with his feet on the corner of his desk, cheeky sod he thought but John was the bringer of untold riches to Dave, just when he'd thought a very ordinary retirement for him was just a few years away. Now he was looking forward to a very promising future and retirement was very definitely on the back burner. 'Dave mate', John said brightly as he jumped to his feet and proffered a firm and friendly handshake. Dave poured them both a single malt in a pair of recently purchased Georgian Irish cut glass tumblers that complemented his period office look. John almost fell into the chestnut-coloured leather club chair as he said, 'nice glasses, spending the profits eh'. Dave looked and then smiled, 'it's made to go around John, enjoy it while you can, what's the point in being the richest man in the cemetery, anyway you look as though you're spending as well, nice suit, if not a little 'Farmer Giles-ish'. They both laughed as John pointed out that it was all the rage, 'you can put tweed with anything now, it's not just for crusty old colonels you know'. John continued, 'so, how's it going? Sales still strong?' Let me put it this way John, you couldn't paint them quick enough mate but it's all about supply and demand, there's a fine balancing act between a drip, drip, approach to the market to maintain exclusivity and getting the sales before trends change and they will, believe me they always do'. Dave now in full flow continued, 'I would tell you to go and have a look around the exhibition, but I know you can't be seen out there, this 'anonymity thing' is a bit of a nightmare to maintain but it makes great press, the papers love it'. John smiled and he said 'Well, there's only a handful of people that know the 'real me' so to speak '. 'Too right, happy days John, you, me, and Frances and maybe one or two of your former lay about arty friends'. 'Yeah, you never did get that squatting 'vibe thing' did you Dave'. 'Definitely not' replied Dave, remembering what damp, dilapidated shitholes most of them had been. He continued, 'it was just somewhere to doss till I made some cash and got myself going, it's never easy moving and surviving anywhere and London is probably the hardest but needs must, eh'. 'Is that how you saw us when we set up that squat together in Camberwell? As artistic dropouts, me, Fran, and the rest of them' replied John. 'Yes, there were some well...', he hesitated, 'shall we be kind and say some right characters eh, especially Ross', said Dave, no sooner had the 'name' left his lips and he realised his 'big' mistake. Dave quickly grabbed the bottle of whisky and gave John's glass a large top up and attempted to move the conversation on. It was too late, the very mention of Ross was an anathema to John, his smile disappeared along with the contents of his glass. 'What? That bastard, you must be joking, hopefully he's dead or maybe he's joined the ranks of his contemporaries on the streets, the downtrodden and the great unwashed, that loser disappeared from my life years ago, what a fuckin waste of space'. Dave waited for John's vitriol to subside before he joined in the conversation again. 'Hey, come on, be fair, none of you had a particular purpose in life then, did you? Art college during the day and daubing public buildings with ...', Dave almost made a second error and said 'graffiti' but corrected himself just in time to save himself from John's wrath yet again, '.... street art at night, about life's unfairness, it was all pretty pointless, wasn't it?' Dave continued attempting to thwart John's negativity, 'don't get me wrong, I did agree with your protests, but it took you a lot longer than me to see that protest alone doesn't make much of a difference to anything'. 'Little people' are powerless, and they can't change big things, the establishment won't allow it, there's people 'with' and people 'without', there'll always will be, and as they say, 'that's life'. John stared at Dave then slammed his glass on the desk and gave a loud ironic laugh and said, 'you're right, who gives a shit, more booze Dave'. 'That's more like it John, forget the past and take what you can and just remember what Getty said, *'The meek shall inherit the Earth but not the mineral rights'*. They both laughed at Dave's unexpected literary quote and then toasted their success with yet another fine single malt. Across the city in E8 'down East' Hackney, in the fading Turneresque orange winter light, wrapped up against the cold, Ross arrived back at his cold, empty and unwelcoming flat. As usual the lift was out of order, and he'd climbed the urine smelling stairs to the third-floor council flat he was lucky to have. 'Lucky' because without it, Ross would be joining the growing army of disillusioned and disadvantaged folk sleeping rough at night on the streets of one of Europe's premier and richest capital cities. As Ross approached his flat, his right leg seemed to drag and ache even more than usual, it was relatively imperceivable limp that seemed to worsen with the cold, an unfortunate childhood illness had left him with an affliction that had plagued his early life and some days its discomfort was a reminder of unhappier times. As he stood in front of a paint flaking and battered front door, he thought for a brief moment, wrongly as it turned out, 'well' at least the council will have fixed the door that was kicked in during a burglary over two weeks ago. Probably just bored kids had done it, stolen what few 'luxury' items he had, that's what Ross jokingly called them. A Bush portable TV from the 1970's which had been a birthday present when he was thirteen and his vintage JVC ghetto blaster that had entertained him and his friends on many a long hot summer afternoon in London's parks when they had very little else to do. Ross knew they were worthless but to him they were hugely sentimental items and some 'nobody' had stolen them, why he didn't know, they were about as saleable as a VHS Joan Fonda 'work out' video. Sad bastards he thought to himself but what really annoyed him was that they would end up dumped as trash somewhere around the estate when the thieves found out they had no value whatsoever. OK they weren't worth anything he thought but they carried happy memories and warm smiles from his past, unlike the present that didn't smile too much to him, but things were about to change dramatically not only for Ross but also for John Noble.

Chapter Two
Blue Ochre

'Asbestiform mineral, Sodium Iron Magnesium
Silicate Hydroxide'

Dark Blue

Ross looked around his dated and rather sober surroundings, at times he had been tempted to 'decorate' the walls with some of his own street art but didn't fancy being reported yet again by interfering neighbours to the local council for misuse of their property. The flat was to say the least, basic in the extreme, but he was a lot luckier than some of the poor souls he saw sleeping rough on the streets. Ross sat at his kitchen table that had at one time been a large wooden drum for electrical cable, he called it the 'Big Yo-yo' and had man-handled it himself from a disused construction site. He rolled a cigarette from what little tobacco he had remaining, shook his lighter, flipped open its metal top then spun the wheel with his thumb and the flint ignited a pale soft yellow petrol-based flame that flickered and provided the necessary spark for his inspirational cigarette. Taking a long slow drag he inhaled calmly and deeply, his body rose and fell with its stimulation. He gazed about the room and thought 'what did he physically have to show for thirty odd years living in London', very little apart from a handful of well-thumbed art books, which included his favourite 'giants' of the Pop and fantasy art movement, Andy Warhol, and Frank Frazetta. Standing upright and leaning against the books stood two photographs that were Ross's only conduit to his past, one a fading Polaroid colour photo taken in the 1970's with his baby sister Joanne, she would be in her late forties now, he would have been about nine when the picture was taken. The other photo showed him, John Noble, and some fellow students when they were at art college together in the early eighties, he recalled the day as though it were yesterday, remembering the laughter and good times, they had at one time been the very best of friends. The photo had been taken at the end of their first term just prior to the year Ross would be expelled for swearing at a lecturer who had considered his work too near the knuckle of bad taste, Ross had always pushed boundaries but on this occasion, he had pushed too far. This incident had galvanised his interest in street art, and he had never looked back, street art fuelled his passion for extremism and social justice as he saw it. John Noble stayed on at college and gained a reasonable if somewhat pointless qualification, but they remained close friends and formed a lethal and forceful street art partnership. Ross however had always been the real idealist, politics, the police, in fact any form of authority he saw as more than fair game and there was never any shortage of issues to target when Margaret Thatcher came to power. Ross took another drag on his cigarette and surveyed his dimly lit one bedroom council flat and thought if this is all I've got, then what have I got to lose, he was determined now more than ever to make a stand, he'd done it before but now it felt 'personal'.

In leafy Surrey, John Noble was returning home, he had left the grime of inner London some years ago when his fortunes had changed and money became less of a problem, he powered his Range Rover Vogue up his long tree lined drive. It was no ordinary 4WD either, this was the top of the range complete with all the requirements for his country lifestyle, with Louis Vuitton cases and a small but perfectly formed walnut veneered mini bar complete with vintage scotch. He aspired, when he'd made the right connections, to join rural shooting events frequented by the 'local gentry', after all there wasn't much point in looking like the country set in tweeds if you couldn't enjoy their pursuits. Now stepping out of the Range Rover he surveyed his detached period residence with pride, it was a style known in architectural circles somewhat disparagingly as 'Mock Tudor'. 'Yes', he thought to himself, 'nice one' John, not bad for a former London squatter and street artist. 'SPOOKZ' John's tag had appeared on all his street art, right from his late teens. All street artists had a tag, it identified them and their work to fellow artists and the casual passer-by, if they were prepared to look up from mobile phones or newspapers on their train journey as they commuted through the less salubrious areas of London. As John entered his hallway, he could sense that his wife Frances was in, perhaps it was one of those inexplicable senses that you just knew someone was there even though you couldn't see or hear them, maybe, he thought it was a sixth sense nurtured and finely tuned from years on the street avoiding night watchmen, the police, and other enforcers of the law. 'Frances', he shouted as he threw his car keys into the pot on the hall stand, no immediate recognition came, then eventually Frances's voice sounded from up above on the landing, 'be down in a minute just on the phone to mum'. Not that bloody woman, John thought, she had done everything to try and split them up over the years, always thinking that he wasn't 'quite' good enough for 'her' precious daughter. What really narked John was that the mothers dislike of him hadn't stood in the way of her accepting a nice little house in the country, from him, when her husbands 'investment Portfolio' had gone, as John succinctly put it 'tits up'. Frances had been one of the dread lock, sandal wearing hippies at the squat when John first met her. He used to mimic what he called her 'posh accent', Frances had always called it atonic, he wasn't sure what that had meant, he just knew she was well off and unlike most of

25

the other inhabitants of their squat, it didn't have to be a way of life for her. However, John knew that it was this eclectic mix of people from all walks of life that made the squat what it was, equal, honest and a constant source of entertainment. Frances had descended the stairs as John was still reminiscing, she had time to get near him and give him a nudge with her elbow, 'Earth calling John' she said, 'sorry luv, I was miles away' he replied. 'Somewhere interesting?' said Frances, 'yeah, I suppose, just thinking about our days at the squat and how much I fancied you, when you were a dreadlock, sandal wearing, vegetarian freak', 'I'll take that as a compliment' said Frances, half smiling. 'It was meant as one, I always wanted you' said John now staring intently at her. During their early years in the squat, she had been Ross's girlfriend, but he was careful never to mention 'that' name, it was all in the past and as he well knew, you didn't look back because you would, sooner or later trip up. 'So how did the meeting with Dave go?' said Frances, 'well, Dave is just Dave isn't he, that bloke could sell anything, but he's got some quality with me and that makes his life a lot easier doesn't it'. John continued, 'sometimes I wonder if I actually need his services, after all his gallery is creaming a good forty percent off the profits, that's a lot of money, just imagine what I could do with that'. 'Don't you mean us?' said Frances who took offence to John's selfishness and his ever-growing indifference to her feelings. John attempted to retrieve the situation, 'Well, err, obviously I mean us' he said quickly but Frances had felt for some time that she didn't necessarily figure in his long-term plans. 'So, I take it the current show is selling well if you're complaining yet again about Dave,' said Frances. 'I not complaining, I'm just saying he does very well on the back of me' snapped John. Frances shook her head, she was sick of his never-ending self-pity, 'yeah, we all know that but don't forget it was Dave who got you noticed and set up the gallery, you have the talent, and he has the connections, that's how a good business works isn't it?' Frances hated John when he went on like this, it had become somewhat repetitive the last couple of years, thinking he was the only one who did anything, she had supported him, without any thanks for over fifteen years through the 'ups' and the 'downs'. As Frances looked back, there had been a significant number of 'downs' she thought, John had got lucky that was all, and that luck was in no little part due to Dave who had suggested that he should go solo and leave the street scene per se to the radicals. Radicals like Ross, who would never amount to anything because their morals got in the way of making money. Frances now reminisced with fondness about their early years when they all shared their last squat in Camberwell, she had left art school without any qualifications, well, it didn't really matter because you didn't need a fine art degree to be creative or indeed be successful. They had many wild times in Camberwell, some of the parties were legendary, life seemed fun and straight forward, people just wanted to enjoy themselves. Nobody took anything seriously and John, Ross and even Dave who had always had an eye for a 'dodgy deal' and making a quick buck, seemed to sail through life without thinking too much about the present, let alone about tomorrow. Frances thought that she wouldn't mind going back to those days, when everything seemed simple and attainable, she had been happy then, there had been some happy times with John over the years but now things had changed between them, money had overtaken him, and it wasn't a pleasant addition to his far from flawless character. He seemed almost ruthless at times, and everyone and everything seemed expendable. Not that she had ever mentioned this to him, as he would always come back with the argument 'well what do you want out of life, I wasn't born with a silver spoon in my mouth like some' meaning Frances, she knew he could be a real tosser sometimes. It was funny that the very thing that most of them hadn't cared about became their undoing. They had squatted in Camberwell long enough to have some sort of rights under a legal system that they ironically had no regard for. With ever rising property prices in the capital and less desirable areas becoming newly intended places for gentrification, the owner of the property had offered them all a good sum at the time of two thousand pounds each to vacate the property. This in turn meant he could re-develop the property without any unnecessary publicity or legal costs. Most of the squatters were in favour of a nice little free handout, however Ross had refused point blank, he saw 'ownership' as an unnecessary and unfair distribution of wealth. Dave saw it as his opportunity to make a start in business and he would eventually use the money to start up a second-hand car business. John had mixed feelings, but he had always had a desire, especially as he grew older to look for the better things in life. Ross wouldn't take the money, and this caused a huge rift between him and John. They never really reconciled their differences and Ross never forgave John for selling his soul for as he put it at the time 'thirty pieces of silver'. Frances thought Ross was being unreasonable, she knew he had principles but that he was taking them just a little bit too far. Frances looked at John now and cursed her lack of judgement and control that had brought her relationship with Ross to an abrupt and painful end. On reflection she consoled herself that she had been young and foolish but her ignorance of the true facts surrounding the real reason for the breakup with Ross then and as it turned out even now were still unknown to her.

She was still unaware that John had tricked her at the time and had mistakenly clung to him as it appeared he was doing her a favour by offering a friendly and unbiased shoulder to 'cry on', how wrong could she have been.

Back in his one bedroomed council flat Ross had been drinking and a sudden rage raced through his whole being, who was he? What had he done with his life? He stood unsteadily, now somewhat drunk, but 'charged' by remorse, anger, and disbelief at his wasted life. Grabbing hold of the table he then upended it, cans of lager, books, papers, and the photographs fondly looked at not more than two hours ago were now scattered across the room. He kicked out at everything that could be reached and threw any item not fastened down about the flat, a muffled voice shouted from the flat next door 'hey keep the fuckin noise down dick head'. Ross shouted 'bastards' and continued to destroy his flat and its contents. After what seemed like an eternity of uncontrollable rage he slumped to the floor and passed out. When Ross awoke in the early hours of the morning, he had a thumping headache, his mouth was as dry as soot, at first, he couldn't remember what had happened but as he surveyed the destruction within his flat, it all came flooding back, the rage, the anger, the hopelessness he felt inside. As he looked at the destruction surrounding him, amongst the debris lay a Lou Reed CD, he stretched out his hand and picked it up, it still carried its original handwritten message on a faded white label 'Merry Xmas Ross love Frances xxxx'. He glanced through the list of tracks, he struggled onto his knees and placed the CD into his remaining 'worthless as it had seemed to his burglars' bargain car boot buy Stereo System, it had been one of the few items he hadn't managed to trash. As the first few chords of the piano sounded, a tear rolled down his face, his throat dry and feeling choked with his croaky voice he sang along and when he mouthed the words 'Perfect day' his heart lifted briefly, he wasn't really an emotional person but this song was 'their song', it always moved him and made the hairs on the back of his neck rise, and as he listened, one by one the tears began to roll down his face. As the song drew to a close, he mouthed the final lyrics '*you reap what you sow*' and in that moment knew that you had two options when you got as low as he was now, you spiralled into mind numbing drunken despair or you got angry and started to fight back. He had fought back before, life wasn't easy when you were on the bottom rung of life's ladder of success and living in squats had taught him much, but mainly how to survive. 'Yes', he was a survivor but more importantly also a fighter and could go a good fifteen rounds with the best of them. He'd been there before, he'd left squats, half dressed in the early hours of the morning when 'encouraged' to move on by some thugs hired by an absentee owner. He would then spend several weeks on the streets sometimes sleeping rough under railway arches, he'd even spent the odd night in a builders skip under a discarded carpet. 'Yes', he knew how to survive and years on the streets had made him wiser if not any richer. As he surveyed his nights destruction, he was savvy enough to know that he didn't want to be evicted by the council and knew the first step to stopping this action was to tidy up and get his flat and ultimately his life into some sort of order. He attempted to stand up, his knees ached with pain from years of kneeling on concrete pavements and roofs while creating his street art. 'God' he exclaimed as his face contorted in response to the pain, gradually as he stood up the pain began to subside. As he surveyed the mess in his room with its contents trashed and strewn across the floor it made the contents of your average skip seem almost designer chic. Ross started by putting the upturned table back on Terra-firma, he then picked up his precious and only physical connection to his past, the photographs and placed them on the table. He then pulled a chair upright and sat down staring at the photos, the one that depicted him with John and Frances at college now acted like a catalyst for his current thoughts, here were the two people that had moved him and his life the most, one he still yearned to 'love' and one he now yearned to 'hate'.

Chapter Three
Antimony Orange

'Antimony trisulphide'

Bright Orange

Several tedious hours later after squaring up what was left of his flat, Ross walked into his 'second home', well that's what Val described it as. 'My God!' she exclaimed 'you look terrible, what have you been doing?', 'bit of a rough night that's all, one of your breakfasts will sort me out, or finish me off if your regular level of cholesterol is anything to go by'. 'Cheeky beggar!' Go on take a seat then' said Val, laughing as she did so. As she disappeared with his order into the kitchen Ross carefully unfolded the piece of newspaper that he had kept from his previous visit to the café, the one that described the media's favourite 'Unknown Street Artist'. Ross knew that he would have to be careful and the method of any attack on John Nobles' Street art would have to be meticulously orchestrated as his 'target' would now undoubtedly have money and influence. He laid the article on the table, flattened it down with the help of a sugar bowl and an empty saucer left by the previous tenant of his table. He scanned the article again looking for the locations of John

Noble's most recent works. In a world of his own he was interrupted by Val 'come on put that away and get this down you' as she placed a large plate of eggs, bacon, sausage, and his favourite fried bread. 'I can't afford this' Ross said, looking at the overflowing plate in front of him, having originally just asked for a lowly sausage sandwich, the cheapest hot item on the menu. 'Don't worry about that' replied Val as she pulled a chair out and sat down next to him. She placed her hand on his forearm and said 'is there anything I can do for you, is it money?' 'It's always about money one way or another Val, but this time it's something more than that'. Ross had a steely determination in his eyes as he spoke, she was surprised at his directness, he was usually so relaxed, almost horizontal to the vicissitudes of everyday life. 'If its cash you need....' said Val, Ross interrupted 'hey I'm fine and you know I never borrow money'. 'Well, if you want to earn it instead there is always re-painting the sign at the front of the shop' Val replied. Ross jumped at this opportunity to pay for his breakfast 'OK, I'll take you up on that', he muttered as he chewed on a piece of particularly tough bacon. Val left the table and Ross tucked into his breakfast, he felt rejuvenated with every mouthful and his searing hangover began to subside. Wiping his plate clean with a final scrap of bread, he then sat back with his mind now keenly focussed on his quest and moved his empty plate to an adjacent table. He then stared at the newspaper article, which was now complete with a tomato ketchup stain, for the first time in hours he laughed aloud as he thought how appropriate because this could well be a bloody battle. Ross scanned the page looking for each location mentioned within the article, and his attention was drawn to the sentence 'where *the Art connoisseur or casual London tourist can visit and appreciate 'the unknown artists' best examples'*. Ross read on, he knew most of the locations mentioned and wanted to visit the most remote site first as an attack there would be easier than on one of the more centrally located works. It didn't take him long to select his initial target. The first engagement with the enemy would take place at a semi derelict builders' yard in the up-and-coming Borough of Stratford, where the New Olympic stadium now glistened in the golden winter sun as a beacon to all the property developers that would make another fortune out of one of London's poorest and neglected neighbourhoods. Ross knew the area reasonably well, he had a good idea where the yard was, there were a lot of new buildings under construction, so inevitably there would be night watchmen to be concerned about. It would be a challenge, but Ross wanted something to get his teeth into and this would take planning and guile, but he was good at that, and it would focus his thoughts. He was on a mission, and nothing was going to stand in his way. Val returned to Ross's table, 'feeling any better?' she asked, he nodded and replied, 'well you could say things are certainly shaping up for an interesting future', he then stood up and uncharacteristically for him, he kissed Val on the cheek and thanked her again.

Later, back at his flat Ross pinned the newspaper article to the wall on top of a map of inner London, he smiled looking at it thinking it looked like something from Churchills secret war bunker. He started to draw a series of freehand lines that linked the tourist addresses for the 'works of art' he laughed at the thought of the media description, the lines stretched from the article to the map like a spider's web indicating the prey's location. Now he proceeded to number them in ascending order of complexity, they would be targeted in a sequence of increasing difficulty with reference to their security features, whether they were overlooked and the remoteness of the location and so on. He knew most of the locations, but all would require a 'rekkie' as he didn't want to slip up before he had even got started. Ross hadn't been active on the streets for some time so he thought he would celebrate this momentous undertaking by checking out the 'tools of his trade' as he called them. From the cupboard that housed the electricity meter and a host of unwanted items he searched for and retrieved a 1970's haversack emblazoned with a large hand painted image of *Pink Floyd's iconic* prism on its flap. The prism had always represented a sort of new beginning for him, it had been his baptism into 'real music' as a teenager and now the idea of 'rebirth' seemed erringly apocryphal. He unceremoniously tipped its contents out onto the floor and variety of items clunked and clattered as he shook the haversack until it had revealed all its secrets. A selection of old tools which included a 'hammer' the multipurpose tool for all difficult scenarios when all else failed, a pair of bolt cutters for the unwelcome padlock or two. Then there was his 'piece de resistance' or as Ross called them 'his pieces of resistance' a variety of spray cans 'a rainbow selection' although black was probably his favourite colour as it gave symmetry to most street artists work. 'Black' highlighted and articulated his message, it was something of a magician's wand, and that's partly what Ross saw himself as 'an entertainer and a preacher', he took a bare wall and created movement and hopefully enlightenment. Long forgotten buildings were his canvas, walls that had once been a part of something vibrant and alive, a thriving factory, a bustling school, they all once had life within their confines and now they became his blackboard for a visual sermon. If people got his message that was 'job done', if they didn't, then maybe his artistic flair would capture their imagination and his message may then seep through over time like sap into a knot of a newly cut piece of timber, it would appear slowly at first but in time it would harden and become something more permanent. Just like soldiers on parade he lined up all his tools, now they were all present and correct, an army awaiting their commands. Ross, even though he was short of cash knew he would have to invest in some more aerosols, you didn't run out of paint during a sortie – only amateurs did that. Feeling buoyant having now set in motion his course of action, Ross decided he could afford a visit to the pub, he kept some emergency cash in a special little tin. An old St. Bruno tobacco tin, it had belonged to his grandfather, and it carried warm memories of a safe and distant childhood, it still had the faint aroma of tobacco even after nearly forty years. Its aroma stimulated his senses and conjured up memories of his grandfather letting him try to 'roll' a cigarette for him, although he always failed miserably, they were happy times for him, but like the tobacco now long since gone. He took some of the cash and popped it into his back pocket, grabbed a jacket and slammed the flat door behind him. As usual a group of youths were blocking the stairway and made no attempt to let Ross past. He took one look at them and thought about asking them to move but then thought 'what the hell' and took a bit of a run and just hurled himself into the group parting them and rolling them aside like skittles. Ross's inertia kept him moving forward and he simply rolled onto his feet and went on his way laughing. It felt good, he hated kids that had no respect for others and always thought 'the direct approach' like this would perhaps open their eyes, he knew it was probably wishful thinking, but thought 'you had to try'. Ross took the long way round to *The Grapes,* a cosy little old-fashioned pub that smelled of fag ash and stale booze, a traditional pub where people sat, drank, and chatted without incessant head banging music or worse still the aroma of cooked dinners and kids running around. *The Grapes* was built in 1890, at the height of Victorian imperialism and it still showed, ornate plaster ceilings and impressive frosted etched glass windows extoling the virtues of India Pale ale and other notable beverages of their time. Ross scanned around for a friendly face, but today there didn't seem to be any, well at least none he wanted to pass the time of day with. He looked again for old Bob, but he wasn't in, Bob was a friendly old fella who had worked for the *Courage Brewery* delivering ale with a dray and horses in his younger days and had a host of stories to tell. His favourite, Ross assumed it must be his favourite, as he seemed to recount it every time, he sat with him. It concerned the 'trick' of how to lift a very heavy full barrel of beer by rolling it and using the weight and movement of its contents to help manoeuvre it up and onto your wagon without doing yourself 'a mischief' as Bob put it. Ross made his way to the bar and was suddenly jostled by a young kid in a hoody, just as he was about to remonstrate, the kid pulled off his hood and said, 'Hey man watch where you're going you old git' then laughed, 'I was just about to give you a right mouthful' said Ross, he knew the kid, it was Karl, something of an understudy of his. He had taken him under his wing after dragging him from the path of an on-coming train a couple of years ago when the youngster had been trying to apply his tag to a building at a local depot. Ross didn't know how old Karl was, he guessed maybe seventeen ish, but not more than twenty, he was a likeable kid but more than a little on the reckless side. Ross had been like that at his age, Karl still enjoyed the thrill of the chase whereas Ross now preferred to be 'in and out' without any trouble. The kid still frequented the train stations and railway depots, it gave him a thrill, a rush of adrenalin, but Ross had lost friends and seen people lose arms and legs, dicing with the danger of moving trains. He understood the thrill of seeing your artwork on a passing train but sometimes the price to be paid was too high and he just didn't think it was worth the risk. The more Ross thought about his forthcoming quest, the initial first attack on the building site, the more he wondered if he could still do it, reticence grew, and his confidence seemed to ebb with increasing age.

Ross had seen this 'gremlin' appear in   older friends and now hesitated and thought maybe he could use an extra pair of eyes on this first job and anyway it wouldn't cost him more than a couple of pints, he decided to ask Karl for his assistance. Ross bought a couple of pints, and they sat down in a quiet little corner of the pub. Not wanting to tell the full story of what he was planning, he felt a little guilty about this deceit but thought about his grandfather's saying 'loose lips cost ships', 'no' he thought, it was strictly information on a need-to-know basis. Two more pints later and Karl was persuaded, he didn't ask any questions, well none that required a direct answer. Ross just said it was a grudge thing with a fellow artist, the street artists were usually a close-knit community but like gangs they had their own 'Post codes' and you entered another's territory at your peril. Ross simply said that some 'Tag' had stepped out of line and needed to be 'taught a lesson' as he put it. Karl didn't stay in the same place very long and he started to look agitated, Ross thought maybe the coppers were after him, or maybe it was something a little more basic and the kid was in desperate need of a little illegal 'high'. Ross was glad he had never been down that road, alcohol, and tobacco were the only stimulants he had ever consumed, they were the limit of his addictions. Karl said he was up for it 'it would be a blast' so the time and date were arranged, Tuesday night at 11p.m, just two days away. That's if Karl remembered thought Ross, he wasn't the most reliable of kids, but it was out of his control, if he didn't turn up, he would just have to do it himself. 'Yes', it would be a little more difficult but 'what the hell' thought Ross, he'd always achieved 'more with less' that had been just one of his many lifelong mantras. Karl now yawned and then got to his feet and then stumbled, obviously he wasn't that much of a drinker Ross thought, he now gave his new recruit a 'Tenner' in the hope that it would encourage him to turn up and do his bit. As Karl left the *Grapes*, Ross sat back contentedly in his seat and finished off his pint, he felt elated, he now knew something was actually going to happen. He had put the wheels in motion, and nothing was going to stand in his way, look out 'Noble' he said to himself as the proverbial 'shit' was about to hit the fan.

Chapter Four
Black Tourmaline

'Semi-precious stone composed of a complex
crystalline silicate comprised of aluminium,
boron, iron, and magnesium'

Blueish to Greenish black

Tuesday arrived without warning 'like an
April hailstorm' for Ross, as he sat in his
flat and surveyed his tools and spray cans.
He had initially thought about adding some extra
graphics to the so called 'artwork' he intended to
deface. However, the more he thought about the
attack, the more he realised there wouldn't be
enough time to do anything clever, he just needed
to deface the image and get out without being
caught. Now studying the photo which depicted
the artwork he would come face to face with that
very night, he felt a momentary pang of guilt at
what he was going to do. He and John had been
such close friends and they had collaborated on
dozens of pieces of street art over the years, one of
their joint efforts had even appeared anonymously
in a Sunday Times magazine on an article about
social injustice in Thatcher's Britain. That image
carried the title *'The foundations of capitalism'* it
depicted 'Iron Lady' dressed as a land girl wielding
a pickaxe, the sky is electric blue with a single fluffy
white cloud, she is surrounded by a green

unadulterated landscape, as her pickaxe enters the ground it pierces the helmet of a miner toiling away below her feet in the dark, with only the light from his helmet to illuminate his tomb like existence. Even after all the years that had elapsed after their friendship ended, he knew this image still carried a huge resonance for him and its message then as now predicated a bleak future for the working classes. Ross had to admit that John had once shared his strong feelings about social injustice, but these feelings had obviously long since left his consciousness. Ross now cleared his mind of what he viewed as pointless reminiscences; he now turned his attention to tonight's target. An 'animal protest' image, it moved him but also engendered anger and rage within him, how could somebody he had admired both as a friend and artist turn his back on reality and pander to some middle-class lefties whose idea of political protest was probably reading the *Guardian*. No! Ross thought, there was no room for sentiment, this wasn't just a battle with John Noble, it was also a war against the corruption of street art, its morals and raison d'etre and it started tonight. Ross now had his mind focused on the task in hand, he packed the tools of his trade along with his versatile multi-functional tool, the 'hammer', well you never quite knew what obstacles you would come up against in the field, they fitted nicely into the 'sacred' Pink Floyd haversack. For the first time in what seemed like years he was energised and excited, life had a purpose again. He felt on a high and to celebrate he sat on the floor with his back against the wall with his knees against his chest and lit a cigarette just like a soldier in the trenches as he prepared to go 'over the top' for his late-night sortie with Karl. As Ross sat contemplating the evening to come in his cold and damp one bedroomed flat, down in leafy Surrey, John was settling back in his Victorian leather club chair in a very warm and comfortable, centrally heated man cave. A luxurious oak panelled room with a deep pile carpet, it was just one of many rooms in his 'as he thought' modest country home. He sat with his feet up on the corner of the mahogany partners desk, he didn't know why it was called a 'partners', that was its description in the auction. It sounded good, impressive and carried something of a legal and authoritative tone he thought, anyway its size made him feel important and that's what mattered. A bottle of Chateau Lafite 1958 stood on the desk, at present unopened but it wouldn't remain that way for long. John pulled open the desk drawer and rooting through some old letters and photographs he came across a picture of himself, Frances, Ross, and some fellow squatters from Camberwell Road. They all looked half pissed, not that that was unusual in those days, they mightn't have had much but they always had enough for a good drink. Even now he still stared enviously at Frances captured in a passionate embrace with Ross, they had been together for over four years then, they always seemed happy, but John had always been jealous of Ross. Frances was a 'looker' and a 'posh bird' that's how he'd viewed her. She was the epitome of what John wanted and 'wanted' to be, relaxed, accepted in most walks of life, oozing middle class confidence and her family had money, there were Solicitors and Corporate types in her family. It was a strange anomaly of John's character that on the one hand he detested the middle classes for their apparent ease with which they made their money, but on the other he also wanted a bit of the action. He knew even as friends he'd always been envious of Ross, but Ross like all people had his Achilles heel, he was a die-hard radical and would never change and sooner or later his beliefs and more importantly his lack of money, could if orchestrated skilfully by John force a wedge between Ross and Frances's seemingly unbreakable relationship. John's opportunity to do this had come the very night of the party which the photo depicted, tensions were growing over their opportunity to make some money by moving out of the squat, something Ross had fought strenuously against. Frances saw this as an opportunity for her and Ross to move on, but he was having none of it, they rowed and fell out, drunk and feeling annoyed Frances was looking for a shoulder to cry on and John had seen his opportunity. They had talked for hours before Frances had eventually passed out fatigued with the sheer frustration of Ross's stoicism, she had also consumed a large amount of alcohol supplied by John. When Frances awoke the following morning, she was lying in bed unclothed next to John. Frances couldn't remember what she had done, the truth was, she hadn't done anything, but he had seen his long-awaited opportunity to get Frances to himself and break up her relationship with Ross. John had undressed an unconscious Frances and slept beside her, and the following morning gave her the impression they had slept together. Not knowing the truth or being aware of his intentions she accepted his story and then took what she saw as her only course of action and came clean with Ross and told him John's version of the truth. The rest was history, Ross was stubborn but an honest and faithful man and now incapable of understanding what Frances had done to him and to 'them'. Frances regretted every moment of what she 'thought' she had done, but this act of betrayal coupled with the money grabbing breakup of the squat bore witness to the end of their relationship.

Ross was now standing in the shadows, just across the street from his target, located in a disused building yard in Stratford. It was a dark, dimly lit site but he could just about see the street art that would be the focus of his attention. He inhaled deeply, the cold crisp night air rushed into his lungs, it was numbingly euphoric and gave him a renewed sense of vigour, but the moment was short lived. What he hadn't realised was that the site although not technically in use, was also now a storage site for a new building project adjacent to the current location, consequently a large supply of valuable building materials was stored close to the disused garage building on which the image was sprayed. He knew the presence of the building supplies could mean only one thing, extra security and sure enough there was the nemesis of every street artist 'the night watchmen'. The watchman stood in the open doorway of his wooden hut smoking a cigarette and blew smoke out into the cold night air, where it was captured and carried away by a cruel winter wind. Ross stared at the security guard and initially cursed his bad luck but there was one thing in his favour , the watchman was decidedly overweight and Ross reckoned the one hundred metre sprint wasn't a likely event for him .There was also another bonus, there didn't appear to be a guard dog, they were bad news as Ross hated dogs, he had been badly mauled by an Alsatian during one of his nightly sorties many years ago and the scars both physical and psychological were a constant reminder of his cynophobia. Ross consoled himself in the fact that the night watchmen probably didn't give two hoots about Mr Noble's art installation, scrawled on the side of a semi derelict garage, he probably viewed it as nothing more than mindless graffiti, rather than the high art that the local council had elevated its status to. However, a more pressing problem for Ross was, where was Karl? More than ever he really needed assistance now. Ross watched the guard as he casually flicked his still burning cigarette away, it spiralled like a firework in an upward trajectory, its orange glow tracing a brief aerial pattern in the darkness before it fell to the ground and disappeared into the detritus that littered the yard. The watchman then shut the hut door and returned to the welcoming warmth of his cabin. Ross stepped out of the shadows and glanced left, then right down a rather long and deserted road, there was no sign of Karl, in fact there was no sign of anyone. Ross now had to think on his feet, how could he tackle this on his own, perplexed he chose some artificial stimulation to help the process, he proceeded to roll a cigarette. Stepping back out of the dim streetlight and into the shadows, he turned his head towards the wall to light his cigarette away from the prevailing winter wind that was beginning to rise in force and coldness. Just as he lit his cigarette a hand touched his shoulder and a deep comic voice said, 'ello, ello, what you doing then laddie', Ross turned abruptly, only to see Karl's youthful grinning face looking at him. 'Shit, what the fuck are you doing, you idiot' said Ross, 'cool it man, it was a joke, a joke, everything is cool, easy man, there's no hassle, relax, relax, give us a rollie' replied a nonchalant Karl. Ross's heart was still racing as he continued to rant, 'what the hell did you do that for, 'I nearly crapped myself, you should know what it's like when you're on the streets at night, you fuckin idiot'. 'OK, OK, I'm sorry man, don't freak out', I get the message' said Karl realising that perhaps he'd overstepped the mark. The kid now took a long drag on his cigarette and tilted his head back and away from Ross and coolly blew an elongated jet of smoke into the freezing cold air and then said 'so what is this job then? Ross hadn't told him anything about what he was intending to do over the coming weeks, not even about tonight's job, as Karl was likely to shoot his mouth off to anyone who'd listen and then probably give the game away before it even got started. Ross pointed over to the compound with the last embers of his faintly glowing cigarette acting like a laser pen. 'There, that's why we're here, the image on that garage'. Karl took a long hard look before saying 'but why? Another Tag has already been there'. Suddenly the penny dropped, and he recognised the image, 'no way, shit man, that's one of the images that bloke who's always in the papers done, that's Spookz's stuff init'. 'Well done, ten out of ten, go to the top of the class', said Ross sarcastically, 'he's our mark, I want to get a closer look at his work'. 'So, what are we doing? Spraying something new, hey maybe we could get some coverage in the papers as well, sounds cool to me, yeah man, let's do it' Karl replied. He then took one last long almost never-ending drag that reduced the cigarette to ash and a barely holdable stub, which he then tossed away. Ross didn't reply to any of questions or observations put to him, what did it matter to Karl, whether it was a new bit of work or what Ross really intended 'a major modification' re-total obliteration. 'I've had a good look around, and because we've got a watchman to contend with and these streetlights' as he glanced upwards, 'I think we should go down the far side of the compound where there are no lights and it's not overlooked,' said Ross. He continued 'once we get through the fence, we can make our way to the back of the garage and then you can just keep one eye on the watchman's hut, and because it's so damn cold, I'll doubt he'll come out for anything more than a cigarette or better still the fat bastard will be asleep'. 'Come on then Karl', 'let's do it, get your gear' said Ross, 'gear, what gear?' replied a surprised Karl now looking blankly at Ross, 'tools man, fuckin tools, wire cutter that sort of thing,' snapped Ross. 'No way man, I don't bother with all that shit, just break in any way I can' said Karl. Ross shook his head, what an 'idiot' he thought, but he needed help, so he said nothing. Ross and Karl stepped out into the light and immediately made their way down the street where they crossed the road and ran down the side of the fenced compound. Ross took the lead even though his much younger associate was a great deal quicker and fitter than him. When they reached the end of the fence he was breathing heavily, Karl looked at Ross and laughed before saying 'come on old man, let's hope the coppers don't turn up, you'll never manage a runner'. 'Never mind about me, just get on with it' said Ross attempting to regain his composure. Ross was surprised just how out of breath he was, maybe it was the fags or the onset of old age, but he dismissed both negative thoughts in favour of stress, he wanted this so badly it hurt. They crouched down while Ross looked for a suitable weakness in the fence, and that was usually near the bottom, he opened his trusty haversack and took out his wire cutters and attempted to cut through the green plastic-coated wire. He tried cutting in a few different places but each time the cutters only bent and twisted the wire, a bit like himself they had lost their 'edge'. 'Sod it, useless bloody things' said Ross in frustration. 'Hey, it's no hassle man, watch' Karl said, as he then proceeded to grab hold of the bottom of the fence and pull it out of the ground where it had partially disintegrated with the dampness from the bare soil. With a little assistance from a hacksaw blade, they manged to create a hole big enough for them to crawl through. Ross pulled up the wire and motioned for the kid to get under first, 'no way man, it's your job, you go first' Karl said. At this Ross grabbed hold of kids sweatshirt and pulled him close, 'Don't piss me about, 'don't argue, just get under it' said Ross, with his voice raised. Karl still grumbling, reluctantly got down on his belly and started to crawl under, but his top became caught on the cut wire edges. He now twisted and jerked himself from side to side in an attempt to free himself, but it was all in vain, without warning he raised his voice, 'I'm stuck man, shit, shit', he continued struggling. 'Shut up! Shut up! Keep it down! Ross exclaimed. Ross might have known, it was just his luck, as Murphy's law now came to the fore 'if it could go wrong, it would', he struggled to release Karl's clothing from the fence, he tugged and pulled with such force that the sweatshirt partially ripped apart. 'Fuck man, that cost me two hundred quid' shouted Karl, 'just shut up and get in' said Ross, while still continuing to push and pull to release him, eventually the kid was freed from under the fence. Ross then pushed his bag through and then carefully eased the wire a little higher so he could squeeze his larger frame through. Once inside Ross motioned for them to get behind the garage building where they then crouched down for a 'breather' in an attempt to regain an element of calm. Ross patted Karl on the shoulder 'well done man, were in, were in', but there was no time to lose. He got to his feet and crept around the corner of the garage and eyeballed the security hut, the door was shut, and the light was on, all seemed quiet, he crept back and motioned for Karl to follow him. When they got to the front of the building, the image was in full view but unfortunately so were they. Karl looking at the image said, 'so where do we start there's not much room left for our stuff'. Ross was now forced to reveal the truth, he quickly explained that they weren't adding anything new, they were going to 'alter', Ross's euphemism for 'deface' what was already there. Ross's young protege seemed unusually freaked out by this, as he protested, 'man, I'm not touching this, it's been in the news and anyway you know you don't mess with other 'Tags' work'. Ross replied dismissively to the kids misgivings,' look, I'm doing this, you don't have to touch it, just keep a look out'. 'OK man, but you should have told me', replied Karl. 'I would have', thought Ross, if you didn't shoot your big mouth off to any loser that would listen. Karl somewhat reluctantly took up a position which gave him a good view of the watchman's hut but was also near enough to warn Ross if he came out unexpectedly. Ross now stood in front of John's work, he had to begrudgingly confess it was good, but knew this had to be done. The work was protected by a Perspex screen which Ross intended to remove, but there was a problem, as he looked at the fastenings, to his dismay, he realised they were anti-theft bolts and there was no easy way of removing them. Ross was initially stumped with this unexpected problem but there was no time for indecision, ideally, he wanted to spray directly on top of the image, but this action now wasn't possible, and removing the screen seemed a near impossible task. In desperation Ross decided he would try and create a gap between the image and the screen by using his multi-purpose tool 'the hammer', he would then pour paint down the gap to deface the image. He knew his solution wasn't in the least compatible with his usual artistic notions but at the very least the image would be well and truly destroyed if he could get enough paint into the gap. Ross with some considerable force manged to ease part of the protective sheet away from the image, he then quickly grabbed an aerosol can and started spraying copious amounts of paint into the gap, black tears of paint ran down the face of the image. Ross continued unabated, suddenly Karl whispered, 'hey man look', Ross stopped abruptly and looked as his conspirator pointed in the direction of the security hut, the security guard was now standing outside again, they watched nervously as he surveyed the compound and then lit a cigarette. Ross watched him taking short drags on his cigarette nervously and impatient, it looked like he just wanted a quick fix, a token gesture of pleasure. The biting icy wind ended his pleasure abruptly as he couldn't face the cold any longer and he discarded his half-smoked cigarette, as it fell to the ground, he screwed it relentlessly into the dirt with his steel toe capped boot. Karl now bored of waiting for the watchmen to go back into his lair, momentarily relaxed and then inadvertently fell backwards dislodging a pile of bricks in the process, they fell to the ground with a deathly thud. The watchman immediately looked in their direction, then took a torch off his belt and shone it roughly where the noise had come from. Karl panicked as the light illuminated the area around him, almost involuntarily fear made him jump to his feet and the torch light then dazzled and blurred his vision. The watchman shouted at him, 'hey what you up to? Stay where you are', the light started to sway from side to side as he started to move towards Karl. The watchman may have been overweight, but he knew these stocky blokes would give a kid like him a good hiding. Karl was having none of it, he immediately took to his heels and sprinted in the opposite direction towards the front of the compound which looked out onto the street. With the momentum of his run carrying him forward, he jumped effortlessly onto a pallet of bricks which gave him just enough height to leap up and clear the perimeter fence, he then spilled unceremoniously onto the pavement. Adrenalin immediately forced him onto his feet as the night watchman closed in and shouted abuse at him. Karl now sensing his freedom just turned towards the watchmen laughed and shouted, 'you fat bastard', gave him the 'V' sign and then ran off down the street. Ross now stood in the shadows with only one associate 'his dilemma', should he stay and finish the job and risk getting caught or should he bolt why he still had the chance. Ross crouched down, his heart was pounding, his adrenalin had kicked in, it was 'flight or fight' time, the watchman had now turned around and was moving back towards Ross's hiding place. He tensed as the watchman approached, he briefly considered making a break for it, but decided to take the chance and 'sit' it out and see what happened. Ross knew if he didn't finish this job, it would be the end of his 'Quest' before it had even started, 'no' he said forcefully, it had to be done, what had he to lose. Ross knew he was taking a chance because as the watchman approached, he could see he was a bit of a 'bruiser' he was slow moving but big and Ross had been on the receiving end of a few beatings in his time from security staff, who'd rather give you a 'good hiding' as a warning to keep away from their site rather than call the Police. Ross now crouched between two large stacks of timber and picked up a two-foot length of wood for protection. The overweight security guard now stopped, Ross could smell him he was so close, stale sweat, yesterday's booze and fag smoke greeted his senses. The watchman began swinging his flashlight in a sweeping motion around the yard like a wartime searchlight, the beam glanced across and highlighted random objects, eventually it stopped on the image that had just been defaced. Ross now thought he was going to take a closer look, but lethargy and the winter chill in the air replaced the watchman's momentary curiosity for the more pressing desire to return to the comfort and warmth of his cabin. Feeling a tremendous sense of relief as the watchman closed the door of the cabin behind him, reprieved, Ross sank to the ground and sat legs outstretched while he exhaled the 'fear' from his body and attempted to regain his composure. Now sitting on his backside in the dirt, he questioned his reasons for doing 'this', was he mad? Maybe, he thought, there he was, a fifty something year old bloke in a builder's yard at one o'clock in the morning on a freezing cold winters night, having narrowly escaped a good kicking. Then the realisation of no family, a crap council flat and no future, these thoughts combined with several deep breaths of freezing cold air gave him the reason and impetus to push on. He got to his feet, dusted himself down and took several tins of spray paint from his haversack and made his way back to the image. As he stared at the now defaced image, he realised the job was almost done, he had given his next move a great deal of thought over the last couple of days. With graceful sweeping motions like a window cleaner in slow motion he sprayed the words 'ART WHORE' in two feet high letters across the Perspex screen. He then finished the job by creating a five feet long spider with glowing red eyes on stalks, he then completed his task by adding his tag 'SPYDER'. He finished the final letter with an exaggerated flourish that added an upward sweeping tail to the 'R'. Overcome with a rare sense of achievement, he had thrown down the 'gauntlet' to John Noble, and there was now, no going back.

Chapter Five
Green Earth

'A phyllosilicate of potassium, iron in both
oxidation states, aluminium, and hydroxide'

Green to Olive green

As Ross added the final flourish to his SPYDER tag, in Surrey, John awoke abruptly from a deep sleep in his mancave and then inadvertently knocked the remaining contents of the bottle of Château Lafite over. Luxuriant red liquid, the colour of deep crimson rushed like a white-water rapid down the mahogany desk and onto the cream carpet, something he had chosen even though Frances had warned him that it would never stay clean. 'Shit', he exclaimed as his previous dreamlike state of euphoria rapidly dissipated, he had enjoyed the best part of two bottles of the one thousand pound a shot wine, that had now matured overnight into a considerable hang over. As he attempted to clean up the wine, he could hear Frances shouting to him, 'what are you doing in there? You said you were coming to bed hours ago'. Frances opened the door to the mancave and immediately saw the wine and John now on all fours attempting to clean the carpet without much success. She looked at him in his scruffy tea-shirt and boxer shorts, what a pathetic sight she thought and said, 'that won't work, you'll need to put plenty of water on it, for goodness sake just come out of the way, in fact just go upstairs to bed and I'll sort it out'. John didn't argue and slowly still half-drunk made his way upstairs. Frances now fetched copious amounts of water from the kitchen and poured it onto the stain, she scrubbed at the blood red invader but couldn't budge it. Now kneeling with her night dress soaked with water and wine, hot and bothered she brushed now drooping hair from her face with the back of her hand. She stared at the stain on the carpet and shook her head and thought what a fool she was. Frances had been wondering for some time about her relationship with John or non-relationship as it had turned out to be over the years. She partly blamed herself, after all she was the one that had slept with John, it was her fault that Ross had left, his trust in her shattered. Why did her thoughts always go back to Ross, 'yes', she had been in love with him but that now felt so long ago, Frances thought she had moved on, but just like the dangerous hidden currents in a river, tucked away in her soul the 'truth' was she never had. When Frances looked at John nowadays, she just saw a grasping, self-centred man, who thought only about his own pleasure and desires. 'Yes', she thought, he must have had a social conscience 'once' or why would he and Ross have done all those images over the years protesting against animal testing, political injustice, war, famine in the third world, no burning topic of their day had remained untouched. Surely, he must have cared, or was John's sincerity as fake as his love seemed for her. Now turning this over in her mind, she concluded that maybe Ross had been the driving force after all, the real anarchist, the street rebel that provoked people to think about the suffering of others. Frances didn't feel sorry for herself, she knew ultimately it was her fault. However as with life in general, like the process of genealogy that allowed you to trace your descendants, you could also trace the chronology of your emotional life, your friends, your partners, your highs, and lows and somehow try and link it all together in some sort of way that made sense. Why was it you focused on the mistakes, rather than the successes in life she thought. One thing she knew her life had lost direction, she wasn't happy and the more she thought about her time with John, now realised she had never been happy. Yes, she now had a very comfortable lifestyle, there was money now, more than she could ever have imagined. John could be generous, but it was always on his terms, he controlled everything, he had to be there when she bought her clothes and jewellery, she could have almost anything she wanted but only if he approved. Her life was like the carpet on which she now sat, it looked clean and ordered but it was easy to stain, and she carried more than her fair share of stains, some of which, like the one she was staring at couldn't easily be removed. Self-pity wasn't something that Frances did, she knew there were people much worse off than herself, but her mind always came back to Ross. She wondered where he was now, and fondly recalled his 'SPYDER' tag and accompanying 'Tarantula of doom', it was so Ross, 'yes' his work had been dark at times but there had also been humour within him and his art. He had always said, 'if you wanted to reach out to people and implant your message in their conscious, you had to make them think and a touch of comic irony certainly helped'. Frances had to admit that she often thought about Ross. She recalled their penniless lifestyle in a series of abject squats, but most of those times had been good ones. They had met at art college, she was a couple of years younger than Ross, he was wild, dynamic, always pushing boundaries, he had no time for authority and its control over people's lives, his anarchy made him seem so 'cool'. Frances at the time was sharing a flat in London with two former schoolfriends, her parents had agreed to her moving to the 'big city' from the home counties but only if she was with people they knew and approved of. Her parents weren't happy about her going to art college, most of her family had careers in the legal profession and her elder sister was their 'favourite', having agreed to study law at university. The very idea of law had always bored Frances to tears, dry and pointless, that's how she had viewed the idea of studying for the legal profession. Eventually her parents had relented and allowed to her to go to art college, big of them she thought now, after all it was her life and she should have been able to do as she pleased, but ambitious parents didn't make for a simple and carefree life when you were young. After Frances had made her escape to Art college in London, away from her controlling parents, she let go of their middle-class sensibilities and simply enjoyed herself. When she first met Ross, he was already living in a squat with some fellow students and as Ross was fond of saying 'it was a hell of a lot cheaper than paying for digs and left more money for alcohol, life had been just one big party, and nothing seemed to matter. Her parents seldom visited Frances in London, so when she finally moved out of the flat and went to live in a squat with Ross, they knew nothing about it. Now sat staring again at the wine stain on the carpet, Frances put her head in her hands and started to sob at the hopelessness of everything, had the magic formula that once created those special moments in her earlier life, now gone for good? Could she possibly alter what she viewed as a bleak future, maybe re-order it in some way and bring back that fun loving, carefree person she had once been. These thoughts were now the only thing that kept her going and gave some form of hope.

Ross was now making his way home after his first successful attack on John's Street art, he moved through the dimly lit back streets that he knew only too well. He was conscious of the now widespread use of CCTV and knew, as it was common knowledge with the 'night-time' community, that most of these cameras could be avoided. He decided he would keep a low profile for a while and use the time to plan his next attack. After an almost unbearable couple of days being cooped up in his flat, Ross needed to escape and paid a visit to the 'Flamingo', strangely the idea of visiting the café always gave him a lift. He liked Val, she felt like a favourite aunt, a friendly face that was always pleased to see him. Everyone needed a friend or some form of companionship, Ross had seen too many 'loners' whose lives had spiralled into desperate levels of despair on the streets without any friends to give them hope and some sort of solace when times were hard. Ross bounded towards the café, he was on a high, his quest was underway and had been reasonably successful, the next stage was already in the planning. As the old-fashioned metal bell shaped cafe doorbell jingled against the frame, it announced his presence like a butler sounding a dinner gong, whistling as he swung towards an empty table, he felt good and the warm and inviting café, as ever, seemed to welcome him. Val turned at the sound of the bell, and immediately noted his upbeat demeanour, having not seen him for almost a week, Val said, 'mm I know the face but can't quite put a name to it', 'OK, very funny', I know it's been a while, but I've been a busy', replied Ross. 'You! Busy' said Val, and laughed sarcastically, 'You'd be surprised, when I put my mind to something...' Val interrupted Ross, 'well how about putting it to painting my shopfront while you're having such productive thoughts'. 'I will, I will, that's why I came in', said Ross laughing, 'well that and the big breakfast you're now going to cook for me'. Val smiled, 'cheeky beggar you are, please take a seat sir, I'll be right with you' she replied, as she gracefully and sarcastically proffered her outstretched hand towards a table. As Ross sat waiting for his breakfast, he studied the wide variety of people that passed the café's window, people fascinated him, the who, why, what, where, he had the journalists curiosity of purpose, and it energised his mind. The local area had changed remarkably over the last few years, there were a lot of what Ross still referred to as old fashioned 'Yuppies', today they were called 'single young professionals', same thing, different name that's all, he thought. They brought money and little else to an area, there wasn't any community spirit as far as he was concerned, everyone seemed to be thinking of number 'one'. He missed the former sense of community, it was too easy just to blame social media for its disappearance, but it must have had its impact. Ross thought he was doing his bit to 'protest' by not participating in Facebook, Twitter, or any of the other multitude of social websites that offered anonymous 'friendship' at a price, usually your personal details and privacy. Ross was suddenly shaken from his mental protestations as his eyes strayed onto a rather attractive girl passing the window. She wore figure hugging jeans and a green 'Parker' with a fur trimmed hood, now pulled up to protect her from the biting cold wind. Her outfit was complemented by the now fashionable 'again' Doc Martins. In his youth, CND wore green Parkers and skin heads had their Doc Martins, as ever fashion regurgitated its past triumphs for a new audience, who were ignorant of their past associations good and bad alike. His eyes followed the girl, 'very nice', he thought as she slinked by the window. Suddenly Val disturbed his thoughts by clunking down an overladen but rather fine-looking breakfast in front of him. 'For the man who isn't interested in romance, eh' she said. 'Wow Val that's some breakfast', said Ross, 'well if you're thinking about 'that sort of thing' you'll need to keep your strength up won't you, oh and your morning paper Sir' she added with a laugh, as she placed a fresh copy of the latest free local paper alongside his breakfast plate. Ross ignored the paper and enthusiastically tucked into his 'full English', he loaded his fork to capacity with sausage, bacon, and egg, and was just about to shovel it into his mouth when he saw the headline on the paper, his momentum floundered, the fork didn't make it to his open mouth, the food fell from his fork as he read '*Mindless vandals deface valuable street art*'.

Ross dropped his knife and fork onto the table and pushed his breakfast to one side, he frantically unfurled the paper, and started to read. Initially he was affronted by the description of himself as a 'Mindless vandal', but as he had always thought, the right-wing press would hardly describe anyone that confronted authority as anything other than anti-social. The article began' *In the late hours of Tuesday night in London's East End, on the site of the new Jubilee Housing development, vandals attacked and virtually destroyed a council protected piece of street art, created by the unknown street artist simply known as 'Spookz'. Hapless vandals that were unable to remove the protective screen simply poured paint between the screen and the image, destroying a piece of work that celebrated 1990's political and social brinkmanship. A local council spokesman described the senseless act of vandalism as a pointless and cowardly attack on Contemporary Street art that had been saved and protected for the enjoyment and pleasure of residents and tourists alike.* Ross laughed to himself at the articles misleading pretence that it was being saved for the enjoyment of local residents, most of whom barely had two pennies to rub together and couldn't possibly comprehend how a piece of random street art could be worth some half a million pounds. He read on, '*the piece of art although on council property is sponsored by a private art dealer and gallery owner Mr David Hemmings. Who, speaking from his fashionable contemporary gallery in Chelsea said, 'he was shocked and disappointed, he appreciated that all forms of street art had a place but was confused by the attack, as he understood (mistakenly it seems) that a code of mutual appreciation of other artists work existed on the street scene'. Mr Hemmings also said that he was offering a ten-thousand-pound reward to anyone that had information about the attack.* Ross was shocked to see that Dave Hemmings was fronting John Noble's work, 'yes', he thought, they all knew each other from years ago but he didn't know they were still that close. The idea of John hiding behind Dave made a lot of sense the more he thought about it. Ross now recalled the heated debate they once all had about taking 'a payoff' from a rich 'absentee owner' to vacate their Camberwell squat. Then Dave had been a budding entrepreneur 'a wheeler dealer', always looking for a fast buck and an angle. John wanted money, but he didn't have Dave's business acumen, so their coalition then and now made such obvious sense. Ross continued reading, *'the council have said that the police were investigating the attack and that they took this wanton act of vandalism and unlawful trespass extremely seriously'. The Police are now reviewing local CCTV footage.* Ross laughed at this, they always say this he thought, reviewing CCTV, what bollocks, but as he read on, he realised he was wrong this time. *A spokesperson for the Metropolitan Police said, officers are looking for a youth who wore a branded Sweatshirt and was seen running from the scene of the crime.* That bloody sweatshirt Karl had worn, cursed Ross, he knew it was very distinctive, perhaps it had even shown up on the CCTV images. Karl wouldn't be able to keep his mouth shut, he'd squeal, what would he have to lose, and they would more than likely sacrifice charging a young kid to catch 'the bigger fish'. There was nothing Ross could do now he thought, he decided it was probably all a bluff to make the council look better in the public eye, to prove they cared about people and were enforcing their zero-tolerance policy with regard to anti-social behaviour. What's wrong with anti-social behaviour Ross thought, if it wasn't for it, this work would never have been created in the first place. Hypocrites he thought, the more he read the more determined to carry on he became. One thing was for certain he would have to go it alone from now on. Karl and people in general, as he had discovered over his lifetime were unreliable and a liability. Ross folded up the paper and returned to his breakfast, he now had a looming battle on his hands, because sooner rather than later, Dave and John would realise who was behind the orchestrated attack and the real 'fun' would begin.

As Ross pushed his now scrupulously clean breakfast plate to one side, Val came over to clear his table, 'want anything else?' she said. 'To be honest I could do with strong cup of ...', Ross didn't finish his sentence but hesitated, 'on second thoughts, no thanks, I've just about got enough money to pay for what I've had'. 'Don't worry about that, I thought we could come to some arrangement' said Val, Ross interjected but 'I'm shocked Val, I barely know you' he said laughing'. 'You should be so lucky, you silly sod' said Val laughing with him, no, you remember we talked about re-painting the front of the shop, that's worth a good few breakfasts to me Ross, how about it?' 'I've got the paint and the brushes, it just needs a gifted artist like your good self to slap it on'. 'Yeah, right, slap it on, that's me, look you've been good to me, and I appreciate what you've done, I'll pop in one day and make a start'. Val was pleased to see Ross had regained his usual spirit for life, she had been more than a little worried about him lately. Having witnessed regular customers come and go from her café over the years, she quickly attuned herself to peoples moods and could, she thought, recognise the danger signs of spiralling despair and depression. You didn't have to be some sort of qualified psychologist she thought, to help people, sometimes just a kind word and a cuppa could work wonders, it wasn't therapy a lot of folk needed, it was just a connection with a fellow human being.

Chapter Six
Platina Yellow

'A yellow crystalline powder of potassium chloroplatinate'

Orange to yellow

Dave Hemmings was just about to settle into his favourite vintage chair with a fine blended malt after a long but profitable day at his gallery. He gazed out of the immense glass windows that offered an unrivalled and panoramic view across the Thames from his third floor Battersea apartment. No sooner had he reclined to admire the fading light of the day and watch the twinkling multi-coloured lights hung like a string of pearls meandering along the bank of the river, when his mobile rang, he stopped the ringtone almost before it even got started. He looked at the caller information, it was John, he wouldn't interrupt a fine scotch even for him, so he continued to adjust his posture for maximum comfort in his leather and laminated Eames chair. This is such a comfortable chair he thought, but then it should be, it was an original and had cost him eight grand, but if you wanted the best you had to pay for it. Sipping his Scotch, he reflected and agreed with himself, 'yes', all the planning and hard work had been more than worth it as he surveyed his flat with its unrivalled river views.

Dave was gently swinging his seat from side to side, the motion produced a tranquil feeling of contentment, he had every right to feel rather pleased with himself. His gallery had sold nearly two hundred thousand pounds worth of John's current exhibition and it had only been running for a week. The whole enterprise had happened completely by chance a few years ago, after Dave had read an article about Charles Saatchi and how he had created the current thriving contemporary art market on the back of up-and-coming young British artists like Damien Hurst. It had been so clever and yet so simple Dave had thought, the article had described how Saatchi firstly bought up large amounts of contemporary artwork. He then exhibited the pieces, courted the press, got some big names on board, and then slowly drip fed the work into the arm of a gullible art market, he created the demand, then satisfied the investors and collectors urge to be involved in this speculative 'new trend' in art. Dave's plan had run along similar lines, he began by buying some of John's Street art at highly inflated prices while at the same time anonymously tipping off the press. The very first article, now framed and hanging on his wall, proclaimed '*Art dealer buys street art for fifty thousand pounds*'. Even now, long after this first purchase, he laughed ironically at the press`s description of it as 'art', he took another sip of his premium malt, it was and always would be pointless graffiti to Dave, however this 'graffiti' once housed on a derelict garage wall was dismantled and rebuilt in his new High Street gallery. It caused quite a stir in the press at the time, this set the ball rolling and further purchases added fuel to the growing flames of media interest, this fire roared into what became the 'street art' movement. Investors flocked to buy and grab a piece of the action, as ever money bred an insatiable level of greed, and its demands knew no bounds. Dave poured himself another big Scotch and thought about ringing John back, but could he really be bothered tonight? It was late and surely it could wait. As he pondered this, he cast his mind back to the days when he had shared a squat with John, Frances, and the rest of the crowd, most of whom were just drifters, without any particular purpose or direction. He hadn`t, unlike most of them, been a student, his dad had kicked him out of the house to survive on his own when he was barely sixteen. One of life`s survivors, he would do any 'crap' job that came his way and he scraped and saved for years just waiting for an opportunity, a 'sure fire scheme' to come along. Like most self-made and successful entrepreneurs, it had taken about twenty or more of these so called 'sure fire' schemes before success came his way. Dave knew things didn`t come to you, you had to be, to use the populist phrase 'proactive', he just saw it as grafting for a living, constantly looking for contacts, everyone was after money and there was always a deal to be struck. He had despised some of the wasters he'd shared squats with some of them came from good families, they were just bored and looking for excitement. It was easier for them, because as soon as they became disinterested or things became genuinely difficult, they could always ask mummy and daddy for a helping hand, one which their long-suffering parents were only too pleased to offer if it placed their darling offspring back on the road to middle class respectability. Dave had had a willing cohort in John, who although had no business acumen whatsoever, did have a talent for art, in particular street art which was driven by his one-time social conscience. Dave didn't then or even now give a toss about 'social fairness', he'd always seen that as the preserve of the 'sandal wearing, nut cutlet eating lefty's as far as he was concerned. However, Dave was a pragmatist and therefore prepared to embrace anything if there was a few 'bob' in it for him. It was strange when he thought about John and how they'd met, they had both been on the poll tax marches that had turned 'ugly' during the height of Thatcher's far right-wing grip of the economy. He had gone along just for a laugh, got carried away and was charged with `minor affray` and had ended up sharing a cell with John for a night. They got talking and Dave had said he needed somewhere to kip, and John had suggested he should come along to his current squat. Dave had been desperate, so he had taken John up on his offer, intending to stay just a couple of nights but nights as usual turned into months. They were a 'good crowd' and he had shared many laughs with them although they were a little too ideological, it wasn't for him, but he had been desperate and agreed to go along with anything at the time, until something better turned up. It was getting late and reminiscing about the past had made Dave drowsy, he fell off to sleep still holding a half empty glass, cradled against his chest. Suddenly his mobile burst into song as it rang again, *'Peaches on the Beaches by The Stranglers'* awoke him with a start, he spilt his whisky, 'Damn' he shouted and thought who the hell was this time. It was John yet again, 'for fucks sake, does that bloke never give up' he thought, he hoped it wasn't John in one of his late-night drunken stupors about to bend his ear after yet another row with Frances. Dave reckoned John had always punched well above his weight where Frances was concerned, she was a good looking and intelligent woman, what on Earth had she ever seen in John? Dave could never work it out, she deserved better, much better. He took a deep breath, then exhaled alcoholic fumes that would challenge the capabilities of even the most robust of breathalysers, now feeling composed he answered John's call. 'Evening or is it morning, you OK mate'? said Dave. No pleasantries came from John, he launched straight into a rant 'you've read the papers, have you?'. Without even waiting for a reply, he continued unabated, 'some 'dick head' has just gone and destroyed one of my works, chucked bloody paint all over it, but I guess you already know all about it Dave, since you're quoted in the article, why the hell didn't you tell me about it?'

'John, John, relax, I was going to ring you' said Dave, he was lying, he had completely dismissed the incident which he had viewed as unfortunate but at the same time saw as a timely source of free publicity for the new exhibition. 'Look John, it's good publicity for us, so what, some stupid kid has had a go at one of 'our works', he stressed the 'our', it just raises the profile, you'd pay good money for press coverage like this'. Dave was determined to have his say now, he'd had enough of listening to Johns' rant, 'I even mentioned the new exhibition in the article, man this is good news, not bad news, remember what they say, any publicity is good publicity as long as they spell your name right', he then laughed. John didn't share Dave's humorous take on the incident, he saw it as a huge personal sleight, 'did you go and see what they've done, they called me an 'Art Whore', the bastards'. Dave attempted to lighten the mood, 'well we both are, it's just I'm better looking than you and it is good money'. 'This isn't fucking

funny Dave, it's me they are having a go at, it's not
your work plastered with the words 'Art Whore' is
it? shouted John. `You make it sound deliberate
John, get a grip man, some stupid kids that's all,
there all no hopers, what the hell, just forget it,
were taking good money at the gallery, this can
only enhance that'. 'You just don't get it do you
Dave, said John angrily, this isn't about money, it's
about respect and these aren't just kids and what's
more I know who did this'. Dave thought, what's
he going on about, he's making fantastic money,
what's all this precious 'art crap, respect thing', this
always happened to people when they had turned
their talent into real money, they became
protective and insular about 'their' precious work.
Dave resisted the temptation to push John
anymore, he could sense his growing anger and
frustration. 'How can you possibly know who did
this, it said some kids in the newspaper' said Dave,
'this wasn't any kid, it was Campbell, Ross 'fucking'
Campbell! John's anger went up a notch, his voice
noticeably louder as he said Ross's name. 'No
way', said Dave, shaking his head unseen to John,
why would he?' Dave knew about the quarrel in
the past over the money to move out of the
Camberwell squat but couldn't understand John's
paranoia about Ross, but he was unaware of John's
lies to Frances and how he had used that deception
to split Ross and Frances up. I don't know,
perhaps he's jealous, I'm a success and he's a

loser, who knows, I mean, he didn't have any ambition, he's an idealistic nobody,' said John. Dave attempted to allay what he saw as Johns unfounded fears,' come on man, how can you be so sure it's Campbell', 'cos he sprayed his fucking 'SPYDER' tag on it, that's how, its him, I just know it,' said John. 'Come on man anyone could have used that tag' said Dave, 'no its him, I recognise his style, I've worked with him on enough 'bombings' to know'. John was just about to continue with his rant when Dave interrupted to diffuse the situation. 'OK, OK John, let's just assume you're right, but think about it, what difference does it make, as you said, he's a loser, a nobody'. Dave continued, 'it's one image, put it into perspective, just think about it, he's given us a nice piece of free advertising and on the plus side, I have that work insured, I can claim for it, it just gets better the more you think about it'. John retaliated immediately 'You still don't get it, do you Dave, this isn't about money, its personal, yeah maybe if it had been some daft kid, I would probably agree with you, but given our past, if I know Campbell this is a 'beginning' and not an end'. John continued unabated, 'Campbell isn't the kind of person who does a one-off random thing, he's a thinker, a philosopher if you like, I know him, and this shit isn't going to stop'. 'Look John if your right and I'm not saying you are, leave it to me, I have some contacts in the force and I'm sure I can sort this out quietly and without too much fuss, surely that's the best way'.

'No, No, no way', I'm not having this, Campbell and I have history, most of it bad, and if he does continue, I will sort this out myself'. Dave waited till John stopped talking, he could sense his immovability about Ross and attempted to placate him. 'OK John, its late, I get where you're coming from but for goodness sake don't do anything stupid, Campbell's not worth it, all I ask is that you don't do anything rash, just remember we have both done extremely well out of this 'anonymous artist thing' we have created, don't screw it all up now, not now'. John rallied again 'why, why the hell should I, he's taking the piss' but Dave sensing more vitriol was coming his way, decided to jump in and cool things down as he suggested. 'OK John let's call it a 'night' man, its late and your rightly annoyed', although he really thought John was being an overprotective idiot, but knew he couldn't say it, 'look, I'm tired, you're tired, let's call it a night eh, just sit tight for now'. Dave continued not allowing John the chance of interrupting, 'get a decent night's kip man and we can talk this over at the gallery, OK, OK'. Dave waited for some confirmation from John, but none came, only silence. 'OK John', he repeated with a firmer more authoritative tone, eventually John grunted in agreement to his request, but Dave could tell this was a 'big' issue that if not resolved quickly could easily spiral out of control.

No sooner had their conversation ended and Dave sank almost immediately into a warm alcoholic induced cocoon of sleep while John now back home and seemingly inconsolable, continued to fuel his anger with even more alcohol. Meanwhile Ross sat alone in his flat reading the press article about his 'destructive' nights work, again for the umpteenth time, it gave him a huge sense of achievement, he hadn't felt like this for years and this was only the start. He had tidied up the flat and made it look quite presentable for the first time in months. There were also some new additions to the flat, prompted by recollections from his childhood when he sat and watched old black and white war films with his grandfather. In the films there were always war deployment forces in underground bunkers where usually young Wrens moved toy soldiers and tanks around on tabletop maps. In a homage to this memory, he had created a large wall chart in greater detail than he thought he was capable of, it displayed a series of sites that marked the location of John Nobles' priceless and protected art works. This was now 'his' war room, the chart marked the best routes to and from the sites, any buildings that overlooked the sites and the best sides on which to approach them, and more importantly the quickest route of escape. Ross pinned his prized article from the press to his newly created scene of crime board and hoped it would be the first of many such articles, that was unless the press lost interest which was more than likely, but he knew that could also work in his favour.

Chapter Seven
Violet Hematite

'Natural Iron Oxide

Light violet to deep dark violet'

Frances turned over in bed and stretched out her arm expecting to touch a sleeping stone of a husband, instead as had become the case recently there was just a cold empty space. She turned her head and squinted at the bedside alarm clock, red numbers glowed in the dark and illuminated a full glass of water from which she took a sip. Sat halfway up in bed and gathered her thoughts after a comfortable night's sleep and considered getting up to see what John was up to? But was it even worth bothering, as she had a very good idea where he would be. Frances decided to try and go back to sleep, but once her mind was churning with negative thoughts, principally about John, it seemed impossible to return to the safety and anonymity of sleep. She threw back the bed clothes and stood up but hadn't made her mind up about going back to bed yet again, so pulled the blankets back into place to keep the nights heat in and then made her way downstairs to the long hallway that lead to the study. John was usually sat at his computer having a drink, but on this occasion, he was fast asleep on a club armchair with two empty bottles of red wine lying on the floor beside him. The sight of John asleep and comatose annoyed Frances, but she also felt pity, not for him, but for herself. Why had she stayed within this claustrophobic and unhappy relationship for so long? Yes, he had money, plenty of money and she could have whatever she wanted if John agreed, but that was the root of the problem, he was in control and always would be. Looking at him opened mouthed and snoring away in his wine-stained grubby off-white T-shirt and two days' worth of beard, what a slob, she thought. Her eyes moved from John as she became distracted by the sight of his bulging Louis Vuitton wallet lying on the desk beside him stuffed full cash. The escape plan she had hatched some time ago now gathered further momentum. Frances deftly removed a good third of its contents, knowing he wouldn't miss it, as his wallet seldom contained less than two or three thousand pounds in notes. This was at the heart of her escape plan, she needed money to just 'go' and leave him without warning, when the time was right. Frances had saved, yes 'saved' she reaffirmed the word in her mind, not 'stolen', a considerable sum over the last two years. Sometimes Frances looked back and wished she had tried harder to persuade Ross to stay in Paris instead of returning to Camberwell, then she wouldn't have ruined their relationship and wouldn't have ended up in this mess with John. Paris had been carefree and fun after leaving art college, she wanted to travel and see something of life. Ross saw the French capital as a huge adventure and hoped it would give him the chance to learn from some of the foremost street artists in Europe who gathered there. Not only to see their work but collaborate on some of their projects. The French had always had an eye for radicalism and anti-political stances, most people attributed this to the 'Revolution' and Ross had seen some merit in this belief or as he had put it at the time 'cos basically the French fuckin hate authority'. 'Yes', she now thought and smiled at Ross's succinct protestation, but that was him all over. She'd had some misgivings about his beliefs at times but had always admired his honesty and integrity for doing what he believed in, and as she reminisced, now knew, she had never stopped loving him. Frances's momentary lapse into the past was suddenly rudely interrupted as John let out a huge snorting guffaw of a snore and shattered her train of thought. She glared at him, drunk, oblivious to the pain he caused, and now knew she had to get out of this sham of a marriage, this 'mere existence' before it sucked every morsel of life from her soul.

At breakfast later that morning John and Frances were sat at the table in their 'Shaker' style kitchen complete with another of John's 'ladder climbing' purchases, which included the ubiquitous statement Aga, that presumably announced that you had 'arrived' and joined the country set. Not that they used it much, like most things that involved money it was more for appearances and the microwave provided more than enough cooking power for John's limited culinary requirements. Frances stared at John, sat wearing his boxer shorts and crumpled wine-stained T-Shirt, he was dishevelled and still hung over, she shook her head as she said, 'you look terrible, do you have to sit up half the night drinking?'. John barked back a reply at Frances, even though his raised voice made his hangover pound even more, 'don't start, just don't start, I've got problems, that's why I drink'. Frances was used to John just cutting her off, excluding her, but she remained calm as she said, 'can't I help, what's happening, what's wrong?'. 'I don't need anyone's help' he replied curtly, and Frances knew when she wasn't going to get anywhere with him but felt it was worth trying. 'I don't understand why you always exclude me, I might be able to help, is it such a big secret that you can't even tell me', she said. John couldn't and wouldn't even mention Ross's name, he choked at the very thought of it. 'It's something and nothing' he replied, trying to calm down the situation, not to save Frances's feelings but in an attempt to relieve his now pounding headache. 'Look let's not argue' said John as he rubbed his face with his hands, 'I need to visit Dave at the gallery this afternoon, why don't you come along and take a peek at the exhibition, while I talk things over with him'. Frances thought about his offer, was it an 'Olive branch' or did he just want to shut her up, and furthermore did she really want to watch a 'bromance' as they slapped each other on the back while toasting their success with yet another congratulatory whisky. Could she bear Dave extolling the virtues of his latest 'single malt' acquisition in their pathetic man cave. Frances was about to decline John's offer, when she thought about the opportunity it provided her with, to take the cash she had removed from John's wallet and deposit it in the Building Society account, opened more than two years ago. 'Yes', I'll go she thought to herself and maybe he'll give me some more cash to buy something to keep me 'sweet' and this can go into the fund as well. Smiling she said, 'yeah that would be great, it will be nice to see Dave again, it's been a while'. Frances was good at lying to John, and should be, she'd had years of practice and now even though her middle class upbringing still balked at her deceit, she didn't feel any form of debt to him. She also assumed that John didn't tell her the truth about lots of things and this also relieved her sense of guilt and made the 'cat and mouse' game with him easier and life just that little more bearable and even entertaining at times. John poured himself another black coffee, sat back on the kitchen chair and sighed, mainly because of the discomfort of his now slowly subsiding hang over. Frances started to clear away her breakfast things and said, 'just as well you're drinking expensive wine, imagine how you'd feel if it was cheap crap'. She laughed as the plates clattered into the sink, now aggravating his hangover further, and then went upstairs just so she didn't have to put up with Johns' constant moaning and groaning.

Later that morning Frances was sat in the front passenger seat of John's Range Rover or 'Rage Rover' as she called it, as they made their way into central London. They hardly said a word to each other for most of the journey. Frances assumed he was still 'hung over' and probably shouldn't even be driving as he was more than likely still well over the legal limit after his nights drinking, but this just summed up his selfish attitude, he didn't care about anyone but himself. Cocooned from 'real life' in John's triple glazed, Burr walnut 'Gentleman's club' on wheels, the outside world couldn't penetrate his universe as he threaded his way through the traffic at speed. On approaching a pedestrian crossing in London's East End, he failed to notice a hooded teenager in a Gola sweatshirt stepping onto the crossing. Suddenly awoken from his catatonic state of self-indulgence, he was forced to slam on his brakes at the last second, even the car's anti-lock braking system failed to react in time as the car lurched sideways as he swerved to avoid the youth. The teenager realised how close his shave with mortality had been, and now let forth a string of expletives directed towards John's and his car as it came to a halt. He gripped the steering wheel and shouted, 'stupid little bastard, I'll teach him', then quickly undid his seatbelt and was about to get out the car when Frances grabbed his arm and said, 'no John, please not now, let it go, you could have killed that boy'. John pushed her hand way and thrust himself back into his seat, he then pushed his hands through his hair and then repeatedly hammered his fist against the rim of the steering wheel. 'For God's sake, just calm down,' she said.' Little shit, put two fingers up to me', shouted John. 'You deserve it', thought Frances but didn't say anything, as she didn't want to start yet another row, just wanting to get to their destination in one piece. Now John just sat staring out of the windscreen not saying a word, Frances decided she'd had enough, 'I'm just going to walk the rest of the way' she said, and before John could respond had opened the door, got out, slammed it behind her and started walking away. This action only infuriated him even more, he restarted the vehicle, floored the accelerator, and then roared off down the road without paying even a cursory glance to his wife on the pavement. Frances found herself walking quickly and not paying attention to where she was going, now randomly crossing streets, and just hoping it was the right direction, but unfortunately it was a part of town she wasn't familiar with. Uneasy and disorientated, she rushed along zigzagging past slow moving pedestrians until her mind started to calm down. She forced herself to walk slower and gradually an inner peace grew within her and the mornings problems seemed to gradually dissolve and go to the back of her mind. After walking for mile or so, now feeling calm and collected Frances came across a small café called the 'Pink Flamingo'. It looked like an old-fashioned friendly Tea room and not one of your modern pretentious 'café culture' eateries that jostled for business on many of London's streets. Its paint peeling window frames added character and gave it a warm and friendly appearance, that suggested what lay within was more important than its shabby exterior. She peered through the slightly steamed up windows, there were a few builder types in, but she didn't mind, at least it had a look of normality instead of the usual 'chrome and laminated' café interiors that were full of 'Young Professionals' who made a coffee last two hours and never lifted their heads or tapping fingers from their laptops. On entering the café, a small bell tinkled on the top of the door, and she thought how quaint, it was a blast from a comforting and fading past. A cheery older lady stood in the cafe, tall and elegant, an elegance somehow achieved despite the best efforts of a not particularly flattering knee length blue nylon overall. The lady smiled and in a warm and friendly cockney accent said, 'hello dear, take a seat and I'll pop over and take your order'. Frances sat at the nearest table which just happened to have a good view of the street, she enjoyed the art of people watching, 'live TV' she called it, small dramas played out in the maelstrom of everyday life. It was nice to be out on her own away from the suffocating atmosphere of home and John's every increasing anxiety and frustration with life in general. Frances ordered a good old fashioned Bacon sandwich and a white milky coffee, not a Latte, she hated the way people called it a 'Lah-tay' which she always found pretentious and irritating. The lady who had welcomed her had a pink streak in long greying tied up hair, her elegant demeanour transcended the friendly but somewhat prosaic surroundings and Frances thought this must be the 'Pink Flamingo'. She seemed a friendly soul who seemed to mirror the old-world charm of a bygone era, when people passed the time of day with their neighbours, washed their cars on Saturday mornings, then people happily seemed to co-exist without the 'must have now mentality' and pervasive world of social media and the Internet. It gave Frances a warm feeling and made her think things weren't quite as bad, as they were portrayed by the media, how Frances longed for normality, even if it did seem to belong to the past. Sitting and clutching her large mug of coffee, she sipped intermittently and 'people watched'. On the opposite side of the street, she saw the young kid that John had almost knocked down, even with his hood up she recognised his Gola sweatshirt. She stared at him with a huge sense of relief, 'thank God he was alright' she thought, he was now walking with an older man possibly in his late forties or early fifties. Intrigued and to gain a better view Frances wiped the condensation from the window with a tissue and on seeing the older man she immediately felt an uncontrollable yearning. The hairs on the back of her neck now pricked up for some inexplicable reason, it was uncanny, her heart rate began to race, and she became hot, almost lightheaded, 'my god, is that Ross', she thought. Frances hadn't seen him for years, she immediately looked for his unmistakable stilted walking action, the stranger walked awkwardly, his hair was different, longer than she remembered, but she was convinced it was him. Without thinking, jumping to her feet, and inadvertently spilling her coffee, she rushed to the door and stepped outside. Just as she was about to step off the pavement to get a closer look, a large lorry rushed past sounding it's horn, a deafening droning sound numbed her senses, she jumped back with a fright, on regaining her composure and looking again the two figures had gone. Maybe it wasn't Ross she thought, after all it had a stressful morning, and perhaps it had all been in her imagination and somehow her subconscious had created these images. However, the strange sensation that had come upon her remained and these feelings alone were enough to make her think that it was Ross she had seen. As Frances stood in the doorway, she wondered why she had such an immediate and uncontrolled reaction to apparently seeing him again. If there had been even the remotest doubt in her mind about her feelings for Ross after so much time apart, she now knew for certain their past bond was still strong and very much alive. As she stood transfixed by her reaction and emotions, a hand touched her shoulder. As she turned around Val was standing beside her and said, 'are you alright dear? You knocked your coffee over when you left in such a hurry'. 'Sorry, sorry, I'm so sorry, I'm', a still stunned Frances could hardly string a sentence together, 'I'm OK, it was nothing, it's just I thought I saw...', she was just about to say Ross's name, hesitated, then stopped herself. Now thinking, what did this matter to a complete stranger, why would she be interested. Frances knew she could so easily outpour all her current emotions and this lady would probably listen and may even understand, she felt desperate to unburden her mind. However, Frances just couldn't do it, couldn't let go, her upbringing had always been regulated by an unnatural level self-control, 'you don't confide in strangers' she could hear her mother saying, and this emotional straight jacket years on, still bound her as tightly as ever. 'No, honestly I'm fine, I'm fine, just thought I recognised someone' Frances eventually said. The disappointment in her voice was undisguised as Val touched Frances's arm and said, 'come on, I've put you another coffee out, just come back in and finish your drink'.

John now arrived at Dave's gallery, he pulled his Range Rover round the back as usual, so he didn't appear too conspicuous, sometimes he hated the clandestine nature of the 'Unknown artist' persona, that Dave was so keen to protect. However, he had to admit that it had been very lucrative for them both. He switched off the engine and allowed the car stereo to keep playing, Mozart sometimes helped to pacify his mood and that was something he badly needed. John sat listening to the music and re-ran the mornings events in his mind. Sometimes it felt as though he was going mad, he had money, the type of house he always wanted, but somehow just couldn't relax, why does everything always feel like a problem, he thought? Incapable of just letting things 'go', he had the kind of personality that held onto grudges and complications, they were his daily mental fuel. Frances had suggested he visit a psychologist, maybe they could 'earth' his negative energy and run it to ground, but he thought therapy was for failures and misfits. 'No!' he thought to himself, he had to resolve his own issues, because when you relied on other people that's when things went wrong. The music now pervaded his thoughts and somehow seemed to dilute and reorder them in a logical fashion, his mind settled, and he felt able to contemplate his next move. He now felt ready to tackle Dave about the incident they had argued about the previous night. John called Dave on his phone, it rang and rang and rang, he could feel his momentary calmness eroding like a glacier in full sun, frustration grew with each ring of abandonment, eventually he answered. 'About bloody time, I'm at the back entrance, can you let me in' snapped John. He then rang off before without even waiting for a reply, Dave just shook his head disconsolately and held his phone aloft and sarcastically said aloud 'Hi Dave, you ok mate', how's it going, thanks for everything you've done for me...', ungrateful sod he thought, but now he was more than used to John's insouciant manner and ignorance. Standing at the back door to the gallery, Dave was staring down at his shoes, they looked unusually grubby to him, so he wiped them on the back of his trousers till a semblance of shine reappeared. He wished it was that easy to restore ones self-confidence by just giving your personality a quick wipe. The rear metal door to the gallery now swung open uncontrollably and John had to step back quickly to avoid being knocked off his feet. Framed by the doorway, Dave stood sharp suited, alert, and ready for action, he spoke first, 'didn't expect to see you so soon' he lied but knew otherwise especially after last night's frantic and ill-tempered call. He also knew that last night's heated conversation was probably just the start of something with John, he could read him like a book. John stepped into the gallery's storeroom, they walked past a series of paintings wrapped and stacked ready for delivery, it exuded Dave's personality, orderly, confident, everything under control and the constant expectation that bigger and better things were yet to come. John followed his business partner through the narrow corridor that led to his office at the back of the gallery. Since his last visit Dave had installed a large tropical fish tank, they both stood and watched as a multitude of brightly coloured Angel fish gracefully glided through the water as though in slow motion. John was mesmerised by their fluidity, grace, and lack of urgency, but he knew if his mind were an aquarium, it would be full of Piranha's.

'Cool aren't they' said Dave with an air of smug satisfaction, 'I can just sit here and relax with a nice drink, it's so calming you should get one John', you really, really should, Dave thought as he looked at John's stressed and troubled expression. 'So, what can I do for you mate?'. Even though he knew exactly what John wanted, he attempted to head off the inevitable scenario of John blowing a gasket and Dave trying to cool him down. He started on a positive topic before John could start moaning, 'want to see the sales figures, they make great reading, took nearly three hundred grand this week alone and we haven't even hit the weekend'. John looked surprised at the idea of having made so much money, 'No, I mean yeah, that's great but it's not all about money is it', Dave hated philosophical debates where money was concerned 'cash was the undisputed King of his world'. 'Well, I did try' thought Dave, as John's vitriol about the previous night now burst forth like an unstoppable avalanche, 'it's about last night, the attack, bloody Campbell,' said John. Dave was about to interrupt John and say he should calm down and not let this obsession with Ross get the better of him, but he recognised that John was a runaway train and the brakes had failed, there was no easy way of stopping him. John's desire was fixated on resolving the matter, Dave now interrupted 'look John, as I said last night, I want to find out who did this, just as much as you do'. John just shook his head uncontrollably from side to side, his face reddened as his anger grew, he resembled a 'Laughing sailor' arcade automaton, except he wasn't laughing and just like an automaton he would run till he stopped of his own accord. Dave had no choice but to listen, not something he particularly liked or was accustomed too. 'I know who did it, why doesn't anyone listen to me, it's Campbell, Ross bloody Campbell, his name is all over it, the style the...'. Dave interrupted, 'hey come on John, you can't be that certain and..'. John now interrupted 'I so am, I told you, it's even got his tag on it, I'm not stupid, how many 'SPYDERS' are out there do you think? I'll tell you, just one as far as I'm concerned'. Dave thought John was like every punter who buys a lottery ticket, they have a blind belief in their judgement, they are totally convinced they have the winning ticket even though the hard cold evidence and odds of 'fourteen million to one' against, say otherwise. Dave motioned for John to take a seat, as he said 'here get this down you', then proceeded to pour a very large ten-year-old malt and pushed it into his gesticulating hands, John gulped it down, 'hey, take it easy, take your time man, this isn't some sort of challenge', he quickly topped up the glass, if it could act as some sort of sedative for John's current mood then all the better. Dave was in a difficult situation, he could see John's volatile nature was gathering pace and needed to placate him in some way, he was after all the gallery's 'Golden Goose' so to speak. He needed to act quickly and calm John down if their fruitful business endeavours were to continue. Now sat on the corner of his desk he looked straight at John, like a barrister about to advise an irascible client, 'look, hear me out, just listen for one minute, forget hearsay and gut feelings, just because you believe your version of the events it doesn't necessarily make for a watertight case'. John remained still for a brief moment but started to shake his head again, Dave pressed on regardless, 'OK then, let's just suppose you're right and this is Ross, ask yourself these questions, why would he do it? What motive could he possibly have? Think logically about it, you haven't seen him for years', he then hesitated at his own assumption, 'have you'? The Whisky seemed to be calming John down and he appeared to be listening. 'No! Course I haven't, but I just know, I just....', but before John could continue, on what Dave saw as yet another blind alley of paranoid delusion, he quickly interjected as his patience was now almost stretched to its limit, 'come on John pull yourself together, this doesn't make any sense, it's just got to be some daft kid, trying to impress his mates, that's all'.

Outside, in the main gallery, Frances had just walked in, having reconciled herself to the fact that she couldn't avoid John all day. Thinking he must have calmed down and couldn't possibly still be carrying the rage he had displayed this morning, or so she hoped. Frances decided to walk around the gallery and see some of John's recent works, they were she had to admit very impressive. One or two of the works still carried his hallmark political angst but she reckoned those must have been some of his earlier street works, whereas most of his recent work was unashamedly commercial art. John's transition from street artist to studio artist had been a skilful piece of entrepreneurial manoeuvring, orchestrated almost solely by Dave. John's new style of work was indeed striking and thought provoking, but she thought it seemed quite dark and verging on the macabre. John's artwork had never been by any stretch of the imagination 'colourful' like the impressionists, but this latest body of work seemed introspective and disturbing. The images depicted top hatted and dark cloaked Victorian 'Ripperesque' figures with grotesque or hidden faces, the characters were juxtaposed alongside historic parts of London in darkness or swirling mist, while contemporary graffiti adorned the walls. His work was pure genius, but they made her feel very uncomfortable, they were uncanny and a product she feared, of a disturbed mind. Frances now strolled towards Dave's back office, she knew John would be in there, as he was never seen in the gallery itself. She'd had enough fighting for one day and felt in a more positive frame of mind, but just as she was about to knock on the office door, when she heard the raised voices of Dave and John arguing. Her heart sank as she thought, was there no escape from this never-ending mental torture that threatened to overwhelm her life.

Chapter Eight
Logwood Black Lake

'Hematoxylin oxidized to Hematein, ingesting
large amounts can be poisonous'

Blueish to purple black

Ross sat in his flat looking at the information
he had collated about John Nobles'
artwork. It was a comprehensive list of all
his protected public works, very conveniently
supplied by one of the major Broadsheets,
presumably he thought to attract the 'tourists' not
'anarchists' like himself. Number one on the list,
the 'Thatcherite protest' work, he had to admit
had been a somewhat bungled affair but ultimately
successful. There were now seven other sites listed
in the newspaper article, but Ross knew he would
have to work on his own from now on, so he
decided to select the next target based not so much
on the desirability of the work but more on the
practicality and ease of the attack. He couldn't
afford to be caught this early on in his campaign,
so he scanned the addresses of the works to
identify an area that he was familiar with. He
narrowed this list down to two possible targets, the
more challenging locations would have to wait
until later.

His selected targets were an urban triptych called *'The Good, The Bad and the Ugly'* which was he thought, well constructed but now found its message somewhat trite. The second image *'Ballistic'* was in a different league, it still carried a powerful message twenty years on from its inception. It was a work he particularly admired, albeit grudgingly as Noble had been its creator, but more importantly he thought, it was undoubtedly a work that meant a great deal to 'Mr Noble's' growing sense of inflated self-importance, as it had recently been given a Grade two listing by the local Borough council .The work itself focused on the nuclear arms race and depicted amongst other things an enormous image of a cruise missile with the words *'To Russia without Love'* it was dramatic and painted on a large scale, any attack upon it would definitely make the newspapers again if he targeted this one. Ross thought about the previous attack and had one major regret, and it wasn't that he was damaging John Noble's work but more that his protest went unrecognised, and the attack had been reported as nothing more than mindless vandalism. This portrayal by the media was a major issue for Ross, he was still achieving his remit, but it would have greater satisfaction for him, if there was a more artistic edge to his protest. Towards this end he decided to employ a technique that was popular on the current street scene, he would use a stencil, they were fast and easy to use and created the instant 'ready meal' of a protest. He had designed and cut a stencil of John Noble's face, whose craggy features and prominent nose were a caricaturists dream. Ross thought that Noble's secret status wouldn't last for long as soon as people started asking questions about the 'face', and the press would undoubtedly take an interest. Time and circumstances allowing, he could still improvise, the 'SPYDER' tag would always be hand done, he could create his 'tag' blindfold and just like a great sportsman his technique was tried and tested and was delivered with effortless ease, grace, and consummate skill.

Later that evening, John was at home and presently lay comatose in his man cave after several bottles of what his vintner had described as 'a good quality and reasonably priced red', a bargain at eighteen hundred pounds for a six-bottle case'. Upstairs Frances tossed and turned restlessly in bed, mulling over the day's turbulent vicissitudes. Dave Hemmings on the other hand was sat observing the 'late night life' across the Thames and scanning through yachts for sale on his newly purchased Surface Pro, his latest gadget. He wasn't a Tekkie, he could pay some wet behind the ears school leaver to take care of work-related IT for him. No, this was pleasure, he liked a gadget or two, in fact he liked anything that gave him an edge in business or in life and an eighty-foot Sunseeker yacht on the coast near Antibes was high upon his wanted list.

Over in a not so 'fashionable' council flat in East London, Ross laid the tools of his trade out on a scratched and stained 1960's Formica topped table, the table, just like Ross had suffered the rigours of life and had taken everything that people could throw at it over fifty or so years of use. It had even survived being dumped in a local skip thanks to Ross's intervention. Hammer, screwdriver, and wire cutters lay side by side, he didn't want another episode like the 'last one' with Karl, no wire fence was going to de-rail his night before it had even begun. Tins of spray paint, just the basics nothing too elaborate, black, red, white, and silver, all newly purchased with nothing left to chance. As he looked at his 'weapons' laid out on the table, he recalled his grandfather's booming voice, 'remember the five P's boy, 'Poor Preparation leads to Piss Poor Performance' his grandfather liked recalling his army experiences, well the positive ones Ross always thought. He loaded his tools and cans into his *Pink Floyd* emblazoned haversack, not perhaps the most unobtrusive way to carry them but he regarded it as his Talisman and knew he would need every bit of luck that could be mustered. As Ross left his flat, he was forced to slam the front door to close it, he hadn't wanted to make a noise and draw attention to his departure as he couldn't trust the neighbours but with its ill-fitting lock, it was the only way of shutting it. Once outside the air was icy cool, the sky a deep almost black shade of purply blue, it was clear, and the stars and moon lay like jewels on a bed of velvet. What an 'awesome' sight he thought, imagining the endless and awe-inspiring idea of distant untouched and uninhabited planets, but unfortunately for him, a moonlight night wasn't necessarily conducive to his clandestine activities. Ross had decided this was the night and now there was no turning back, a solitary dog barked in the distance, a dust bin lid rattled somewhere on the estate, there were signs of life, but they were limited and transitory. As he descended the stairs the few sickly pale yellow emergency lights that hadn't been vandalised, flickered on and off, two kids stared at him but said nothing. They had their hoods up and turned their backs to him as he approached. He didn't know if they belonged in the block of flats but that was part of the problem today, he thought. Nobody cared any more, people just ignored each other, no social integration, no recognition, it dismayed Ross, but this form of social anonymity suited his purposes well, at least for tonight. Outside on the street there were increasing signs of life, people returning home after a night out, people just about to go out for the night, it was a twenty-four-hour existence, people, cars and more importantly noise, it would all help to conceal and distract people from his movements. Ross always thought how strange it was that you could sit in your flat in relative silence and think the world around you were doing the same form of 'nothingness' but you could step out onto the streets at two a.m. and the world was alive with life, a life with its own sub-culture and rules. Ross made his way across the road and disappeared down the nearest alleyway, from here he could make his way along the backstreets to his target. It was roughly two miles away, a thirty or so minute walk he had calculated. He seemed to glide along with ease, he was pumped up and the adrenalin of expectation was racing through his veins, it was excitement tinged with fear. He now realised he had missed this 'feeling', it reminded him of his younger days, when he would have been out all night looking for locations for his artwork. As he came out of a side street and stepped into the road, he was dazzled by car headlights, he instinctively stopped and the car broke and swerved, it all seemed to happen in slow motion, the car skidded and caught Ross, it lifted him off his feet, he rolled over the top of the wing and then landed awkwardly on the ground. He lay stunned and motionless for what seemed like an eternity, slowly he gathered his thoughts, he sat up and removed his haversack, instantly he felt a searing pain in his shoulder. A young man and a woman had now got out of the car and stood over him, they then kneeled on the ground, the man took out his phone and said, 'I'll ring for an ambulance'. Ross felt dazed but the word 'ambulance' instantly cleared his head, an ambulance meant unwanted attention and worse still the Police, then questions, the whole works. He could almost hear the questions, What's your name? Where are you going? What's in your bag? He had to get going, he grimaced and struggled to his feet, his shoulder throbbed with an intense pain, his leg felt numb, but he could just about move, albeit like an ageing cart horse, but now knew he would be unable to move as freely as he had previously. The man now tried to steady Ross, 'I'm OK mate', just a little sore, that's all, but I'll manage, just got to take it easy' he said. Ross struggled again to bend down and pick up his bag, he then slowly moved on his way. The woman was now shouting at her partner 'to do something' but he just shrugged his shoulders, Ross had done him a big favour, no Police, no questions. Looking at Ross in his camouflage trousers and jacket, the young man assumed this waster was probably dealing drugs and didn't want the Police to come and discover the truth of what he was up to. He thought to himself, maybe he had almost done society a favour, by taking out this 'dealer of death' on the streets. Ross struggled into the nearest alleyway and disappeared out of sight, initially he stood with his back to the wall in the shadows trying to convince himself he was OK, but slowly like a felled tree, his legs gave way, and he keeled over and lay on the ground. He felt a stabbing pain as he tried to turn his body to the right and get on his feet again. It was no good, he needed to gather his thoughts, cars and sirens rushed by on the main street no more than hundred yards from where he had now struggled into a seated position. He fumbled in his pocket for his cigarettes, every movement seemed to be a challenge, eventually he lit a cigarette and the smoke from it seemed to hang in the freezing late-night air, the orange glow as he drew on it was the only sign of life in the dark, rubbish strewn and filthy back alley. Ross was now a desperate and wounded animal, alone and vulnerable, he had a dilemma, should he continue his nights quest or should he return to the relative safety of his flat. He immediately dismissed his 'safe' second option, knowing he had come too far that night and life in general to stop. OK he was hurting now, but surely that would pass, pain usually did when you focused your mind onto a target or an object. That's what his grandfather had told him they had to do if they were captured and interrogated during the war, focus on an object, stare, and stare at it, till the reality of what was happening to you just disappeared. Ross focussed on his cigarette, inhaled deeply and then exhaled with a sense of relief that he had at least survived the accident. The nicotine now raced through his body and numbed the pain he had suffered, gradually it gave him the impetus to pull himself together and proceed with his journey. He struggled up onto his feet, everything now seemed to ache, 'yes', he was suffering physically but psychologically was still surprisingly in a good 'place'. He gathered his positive thoughts and attempted to loosen himself up with some gentle side to side movements, the pain had subsided slightly, but he could still feel a debilitating level of discomfort in his shoulder and leg. Could be a fracture he thought, 'no' he said and confronted his negative thoughts, more likely just bruising. On a positive note, he was now more than halfway to his target, he had approximately a mile or so to go if he made his way indirectly through the backstreets and alleyways. It would make the journey a little longer, but he could just take his time and hope he didn't come across any more trouble, but this was a big risk given the number of gangs that roamed the streets at night. Ross certainly didn't feel up to fighting and running away from any trouble given his present condition was out of the question.

Ross slowly made progress through a series of backstreets many of which he was familiar with and some that he wasn't, he was still suffering from discomfort, but the night's winter chill and his determination nullified the pain somewhat. Eventually he arrived at 'the target', he stood in the nearest shadows to survey the image, and there it was, a twelve-foot-high former protest against the nuclear arms race, it was much bigger than he remembered but strangely given the way his night had unfolded so far, luck was now on his side. The image was too large to be protected by a screen or perhaps the council were just too embarrassed to spend the taxpayers money in case it incited a backlash in the papers. '*Council spend thousands protecting vandals graffiti*', he could just imagine such a headline in the tabloids, but who cared about the papers he thought, they were full of lies, fabrication and twisted truths. 'Come on focus' Ross said to himself, luck is on your side for once, there was scaffolding up the wall on which the image was painted. He decided the council must be carrying out some sort of repairs, but whatever the reason, his task had suddenly become a much easier prospect for a successful outcome. Initially because of its size, he had prepared for a ground assault maybe reaching at most seven or eight feet high, but the scaffolding now presented him with an unexpected opportunity. As he stood in the shadows contemplating how to get onto the scaffolding, suddenly a dust bin rattled and fell over behind him, then a gruff voice shouted at him from the shadows, 'here, what you up to, you little scroat'. Ross turned to see an amorphous looking rock shape made from material slowly move and rise to take the form of a man, a huge man who resembled Shakespeare's bearded Falstaff. His outer garment was a long ex-army great coat, tattered, torn and battle scarred, he had a mass of tousled unwashed hair that stood up like a cliff from his forehead and a face almost black with ingrained dirt, his white eyes shone like beacons through the blackness, his face was framed by a stalactite beard, long, grey and bedraggled. He shouted again 'you bloody kids always up to no good'. A 'kid' Ross laughed, kid, a kid he repeated to himself, daft old sod he thought, I'm fifty-three. 'You alright dad', Ross said to him, trying to diffuse what could easily become an awkward situation, the last thing he wanted was some copper turning up because of someone reporting a disturbance. Ross knew what a rough life it was on the streets and usually all people wanted was some little comforts, the kind of things most people took for granted. Ross moved towards the man and held out a cigarette, 'here mate have a fag,' he said. The man wary at first, now shuffled towards Ross, he was a big man and even though stooped by age he was well over six feet tall and although both his body and mind had seen better days, Ross was sure he could present him with a problem if things turned physical. As Ross lit the man's cigarette, the lighter's flickering flame highlighted the stranger's face with a pale-yellow glow, he looked like a bystander in Joseph Wright's oil painting '*The Experiment*', with craggy lines around sad looking eyes that were transfixed by the glare of the lighter. He looked to be at least seventy years of age, but Ross could tell from his own experiences of living on the 'streets' that this poor soul would be sixty, if that, and that the ravages of British winters, lack of decent food and friendship had robbed him of at least one fifth of his life if not more. Ross felt sympathy for him, but he could tell that there was no great connection between them, this man had spent too long on the streets and any social skills he may have had at one time, had now been replaced by a single-minded desire for survival, almost robotic, his connection with reality irreparably severed. The man took a long manic drag on his cigarette then coughed uncontrollably, his voice hoarse with smoke, he then got his eye on Ross's camouflage trousers. The man nodded respectfully at the trousers and said 'army, you been in the forces my lad?' Ross now saw an opportunity to calm things down, even though the closest he'd ever been to the army was being on the receiving end of one of their water cannons at a protest that turned ugly in the early 1990's. He took a gamble, spun an imaginary roulette wheel, and plumped for his grandfather's old regiment, 'Royal Engineers' said Ross. 'Ahh REME, eh', the man said, nodding his head at the same time, 'good blokes them sappers, could fix anything, me, I was Irish Guards, twenty-five years, twenty-five years' he repeated with pride. The man's aggressive demeanour seemed to soften at the realisation of their 'brothers in arms' connection. Ross's gamble had worked, the man now stood in silence, he then nodded and gave a purposeful almost tragic comic salute, he then shook his head and muttered something incomprehensible under his breath, turned away from Ross and began to shuffle off back into the darkness of the alley from which he had first appeared. Ross followed him and pushed some of his own pre-rolled cigarettes into his hand. 'One Squaddie to another eh, take care man,' said Ross. The man turned and looked at him, there was a glimmer of recognition in his troubled and now watery eyes, kindness had been a stranger to him for too many years, he didn't say anything but just nodded his appreciation, Ross felt as though he had touched his soul. The man now moved on and Ross took a long drag on the remainder of his cigarette, tilted his head back and blew a plume of white smoke into the freezing cold air. Now thinking, could anything else go wrong tonight, he had started out with one mission in mind, that would be difficult enough on his own, but so far, all the careful planning had gone somewhat astray. He now moved back to the shadows again, which overlooked the 'target'. Everything seemed strangely quiet, too quiet he thought and there were no security guards this time, the target sat almost submissive awaiting his attention. He crossed over the road and surveyed the scaffolding, no ladders were available, so he would have to climb onto the first level. His side still gave him considerable pain but now he was in the 'zone', he threw his bag of tools up onto the first level and then took a firm grip of one of the scaffolding poles, he would have to get one foot onto one of the metal clamps that held the scaffolding together and then pull himself up. He got one foot on the clamp but as he attempted to pull himself up the pain was intense, 'Ahhgh bastard' he said aloud, grimacing he pulled and pulled and somehow managed to launch himself un-ceremoniously onto the landing, while at the same time attempting to avoid rolling onto his painful side. Lying on his back he breathed deeply waiting for the pain to subside, the scaffolding boards were hard and unyielding, but they were the most comfortable resting place Ross could ever have hoped for. He had carefully planned how he would disfigure the work and now sitting up, he proceeded to empty the contents of his bag onto the staging, it clattered noisily in the cold night air. First things first he thought, he needed to be roughly just off centre of the image to spray the word 'SPYDER'. The tag was completed in its usual livery of black and silver, in the cold air the spray cans spluttered and coughed and were loath to flow freely, but Ross persevered to maintain the standard he always set for himself. Once the tag was done his next job was to spray a large Spiders web across much of the image, he would start this on the scaffolding but would have to get down to ground level off to finish it off. The completion of the 'web' took longer than he had expected but he was determined to create something that was both artistic and striking and wouldn't be regarded this time by the media as an act of mindless vandalism. Next, he positioned the template he had created of John Nobles face within the web, taped it into place and took great pleasure in spraying onto it, he sprayed a little too zealously as the paint ran down the front of the template and Ross had to give it a few moments to dry before continuing. The moment had arrived, he slowly peeled back the template to reveal John Noble's crying face complete with outstretched hands grabbing onto the spiders web, he was trapped, struggling and unable to escape. Ross surveyed his nights work, he nodded agreeably and was just about to pack up his 'tools', when on impulse he grabbed a tin of white spray paint and artistically fashioned the words 'ART WHORE' in two-foot-high letters below John Noble's image. Ross now laughed out aloud and shouted 'yes' this would be 'Nobles' new tag from now on.

Chapter Nine
Quinacridone Burnt Scarlet

'Mixed crystal phase quinacridone'

Dark Orange to violet Brown

The morning after Ross's night of artistic destruction, Dave Hemmings poured himself a fresh glass of orange juice as he sat in his riverside apartment. Dave was wearing his usual crisp white shirt complete with cufflinks and a 'borrowed' MCC gold and red striped tie. A tie someone had mistakenly left in a Gentleman's club washroom, and he had seized the opportunity and taken it. He sometimes wore it for a laugh, he knew nothing about Cricket and didn't want to, but as with most things in life just displaying a connection to something 'establishment orientated' usually impressed people and opened doors. It was six thirty in the morning and he was preparing for the forthcoming day's business by grabbing a relaxing ten minutes in the 'Eames' before leaving for the gallery. It was still dark as he looked across the Thames, but all the usual signs of life were there, he loved his adopted city, its vibrancy, its twenty-four-hour culture if you wanted it, it was every entrepreneurs dream. Dave put his feet up, sipped his orange juice and took out his mobile phone and scrolled through his most recent messages, nothing of any importance caught his eye. As he neared the bottom of his e-mail list' suddenly one message drew his eye like iron filings to a magnet. '*Ballistic*' was its heading, as he opened the message there was a picture attachment along with several lines of text. Dave didn't read the text, he just loaded the image, at first, he thought it was someone trying to sell him some street art, he received many requests from 'wannabe' street artists who wanted to trade their urban poverty inspired art for high street gallery stardom. He was just about to delete the image when he realised what the picture was, it was John's iconic '*Ballistic*' image or what was now left of it in Lime House. He scrolled back to the text, it read '*thought you would want to see this, someone has defaced our image*', the 'our' referred to the fact that the image had been donated to the local council by Dave Hemmings. An act that had represented a carefully managed publicity stunt and not the social philanthropy expressed in the press at the time. The text described how the image had been defaced and that the attack was all captured-on CCTV, the images it said were grainy and dark, but it appeared to be the work of just one person. The sender of the text was local councillor Joe Denton, an 'old school' councillor, in Dave's jargon 'bent', he often gave Dave some useful inside information on lucrative local planning applications in return for what Dave described as the monetary equivalent of a 'little drink'. In fact, if it hadn't been for Joe, Dave wouldn't sitting on a large and valuable portfolio of property acquisitions in what were now fashionable areas, which had at one time had been some of least desirable and poorest boroughs in London. Dave expanded the image by stretching it with his fingertips on his touch phone, he managed to zoom into the newly added image of John, trapped in a web, at first, he laughed at the caricatured and tormented representation, but then realised this was going to be a big problem for him. He knew that John would be 'incandescent with rage' and it would be impossible to placate him again after their previous heated debate. Dave was almost tempted to have a stronger drink than his current orange juice, as he watched the city come to life as light by light appeared in sleepy bedsits and buildings crammed cheek by jowl along the Thames. He knew he needed to act quickly to head off the impending psychological weather front of 'storm John' but was unsure as to the best way forward. He needed to calm him down and keep him focused on producing his artwork, rather than losing the plot and becoming so obsessed with what Dave knew could become a purely 'Ross focussed' all-consuming paranoia. He knew Campbell, but hadn't seen him for many years, and had always viewed him as a dreamer and an anarchist, someone always on the side of the underdog, but more importantly he knew that you couldn't buy him off. Dave recognised weaknesses in people and knew how to exploit them, be it the offer of sex, money, or drugs. However, people like Ross were a major problem, principled and a maverick, traits he saw as a lethal combination, these kind of people were dangerous and unpredictable. If it transpired that Ross was behind these attacks and Dave still wasn't totally convinced about that, so he decided to approach some contacts he had in the Police force. He would call in a few 'favours', maybe they could harass Ross a bit, warn him off, and maybe, just maybe this would calm things down, or rather calm John down more importantly.

Dave arrived at the gallery earlier than usual, he wanted to try and get hold of his contact in the 'force' before the inevitable phone call or worse still, a visit from John. How long would it take for John to find out would be anybody's guess, but at least Dave had been forewarned. He didn't want to use text or any other form of social media to reach his Police contact. He didn't really trust mobile phones either, heeding the media rumours that all calls were listened to or worse still recorded. His contact wasn't on speed dial in case his phone was ever lost and then subsequently interrogated. Dave tapped in the number, contacts he had memorised 'on a need-to-know basis'. The number barely rang twice before a voice simply replied, 'Mr H long time no see, so what's the problem?' The voice on the other end of the phone didn't receive social calls from Dave, he simply provided a 'service'. Dave wasted no time, he outlined his problem, providing only essential details to his 'man in the Met'. The 'voice' said they could take a look at the Council CCTV footage and if they could identify the culprit, they could bring charges of criminal trespass and wilful damage to council property. This all sounded just like a little slap on the wrist as far as Dave was concerned and he asked if they couldn't perhaps hassle even rough him up a bit, as he thought this direct approach would be more to John's liking. The 'voice' laughed at this request 'this isn't the 1960's anymore, everything must be done by the book, there are so many watchdogs and official bodies, you could never get away with it Mr H'. Political correctness gone mad that's what Dave thought, but his contact was adamant that his best course of action was to do it strictly through the legal channels. Dave had to begrudgingly admit to himself that this course of action was probably right. After all he had a totally legitimate enterprise that had a sound and useful press profile and any hint of scandal could irreparably affect his hard-won business success, but more importantly strangle his cash flow. Dave sat in his office for a good hour mulling over the best way to approach this current problem. He prided himself on being a 'fixer' of most things but this issue if he wasn't careful could become his very own UXB. Chewing on his thumb nail he contemplated his next move, should he grab the initiative and ring first before John called him, this way he would have some control. Getting in first, maybe just maybe, could keep things calm, because if John found out from another 'source' the blue touch paper of his rage would be lit and then the chances of keeping him grounded and sensible would have long diminished. He decided that attack as usual was his best form of defence and he therefore resolved to call John up and take the lead.

As Dave selected John from his contacts list, unusually for him he felt a certain sense of reticence not because he was 'afraid', that emotion wasn't part of Dave's vocabulary, no he thought it was more the sense of the unknown. He normally read people quite well, but this seemed different, just as he was contemplating his opening gambit, John answered. Dave's initial thought was, well at least he doesn't sound 'hung over' which was unusual. 'John mate' said Dave confidently wanting to take control from the outset. 'I was going to wait and see you in person before I told you', he lied, 'but we have had a problem with another attack on one of 'our' works', he stressed the 'our' in a feigned attempt to demonstrate his shared annoyance and support. John immediately snapped back a reply, 'what did I tell you, but no one bloody listens, I told you didn't I, which one is it?' 'Limehouse' replied Dave. '*Ballistic*, that's one of my best ones, that bastard, I'll ...' retorted John, Dave swiftly interrupted, 'just let's keep calm, it's annoying, but like I said last time it's not the end of the world'. Dave continued unabated not allowing John to speak 'look I've had a word with my contact in the Met, they might be able to find out who's doing this, and then it can all be done by the book, no need to get our hands dirty'. Silence came from John, followed by half-crazed laughter, 'forget it Dave, I know who it is and so do you, just admit it'. 'Hey, come on John, let's not jump to conclusions yet again, before we have some hard facts, let's try and keep an open mind. John remained silent, 'OK?' said Dave seeking some form of agreement. 'Yeah, whatever you say' replied John, but he seemed nonchalant and somewhat distracted, his mind somewhere else. Maybe he was hungover after all thought Dave, but he was more than pleased to accept John's seemingly insouciant attitude to his request and thought this whole incident might after all just blow over. Dave decided to quit while he was ahead and leave things in a state of acceptable flux for the time being and said he would catch up with John later and let him know of any developments, although secretly he hoped there wouldn't be any.

As the call ended, John sat in his boxer shorts and vest in his man cave, surrounded by the usual array of empty and half empty bottles, he wasn't hungover as such, but felt mildly 'off-colour' after another night of binge drinking. He assumed that he was becoming immune to the worst aspect of alcohol 'the hangover' as the mornings weren't as bad as they used to be, but fortunately alcohol still helped him rationalise or better still sometimes forget his problems. He swept his hair back over his head and rubbed his face, he could feel two days stubble rasp against the palms of his hands. The recent conversation with Dave had provoked a realisation and a determination that he had to pull himself together and get this issue with Campbell and 'yes he knew' unlike Dave, 'yes', he was one hundred percent sure hir tormentor was Ross Campbell, he could just feel it. He was experiencing that 'sixth' sense that people have when there is something inexplicably wrong, the German's called it 'unheimlich' the 'uncanny' a wariness, a recognition of an uneasiness that just won't subside. Now gripped by an ever growing and uncontrollable paranoia, he was convinced that no-one apart from himself, could possibly understand or resolve this problem to 'his' satisfaction. He decided he had to take control, the thought gave him an impetus that had been lacking in his life for some time. The more he thought about Ross the more his rage flared like ignited Phosphorous, glowing white and seemingly inextinguishable, now consumed by anger he slammed his fist down on the desk and then with his outstretched arm swept an array of bottles and ornaments across the desktop and sent them crashing onto the floor. He then leapt up off his chair with all the urgency of an Army private jumping to attention on seeing his commanding officer enter the room, he now made his way to the bathroom. As he walked through the hallway in his bare feet, the cold tiled floor invigorated his movement, he didn't even notice the note Frances had left him on the hall table.' *Out shopping in town, won't be back until late afternoon*' but that wasn't unusual, as she did her best to avoid John in the mornings to allow him time to sober up. He now stood in the shower with his eyes closed, the warm soothing water cascaded down onto his head and ran in rivulets down his body, the action didn't just cleanse his body it seemed to free his mind, negative thoughts seemed to disappear and were replaced by a calm and warm sense of euphoria. By the time John had decided to get out of the shower, he had already formulated his plan. Firstly, he decided he would visit the site of the '*Ballistic*' image and see at first-hand what Campbell had done, this he decided was a pre-requisite to galvanise his thoughts and forthcoming actions. He would dress down for his visit to Limehouse, not wanting to stand out, he would park his Range Rover some distance away and just walk to the site. John had an uneventful almost mesmeric journey to Limehouse, suitably 'camouflaged' he thought in jeans, sweatshirt, and a black hooded top. John got out of his Range Rover, glanced about him then flicked the button on his remote to lock his car, the orange lights flashed, and the Rover made an audible high-pitched sound, confirming that it was 'armed'. He had chosen a quiet back street about half a mile from the '*Ballistics*' location. As he stood looking at his car and getting his bearings, he turned around and some way off, two young lads were watching, he stared at them and they unnervingly for him, just stared back. They seemed to have no fear, there was a time that he could remember if cheeky kids looked your way and you stared back at them, they would look away or just move on, but not these days. He didn't want any trouble so decided on a direct approach, they looked about eighteen or nineteen. John now walked towards them, 'all right lads, see it doesn't come to any harm eh' he said, now pointing with pride at his beloved Range Rover. John then handed the kids a twenty-pound note, almost speechless they barely managed a cursory 'cheers mate, err... no problem' as their eyes lit up at the sight of ready cash. It was worth a gamble John thought, he saw it as a 'basic' insurance policy and cheap at twice the price if his car was untouched upon his return. John had no idea who the kids were, just two no-marks as far as he was concerned, but he felt good, and thought he could still connect with 'the kids' even though he had an underlying contempt for them. As he turned and walked away, the kids looked at each other and then one of them staring at John now some distance away, said, 'see that flash git, he nearly killed me a few days ago on a fucking Zebra crossing, the bastard'. Karl hadn't immediately recognised John, when he had approached them, but he did know his cars and white Range Rover Vogues with specialist AMG styling kits and twenty-four-inch diamond black alloys were very rare, especially in their part of town. Karl decided to seek revenge on his 'new benefactor' and immediately took out his spray cans from his Gola Satchel bag. He gracefully and without any surprising hurry, as he didn't need to worry too much about being disturbed in an anonymous shitty back lane, proceeded to write the word ' *Wanker*' in two feet high 'fat boy' script, down the driver's side of the 'Voguey'. It was a simplistic and abusive assault that even John might have appreciated in his younger days. The use of mainly black lettering with silver allowed for a highlighted star effect to the 'W' and the 'R'. The whole process of spraying the car seemed like the beginning of some sort of pagan ritual, a ceremonial decoration before the slaughter. Karl's mate looked on in pure disbelief, not a fellow street artist his contribution was to shout 'tosser' and hurl a house brick at the cars windscreen. It didn't shatter the car's screen, it bounced off, but not before it took the impact like a boxer soaking up a well-directed punch, the brick crazed the screen and left a large concave indentation, the car was badly bruised but not knocked out. The cars alarm sounded immediately on the brick's impact and emitted a deafening high pitched repetitive scream, like that of a wounded and cornered animal, then the hazard lights joined in to register the car's 'pain'. Karl and his mate immediately stopped and stared at each other, their violent retribution was temporarily frozen by the brain numbing and ear-piercing noise. The alarm's sound now seemed to reverberate and bounce off everything in its path, dustbins, doors, even walls, shared in the electronic 'symphony of fear'. Sensing the possibility of discovery for their act of vandalism they jubilantly and quickly 'high fived' each other and ran off in the opposite direction to the car's owner. John feeling buoyant walked on completely unaware of this most recent defilement of his property, he knew most of the backstreets, although it had been some years since he had wandered about on foot in less salubrious areas like this. He had spent years in his younger days as a feral street artist dodging the Police and Council workers, basically anyone who had the authority and muscle to thwart his aims of spreading his message of social injustice. There were, he had to admit begrudgingly to himself been some good times with Ross. They had been very close and had undertaken many 'Missions' together, but the bitterness he felt towards Ross now, quickly extinguished any nostalgic thoughts that had briefly flashed through his mind. As he approached the side street that overlooked the 'image', his progress slowed as he neared the end of the alley. He could see the scaffolding that partly obscured the image, the very platform that Ross had struggled to climb onto. As he moved closer, the defacement became all too apparent, as the words 'SPYDER' seemed to almost 'glow' nuclear like on the wall. 'Bastard' he shouted, as he surveyed the calligraphic snub. He now stood across the road, just as Ross had done', suddenly he heard a scuffling sound behind him, he turned quickly thinking someone was going to mug him. Turning around quickly he saw a tall and slightly stooped figure, a 'bedraggled dosser', that was how John perceived him, it was ironic, given his early years in squats and the odd night on the streets sleeping rough, that he had no sympathy for people who he should have understood, his only feeling now, was one of contempt. He was just about to tell the old man to 'Piss Off' assuming he was going to ask him for money, when the man said 'I saw him do that you know, watched him, didn't see me though, I've done surveillance see, army and that' .'Is that right dad' replied John, it was bizarre thought John calling the man 'dad' as he probably wasn't much older than himself, he just looked older , a lot older , the ravages of street life had taken their toll, but he had no empathy, and cruelly he thought 'you got what you deserved in life'. 'So, who was he? Just some kid I suppose' said John probing for the confirmation he so desperately sort. 'Kid, hell no, he was ex-army like me, fatigues, balaclava, the lot, good sort as well, gave me fags he did, army blokes look after each other, we've got to, cos civvies don't understand us you see, think were odd, they can't understand what 'we' go through'. Then the man just started mumbling incoherently to himself and out came an inaudible fog of words created by years of psychological withdrawal. John was impatient to get the information he sought, so he took out yet another key to unlocking the souls of the desperate 'money', a crisp new twenty-pound note. 'Here dad, get yourself a few beers, I've always admired you army blokes, selfless that's what you are, Queen 'n' Country and all that, not like these bloody lazy kids these days'. The man nodded in agreement, John had the man's attention, so he pressed on, 'So this bloke, which regiment was he in', the man shook his head, 'don't remember', Scottish bloke though, they like a drink don't they, the Jocks, eh', he then coughed uncontrollably and spat on the ground. John initially swayed backwards with disgust but then approached and held the money up in front of the man's face, like a red card to a footballer, he then folded it neatly and pushed it into the top pocket of the man's filthy and torn coat. The overcoat had seen better days, a piece of frayed string was used to fasten it around his waist as it had no buttons, this simple act mirrored his frail grasp on life, things just about held together but were liable to break at any time. John had all the information he wanted, he knew it was Ross, not only had he put his SPYDER tag on the work but the fact that he was Scottish sealed the deal for John. It was all he needed to know, he didn't care if anyone else, especially Dave believed him or not, he now knew for sure and that's all that really mattered. He decided that even though it was like a knife twisting in his side, he would take a closer look at Ross's vandalism, that's how he now perceived it, wanton mindless destruction. The Spiders web Ross had painted covered a good two thirds of '*Ballistic*'. The additional image of John trapped within the web struck a desperate chord within him, it was a metaphor for his life, he did feel trapped, trapped in a marriage that wasn't working and trapped by a problem that nobody wanted to resolve. Buoyed and feeling more than a little smug by his earlier success in persuading the two youths to 'keep an eye' on his pride and joy, the Range Rover, and now finding out from the tramp about Ross, he now felt a sense of achievement and power. He was still angry but strangely now felt in control, he cast his mind back to Dave's advice about 'staying calm'. Maybe Dave was right, in a way he almost felt pity for Ross the pathetic no-hoper, there he was, a 'fifty something' radical, still mixing with the 'down and outs' in the early hours of the morning. Still spewing out his pointless 'street' rhetoric with a spray can, what a pathetic loser he had become. John decided to ring Dave and see what could be done about sorting Ross out without him having to be personally involved, that's what Dave wanted, so he would put the ball in his court. He rang Dave on his mobile whilst staring at his ruined and defaced image, but the words 'Art Whore' which stared back at him gnawed at his very tenuous grasp of humility. The phone rang and rang and rang, eventually his answer phone cut in with a quirky impression of Michael Caine, 'Dave's not in at the moment, not a lot of people know that.' the voice said followed by a long pause. John was just about to leave a message, when he heard Dave's voice, 'John, mate, everything OK?'. Sat in his office, with his feet on his desk, he had his laptop displaying yet another luxury yacht for sale, 'two secs mate I'll just...' he said, now putting his laptop down and taking his feet off the desk, he sighed and thought to himself 'what now'? 'Sorry about that, so what's happening'. 'I'm here', John said, he assumed that everyone else was as fixated as much as he was about Ross. 'Just update me, where's here?' replied Dave. This almost nonchalant response irritated John, his brief flirtation with his inner Karma disappeared with all the grace of a punch in the face. 'The Limehouse site, why else would I call you, have you seen what that Scottish twat has done, Spiders bloody web with me trapped in it'. Before Dave could get another word in, 'fucking *Art whore* that's what he's called me, the bastard', shouted John. Dave shook his head, here we go again he thought, 'steady on, we don't know for sure its Ross' replied Dave. 'I bloody well do' said John his voice now raised, Dave now beginning to lose his patience snapped back as he said, 'so come on then, how do you know for sure'. John continued 'because some down and out watched him do it, he even spoke to him, Scottish bloke he said, come on Dave don't try and convince me otherwise'. Like a verbal machine gun John rattled on 'I want something done about him, he's making me look like a joke and I've had enough'. Like a fish out of water, John took a huge gulp of air and continued almost without stopping, 'Can't your mate in the force have him warned off, fitted up for something'. Thinking of what his contact in the force had said. Dave just repeated it in a language John would understand, 'this isn't 1960's London with bent coppers on the take and the Kray twins running amok, this is 2016, it has to be done by the 'book', everything gets scrutinised, it's got to be done legally, but we've got the time and money, we've got to be patient mate'. 'Bollocks to all that', It's not even a fuckin slap on the wrist, I can sort this myself,' shouted John. 'I've told you before John, don't do it, don't get involved you've got a lot to lose', 'don't you mean 'we', countered John smugly. This retort grated on Dave, selfish sod he thought to himself, when I think what I've done for you, you'd be nothing without me, but Dave held his tongue and simply agreed 'OK then John, I'll rephrase that, yes, 'we' all have a lot to lose'. Dave could feel his hackles rising, 'yes', he needed John, but he also had a lot of cash tucked away and didn't need him forever, but realised he had to keep the 'things' together for now. Now it was Dave's turn to have his say, 'So OK then John, suppose you find Ross, then what?' Give him a good kicking, would you? Then risk him going to the press and then watch everything you've worked for, just go down the drain, what does that achieve, and would you go to prison then, for, as you put it, that Scottish twat, that nobody, that waste of space'. John fell silent just listening to Dave's rant, which was calculated and targeted like an arrow to pierce the armour of John's aggressive fervour for revenge. He remained silent for what seemed like an eternity to Dave, when he finally spoke it appeared to Dave that he had managed to calm John down. 'Yeah, OK then, have a word with this contact of yours, see what he can do'. John seemed somewhat distant as he spoke to Dave, his mind now clouded and befuddled, his former intractable determination wavering slightly, confused, and unsure he needed to buy himself more time. Dave sensing a possible break through didn't want to labour the point, he was satisfied with what John had said and thought that perhaps his direct 'no-nonsense' approach had eventually hit home. Dave said he would catch up with John and was relieved that he had apparently 'seen sense' and wasn't going to do something 'they' would both regret. John now stood and stared at his defaced image, he ended the call without saying a word, then placed his phone back in his pocket, turned and looked around for the tramp, but he had gone. What a fucking life John thought, as he shook his head and looked at the overflowing bins of rubbish that littered the alley in which he stood. It was probably the tramps home for the night, the phrase 'you made your bed and slept in it' flashed through his mind without stopping to be processed by his conscience, he simply dismissed the tramps grotesque misery from his mind 'like swatting an errant fly' and started to make his way back towards his car. As he walked the jagged thoughts of revenge were smoothed slightly, he was still angry but what Dave had said to him perhaps had some merit. As he turned the corner to where his vehicle was parked, he immediately heard his car alarm and saw the hazard lights flashing on and off like an American street walk sign, shocked and now pumped with adrenalin he sprinted towards his car. As he got closer, he saw the graffiti and the smashed windscreen, he then just exploded with rage. He grabbed the nearest bin and hurled it some yards through the air, as it smashed down onto the ground its contents of tins, paper and all the general detritus of human existence sprawled across the ground. 'Bastards' he shouted, 'fucking bastards' I'll kill them and that Campbell as well'. The incident had now pushed John over the edge of any rationality that may have temporarily entered his mind, it was now that he decided to sort this matter with Ross in his own way. He was sick of being fobbed off with excuses and treat like an idiot, now, he wanted to retaliate in his own way, and knew just the people who could do it for him.

Chapter Ten
Han Blue

'Pulverized Ceramic, Barium copper silicate'

Deep reddish blue to purple Blue

John had returned home and was sat in his inner sanctum and on his second bottle of wine, opened only minutes previously and now already more than half consumed. He unlocked the top drawer of his desk and removed a spare mobile phone not registered under his name, this was a 'special' phone for his conversations and deals that had to be kept private. Wine and delusion now engendered scant regard and little consideration to what Dave had said on the phone about not getting involved with Ross Campbell. John had now decided to employ somebody else to do his 'dirty work' and thought it the perfect solution. Ross would be dealt with, and as far as Dave would be concerned, he wasn't personally involved. Feeling confident that the call he was about to make would solve all his problems, with an insouciant confidence he thumbed in the contact number. The phone rings and rings, 'come on, come on' John says aloud, he is desperate to get the 'game' started, 'answer the bloody thing' he demands in his mind. However, there is no reply and eventually the phone engages it's answering machine, there is background music, a droning Church organ playing the kind of music you would hear in a crematorium and then a deep slow creepy voice announces that 'the chapel of rest is closed at the moment, but please leave a message if you require our *specialist* out of hours services'. John was familiar with this message, however it still freaked him out, his newfound confidence ebbed at the thought of leaving a message, he decides to just ring off, doesn't want to leave anything that could link him with the service he hopes to take advantage of. No sooner had John put his phone down and gulped another mouthful of red wine when his 'special' phone vibrates with life, he stares at the phone, the motion makes it wiggle from side to side on the desk like a twitching dead animal. This 'is it' he thinks and knows that once he engages the services of the people on the other end of this phone, there is no turning back. With the phone now held in his hand like a grenade, he knows that once answered, the pin is out and what follows could be explosive and uncontrollable. Another gulp of wine and then he presses the 'accept call' button, a confident but 'matey' East London voice answers the phone and in a deep voice jokingly says, 'You rang', 'Frank, its John, I need your help with something, and I thought you might be the man to sort it'. John could hear a mixture of noises in the background of the call, the chink of exercise weights clanking together, voices shouting encouragement to go to the limit and the incessant gloving of punch bags, the 'oosh oosh' sound of controlled and targeted blows of punishment. Frank Swift ran a legitimate boxing and fitness club but also had a less dubious side-line in drug dealing and security, he described himself as a 'crowd control executive', which most people accepted was his euphemism for running the doors of local pubs and clubs where he supplied the bouncers. He was more than happy to give anyone who stepped out of line a little 'reprimand' as he called it. This sounded innocuous, however people did get hurt from time to time but generally it wasn't a problem as the Police usually sided with the doormen during late night scuffles with drunken punters. 'No problem' replied Frank, do you need something for a little party, 'No! it's nothing like that this time, it's more of a personal nature' replied John. Frank provided many 'services' and John had used this dubious 'contact' to supply some 'get the party started' substances in the past. 'Thing is, I've got a problem with a 'nobody' who's interfering with my day to day business and I need someone to, well ...' John hesitated, Frank interjected 'give him a little reprimand', 'well possibly' said John, 'but initially I just want you to warn him off, let him know that if he doesn't back off and behave, he could get hurt, something like that, know the sort of thing I mean?'. Frank laughed and then replied, 'Yeah, I know exactly what you mean, that's not a problem man, 'Cosh' my trusty sergeant at arms can take care of this for you'. John had met 'Cosh', a man that took verbal austerity to an extreme and someone he remembered as an evil looking bastard. Colm O'Shea known by his friends and enemies alike as 'Cosh', stood six foot tall and seemingly as wide, with a Japanese style dragon tattooed on his shaved head and a Scorpion on his hand. The Scorpion was a homage to his not so illustrious military service days in 'the Tin Bellies', a tank regiment more commonly known as the Blues and Royals and their motto suited him well *'Honi Soit Qui Maly Pense,'* Evil to him who evil thinks. John now explained to Frank about Ross but didn't go into too much detail from their past, he didn't need to know their 'personal' history. John said he didn't know where to find Ross, and glibly joked 'he's probably sleeping rough in some back alley'. Frank assured John that he had 'contacts' and could find anyone even in London where most people mistakenly think you can easily disappear. Frank wanted two 'grand' to sort the problem out and John regarded this as a cheap solution to his current woes, and with Ross warned off and out of his hair he could return to his normal life or so he imagined.

Over in Hackney, Ross was on his way out, he attempted to close his front door as best he could by slamming it repeatedly against the door frame as the council had still not repaired it, once shut a padlock was attached for added security. He didn't have much worth stealing but had been burgled before and not finding anything of value, they had simply just trashed his flat for the 'hell' of it. He descended the four flights of stairs to the ground floor and made his way onto the main street. With him, he had his only real possession, the Nikon camera, its black and white logo embellished strap wound tightly round his wrist to stop anyone just snatching it. Ross exercised his passion for street photography by always making his way through the back alleyways, that's where the uncut 'real side' of life was. He'd seen it all over the years, people sleeping rough, confrontations, explosive gang culture, you had to be more than a little savvy and keep your wits about you. A lot of the people he saw 'kind of' recognised him and didn't particularly see him as a threat, as they would a 'stranger' that could be an undercover copper or something of that ilk. Ross had photographed the people and backstreets in and around where he'd lived for many years and had a comprehensive collection of socially challenging and disturbingly sad images. Ross's interest in photography and the championing of the deprived had been ignited in his college days when he had seen an early form of Victorian photograph known as an 'Ambrotype'. The image had featured a British Napoleonic war veteran, captured for posterity on a glass plate wearing a battered stove pipe hat and an eye patch, his long overcoat was tattered and torn and displayed upon it was his campaign medal, he was poor and seemingly almost destitute. Looking dejected and bemused he and his wife are staring straight at the camera, his war time efforts, were worth a mere small piece of silver fashioned into a 'heroes' medal. His eyes pierced the future, captured for posterity, his image was a sadness from the past looking into the present. Ross had seen thousands of images in his time but this one photograph above all others remained in his consciousness and pricked any bubble of complacency that he might have, that 'things' as the politicians kept saying, were much better for 'all' people today. He always used black and white roll film, he didn't like digital photography, 'yes' digital photography was easier and quicker, but he felt that to capture something of a person's 'soul' the film needed to be something physical almost alchemy like. So much of the digital photography he had seen over the years had been manipulated in some way and it was difficult to see the truth within the image, and if you didn't have truth what was the point. Ross's photos were about recording the social injustice he witnessed day in, day out on the streets. He couldn't give the people he saw any money to get a drink or something to eat, he barely had enough for himself, but he could give them the time of day, a friendly word or a spare fag and publicise their plight and suffering at the bottom end of society by scanning and then publishing their photos on his own basic no-frills website 'Down_but_not-out'. His website didn't make any money but on the plus side he always thought it didn't cost him anything either, as his local library had computers for public use, and he had made the most of this free social facility. When he could, Ross always carried his camera because he knew you didn't 'think' about taking a photo if you saw an opportunity, the professional or keen amateur just 'snapped' first then reviewed the images 'artistic worth' after the event. As he had grown older the photographic side of his life had become increasingly important as the desire to trawl the streets at night looking for opportunities to protest via his street art had become harder, at times dangerous and in some respects less rewarding. Maybe he was getting too old for the intrigue of clandestine street art, the car injury he'd suffered some nights ago was still painful and knew as he became older that the aches and pains didn't seem to dissipate as quickly as they had when he was younger. Ross's feud with John Noble was fuelled by adrenalin which fed his anger. However, today Ross wasn't angry, he felt good, his mind was in a 'good place' and this enhanced his newfound positivity and creativity. As he strolled through the backstreets looking for subjects that caught his eye and imagination, he decided to make his way towards the Pink Flamingo, after all he hadn't been there for a while. Ross missed his little chats with Val, and he also wanted to repay her the help and advice that had kept him going during some of the darker moments of his life. As he moved towards the café, he noticed a figure slumped on a pile of carboard boxes that announced '*Drink Responsibly*' amongst their advertising. Now staring he realised, this was the Irish army man who had accosted him in the early hours of the morning when he'd been about to launch his assault on John Nobles second artwork. The old man lay unconscious and in an outstretched arm grasped in one of his large and grime encrusted hands was an empty whisky bottle. Ross was personally all too familiar with this form of escape from reality, sometimes it's all you have he thought, as he stared at the drunk pathetic figure, it was difficult to imagine he'd once been a proud and respected soldier. He well remembered the feeling of euphoria alcohol can bring and the mistaken thought that the uplifting feeling it generates will last, but today Ross was at least in a better frame of mind and for the time being he had a new purpose, one that even alcohol couldn't compete with. Ross tentatively raised his camera before taking a series of shots of the man lying like some huge immobile and forgotten dinosaur, he felt immense guilt at taking photos of this tragic figure but if he didn't capture these images and use them to record his plight, the ex-soldiers suffering would count for nothing.

Frances sat looking out of the window of the 'Flamingo', she had decided to return to the café as its natural worn interior and untouched feel took her back to her childhood. There were no state-of-the-art coffee machines or metal chair legs screeching on tiled floors. 'No' it was 60/70's retro glamour with its Formica topped tables, Linoleum flooring and a large glass topped counter incorporating cabinets with sliding glass doors. They contained a treasure trove of recognisable treats from the past, 'her' past, Custard slices, Bakewell tarts and the ultimate sweet for Frances, Tunnocks chocolate tea cakes. The Café had a genuine warmth, that made you feel somehow safe and wanted, she was so pleased to have discovered it, albeit by accident on her ill-fated last visit to town with John. As she stared out of the window the warm sun made her feel like a cat, curled up on a sunny window ledge safe and contented, her recent and on-going problems with John seemed to disappear into the invigorating coffee aroma that permeated the cafe. Blissfully daydreaming she was brought back to reality by Val who was clearing Frances's empty plate from her table. 'Penny for them' said Val, Frances smiled at the phrase, it was something she hadn't heard since her school summer holidays when visiting her aunt and uncle on the South coast. 'I don't even think they are worth that' she replied, and they both laughed. Val could recognise when people were struggling psychologically or seemed consumed by some other personal issue, this was something she had gleaned from working with the public for over forty years. Amateur psychologist that's how Val saw herself, and convinced herself that she wasn't nosey, but just 'cared' and if people wanted to talk, she had a sympathetic ear. 'Is it a fella?', it usually is? Said Val

Frances laughed at Val's all too accurate diagnosis of her problem, 'well sort of, in fact I think you could say its two' replied Frances, 'huh, alright for some, I can't even find one', said Val laughing. 'They say there's someone out there for everyone, you're just fortunate if you pick the right one and I think, no I'm sure, I definitely haven't,' said Frances'. 'Well can't you change your mind lovey', 'If it were that simple, I em...' said Frances now hesitating. Val interjected, 'it never is', the only advice I can offer is, don't stick with something that doesn't work, believe me, I've done it and always regretted it'. Frances was just about to let loose some more home truths to this friendly 'stranger' , but her middle class reserve and the ever-present memories of her parents saying 'you never talk about family matters to strangers'. Why? She could never understand, as it was so much easier. Unfortunately, their attitude to emotions had propagated a reluctance to engage and 'let it all out', this feeling of inner restraint had always held her back, and as ever just like an army fearing defeat before the battle had even started, she withdrew and just smiled. 'I'll work it out, I've been here before' and with that Frances finished her last mouthful of coffee and then touched Val's arm and said, 'but thanks for the sympathetic ear, who knows I may use it again someday'. 'Anytime lovey, and just remember pick the one that makes you smile, it's never too late, don't just settle for safe, safe is the cowards way out' said Val. Frances knew what Val meant and deep down realised she was right but they both knew without saying it, that life just wasn't that simple. Frances put on her coat, thanked Val for the coffee and her wisdom. Her brief time at the 'Flamingo' had made her smile and laugh again, even though deep down she knew the reality of her desires was probably unattainable. Now putting her hands into the coat's pockets, she could feel another part of her escape plan, it was the best part of two thousand pounds taken in dribs and drabs from John's wallet and this was destined as usual for her building society account. As Frances closed the café door behind her, the little insignificant bell suspended above it to 'welcome' and say 'goodbye' to customers tinkled briefly, but she knew somehow, she would return. Frances decided to walk the not inconsiderable distance to her building society, even though the streets surrounding the café were not without danger in terms of street crime. As she left the café and headed away up the street Ross was just turning the corner some hundred or so yards behind her. Camera in hand he suddenly and inexplicably stopped dead in his tracks. He was immediately overcome with a feeling of both euphoria and dismay as he stared at the woman heading away from the café some distance in front of him, the feeling within him was uncanny, almost spiritual. Frances's face immediately came into his thoughts, it was her, he was so sure, but how could he possibly know? He couldn't even see her face, it seemed impossible, after all, he hadn't seen Frances for so many long and painful years. His heart still yearned for her, he could sense her presence, and recalled them holding hands and the 'feel' of her close to him. The memories of what they had shared together all those years ago came flooding back like a storm wave crashing over a pier, beautiful yet destructive and overpowering, he was suffocated by emotion, he could hardly breathe. Ross wanted something of her, in desperation he raised his camera and frantically took several photos of the 'stranger'. He wanted to shout and run after her, put his arms around her, but his body, his whole being was frozen to the spot. Incapable of any movement, his mouth dry, not a single solitary word would come out, he just stood silent and helpless as Frances disappeared out of sight.

It seemed like an eternity before Ross eventually entered the café, he was in a total state of shock, and couldn't believe the effect that seeing Frances had had upon him. He thought the 'pain' of her loss was all behind him, but he knew deep down in the vaults of his subconscious the turmoil and love he felt were very real and unsatisfied. On seeing Ross, Val was about to launch into her usual cheeky welcome, but tact got the better of her when she saw Ross's ashen face and troubled expression,' my God, have you just seen a ghost or something' she said. 'I've seen someone, and it definitely wasn't a ghost' Ross replied. Val motioned to an empty chair and said, 'come and sit here, 'I'll bring your usual over'. He sat down next to the window, still in a state of shock, not just because he thought he had seen Frances, no it was more the 'hold' and devastating impact she still had upon him after all their years apart. He thought 'his feelings' had died long ago, 'yes', he'd always missed Frances, but this was more than that, surely this was 'love' whatever that was. To Ross, as with most men, 'love' was something that belonged in the movies, he just knew there was an inexplicable desire, a soul wrenching longing for this person who made him feel 'complete' and that without them his life was a mere existence, rather than a fulfilment of present and future expectations shared and enjoyed. Ross's head was now swimming with contradictions, was he carrying out his attacks on John Noble's work because of his disregard for street art and its true social value? Or was it simpler and more of a basic instinct, a jealousy harboured deep in his subconscious, maybe he still loved Frances and wanted her back and he knew John Noble held the key to it all. Or perversely, if he could destroy Noble, the desire to have Frances would somehow disappear into the ether, none of it made any sense and furthermore if he couldn't forgive her at the time when she had betrayed him and slept with John, could he really forgive her now? Just when Ross thought he had regained his direction in life, this sudden and inexplicable desire for Frances had come back to taunt him. There seemed no easy way of resolving the problem, there were now more questions than answers, 'no' he'd always said to himself he couldn't forgive Frances but with the passage of time, could he? Would she still even want to be with him? It was all too much, he hated being out of control of his emotions, after all he was no lovesick teenager, surely, he could put this behind him. Ross stared out of the window and thought, how was it you could be in high spirits, just happily sailing along on life's calm ocean and suddenly something or someone could capsize your boat of apparent contentment. He'd been on a high but had now taken an emotional upper cut from Henry Cooper, his legs buckled, and he was down on life's emotional boxing canvas dazed and confused. Suddenly without warning Val crashed down a large welcoming cooked breakfast in front of him and suddenly it's the end of round one, he's now back in the corner of the ring receiving a wafted towel and a sponge full of iced water in his face. 'Get that down you' said Val, she was tempted to give him some 'big sisterly' advice, but she decided to replace that with some tough love. She continued 'and when you have had that, you can repay me by painting the front of the café, it definitely needs a face lift and I'd let you do me as well if you were a plastic surgeon', Val laughed, and Ross smiled in acknowledgement of her attempt to raise his spirits.

As Ross started to eat his breakfast, the chewing sound he made was not dissimilar to the choking sound being made across town by his young understudy Karl. Whose feet were currently twelve or so inches off the ground and a grip that would be required to hold the fiercest of dogs was tight around his throat. The hand not far off the size of a shovel sported a Scorpion tattoo and held Karl suspended helplessly above the safety of the ground. As his face started to lose its life blood and colour Colm O'Shea released his grip and his hapless prey fell to the ground like a sack of potatoes. He now coughed violently, spluttered, and gasped for breath like a fish landed on a riverbank by an overzealous angler. Slowly his pale face regained some of its pinkish human tone.

O'Shea then stood back, and the looming figure of Frank Swift moved forward and knelt down to the kid's eye level. After John's call it had taken Swift no more than a few hours to start his search for Ross Campbell. Now, Swift's gnarled and misshapen boxing hand grasped Karl's face and made him look at him, 'let's try again or will I let Cosh loose again, just answer my questions' said Frank. Swift fixed a stare upon Karl's watering red and sore eyes, he was just a kid, terrified, tears rolled down his face, he wiped his snivelling nose with the back of his hand, cornered like a rat there was no hope of escape. Frank was calm, frighteningly so, he was used to hurting people, it came as second nature to him, almost primeval. Karl's voice was now distorted to a higher-than-normal pitch by uncontrollable fear, he blurted out 'I done it for revenge, nearly killed me on that crossing, driving like a fucking maniac he was'. 'Listen boy, listen' Frank repeated, 'wait for the question, it's not a bleedin quiz show with extra points for quick answer'. Karl just kept on muttering about a car, 'the Range Rover, the Rover, it was me, me', Frank interrupted, 'shut up and listen very carefully to what I'm going to say,'. Frank seemed disinterested in his confession about the Range Rover, Karl felt a slight sense of relief at this, he couldn't immediately recall any other recent transgressions against society, so maybe, just maybe they would realise they had the wrong person. He now regained a little of his confidence, if it wasn't the 'Rover' he thought, he was in the clear, but his confidence waned as he looked at the menacing figure of O'Shea standing just behind his 'master'. Frank now stood up and then placed his foot across inner part of Karl's ankle, his foot rested gently upon it. Frank then said 'right young Karl here's a nice simple question for you, Ross Campbell, you know him, don't you? The kid was confused, Campbell, Campbell he repeated in his head, he wracked his brain, he didn't know a 'Campbell' but he did know a 'Ross', confused and disorientated he couldn't remember Ross's surname but assumed it must be him, as he was the only Ross he knew. Hesitating, then unconvincingly saying,' nah, dunno who you mean, I've never heard of him', however his loyalty was misplaced and ill judged, 'wrong answer' said Frank, who then proceeded to press down with his full weight. Karl's body tightened like a noose around the neck of a condemned man, he screamed and flinched with pain as the crushing weight of Franks seventeen stone and size twelve Oxford Brogues bared down upon him, crushing his ankle. Swift then laughed as he said, 'It's just like 'Alien', there's no one to hear your screams'. He continued 'come on boy, Ross, I know you know who he is?', Karl's body temperature had now soared, the pain was excruciating, it invoked an immediate survival response as he said 'yes, yes, I know him, stop, stop' he cried. Frank still standing on Karl replied, 'that wasn't too difficult was it, now we're getting somewhere, see, it's easy isn't it'. Frank continued, 'now think very carefully before your next answer', now temporarily releasing the pressure of his foot, he continued with the interrogation. 'I want to know where he hangs out, I need a little friendly chat with him, that's all, mano to mano type of thing, you understand that don't you boy'. Karl nodded his head, the temporary relief from the pain had cleared his head enough for him to realise there was no way out of his current predicament and Ross would have to be sacrificed for his own survival. 'I only ever meet him in the pub' said Karl, 'which pub' Frank barked, the 'Grapes', 'the Grapes', he repeated fearing another reprisal on his pain wracked body. Frank turned and looked at O'Shea who nodded a confirmation of the pub's name and that he seemingly knew its location. 'Good Boy' said Frank condescendingly, the pub's name represented the second piece of the 'Ross' jigsaw for him, and this piece was definitely part of a face and not a random piece of sky. Karl's eventual confession had added to Frank's large mental database of people, places, and events, which as ever was primarily sourced by a litany of threats, confrontations and deals that had to remain under the radar of everyday respectability. He now removed his foot from

Karl's shattered limb, and just stood with his hands behind his back in a school master like pose. 'I'm a trusting soul and am assuming you've told me the truth', he then rested his foot on Karl's other ankle, the sheer look of terror on his face at the prospect of further pain made Frank roar with laughter as Karl bleated out the reply 'yes, yes, yes' as he squirmed on the ground. Frank then proceeded to place his full weight on Karl's foot for a brief second, just long enough for a shock tactic and then said, 'and don't tell Ross we've been to see you, cos if you do, I won't be as easygoing next time'. As Frank and O'Shea turned and walked away Karl sat sobbing on the ground like a child that had been bullied in the school playground, the intense pain they had inflicted throbbed and throbbed like a hammer striking a rhythmic beat on an anvil. He didn't know where Ross was and he didn't care, that was Ross's problem, and he was old enough to look after himself. Never one to rest on his laurels Frank decided to pay an immediate visit to the 'Grapes' to see if his prey was there. He reckoned the 'no-hoper' that John Noble had described to him would more than likely be drinking in the pub on a weekday afternoon. John had painted a verbal image of Ross as some sort of alcoholic waster who trawled the streets causing trouble. As usual he'd been somewhat sparing with the truth about Ross, he had told Frank as much as he thought was required, he had a low opinion of Ross and revelled in any opportunity to share it.

Frank stood outside the 'Grapes' looking at its façade, it reminded him of the good old days when money had a value and people did proper physical jobs not poncy office stuff, it was 'a real man's pub'. It had seen better days, its once imposing brick built Dutch gable and sandstone mullioned windows were worn and blackened with a century of city grime. Ornate glazed mustard and brown coloured tiles decorated the surrounds of three arched windows and two porticoed entrances, one of which was now boarded up with 'paint peeling' plywood and thirty years' worth of old poster staples. The remnants of tattered and faded Union Jack bunting was strung like a necklace across the upper windows and clung like Ivy to a rapidly disappearing past. The pub was as quiet as any 'normal person' would expect on a grey anonymous overcast winters afternoon, most of the local drinkers would come in later when the heating was on. Frank and O'Shea pushed open the frosted and engraved glass double doors that proudly proclaimed the pub's name 'The Grapes' in an attractive Gothic style script. There was probably a dozen or so people in the pub, half of them stood at the polished mahogany bar counter. The rest, a series of odd individuals, sat around randomly spaced Victorian cast iron circular pub tables, enjoying a quiet 'half' and revelling in the opportunity to ogle a pretty barmaid without appearing too much like 'dirty old men'. One or two regulars at the bar turned and looked at Frank and O'Shea as the doors opened and in swept an unwelcome blast of cold winter air. Anyone who looked at Frank's menacing sidekick quickly looked away, he was someone who you didn't want to catch his eye. Even if they didn't know O'Shea's dangerous reputation, his appearance alone frightened most people who saw him, and apart from the odd 'crazy' individual who might be stupid enough to take a liberty, and they would very soon be taught an unforgettable lesson. As Frank and O'Shea strode into the pub, the doors swung backwards and forwards with the force of their entry. They stopped and looked around, it was like a throwback to the 'good old' or 'bad old' days depending upon your view of 1960's London when local gangsters could enter a pub and gain immediate respect purely through fear and intimidation. They moved to the bar and stood side by side and immediately cast their gaze onto an attractive blonde barmaid in her mid-thirties who wore surprisingly few clothes given the inclement winter weather, she was obviously the reason why most of the punters were stood at the bar. Frank kept himself in good physical shape for a man in his mid-fifties, after all he had been an athlete and boxer for over thirty years, he asked for a soda and lime, but asked for a pint, he still viewed soft drinks as something of a 'pussy's drink' but ordering a mere 'half' would be unimaginable, O'Shea had his usual pint of mild. As the barmaid poured their drinks, Frank had heard one of the locals call her by name, he saw his opportunity to start a conversation, 'and get one for yourself Steph' Frank said. 'Is it OK if I put the money aside and have it later,' she replied smiling. Steph was used to offers of drinks and kept the cash to one side as it boosted her paltry minimum wage. 'No problem love, keep enough for a large one' said Frank, as he handed over a crisp twenty-pound note, smiling and laughing she said 'oh, thank you kind sir' in a comic voice', she was surprised at the offer but also a little suspicious. 'Bit quiet in here today Steph', Frank said as he scanned the pub, Steph was surprised this stranger knew her name, but was also flattered. Frank was tall, ruggedly handsome and wore a nice suit and had money, he was something of a novelty in the 'Grapes' and certainly not representative of the pub's usual clientele. 'No one's got any money that's why and there's no heating on, its freezing', she glanced over her shoulder before continuing, 'bloody manager, he's a tight as a fishes arse'. She continued, 'I've not seen you in here before, you're not from round here, are you? 'No, I've just popped in on the 'off chance' of seeing an old mate of mine, we sort of lost touch and to be honest, it's a bit embarrassing, I owe him some cash, just wanted to settle my debts, he's a good sort and it'll probably help him out'. 'What's his name? This friend of yours' replied Steph. 'Ross, Ross Campbell, Scottish bloke, good sort,' said Frank. 'Scottish you say, with a name like that I'd never have guessed' said Steph laughing. Frank wasn't amused or accustomed to having the 'piss' taken, but he just smiled. 'It makes a change someone owing Ross money said Steph', she had taken Frank's bait, 'Ah you know him then' said Frank, sensing a new trail to his prey. 'Ross, yeah, although he hasn't been in here for a while', the big Mans' growing expectation suddenly took a knock, as he didn't fancy coming back to this dump again. Then 'lady luck' smiled upon him as without having to ask any more questions, which he thought Steph may have thought unusual and suspicious, she offered up an alternative location of where to find Ross. 'You could try the little café on the High Street, the Pink Flamingo', 'sounds more like a dodgy night club' replied Frank laughing. 'Well, it was definitely a café last time I looked, and if he comes in here in the meantime, I'll tell him you were looking for him, what's your name?' said Steph. Unusually for Frank he'd made the mistake of hesitating, his usual easy-going manner faltered, he then replied, 'I would like to give him...', he paused 'it's been a while you see, and I'd like to, well...' he hesitated again, before saying, 'give him surprise, you know old mates meeting again, slap on the back and all that stuff, you understand don't you'. Steph now looked at Frank with some suspicion, his hesitancy when she had asked for his name and the ominous figure of O'Shea stood at his side, something just didn't seem quite right and now she regretted being quite so forth coming with the information regarding Ross. Years of experience working in pubs had taught her that strangers asking questions, generally didn't lead to any good. She cursed herself 'you stupid cow', always happy to oblige, sucker for a good-looking bloke and a bit of flattery. In her defence it wasn't something she experienced often, well not from people like Frank, who gained immediate but unwarranted respect from people and had more than a few quid to splash around. Maybe just maybe, she thought, more in hope than anything else, that it could all be true, and was after all, she had to admit to herself, maybe too suspicious at times. However, as her granny was fond of saying 'the road to hell, is paved with good intentions' and presently Steph couldn't possibly imagine just how poignant this parable would be.

Chapter Eleven
Lead-tin Yellow

'Lead stannate, prepared from a heated mixture of lead dioxide with tin dioxide. Contains lead, may darken by atmospheric hydrogen sulphide'

Light Bright Yellow

Ross sat in his council flat with an array of paint spattered spray cans spread out on the table before him, his small army of multi-coloured troops, as ever, ready for battle. To most people they were just as they appeared, an inanimate object but to Ross they represented a voice against authority. He gave each tin a little shake to check their contents and the lighter ones made a short aerial trip towards an open black bin bag on the floor in the kitchen. He had a job, a special favour to perform, and after enjoying his breakfast and pick me up conversation with Val the previous day in the Pink Flamingo, he decided he owed her more than just a little in the form of repayment. As he didn't have any spare cash, in fact he didn't have any cash at all, so had promised to paint the exterior of the 'Flamingo'. On the bonus side he had persuaded Val, to not only paint the exterior but to allow Ross to add his own special touch   by creating a bit of street art for the café name and giving it a new logo. It hadn't been plain sailing though, she had taken some persuading, viewing 'street art' as nothing more than ugly graffiti that had ruined and defaced the area in which she had lived for most of her life. Something 'nice' that's what Val had asked for, something that attracts people, not repulses them, it made Ross laugh since 'nice' wasn't really what he did, but, if 'nice' was required then 'nice' was what she was going to get. On a scrap of paper, he had sketched out a simple design that used the neck and head of the Flamingo to create the 'P' of 'Pink' and the rest of the lettering would be in Ross's own particular brand of street script, after all he thought there had to be something of himself within it. For once, he was actually looking forward to this little assignment because it wasn't some clandestine operation in the early hours of a freezing cold winters night. There wouldn't be any watching over his shoulder, or the continual fear of being arrested or worse still being involved in a tussle with some overzealous night watchman. Ross for the first time in weeks felt a sense of 'calm contentment', something he hadn't experienced for some years, a sense of euphoria, 'yes', he was still confused about his recent feelings about Frances but the angst he had felt towards John Noble had itself receded like an outgoing tide towards a distant horizon. Somehow, he felt as though the attacks he had carried out on Nobles' work, were perhaps more than sufficient to satisfy his anger and clamour for retribution. As he looked at his most recently developed photos from the previous day's street photography, he was especially moved by the image of the drunken ex-army man he'd been confronted by, on the night of the first attack. The image of this man sprawled face down, drunk and helpless, pricked his conscience. Perhaps he thought, maybe his time and energy could be better used attempting to give a louder voice to the less fortunate and forgotten members of society struggling to survive. The idea of 'helping' rather than 'fighting' appealed to Ross in a way he didn't think was possible. As he loaded his bag with the paints and tools he required for Val's makeover at the café, he felt good, 'yes', he definitely felt good, it was a feeling that he enjoyed and hoped would continue.

'Just a little tighter Cosh' said Frank as Colm O'Shea's vice like grip tightened the laces on Frank's boxing gloves. He had worn these gloves over the years, and they were his 'mates', worn, comfortable, a perfect fit and just like old friends they could be relied upon. The gloves had fought in many a battle in the ring and Frank had twice gone close to a shot at the World middleweight title in his younger days. Now for him it was just a matter of keeping fit, he'd given up on the running part of training, problems with old creaking ankles and knees, had necessitated this, but he could still give the 'bag' as it was known in boxing parlance, a good 'going over'. Frank pushed it away from himself and as it swung back towards him O'Shea steadied the bag from behind and held it firm as though he were holding someone's arms behind their back. Frank then unleashed a volley of punches to an imaginary adversary, two quick blows to either side of their ribs followed by a left hook to the side of the head. The unremitting oosh, oosh, oosh sound of the punishing blows drove him on to punch harder and harder and then finally there followed a constant but targeted series of blows that would at the very least seriously maim someone or possibly render them lifeless. Frank stopped punching and stepped and placed his hands on his hips, breathless he muttered the words, 'fuck, that was so good' he then gulped in large quantities of oxygen in an attempt to re-energise his system.

After an uneventful walk along the back streets to the Pink Flamingo, Ross looked for, but didn't see any sign of the drunken ex-squaddie that had moved him so much last time he went on a photo shoot. He laughed to himself at his own mental description 'photo shoot' you would think it was some sort of high-end fashion magazine that employed him, not just a personal quest and moral fight from an unknown individual. Ross arrived at the café, he had his instructions from Val and more importantly a morning coffee. After placing his empty cup on top of the shop's fascia box, that carried the cafe's sign, he repositioned some borrowed aluminium ladders to allow for better access. They were light and easy to pull around but that presented its own problems in terms of stability, as he had no-one to foot them, but on the plus side he didn't fear heights so wasn't too concerned. As he adjusted the ladders one final time, across town Frank was fastening his second cufflink on his shirt. Showered and felling dynamic after his work out he had decided with O'Shea in tow, that he would pay his daily visit to the bookies. After that, they would call into the little café that Steph had unwittingly given him the name of, 'Pink Flamingo', he laughed to himself, thinking what a poncy name. He assumed it would be some posh street café full of wannabee young professionals and lay-about students who spent three quid on a coffee and then spent hours drinking it while pretending to look intelligent because they had the latest laptop. Ross was just sorting out his kit when in-between a constant stream of traffic, he glanced across the road and was shocked to see Karl limping awkwardly with what appeared to be some sort of white plaster cast on his leg. Ross shouted over the incessant traffic noise in an attempt to attract his attention, Karl on hearing his name now looked in Ross's direction, but then immediately turned away and kept on moving. Ross thought maybe the kid hadn't hear him so he left what he was doing and dodging the traffic, walked as quickly as he could after him. As he did, he repeatedly shouted 'Karl, Karl, Karl but he didn't turn around or make any attempt to acknowledge his name. Ross eventually caught up with the slow-moving teenager and put his hand on his shoulder and said, 'hey mate', Karl shrugged off Ross's hand, said nothing and kept moving 'hey man, hold on, what's wrong,' said Ross. This time he stopped, turned, and looked at directly at Ross, there was fear in his young eyes, 'don't talk to me man, your bad news, look at the state of me' whilst pointing at his leg. 'What happened Karl?' said Ross desperate to help, the kid just ignored the question and said, 'just leave me alone'. Ross then put his hand on Karl's shoulder again and said 'come on man, talk to me' but he remained stoically silent and just twisted away from Ross and shrugged off his hand of friendship and struggled on his way. Ross shook his head in bewilderment, then stood and watched as the somewhat pathetic lonely figure struggled away up the street. Ross decided to leave it for now, turned and went back towards the café wondering what he had done. He felt guilty but Karl just wouldn't listen, confused, and frustrated he made his way back across the road, still shaking his head and thinking what else could he have done? Ross started unpacking his paints and tools, but he was troubled and unsettled by the incident, maybe the Police had pulled the kid and given him a warning. However, that seemed unlikely and didn't explain his damaged leg, anyway Ross thought, Karl wasn't frightened of the Police and like most young people he had what Ross saw as a healthy disregard and contempt for authority. 'No', it was more than that, he seemed scared and uneasy, there was more to it, as he seemed too frightened to even talk. Ross's early morning euphoria was now rapidly disappearing, he was annoyed, he hated seeing people in fear, but perhaps things were best left to cool off, maybe he could catch up with kid in the 'Grapes' and make it up to him, 'whatever it was he had done'. Ross decided he just had to get on and do his own thing. As he ascended the ladder his aerial view of people and traffic eased his thoughts as he became detached from life rather than being a part of it. The first part of his job was the laborious one, he had to prep and then paint on some quick drying the primer before the 'real' work began, and reckoned he would be finished in one day. The final artwork wouldn't take long, he knew that because he was used to working quickly on the streets, 'in' and 'out', without hesitation, speed of creation added a sense of flair and creativity to his work. As Ross toiled away up the ladders, below him, destiny beckoned for him in the sizeable form of Frank Swift and Colm O'Shea, they entered the café unaware that their 'mark' was just yards away from them. In the café their combined bulk of some forty stone seemed to fill the café like a 1990's gimmicky glass jar of pickled people squeezed randomly together, consuming every millimetre of available space. Val was quick to recognise new faces and she viewed these two strangers with some apprehension and suspicion. 'Take a seat, I'll be over in a minute to take your order' said Val with her usual bon homme. Swift and O'Shea eased themselves into two seats near the window, their bulk made a normal seat look child sized. Val duly returned 'what can I get you then gentlemen', she said 'gentlemen' in a mocking tone. Frank replied, 'Full English love, two of them', O'Shea seldom spoke so the pleasantries were always left to Frank whose amiability could lull the unwary into a false sense of ease and trust. However, Val had, as they say been 'round the block' on more than one occasion and could recognise a 'wrong un' and she knew instantly that here was a prime example. Frank eased back his chair from the table, 'Nice little place you got here' he said, assuming that Val's pink hair and the cafes name were more than likely synonymous and not a mere coincidence. On hearing Frank's opening conversation, Val immediately felt as though she were back in 1960's London, when her father had endured numerous threats from gangs attempting to extort protection money from helpless shop owners. She expected 'nice little place you got here' to be followed by 'it would be a pity if anything was to happen to it', 'yes, it's taken a while to build it up, but it's been worth it' she replied apprehensively, however the protection 'money line' didn't come from Frank, he just smiled and said, 'two teas as well, love'. Val breathed a sigh of relief, she wasn't frightened but didn't want any unnecessary trouble, and would have told them to sling their 'hook' had they asked for money, just what her father had done some fifty years before. Val smiled made a quick note of their order on her little note pad and returned to the shop counter. She knew there were more questions to come, it was her sixth sense, a gut reaction, that made you feel wary and more than a little uncomfortable. She'd had CID in from time to time asking questions, as they assumed that the people on the ground knew what was going on in their neighbourhood better than anyone, but these two were definitely villains and not the cops. Val returned to Frank's table with two teas and placed them on the table in front of them, 'here love' said Frank and he casually proffered a twenty-pound note in payment. 'I'll get your change' said Val, 'no need, keep it and maybe you can do me a little favour' replied Frank. Val's intuition had been one hundred percent accurate, as the next question came. 'I'm looking for an old mate of mine' he then hesitated as Steph's curvy figure flashed through his mind, 'a little bird said, I could find him here, I'm looking for Ross, Ross Campbell'. Val stayed calm, knowing these were no friends of

Ross, now taking her time before replying in the hope that it didn't look too suspicious. Val paused and shook her head and said, 'mmm, never heard of him', then turned to walk away. Frank put his hand around her forearm 'no need to rush away' he said, taking a firm grip. He continued, 'Scottish guy, medium build, about fifty, a bit of an artist, Ross, Ross, nodding his head as he repeated the name. 'Never heard of him' said Val firmly again now irritated by Swift's persistence, 'doesn't ring any bells, anyway I get all sorts in here, I can't remember everyone that comes through the door, can I', she then shook his hand loose from her arm. Frank could tell a lie from a mile off, if they didn't look you in the eye, you just knew, but he was in no hurry and the café was now quite busy. Too busy for his next line of questioning that usually included some physical persuasion, there were now too many witnesses to take the matter further at present. As Val turned to walk away from Frank her heart was pounding, she didn't normally get frightened, but it was a combination of protecting Ross and her annoyance at this thug coming into her café and having the temerity to cross question her. Val was halfway to the counter but still within earshot of Swift and O'Shea when Abby the part-time waitress walked in through the door to start her shift and was totally ignorant of anything that had gone before her arrival. Abby shouted over to Val, 'Ross says he won't paint another inch of your new sign until he gets another cup of coffee', she laughed but Val 's face told another story. One of regret and dread, she quickly shook her head, grimaced, and pointed her gaze towards Swift as if to say, don't Abby, just keep quiet. Abby's smile disappeared and she was just about to say, 'what's wrong, what have I done?' Frank looked at O'Shea, then smiled and looked at Val and just shook his head in triumph, you smug bastard she thought, as Frank now pushed his chair back and stood up, his actions immediately copied by his faithful 'fighting dog' O'Shea. Val stepped forward to block their path as they walked towards the café door. 'Look I don't want any trouble' she said firmly. Frank brushed Val aside like a rag doll with a dismissive sweep of his arm, he then said sarcastically 'Never heard of him eh', then just laughed. Abby looked at Val who motioned for her to get on with some work, she then watched anxiously as Frank and O'Shea stepped outside and shut the door behind them. Frank stood legs apart with his hands behind his back, he looked like a Regimental Sergeant Major about to shout out the 'drill' as 'private' O'Shea stood to attention beside him. Frank motioned for O'Shea to get hold of the ladders. With the constant noisy buzz of street traffic below, Ross was blissfully working away, unaware of their presence below. Frank nodded to O'Shea who then started to move the ladders slowly from side to side, the relatively small amount of movement at the bottom was magnified exponentially at the top some sixteen feet from the ground. Ross immediately felt the sway in the ladders, it created a sense of being drunk as he seemingly moved without any effort, caught unawares he dropped the paint can and brush he'd been holding and hurriedly attempted to grab on to something solid as the world seemed to move from underneath him. The tin of primer paint clattered to the ground randomly spilling its contents which in turn created a 'Jackson Pollock' like abstract painting as it spread and splashed haphazardly across the pavement. Ross looked immediately down below him, seeing the paint spread across the pavement, he thought that could so easily have been his blood had he toppled off the ladders. Ross then saw the two looming figures of Swift and O'Shea looking skywards at him. O'Shea still had a firm hold of the sides of the ladder and now started to move them violently this time from side to side. Ross with one hand holding the top of the shop frontage and his other hand grasping the ladder attempted to stop the movement, but O'Shea had all the leverage in every sense of the word. 'What the fuck are you doing', shouted Ross now glaring down at them. Frank signalled with his hand for O'Shea to stop and then shouted up towards Ross, 'better come down mate, it looks dangerous up there'. They both now stepped back from the ladders and

Ross tentatively descended, nearing the bottom, he was desperate to get off but wondered 'what the hell they were doing' and what awaited him. Ross could feel an adrenalin rush of 'fear' as he stepped off the ladders and turned around to face Swift and O'Shea. The immediate sight of Frank but more especially O'Shea made him feel cornered, Ross was of medium height, not small but the height of Swift and the sheer bulk of O'Shea made him feel small, almost like a schoolboy. He looked at O'Shea and thought, how could a human get to such a size, his bulk making 'three' of Ross. Before he could even get a word out Frank in a calm and collected voice said, 'just listen, I want to make this as simple as possible, and I don't like having to repeat myself'. For once Ross just bit his tongue and said nothing, usually, he wasn't afraid of an argument or a spot of physical violence but these two represented a daunting spectacle even for him. Frank continued 'you've been interfering in things that don't concern you and have destroyed some valuable works of art'. 'Art, who are you, Brian bloody Sewell' Ross exclaimed, Frank just shook his head and looked perplexed. Ross looked at Frank in his smart suit, and could smell his overpowering aftershave, here he thought was one of those blokes that dresses well and covers himself in a pungent cologne as though it made them somehow clean and respectable. Ross just saw it as a mere shield, something to hide behind.

Ross was now tempted to have a 'pop' at Frank but decided there was no point, one he wasn't convinced he could hurt him and secondly his partner in crime the 'Incredible Bulk' would probably just crush him like an empty packet of cigarettes. Ross decided to continue listening to what he had to say, then maybe, just maybe, have a 'go'. Frank continued, 'My client', the word 'client' triggered something within Ross and his calmness evaporated almost immediately, he interrupted, 'client', 'client', that's a laugh, John fuckin Noble you mean, just say his name'. Frank tutted, shook his head, and repeated 'my Client'. Ross interrupted again, you're a bouncer, a thug, not a bloody solicitor. Frank ignored this second outburst, 'My client has asked 'me' to have a quiet word with you, look and listen, it's nice and simple Ross. He continued, 'keep away from things that don't concern you, in short, mate, do yourself a big favour, stay away from 'street art', it could be bad for your health'. Unusually for O'Shea he laughed and in a deep monotone voice said 'yeah, very bad'. Ross's patience had now run out, the thought of John Noble using two thugs to threaten him was more that he could stomach, 'oh it speaks, does it' said Ross looking at O'Shea. Who, without warning moved remarkably quickly, given his size and bulk, and like a lizards tongue shooting out to capture an unwary insect, his enormous hand shot forth and grabbed Ross by the throat and thrust him back towards the shop window. Ross's head bounced off the plate glass like a rubber ball. 'Woh, Woh' said Frank as he pushed O'Shea's arm away, 'you see what happens when you try to get smart'. The big man's vice like grip had choked the wind out of Ross and temporarily removed his ability to talk, he coughed and rubbed his throat to relive his discomfort. Frank continued 'look Campbell, you've had your bit of fun at my clients expense and now it stops, stops, right here and now, this is me being nice and friendly, don't mess with me'. Without warning a split second after Frank had issued his final warning, O'Shea's open right hand whacked Ross fully across the head, he then immediately stumbled and then fell to the ground, his lightweight frame unable to counteract the force of the blow, he now lay in the wet paint that covered the ground. Immediately the Café door opened, and Val stepped out shouting at Frank and O'Shea, brandishing a broom, 'get away from him, get away'. 'I've got the Police here, right now on the phone', she held up her mobile to them, she was bluffing but was pretty sure they wouldn't take the chance. 'Stupid cow' said Frank as he grabbed the broom from her and snapped it over his knee like a matchstick and threw it into the street narrowly missing a passing car. Frank turned to Ross as he lay on the ground and said 'keep away, learn your lesson, just go back to being a loser, leave the winning to the big boys'. Ross had now managed to struggle into a sitting position but was still stunned. Frank looked at O'Shea and motioned for them to be on their way, as he passed Ross, O'Shea drew his arm back as though he were going to slap Ross again, who instinctively flinched, only to see O'Shea's arm merely swat the air above his head in a mock attack, they laughed as they walked away. Val bent down to Ross's level and put her arm around his shoulder and said, 'what was all that about, are you OK'. Ross just shook his head and replied 'yeah, I'll be OK, but I know someone who won't be'. He rubbed his jaw, it ached like 'hell' and that was just one slap from O'Shea's enormous hands. 'I'll make Noble pay for this' resolved Ross, and if thought he was under attack before, he'd seen nothing yet. Val coaxed Ross to his feet and got him settled in a quiet corner of the café, she brought him a fresh cup of coffee and something to eat but given his current level of discomfort liquidised food and a straw may have been of greater use. He sat almost trance like as Val observed him from the counter, he still looked shocked and confused but Ross being 'Ross' she knew he wouldn't tell her what was going on or want any help. As he picked at his meal, Val tried to get him to talk to, but all he kept saying, was, 'this is about pride now, nothing else, just pride'. 'Ross please don't do anything stupid, you can't mess with people like that, they will hurt you and they don't care about anything apart from money, 'fear and violence' is the currency they use to get it'. Val continued trying one last attempt to get through to him, 'I know you won't tell me what's going on, but can't you just stop what you're doing and turn a blind eye to whatever's going on?' 'I can't Val, maybe I would have said 'yes' before they did this'. He surveyed his paint spattered clothes and grimaced at the throbbing pain from his aching jaw, he continued 'but now it's too late, I can only be pushed so far, and Noble has overstepped the mark'. 'Who's that?' said Val, intrigued and noting a hairline crack appearing in his resolve to remain quiet. 'Forget I said anything, just forget it, I'll be careful', I promise, said Ross hoping his contrition might quell Val's concern and allow him to pursue his objective without having to justify how and why he felt the way he did. The day's altercation with Swift and O'Shea had reconciled Ross to the fact that he was past any attempt at conciliation with either himself or others and could see only one course of action open to him.

As Ross sat recovering from his intimidating and uncomfortable tussle at the hands of Swift and O'Shea, John Noble across town, now received a call from Frank Swift that brought a smile to his normally angst-ridden face. Like a lottery win for a struggling worker who can now leave their poorly paid and mundane job, John felt a sense of not only relief but immense satisfaction at the news that Ross had been well and truly warned off. He was unaware of the physical retribution handed out by O'Shea and didn't want to know the minutia of the incident, but secretly he hoped they had given Ross a torrid time. John had a sense of unnatural and unseemly human gratification in Ross's attack, he had consciously absolved himself of any guilt believing Ross had brought this all upon himself, his hands were 'clean' and now thought he had achieved his aim. With Campbell warned off, John believed his life and more importantly his temperament could now return to normal. As he shut his phone this mood of contentment blossomed further with the thought of spending some money, an obscenely large amount of money. He was standing outside one of Bond Street's premier jewellers and as he peered in the window, the background noise of the daily traffic receded as he became distracted by the glistening spotlights that made a diamond bracelet glimmer and sparkle and send forth a beacon of light. This 'mere' jewel carried the obscene price tag of some seventy-five thousand pounds but was easily affordable to John. Somehow, he imagined that a such a gift could apologise for his recent unstable behaviour and besides, he enjoyed spending money, there was plenty of it and he mistakenly saw it as a way of smoothing over most of the cracks he created within his marriage. Little did he know that Frances had sold most of the expensive items of jewellery he'd bought her, and then had purchased cheap copies off the internet and stored the bulk of the cash in her 'secret' post office account. As John entered the jewellers an attractive brunette in her early twenties, fully but tastefully 'made up' approached him and asked if she could be of assistance. He described the bracelet in the window, he always thought that the assistants in these up-market shops expected you to sound posh, as though they were the only kind of people who had 'disposable income'. John didn't make any attempt to tone down or disguise his accent, he was from the 'East End' and had no intention of hiding the fact. 'It's rather expensive I'm afraid, seventy-five thousand pounds' she said condescendingly, looking at John expecting him to be shocked and assuming he couldn't afford it. He played along with her assumptions and pretended to be embarrassed and even threw in a token cockney 'cor blimey love' for good measure but insisted he would still like to see it. The assistant reluctantly opened the security shutter then took the bracelet out of the window and placed it upon a sumptuous deep blue velvet cloth on the glass counter. 'It's stunning isn't it' said the girl as she picked up the jewel and draped it over her slender tanned wrist, 'very much so, but mmm..' said John, 'a lot more than you thought' the girl said as she mistakenly thought she sensed his embarrassed hesitation. John laughed to himself as he played his little game with her, 'it certainly is', I'll ....' he then hesitated on purpose, the girl interrupted 'have a think about it eh', then moved to put the bracelet back into the window. John now played his ace, 'what the hell, it's only money, I'll take it and I'll have the earrings that match as well'. Speechless the girl put on a fake smile as she now turned to the window and removed the matching earrings as well. John revelled in his bit of fun, it felt so good to have the money to put pompous wannabees in their place. When the transaction was complete John had his final laugh when he gave the girl a twenty-pound note as a tip, the fact that it was a 'grubby' twenty made it feel even better. On a high as he stepped out of the sumptuous confines of the shop and onto the pavement, he became engulfed by the buzz and electric atmosphere of central London. He decided to pay a visit to 'Mr Hemmings' who also enjoyed 'John's' money, 'yes', he thought to himself, it was 'his' money that Dave spent, but had never openly cast that slur upon Dave. John was on a high, better than drugs he thought, and things couldn't get any better, a true 'red letter' day, now hopefully about to be nicely topped off with a fine single malt and a look at his most recent gallery sales.

John caught the Underground to the gallery, he then walked a short distance with his most recent purchase from Van Cleef and Arpel. He had ditched the expensive looking bag proudly displaying the 'V & A' logo in which they were held. After all, you didn't walk around carrying an ostentatious bag unless you wanted to be mugged, for safety he had tucked the boxed jewels into the inside pocket of his country tweed jacket. He could feel the movement of the packages against his chest, it was a constant reminder as to why he felt so good. Standing outside the gallery, he felt a sense of inflated pride at seeing his work proudly displayed for the 'discerning art collector' that's what Dave's advertising blurb said. The description made him laugh, as some of the works on display had taken less than an hour to paint and most carried price tags in excess of fifty thousand pounds. The speed at which John created his art wasn't necessarily a reflection of his artistic talent even though that was undoubted and would be admitted to, albeit be-grudgingly even by his revenge obsessed enemy Ross Campbell. John's speed of painting was directly related to his experiences on the street where time was of the essence, the mantra 'get in, get out' as quickly as possible before someone called the police, had served him well. Today John felt a huge sense of wellbeing and proudly displayed it like a Peacock's tail for all to see, he didn't skulk around to the rear entrance, he ignored Dave's constant plea, to keep his identity secret. As he stepped through the main entrance, his leather soled brogues clattered and echoed on the polished wooden floor as he strolled around watching the 'punters' pensively studying and evaluating his most recent artistic offerings. He laughed to himself as he thought, a thirty quid canvas with twenty quid's worth of paint on it and one sale would pay for the bracelet he'd just bought, that was the way to make money. John was now approached by Simon, keen to make his paltry commission on each sale and to keep Dave off his back, 'anything catch your eye sir, are you a collector or perhaps an investor'. Simon's cultured tone was everything John hated about the art world, its inflated sense of importance and arrogance, but he found it amusing that this person selling his work didn't even know who he was. 'Not my kind of art this mate' said John to Simon, 'looks like bloody graffiti to me' he continued 'do people really pay good money for this crap'. Simon looked with a sense of cultural distaste towards John, 'cockney philistine' he thought, although he probably thought the same as John but his current meagre bank balance and his liking for a 'drink' necessitated a shift in his own cultural appreciation of what he viewed as 'art'. 'You need to see in in a particular context, think of it as anarchy versus authority, the Lilliputians versus Gulliver, the desire to...'. Simon's impromptu art lesson was suddenly interrupted by Dave who seemed to appear from nowhere, and then dismissively said 'Simon, there's a good chap, that young couple over there, why not give them the benefit of your knowledge'. Simon hated being ordered around, especially by someone like Dave who he viewed as ignorant, ill-bred, and essentially illiterate in terms of art. However, he needed the money so he smiled as usual, nodded his head as a foreign diplomat would do in feigned respect of a greater power. 'Nice to see you mate', then he whispered, 'but not in here eh, let's go through to the back office'. Dave noticed how John seemed to have an unusual spring in his step, an alertness that he hadn't seen for some time, maybe John had come to terms with letting his 'Ross paranoia' just blow over and had hopefully decided to get on and enjoy the very comfortable lifestyle he had. 'Drink John, 'nice little single Malt I think' said Dave as he placed the glasses on the polished mahogany and leather topped desk, he poured a generous measure for John and a smaller more circumspect one for himself, as ever wanted to be in control of his surroundings. 'I'm pleased you called in', he lied, preferring to deal with John at a distance, preferably on the phone. He continued, 'I've got something for you', Dave pulled a small envelope from the filing cabinet, removed its contents, then placed a cheque on the desk in front of John. As he did so, he said 'don't spend it all at once eh', nodding and laughing at the same time. John picked up the cheque and read aloud 'one hundred and seventy-five grand, John kissed the cheque and punched the air as he said, 'get in'. Dave continued as he held his glass up in celebration, 'and there's plenty more where that came from mate, if we just keep ourselves below the radar, know what I mean', nodding as he said it. John's exuberance disappeared like a light bulb being switched off as he replied, 'you mean Campbell don't you', 'well you were, rather, how can I put it, animated the last time we spoke, I was afraid you might, shall we say, do something uncontrolled, unnecessary, spoil things, know what I mean,' countered Dave. John sat forward in his chair and said, 'I'm past all that now', he then took a slug of his whisky and continued, 'I thought long and hard about what you said and although I got where you were coming from, I just couldn't sit back and do nothing'. Dave now felt an uneasy feeling creep over him like the incoming tide that rolls relentlessly up the beach, over-powering and carrying everything away in its path, thinking to himself 'what the hell have you done'. John now smiled 'I know what you're thinking', he's not dead, more's the pity' John laughed, 'only joking man, the look on your face Dave, it would look good on one of my canvasses, don't worry, I don't want to say too much, but I've had a chat with him so to speak'. Dave was shocked, 'What! You mean you've seen him'. 'God no, no way, no, hell, I probably would have killed him' replied John but didn't laugh this time, 'no I had some associates have a quiet word with him and they assure me that he will keep his petty grievances to himself from now on'. John took a large gulp of his whisky, eased back into his chair, and then continued, 'these people don't mess around and I'm sure they're right, I have a good feeling about this Dave, they've frightened him off and things can just go back to normal', and as he stopped talking, he waved his cheque in the air.

Dave looked at John and just shook his head, 'what? what's wrong?' said John, knowing fine well what Dave was thinking. 'You shouldn't have involved a third-party, these things are best kept in-house, so 'we' are in control'. Dave continued 'it doesn't take long for people to start joining up the dots and what starts out as a disjointed image, without any shape can soon become a 'picture' of opportunity' and he knew all about this, as he'd taken advantage of situations this way himself. 'Stop worrying Dave, these are just a couple of mindless goons, they're not capable of even joining dots together'. John didn't show it in his face, but he was lying as he knew Frank Swift was certainly no Neanderthal. 'I'll take responsibility for this, don't worry Dave, it's all under control, trust me'. The problem for Dave was that he didn't trust anyone, especially when they knew more than him and he didn't like the sound of these characters that John had 'engaged' to do his dirty work, but it was done, now there was little else he could do. He could voice his displeasure about what had happened and then hopefully that would be that. Dave poured two more drinks and gave himself an unusually large top up, as he said, 'here's to our continued success eh', he held his glass up as a toast, and as he did, added the caveat 'no more phone calls to goons, let's keep this strictly in-house from now on'. Dave held his glass out for John to chink his against, it was an old-fashioned gesture of comradeship that Dave hoped would resonate and stay with John but down in the very basement of his inner thoughts packing cases full of severe doubts were now piling up.

Chapter Twelve
Red Jasper

'Amorphous quartz, coloured red by iron'

Deep red

Ross eventually returned to his flat, the rage he felt inside about his treatment at the hands of Frank Swift and Colm O'Shea had now overwhelmed his earlier more calmer thoughts. Now, he was certain he knew why young Karl had been so frightened. Ross had been about and had encountered trouble on the streets but these two characters that hassled him at the café weren't your everyday thugs, he recognised professionals when he saw them, and these were, he imagined, well paid pros at that. Ross felt he should make it up to Karl in some way but decided for now he would do what his young understudy had asked and keep away from him. He didn't want the lad roughed up again or possibly worse, he was just a kid, why should he suffer for his vendetta with John Noble. Ross thought long and hard as he sat in his flat contemplating his next move, he was no chess grand master, now his moves wouldn't be in the least subtle or crafted. He thought briefly about confronting John in person, but this would render his clandestine night attacks pointless, 'no' he would have to finish this as he had started it 'out on the streets'. The whole situation had escalated in a short space of time, Ross had imagined that he could have spread his 'annoying' targeted attacks over a long period, weeks even months. He knew John could be 'hot headed', but he didn't think he would act as quickly as he had done. Ross now took great pleasure in the thought that he had not only woken the sleeping dog of John's angst but now had this 'mad' dog baying for his blood. He looked at the map on which he had indicated all the positions of Nobles 'street works', they were quite widespread, but he estimated that a good nights work would allow him to carry out his Blitzkrieg approach of destruction and this time there wouldn't be any great artistic merit to any of them, it would be simple SCUD technology, locate and destroy. He hadn't cared about being roughed up himself by John's hired heavies, but their treatment of Karl was in his eyes totally unjustified. He didn't care about his own safety, he knew he could always slip back anonymously onto the streets, maybe find a squat or two and keep a low profile, till it all blew over. John was unpredictable but surely, Ross thought, even he would eventually run out of steam in his desire for retribution. He thought he knew and understood John Noble, maybe he had at one time, but now he had changed and gained a ruthless streak that even Ross couldn't have reckoned with.

John was buoyant on hearing the recent news from Frank Swift, but it hadn't in any way eradicated his paranoia towards Ross or given him any misgivings about the strategy he had engineered to stop him. His paranoia had now gained wings and was soaring unstoppably skyward after his discussion with Dave Hemmings, who had unwittingly planted a tiny seed of doubt about the long-term effectiveness of his impromptu actions towards Ross. John's psyche now became a fertile ground for the cultivation of his doubts, insecurity, and anger. John sat contemplating his next move, he knew there was no point in talking to Dave again, he'd already aired his displeasure at his actions in no uncertain terms. John now felt like a dog that had cornered a rat, his instinct told him to finish the rat off, he just couldn't let go, Ross was cornered, and he wanted the issue settled beyond doubt. He removed his 'special phone' from his desk drawer and instinctively speed dialled Frank Swift's number, this time he didn't hesitate. This impulse gave him a rush of excitement, a feeling of power, he now knew he could orchestrate the whole affair at a comfortable 'distance' by phone. It would be impersonal and distant, like bombing a city from the air, you didn't see or feel the suffering and destruction you inflicted below, it was inhumane and devoid of any conscience, you were only interested in the end result. As usual Frank's answer phone was on, as John listened to the droning organ music and Frank's cryptic message, he suddenly felt hesitant, his bravado waned, should he leave a message? 'No' best not he thought, don't leave any 'dots' from which a picture could be drawn, he hung up without leaving what he thought could become an incriminating message. No sooner had he closed his phone, and now feeling confused and indecisive he needed time to think. Then without warning Frances walked into his office unannounced. He was sat with his 'special' phone in his hand, palm up resting on the desk in frustration, 'are you calling someone?' said Frances. John taken unawares looked furtive, initially tongue tied he instinctively turned the phone face down and covered it with his hand. Frances was immediately suspicious, and knew you could say the right words, but your eyes would always betray you, she should know having practised and mastered the 'art of lying' for years with John. 'Mm, yeah, I em..., just wanted to get hold of err.... Dave, but he's busy' said John, stumbling over his words like a drunken sailor. Frances had caught a brief glimpse of the phone in his hand, it was a small black ancient looking flip phone, she'd never seen it before, his usual phone was always the latest model I-phone, she knew there was something going on. Suddenly the phone John was covering, rang, the ring tone was a very basic tinkling sound that was common on early cheap phones when sophisticated choices were non-existent. John didn't answer it, he sat motionless, it rang and rang, repeating it's annoying tinkling sound, 'well! aren't you going to answer it?' snapped Frances, calling John's bluff. He looked at his phone as if it were an unexploded bomb, reluctantly he picked it up and answered it, 'Hi, Dave, thanks for calling back', he used Dave's name to try and add an air of verisimilitude to his call, but Frances was unconvinced and just stood staring at him, using her presence to create maximum discomfort. He shifted and squirmed with guilt in his chair, he had to get rid of Frances and in desperation he put his hand over the phone's speaker and asked her to get him a couple of 'paracetamol' as he had a blinding headache. At this she just shook her head and looked at him with contempt, turned, walked out of the office slamming the door behind her and was just about to walk away annoyed and frustrated, but curiosity glued her to the spot. She wanted, no 'needed' to listen to his conversation, the doors were constructed from heavy oak planks, and they muffled most sounds, but the odd word did escape. Standing with her ear pressed against the door, it felt like a confessional in a church, she was the priest, straining to hear John's untimely transgressions. Listening intently, Frances caught the odd word, nothing incriminating, then she heard Ross's name mentioned. John hadn't said

Ross's name for years because their friendship had soured so much, his only emotion towards him was one of pure hatred. Somewhat unfairly Frances had always thought, surely that was all in the past and anyway she was to blame for her and Ross's untimely breakup, why did John hate him so vehemently? Unbeknown to her it was insane jealousy, but its magnitude would always be far beyond her understanding or comprehension. As Frances stood listening, she shifted her position slightly and inadvertently stumbled against the door, she winced at the 'dull' sound it created and froze to the spot, like a fly trapped in a web, she prayed he hadn't heard the sound, but John had, and on hearing the noise, had left his seat, and stealthily crept towards the door. Frances watched the door handle intently and to her horror saw it move slowly down, measured, and sinister like a Tarantula closing in on its prey. She was now transfixed with the fear of discovery, suddenly her body loosened, and instinctively she went into flight mode, turning quickly, and scurrying towards the kitchen. John now opened the door and stood holding his phone while surveying the empty hallway, had Frances been listening? Had she heard anything? John couldn't be sure, but he was convinced she had been eavesdropping, stepping back into the room he quietly closed the door. The click of the door catch echoed down the cavernous, tiled hallway, like a cruel whisper.

Before this furtive call, Frances had nothing more than a hunch that John was 'planning something'. Now this feeling had manifested into what she saw as some sort of evidence, albeit circumstantial, she needed to find out what he was up to, but how? How could she do it without him suspecting something. Frank had now returned John's latest call, he could hear the background noise from the gym, it immediately set the scene in his mind. Frank strong and fearless, working out, a mean machine not to be messed with, this image gave John a sense of power that he could pull in the 'big guns' when he needed them. He felt like a general, marshalling a specialist fighting unit, they would do his dirty work. Nice and simple, as easy as dialling for your favourite takeaway meal, however Frank's kind of 'takeaway' service was an entirely different matter and needed to carry a government Health warning. Frank stood in the centre of the gym wearing his usual grey Lonsdale sweatshirt, he was helping some of the young up and coming hopefuls with their training. With the phone to his ear and his other large and powerful hand placed behind a punch bag that was mercilessly being pummelled by a young protégé, he had to shout to be heard above the furious activity around him. 'It's no good John mate, I can't hear you, give me a minute and I'll go to my office' said Frank . He released the punch bag and now made his way through a frantic scene of boxing gloves being placed on hands, gloves being removed from hands, people bench pressing weights the size of car tyres as muscles strained and flexed and were pushed far beyond their intended physical limit. As Frank shut the office door behind him, he wiped the sweat off his forehead with the back of his forearm and then took a deep of breath of air before preparing for his conversation. Frank tolerated John, he called him 'mate' but he just saw him as another punter with too much money and 'no bollocks' to sort out his own mess. The big man sat with his size twelve feet rested on the corner of his desk as he listened to John, 'thing is Frank, I appreciate that you probably have frightened Campbell off ', he couldn't even bring himself to use the name Ross, 'but I want him followed for a while, just to make sure he's learnt his lesson'. Frank interrupted 'that will be expensive'. He didn't really want the job but thought if there was enough cash in it for him, he would do it. 'I'm not bothered about the money' said John sensing that he was going to get what he wanted, his reply was music to Swift's ears, too much money and too little sense thought Frank. John continued 'I just want to make sure he behaves himself', Frank interrupted 'you're talking at least...', he hesitated and was just about to say fifteen hundred a day, then decided to push his luck, 'two grand a day man, that's what we're talking'. John repeated 'as I said, I'm not bothered about the money, just keep an eye on him and if he goes near any street art, I need to know, I want him stopped, I want him incapable of causing me any more grief'. 'Watching is one thing but 'physical dissuasion', Frank's euphemism for a good roughing up, 'will cost more' said Frank', 'just do it' replied John, 'as I said money's not an issue'. Now John saw Ross Campbell as a cornered rat and Frank was the 'Pit Bull' that was about to seize him in his jaws and shake the life out of him and then toss him through the air and crashing to the ground lifeless, crushed and incapable of a single breath. 'If that's what you want mate, consider it done, I'll get on to it from today, although I'd imagine our little 'piss artist' will do all his dirty work at night, but we'll be there, his card is well and truly marked, I'll be in touch,' said Frank. He then pressed the 'end call' button without waiting for any response from John. You didn't have to ask Frank twice, the die was now cast, there was no turning back. As John closed his mobile phone, he relaxed and pushed himself back into his chair, and felt a sense of euphoria and excitement that seemed to stimulate his whole being. He now believed his call would put an end to Ross's aggravation towards him and more importantly his artwork. He drank the remaining contents of a very good red, it had the taste of 'victory', he couldn't remember when he'd opened the bottle, or even how many bottles he had drunk but it couldn't have been that long ago as they never remained full for long. While John celebrated, Frances sat in the kitchen stirring 'an alibi' in the form of a hurriedly made cup of coffee to cover her quick and untimely exit from outside John's study door. As she sat drinking the coffee her mind briefly flashed back to the street café where that friendly woman with the pink coloured hair had offered her a shoulder to cry on, now feeling confused she wondered why the café had come into her mind. Maybe, she thought it was just a case of that Pavlov's 'association thing', the smell of the coffee had somehow triggered the thought or was it that she was feeling the need for sympathy at the mention of Ross's name during John's mysterious phone call. Frances knew that the time she had spent with John over the years had proven him to be unstable and unpredictable and that he had demonstrated on more than one occasion that he was not averse to using violence. Fortunately, though he had never used it against her, but she had suffered his anger and frustration, which could grow disproportionately from the most insignificant of events. What was John planning? She needed to find out, her mind was in turmoil, why was she still thinking about Ross? She now realised one thing, he still had a hold on her emotions, even after all their years apart and she wanted to help him in any way possible. Frances thought if only she could get hold of the phone that

John had been using, that held the key. She knew it wasn't his usual phone and had never seen him use it before. He must hide it somewhere and all reasoning pointed to the 'man cave'. She had found odd things in there from time to time, drugs being one of the items, but had just let that go, she was leaving him anyway and now didn't care what he did to himself. He was selfish and had been for years, probably she reasoned, ever since they had first been together. He was like the proverbial mad dog, once it had bitten someone, it could never be trusted again. Frances would have to bide her time and search his room when he was out or drunk, the latter being the more likely, the way things were now.

In front of Ross on his makeshift kitchen table, lay a detailed plan of the local area on which he had marked the location of the six remaining Noble 'artworks'. Ross hadn't done any research into these particular works, unlike his other attacks which had been carefully planned and orchestrated in an almost military like fashion. However, his patience had now run out, any kind of satisfaction he had initially felt had dissipated, this was now 'petrol bombs in the streets', Molotov's hurled from the front line, dodging rubber bullets, there would be no more planning. The time for direct action had come, a concentrated attack, his own mini-Blitzkrieg', a sweep of decisive aggravated attacks, not pretty, not even artistic. Intended to create the maximum amount of anger, he knew how Noble would react and the thought of this made his furnace of retribution roar and glow white with expectation. Now, he failed to comprehend how only a few days ago, he had imagined that perhaps his job was done and maybe it was time to move on. The thought now seemed ludicrous, and he shook his head in utter disbelief at his own naivety. He had fought battles all his life and nothing seemed to change to give him a break, and knew he would always be fighting, always be struggling and now he didn't care what happened, one way or another he would have his day. Ross had purchased several spray cans of Henry Ford's favourite colour 'black', the attacks would be simple and targeted. He had decided what he was going to do, he had the stencil of Nobles face, he would spray a web complete with Nobles anguished face trapped within it and finish it off with the personalised epithet 'Art Whore' and if he had time, he would tag it with 'SPYDER' but that seemed almost superfluous now, as John Noble would know who had done it. However, the 'tag' was part of street etiquette and although conformity wasn't something that had played a serious role in his life, but he did try and stick to the street code. Ross estimated it would take at least a full night to complete his mission, that was allowing half an hour per attack and then he needed time to get from one location to another on foot, and that wouldn't be easy, given his recent injuries. Fortunately, he knew the backstreets well, and just like a hungry rodent, knew the best runs. He would be able to morph seamlessly with the environment and move unseen through the streets and alleyways to spread his tide of retribution. This would overpower and engulf John Noble and his 'precious' media hyped artwork, sweeping it out to sea and depositing it at the bottom of the ocean, lost, forgotten, and ultimately drowned.

As Frances sat drinking her coffee, she was shocked when John entered the kitchen in his jogging gear. He'd bought it a month earlier, just another fad she had thought, after all he'd hadn't shown any interest in any athletic pursuits before, his overweight and flabby body being testament to that. She reckoned this current desire for sport must be fuelled by alcohol or cocaine as he seemed unusually animated and positive. 'What on earth' she said as she looked at him, John was on a high, he felt the urge to run free and get out in the fresh air, he knew realistically he'd be walking rather than jogging as he was out of shape, but 'what the hell' he thought as it was an opportunity to escape the confines of his mind and the 'man cave'. He was convinced that Campbell was now 'sorted' or soon would be, now it was his turn to break free. Frances was still in a state of disbelief but knowing John she knew he was up to something, and as she stared at him, her mind immediately went into planning mode, and thought to herself, this could be the opportunity she was looking for, 'will you be long? ' she said trying to calculate the time required to search his room and look for 'the phone'? John said nothing and Frances was just about to say 'are you even listening to me' but decided to keep things as calm as possible, as she wanted him out of the way, so she could get on with her search. Frances continued 'yeah, you get out and enjoy the break, it will do you good, you looked so stressed before'. Testing the water and fishing for clues, she now pushed her luck, 'are you in trouble, I mean that call before', she almost mentioned Ross's name but that would sound alarm bells, and she couldn't face a massive argument. She'd had enough of them over the years, so kept her questioning vague, 'it's just you seemed edgy before, in the office I mean, Dave doesn't normally have that effect on you, is there something wrong? Can I help, you can tell me you know', she knew he wouldn't, he never did. 'No, no', said John 'just Dave, the usual, greedy sod wants more artwork, it'll be OK, I'm on top of it now'. To Frances this obvious lie only hardened her resolve to find out the truth. She now asked again 'will you be long', 'dunno, maybe an hour or so, I'll go round the public footpaths and up past the old church, it's a circular route, why? Do you want to come?' Said

John. 'No, No, I'm not even dressed, just interested, that's all'. Allaying any possible suspicion, she further iced the cake of believability,' thought I could get us both breakfast when you get back, that's all but it's not important, just go and enjoy yourself, you deserve a break'. John just lent against the door frame and hesitated, Frances's unusual level of interest and concern confused him. 'Just go, just go', she kept repeating over and over in her head, she couldn't even stand the sight of him now. The feeling between John and Frances was mutual though never stated, did he even need her anymore, 'yes', he had thought, it used to give him a sense of contentment and pride to have an attractive woman on his arm, but their relationship was dead, he knew that. John had always thought about following Dave's example and maybe try and have a 'fling', with a new bit of 'young stuff' as Dave described it, at the gallery. Dave had had plenty of luck with the temporary female staff that he employed as his 'personal assistants'. You have to think about yourself John thought, he knew Frances couldn't abide him anymore and furthermore he no longer cared, 'sod it' flashed through his mind as he stepped out of the door and onto his sweeping gravel drive. The rush of adrenalin on his first intake of cold fresh country air seemed to clear his mind and he broke into a slow jog which took him down to the lane that adjoined his drive. Rolling fields ploughed into neat winter furrows and huge oak trees dotted the country lane as it meandered its way down towards the village. The aroma of nature combined with its sensory kaleidoscope of bird calls and distant animals made him feel lightheaded and engendered a sense of natural euphoria rather than the 'one' he normally obtained through alcohol and drugs. He hadn't run more than a couple of hundred yards before his current hedonistic lifestyle took its toll and his initial jog of enthusiasm slowed to a walk. He now made his way towards the distant village, as he surveyed nature in all its splendour, he realised just how far his life had come since his early days in the grimy backstreets of East London. As he meandered, Frances wasted no time and was in his mancave searching frantically for the key to unlock his desk. She knew what he carried about normally and the small ornate brass desk key wasn't on his key ring so it must be in the room somewhere, but where? John's office was full of bookshelves that contained not only a fine array of art books, but he also had a good selection of collectables, he had purchased anything unusual that caught his eye and imagination over the years. She felt inside pots, opened ornate inlaid wooden boxes, moved books backwards and forwards on the shelves but there was no sign of the key. She slumped into his leather armchair, frustrated after twenty minutes of fruitless searching, 'where would he hide it' she kept saying to herself, it seemed like an impossible task, the epitome of a needle in a haystack. She glanced around the room, being tall, perhaps John had hidden it on top of the ornate Victorian bookcases that towered above Frances's head. She pulled over a stout coffee table and stood on top of it and then attempted to run her hand across the top of the first bookcase but there was nothing apart from a thick layer of dust that now clung to her fingertips. Frances repeated this process for all the bookcases but found nothing, it now seemed like a hopeless task to her, she slumped down again in his chair now frustrated and dejected.

Having exhausted his initial head of steam, John's pace now slowed to a walk as he traced the public footpath's route that circled around the village, then headed out towards the local Saxon church. Hand's in pockets he strolled along, then instinctively felt around inside his trouser pockets where he touched a handkerchief and then a small metal object which he then removed, it was the key to his desk drawer. He was confused, why did he have this with him? Normally he hid it inside the zipped cushion that sat on his chair, now he started to panic, had he locked the desk drawer? He couldn't remember. Meanwhile Frances stared with frustration at the fine antique mahogany partners desk with its brass escutcheons and tooled and gilded red leather top that could hold the answers to so many of her questions. In a pique of anger, she jumped up and writhed at the desk with so much force that one of the large main drawers opened and shot back towards her unexpectedly. Taken by surprise she lost her balance and fell over backwards, the drawers contents spilled out and onto the floor. In front of her, was a now upended nineteenth century Martins Brothers anthropomorphic pottery bird tobacco jar 'the barrister', one of John's many valuable collectables, he'd paid some seven thousand pounds for it at auction from *Christies,* just because it made him laugh. It's head now lay on its side with its comical lugubrious eyes looking sideways at her, the jar's contents had been a 'snow' white suspicious looking powder which now lay scattered upon the floor. Frances shook her head in utter disbelief at her stupidity, John had failed to even lock the desk after all, and she hadn't even thought to try them, assuming they'd be locked. Now panicking on seeing the contents of the desk drawer now spread across the floor, it represented a visual testament to John's deceitful lifestyle. She hurriedly re-gained her composure and started scooping the white powder up with her hands and attempting to put it back into the jar. Her hands were now hot and sweaty with fear and the powder clung to her skin, she touched her face, and a white streak left its mark. She wiped her forearm across her forehead and felt sick with the fear of discovery, sitting motionless in an attempt to calm her nerves, she took some deep breaths, and this seemed to settle the growing state of panic. Staring at the remnants of white powder on the rug, its discovery hadn't been a great surprise as she knew John had been taking it for years and had reluctantly just accepted it's use, along with his other quirks. Frances had, like a dog that cowers from a brutal master gratefully accepted anything that made John a little more bearable, she was happy to turn a blind eye to almost anything for a 'quiet life'. Suddenly her abject despair subsided, as, no sooner had the lid been placed back on the Martins jar, there among the drawers contents lay something just as valuable to Frances as the large amounts of cash she had ferreted away over the years. There, there it was, the target of her search, John's 'secret' mobile phone. Frances lunged for the phone like a prospector grabbing for a large fist sized nugget of gold. Without hesitation she immediately pressed the red button on the phone and the screen came to life. A black grainy screen displayed the most basic of information, the date and time and a message that brought further despair, the phone was locked 'shit, shit, shit', Frances exclaimed out loud, she almost felt like crying. Can't anything go right she thought to herself as her eye glanced from the phone to the mess lying on the floor in front of her. She sat shaking her head and then like a light bulb being switched on in a dark room, she instinctively typed in the digits for Johns date of birth '1' '9' '6' '4' and the screen switched to the main menu. Frances sighed with relief, at least John was predictable in some ways, the phone as far as Frances was concerned was old technology, she was used to the now ubiquitous smart phone where most operations were done by touching the screen. The phone felt clunky and awkward as she struggled to press the small grubby little rubber buttons to move around the main menu in an attempt to find the phones call log. She clicked on the telephone icon, which she thought an obvious choice, but there was no log, where the hell was it? In desperation she tried icon after icon without success, frustrated and about to give up she made one last attempt by selecting a bizarre looking 'cog wheel' and there was the log. She scrolled roughly to the time John had been on the phone and located the number he had called. It was tempting to 'call it' there and then but knew it would show up on the phone, instead she grabbed a pen and paper off John's desk and scribbled it down for later use. Hurriedly she switched the phone off and now had the difficult task of replacing the items into the drawer that were currently lying upturned on the floor. She would just have to guess how they had been stored originally, somehow get into John's mind, not that that were possible or even desirable, and hope that when he opened the drawer, he wouldn't notice it had been disturbed. Fortunately, she thought he was usually so drunk when he frequented his office that it was unlikely, he would notice anyway. And even if he did, she reconciled herself to have it out with him, but she knew deep down, if at all possible, it had to remain a secret for now.

Chapter Thirteen
Ceramic White

'Strontium Titanate, Titanic Acid Strontium'

Bright pure white

Across town at the boxing gym, O'Shea stepped into the 'office', where its décor, a bit like Frank's psyche was stuck firmly in the 1970's. Pine clad walls and polystyrene tiles that drooped slightly from the ceiling stretched the idea of retro chic to an unfortunate extreme. A jumble of junior boxing trophies and old boxing magazines were stacked haphazardly on a shelf behind Franks desk. Proudly displayed behind them and affixed to the wall were a series of thin black picture frames. The frames held a collection of boxing posters in large black and red print that catalogued Franks, some pundits would argue, not so illustrious boxing career. They spanned his early days from Bethnal Green to the star-studded Caesar's Palace in Las Vegas where during training he had once sparred with the legendary Ken Norton. Frank's one time fight for the light heavyweight title in Vegas had been a bad-tempered affair which he lost on points. He had the dubious reputation to be one of only a handful of fighters to have knocked the referee out at the end of the fight, it turned out to be his one and only title fight but as with the rest of his life, he had given it his very best shot. Frank knew you couldn't always win but you could leave your mark. O'Shea who had been helping out in the gym with some of the younger kids was pleased at the chance to throw his large if not particularly muscular frame into a comfortable seat. 'Do you want a can mate' said Frank as he placed two tins of lager on the table. O'Shea gratefully accepted the offer and the click of the ring pull and the 'ssst' sound of escaping gas added to his idea of Nirvana as he leaned back into the chair with a comforting sigh. 'We have a nice little job on Cosh, that geezer I know who wanted that 'loner' warned off, well guess what, he reckons that miscreant', Frank laughed at his choice of description for Ross, 'might just ignore our little chat we had at that café the other day and start causing trouble again'. Frank continued as O'Shea sat in his usual silent mood and just nodded his head 'I don't really want the job, we 've got enough on, but this 'client' is prepared to pay us a grand a day'. Frank had lied, it was two thousand a day, but this little untruth would cut down Colm's share considerably, 'the client wants us to follow this 'waster' for a while and see what he gets up to'. 'Ah you're joking Frank, I mean look at me, I can't do that', 'I mean, I'm not that mobile' O'Shea said, whilst drinking and patting his generous pot of a stomach'. Frank laughed at the big man's animated statement, 'No, Cosh, I realise that you're not exactly a foot soldier anymore, but I was thinking you could take my car and just keep an eye on our 'little friend', and if he gets up to anything you give me a bell and we can sort him out'. 'I dunno Frank, it's not really my kind of thing, I mean this is like a 'dole snooping' it's so fucking boring sitting in a car just watching people'. 'Look Cosh, I need you to do this', said Frank and realising O'Shea's indifference to the task, he made him, which on the face of it seemed like a generous offer. 'Look, I tell you what, I'll split the daily fee with you, come on mate, that's five hundred notes a day'. O'Shea was now shaking his head and looked slightly quizzical, as he said, 'like I say, it's not really my sort of thing', Frank now persisted, sensing cracks appearing in O'Shea's resolve, 'come on mate that's a shed load of money for just sitting on your fat arse, you could make a few grand in a matter of days, for just watching this bloke'. Frank continued unabated, he wasn't going to take no for an answer,' it'll be easy, just follow him to find out where he lives, then it's just a matter of watching, he mightn't even do anything, we probably frightened him off last time, it'll just be for a few days to keep this 'client' off my back, come on mate do me this favour eh', he then placed another lager in front of O'Shea. The can represented Frank's sucker punch and his 'sergeant at arms' took it right on the chin, his will and resolve buckled and gave way as he opened the can and then agreed, albeit reluctantly to take on the vigil and this is exactly what it would be, as most of it would occur during the twilight hours. Frank now sat back in his chair feeling quite smug having successfully secured O'Shea to do his donkey work for him, and at the same time he would be picking up fifteen hundred pounds a day for doing absolutely nothing. As Frank considered what to spend his 'easy' money on, his phone rang, 'shit' he thought, not that bloody Noble again, he decided to let it go to answer phone. However unbeknown to Frank it wasn't John calling this time, Frances had plucked up the courage and dialled, the 'mystery number' she had taken from the 'special' phone. Frances had used her own mobile, the suspense was too much, she couldn't wait any longer, and was curious, 'no' it was more important than that 'she had' to know, who was on the other end of the phone. As she listened to the creepy organ music and then the somewhat cryptic message that accompanied it, a chill ran down her spine. She had hoped somebody would answer the phone and give some clue as to who they were, anything, a name, a voice, just something. The answer phone message gave Frances a deeply 'uncanny' feeling, like the sight of a slowly moving child's swing in an empty park with no sign of the previous user and no trace of anyone. As the answerphone message bleeped and asked for her to leave her details, she panicked and immediately shut down her phone. Thinking to herself what will happen now, her mind suddenly did the hundred metre 'panic' sprint, as she suddenly realised it would have recorded her number. The scenarios of her actions now seemed almost limitless, what if, whoever's phone it was, rang her back wanting to know who she was? Asking where she got their number from? What if they called John and mentioned the number on the phone, he would then know Frances had been through his desk. She knew things could go badly wrong, but there was nothing that could be done now. Frances wanted to find out what John was up to and there would always be risks involved, she would just have to hope that 'they' whoever 'they' were, might think it was a wrong number. No sooner had Frances calmed her nerves through wishful thinking rather than fact when her world crashed in around her. She could hear a phone ringing and ringing and ringing in John's man cave, surely it was too much of a coincidence she thought to herself. Fortunately, at least John wasn't in to answer it, but no sooner has this little crumb of comfort entered her head, when it was mercilessly crushed as she heard footsteps on the gravel drive outside. Jumping to her feet she rushed to peer through the corner of the hall window, her worst fears were now realised, it was John, puffing and panting, his face red and sweaty. As he came closer to the house, he rested an outstretched hand against the front door to steady himself, inside the house the phone continued to ring and ring. Frances could hear herself saying, stop, stop, stop, in her head, as her whole being tensed with nervous despair. Just as John's key entered the front door lock, the ringing subsided, she breathed a huge sigh of relief, but knew that this may only be a short stay of execution.

Ross had now completed his schedule and chosen the day for his Blitzkrieg attack of John's remaining works. To celebrate the 'beginning of the end' as he saw it, he had made his way to the Pink Flamingo. As usual strapped for cash he had to rely on Val's gracious level of bonhomie and very soon he was duly tucking into his usual 'mates rates' full English. She'd felt somewhat responsible for the altercation that had happened only a few days before and was happy to provide some form of recompense, albeit in the form of food and drink or even a friendly ear to take in Ross's woes. Val sporting her blue nylon overall stood in front of Ross and just stared at him until his eyes moved from his plate and then Val said 'well?',' 'mm, not bad, bacon's a little tough' Ross replied'. 'No, I don't mean the breakfast you idiot, I mean 'well' as in, are you going to finally tell me what the other day was all about'. Ross looked ruefully at Val, 'It's a bit like James Bond all this stuff, If I told you, I would have to bump you off'. They both laughed at this, 'No, seriously Val, its best you don't know anything, I mean it's nothing really bad but the less you know the better, anyway it's not something anyone could help with, to put it simply, I've chosen to go down a path that goes through the woods rather than across open fields that's all'. Now shaking her head, she said, 'I've no idea what you're on about, I just hope you know what you are doing, cos I've seen people like those blokes before, and when you mess with people like that you usually come off worse'. 'Thanks mam, for the advice' said Ross, Val just laughed and said, 'you daft sod and I tell you what, If I was your mam, I would probably give you a clip round the ear and say pack it in, just promise me ...', she hesitated then shook her head, 'oh what's the point you won't take any notice anyway will you'. Val then placed her hand on Ross's shoulder, and walked back to the shop counter, that was her way of saying without any more words that she understood but hoped he would be careful.

As Ross sat in the warm and comforting Flamingo café cocooned from the realities that awaited him in the world outside, Colm O'Shea sat in a dented and rusted Fiesta van, that looked as though it had fallen off the top of a skip. He was parked some hundred yards down the street from the Pink Flamingo. Frank had insisted that O'Shea got straight onto the job and had sent him out immediately after their chat at the boxing club. The Fiesta that O'Shea described succinctly as a 'pile of shite' was to be his temporary home for the next few days. He looked almost comical in the car, as his inhuman bulk made this average sized car look like it had been driven straight off a children's fairground ride. It wasn't Frank's 'proper car' no that was a very nice top of the range BMW but unfortunately for O'Shea, Frank never used the BM for work. He didn't like to draw attention to himself, he always maintained that if you ran around in an old banger, no one gave you a second look, especially the tax man. Frank always thought, no one was interested in a loser in an old car and people he assumed were genuinely shallow and judged you by your car, your accent, and your clothes. Frank called this presumption simply 'human nature' while the so-called psychologists gave it a fancier title of 'unconscious bias', whatever it was called, if you were aware of it, you could manipulate almost any situation. Colm O'Shea now sat bored out his mind as he watched the café for signs of Ross, it reminded him of his time in the army, five percent action and ninety five percent boredom. That's why he always assumed he'd become involved in smuggling contraband which led to his court martial, eventual dismissal and being described by his commanding officer as 'weak minded and gullible' at his trial. Although he wasn't the only person who had been involved in the smuggling racket, he was unfortunately the one that got caught. He knew there were many people higher up in the 'food chain of deceit' than him, who had amassed small fortunes illegally, but you just kept your mouth shut and accepted responsibility for your own actions, the unwritten code of conduct read something like 'you took your punishment and didn't grass on anyone'. He left the army in some people's eyes 'in disgrace' but to him it was all 'bollocks', everyone was on the take in all walks of life and sometimes you were just unlucky. Frank had taken pity on ex Private Colm O'Shea, after being impressed with his no-nonsense approach to trouble when he had seen the big man break up a brawl in one of his pubs, he gave him some 'delivery jobs' to do and O'Shea had been grateful for that, as his life, like many of his ex-colleagues was far from easy after their time in the services. Somewhat ironically, O'Shea's 'prey' Ross Campbell, and he, had one thing in common they both stopped and gave time and when they had it, money to ex-servicemen who slept rough on the streets. It was a strange fact of life that even though people seemed polar opposites in views and even cultures, if they took the time to understand each other, perhaps life could be a great deal better for all. O'Shea may have screwed up his army career but the camaraderie he'd experienced in the service of his country had stayed with him despite his bitterness towards authority.

Just as O'Shea slid the driver's seat as far back as it could possibly go and was about to settle down, Ross appeared from the café doorway clutching his trusty *Nikon*. He glanced up and down the street, O'Shea assumed he was probably far enough away not to be noticed, but he instinctively slunk down in his seat just in case. Fortunately, his 'target' walked up the road away from the car, rather than towards him. He started the car, pulled his seat forward and waited for Ross to get far enough ahead before he slowly moved off. Driving slowly, he was immediately tooted at by a car close behind him, and being a man who thrived on confrontation, he instinctively wound down his window and proceeded to present the motorists 'V' sign of indignity to the car behind. The vehicle then sped up and drew alongside O'Shea with the intention of confronting him by shouting abuse but the driver immediately on seeing the formidable occupant, quickly looked away not wanting to even make eye contact for fear of reprisal. The Fiesta proceeded slowly on, and O'Shea watched as Ross dodged up an alley way, fortunately there was only one way out of the alley, so he simply rounded the block and sat waiting at a discreet distance. Ross meandered up the back alley taking a series of instinctive photographs that stirred his artistic and social consciousness, sadly there was never any shortage of thought-provoking images to capture on film. Like a war zone there seemed to be more than the usual number of 'street' people 'the socially disconnected', some sat up, some sprawled full length in doorways, a 'contortion' of human flotsam and jetsam washed up by a tide of political and social injustice, their lives and worldly belongings trapped in a seemingly inescapable microcosm of detritus and despair. As Ross emerged from the alley, he had accumulated yet another selection of photos, and thought how many images did he need to put on his website before the authorities and the useless self-centred politicians would stand up and help these poor souls to turn their lives around. As soon as O'Shea saw Ross emerge from the alley, he waited for him to walk some way up the street before tailing him again. Following Ross became something of a tortuous journey, worse than he could possibly have imagined,' what's the matter with this bloke' he thought, couldn't he move in straight lines, because every time Ross had the opportunity to stay on major roads, for some reason he would just abandon them in favour of a back lane. O'Shea coined a nickname for Ross, he now called him the 'rat runner', as he dodged up every alleyway like the lowest of animals, seemingly driven by instinct and survival. It took Ross almost an hour to make his way back to his humble council abode. Sitting outside the block of flats into which his prey had disappeared, O'Shea presumed this was where he lived, well it was a 'shit hole' suitable for a rat he thought. He would just have to sit it out now, keeping a watchful but not too conspicuous a presence, as this was an area where if people didn't recognise you, it invariably drew unwanted attention. Ross sat at his kitchen table, a 1950's Formica topped affair left in the property by a previous resident. He placed his camera on the table, flipped up the chrome winding handle and meticulously wound the film forward in a clockwise direction until it reached its stop. Ross opened the camera back and took out the roll of film that he would eventually take to his local library, where the community film making facilities would allow him access to a darkroom. He held the tiny roll of abject 'misery' in his hand and then moved towards the living room window, as he stared out onto the street, he was unaware of O'Shea squeezed like a Sardine into a tin, on his uncomfortable vigil. The area looked particularly uninspiring today, dull, windy, and forlorn, empty cans and litter tumbled and rattled from one end of the street to the other, groups of teenagers huddled in suspicious groups, grey and uncompromising, it was the epitome of the 'concrete jungle'. People were trapped by their seemingly hopeless and inescapable surroundings, it was a world away from the idyllic rural village, that a then seven-year-old Ross had been packed off to, many, many years ago. He had been sent to live with his grandparents, when his mother, abandoned, two years previously by her partner, Ross's father, simply couldn't cope with him and his little sister anymore. Ross could remember walking down the steep hill from his grandparents small, whitewashed granite cottage that led to the local village school. As he descended the hill he remembered the view across the small coastal bay, especially when the sun light would glint and add a dash of silver highlighting to the incoming tide that would eventually smother the mud flats. He recalled the sweet scent of the hedgerows blossoming with life, there were vivid coloured wildflowers and butterflies, sparrows chirped as they sat on rusting wire fences, he would trail his hand across the tips of the tall grass growing at the side of the road, the memory of the grass tickling the palm of his hand had never left him. One day while walking to school he watched as a young jet-black crow prepare itself to feast on a partly discarded sandwich that lay at the side of the road. The Crow rested on its belly, and he remembered being confused on seeing the bird in such a strange pose. However, as it attempted to stand up, he realised it had only one leg, and tottered from side to side almost falling over each time it moved. The large bird looked lost and almost helpless when a group of Starlings came and bundled it over and attempted to take the sandwich, but the desperate

Crow didn't give in, and fought with all the energy it could muster and took back the bread and somehow manged to take flight and escape with its prize. He recalled saying 'yes, yes' excitedly as it escaped, he felt that solitary bird mirrored his life at school, where he felt alone and was constantly being teased and bullied by the local children but just like the Crow he also learned to fight back, and he'd been doing it ever since.

Now looking back, although far from perfect, he had enjoyed many happy times, but with most of the good things in life he'd experienced, it was destined not to last. He was forced to return to his mother's house near Glasgow when he was eleven, after the death of his grandparents. His unwanted return prepared him over the subsequent years for nothing more than grim survival. Ross was a 'city boy' now, dodging, and surviving best he could, and prided himself on being able to adapt to his surroundings, like a chameleon he could just morph into the background, a skill that had served him well for most of his adult life. As he recalled his childhood in rural Scotland, he made a promise to himself that when this final phase of destruction was over, he would pack up and move away from the grime and desolation he now experienced in London. He would take himself down to an artist's colony he'd heard of in Pont Aven in Northern France, he would hitchhike his way down there and start a new life. The thought of this lifted his sagging spirits as he stared onto the grim grey streets before him. O'Shea had already called Frank Swift and said that he had found the 'rats lair' as he called it, he viewed Ross very much as a feral animal, something that needed taming or perhaps even putting down. He had his instructions from Frank and although he hoped 'The Rat' might just behave itself, he would be in for a long wait as Ross had planned his attacks for two nights hence. O'Shea duly returned and parked in the same position outside Ross's 'lair' bright and early the next morning but after sitting in the vehicle for nearly two hours he became increasingly restless as his enormous frame groaned with the consequences of inactivity. 'Yes', he thought it was OK for some, meaning his boss, probably sat in a nice comfortable chair, in the warmth of his office, while he slummed it in a cramped and grubby old car. He knew Frank wanted the surveillance kept quiet, but his mind was now working overtime, and was always looking for an angle. O'Shea decided to phone Danny, one of the young kids that came to the boxing club, that both he and Frank had used to run 'errands' for them from time to time. The kid was 'a goodun' and if told him to keep his mouth shut, that's exactly what he'd do. He rang Danny and gave him his current location and decided he would give the kid one hundred pounds a day and let him do some of the baby-sitting duties. If Ross went anywhere the car couldn't go, then the kid could just leave the car and follow-on foot passing on the details to him, what could be simpler he thought. O'Shea sat for another two hours before Danny turned up. By now he was climbing the 'walls' and dying for a 'pee' but he needed to point out Ross to the kid, before he could leave him to it and then take a break which would more than likely be in some local boozer. As it turned out 'Lady luck' was smiling on him as he sat in silence with his new recruit. Colm wasn't a great conversationalist, but it didn't really matter with Danny, because as with most kids of his age, he just sat and played with his mobile phone or listened to music, the art of conversation between the generations was well and truly dead. As they both sat in silence, O'Shea breathed a huge sigh of relief as Ross appeared from his block of flats and stood looking around. He glanced in O'Shea's direction, who then made a vain attempt to slink down in his seat, but his bulk made the act impossible, however Ross was looking with his artist's eye, surveying the scene, not looking at anything specific but taking in an overall picture of life. O'Shea then said to Danny 'that's him, look, there, the one in the combat gear'. The kid didn't pay any attention and hadn't heard him as he played with his mobile and had his headphones in, which were pumping out a rhythmic mind-numbing 'beat'. Frustrated at the kid's lack of response, his temper got the better of him as he pushed Danny with his left arm which in turn knocked the phone out of his hand. The kid now glared at O'Shea but was too frightened to say anything, he then pulled his earphones out with indignation, 'there, that's him', O'Shea repeated while at the same time pointing with one his 'baseball bat' sized fingers. Danny initially looked with indifference at the man, just a regular sort of bloke, but as he looked more intently, realised that he recognised him from somewhere. He didn't say anything to O'Shea, he just said 'OK' and as he stared at the man again his mind seemed to click into gear and he remembered his name, it was 'Ross' and that he'd taken him and some of the kids from his estate through a council sponsored course in art, not 'posh art' but 'street art'. He now cast his mind back and reckoned it must have been three or four years ago. For Danny, education had been a non-starter, he hadn't been in the least academic and very little he saw at school had sparked any interest within him. However, he had enjoyed the 'art' course and this 'target' he was about to follow, was just like himself 'from the streets' and he'd been receptive to how Danny and his mates thought and behaved. Ross had shown them respect and appeared to understand them, this was a rare moment of recognition and appreciation from a kid like Danny. Suddenly he wanted to know why O'Shea wanted him followed, he assumed that Ross must have overstepped the mark in some way and that was bad news where Frank Swift's crew were concerned. What had he done? Danny knew to keep his mouth shut, he'd learnt early on, you don't ask questions, however, he felt a genuine empathy towards Ross, he was an 'alright bloke', and wanted to help him, but did he dare warn him? The thought ate away at him, but he'd seen O'Shea deal out beatings to people and didn't want to be on the receiving end of one of them. As with most of what happened on the streets, he would just keep his head down, do the job and not get involved, it didn't feel good, but life was about survival not morals. As Ross set off down the street yet again, he was followed as usual at a discreet distance, but this time when he did his usual rat run up an alleyway O'Shea didn't panic. He simply instructed his newly recruited 'foot soldier' to leave the relative comfort and warmth of the Fiesta and follow-on foot. Ross wasn't an easy 'target' to follow as he kept stopping to take photos of what seemed like inconsequential and everyday subjects to Danny, people dossing in doorways, cocooned in cardboard and blankets attempting to keep themselves warm. Just when it seemed that Ross was about to move on, he'd stop again to photograph yet another 'down and out' lying in some doorway. Danny became irritated at Ross's inability to get on with it and keep moving but his main gripe was the freezing cold weather and that he'd rather be in the car, even though it did mean sharing it with the 'stone'. Eventually Ross arrived at his destination, even if it was a temporary one, the Pink Flamingo café. The windows were all steamed up and ran with the 'condensation of gossip', and the yellow lights shone like a beacon to the cold and weary. It looked warm and inviting to Danny and he was tempted to follow him inside, but what if Ross recognised him, O'Shea would blow a gasket if their cover was blown, so he rang and told him where he was. He was 'ordered' to stay put and O'Shea would follow on in five minutes or so. As five minutes painfully and slowly turned into forty-five minutes Danny's feet almost turned into immovable blocks of ice, he rubbed his hands and attempted to warm them by exhaling warm air from his breath into them. Where the hell was he, Danny kept repeating to himself as he looked up and down the street for the ancient Ford Fiesta. Just as the fear of incurring the wrath of O'Shea had diminished in comparison to the discomfort of the extremely cold weather, he now considered doing a 'runner'. Suddenly Danny heard the toot of a car horn and the Fiesta appeared alongside him and pulled half onto the kerb. Much to his amazement, as he got in, O'Shea presented him with a McDonald's meal and a cup of lukewarm coffee which he gratefully accepted. As Ross sat in the Flamingo Cafe, it had a comforting warmth, that was only spoilt when the door opened to admit or witness the departure of a customer, when the resultant incoming rush of cold air would dip the temperature temporarily. The café was busy but not packed, idle chatter and the chink of freshly stacked cups and cutlery complimented the friendly atmosphere, Ross tucked into one of Val's specialities, her 'BEST' meal, a mega sized Bacon, Egg, Sausage and Tomato sandwich. He stretched his legs fully out under the table for maximum comfort, at the same time O'Shea sat with knees almost up to his chin in the cramped interior of the Fiesta and Danny sat munching on his now cold McDonald's. Ross viewed his current meal as possibly the last for a condemned man, he had decided that tomorrow night was to be his D-Day, the battle plans were drawn, his grandfather would have been proud of him, well perhaps for the planning but not the Graffiti he thought. His reminiscences in his flat, about his childhood and happier times and the possibility of new adventures in France had brought about a sudden desire to act decisively and 'finish off' what he had started.

Frances sat on the bed in the spare room, this was one the few spaces in their voluminous country house that John didn't use, so she thought of it as 'her room', a sanctuary. She'd never regarded the house as her home, 'no' it was always John's home, and she didn't want anything from him. Frances sat staring at a suitcase lying shut on the bed beside her, the case contained just about everything she would need when she eventually walked out on John. The case had been packed for nearly two years now and she refreshed its contents on a regular basis, not because it needed it, but because it re-affirmed her desire to leave. Frances somehow always knew she would 'go' one day but always convinced herself it was about timing, she now had just about enough money, the only thing that hadn't been decided upon was where to go. She feared that John might come looking for her, but could he be so blind to their problems? Deep down she assumed that even John must surely know their relationship was over, but his increasing level of paranoia coupled with his failure to see her as anything more than a possession or a trophy, could, she thought now, drive him to seek revenge. Suddenly Frances's mobile rang unexpectedly, she jumped, and was shaken out of her mood of contemplation, intuitively she picked it up assuming it was John checking up on her as usual. She could just hear his probing questions in her head, where are you? What are you doing? Who are you with? Those where his usual questions but on looking at her phone, she didn't recognise the callers number. Curiosity and daring made her answer this mystery number, she didn't speak but waited for the other person to answer first. A bright and confident deep East London man's voice boomed down the phone, 'You rang my number'. Frances thought quickly, who had she rang, then like a sledgehammer crashing down on her thoughts, 'oh no', it had to be the number that she had taken from John's secret phone. Now beginning to panic, she was tempted to hang up, but 'daring' got the better of Frances as she bluffed her way into the conversation. 'Yeah, I got it from a friend, who said you might be able to help me', she had little or no idea what he did, but thought it might be possible to glean something from his reply. She was determined to remain vague with her answers, to keep him guessing without arousing suspicion, 'and which friend might this be' he replied, 'oh just a friend of a friend, you know' said Frances now feigning a girly laugh. She could hear strange noises in the background on his phone, people cheering, laughing, and clapping, it sounded good natured, like some sort of club. 'So, what's a nice sounding lady like you, need from Frank then'. 'Frank? Frank? She thought 'who the hell is Frank', John had never mentioned anyone by that name. Now, thinking on her feet Frances took a gamble and said she wanted to find someone. Frances was stopped in mid-stream by Frank, saying he didn't discuss business on the phone, as he prided himself on the personal touch. 'Yeah, I can probably help you, but we would need to meet up somewhere,' he said. Frances hesitated, would she dare meet a stranger, who, if he turned out to be one of John's close associates was probably better left alone. Frances knew if she didn't agree to his suggestion, she would never know what was going on, and what would have been the point of the frantic search of John's room and all of the resulting subterfuge. 'OK then, what did you have in mind' she replied. Frank liked the sound of this 'posh bird' on the other end of the phone, but he was pretty sure she was 'spinning him a yarn', but was intrigued and anyway, he thought it might be an interesting diversion, so why not try his luck. He suggested a meeting over a drink but not at one of his usual haunts, 'no', it would have to be somewhere half decent not some 'dive'. Frances hesitantly agreed to meet for a 'chat' at seven p.m. the following night at a little wine bar in Camden Town, somewhere she actually knew from years ago, this made her feel a little more confident and marginally less insecure. Ending the call, she fell back and lay her head on the bed with her eyes tight shut, she twirled and twirled a long curl of hair between her fingers, it was something that she did subconsciously when stressed. 'What the hell have I done' she thought, this guy could be some sort of axe murderer but the fear it engendered was also tinged with a feeling of nervous excitement, something she hadn't experienced for many years.

The next day came all too soon for Frances, who now stood in the 'Ladies' within a large department store in the city. She had spun John a story about late night shopping so he wouldn't be expecting her home, she had fretted for a full day about this meeting with Frank, now the time for regrets was over. Staring into the mirror, the room lights shone with a bright white unyielding glow that made her look pale and gaunt. This may have been the reason why she applied more than her usual amount of make-up, why was she even doing this? She thought, 'after all this character Frank, was a total stranger and might get the wrong idea'. Now hesitating with her lipstick poised like a pen about to sign a death warrant, she went ahead and applied an extra thick layer of deceit, then hesitated, and was just about to wipe it off with a tissue when she thought, 'what the hell', they were meeting in a busy little bar, that was safe, wasn't it? As she applied the finishing touches with her eye liner, she'd forgotten how good she could look, and it gave Frances a feeling of long forgotten self-worth. On the other side of town Frank was also staring in the mirror in his newly refurbished bathroom in what had been his mother's three bed terrace in Bethnal Green. An ex-council house bought for a song in the late eighties as a gift for his mother, it was now worth south of five hundred thousand pounds. When his mother had passed on, he had decided to give it a complete makeover 'to borrow the TV jargon'. He'd moved in, rather than selling, because his ex-wife had screwed him 'over' during their divorce and taken just about everything including their, as the estate agent had described it 'nice little pied-à-terre' in Kensington. The 'Green' wasn't a bad area, he'd grown up there as a kid, 'yes' it had changed over the years and not, he considered for the better, it was now in the grip of an insidious form of social improvement referred to as 'gentrification' and that was replacing genuine working-class symbols like the local pubs with up-market wine bars offering a variety of 'New World wines' by the glass. There were still a few old timers living in the street who remembered 'big Frank' as a kid, and he had a certain amount of respect in the neighbourhood gained more from 'fear' than anything else. Frank considered himself a fair and reasonable working-class man, but he mistook his respect as genuine adulation for being a local kid who had done well for himself. Frank looked in the mirror, he stretched his face with his fingers in an attempt to make the age lines around his mouth and eyes look a little less noticeable, 'mm not bad for a fifty-five-year-old' he thought to himself. As he glanced to the side of the mirror, he looked at an old picture frame containing two photos of his grandfather 'Gentleman' Jack Swift. One, a fading black and white photo which portrayed him as a fresh faced eighteen-year-old kid in a staged boxing pose from the early 1920's with his gloves up ready for action. The other was a colour Polaroid of 'grandad Jack' in the early years of his retirement wearing his favourite suit and his trademark brown 'pork pie' hat. His grandfather had been a docker and had lived over in South London and like many of his contemporaries had taken up prize fighting as a means of making much needed extra cash. He idolised his grandfather and could still remember holding his large waxy comforting hand when he had taken him out on walks to give his mother a break from him and his three younger brothers. He remembered visiting his grandfather's place of work, a large bank in the city, he joked that he was the 'Bank director', which was sort of true, as he worked as a lift attendant and 'directed' visitors within the building. Frank recalled his grandfather opening the lift doors for city snobs in bowler hats and calling them 'Sir'. The thought even after all these years, still annoyed him, to think that his grandfather had worked hard all his life for very little reward and these 'pinstriped nobody's' had comfortable lives and money, not through hard work but mere 'networking' and privilege. Frank could still recall his grandfather's warm gravelly voice saying, 'it was an 'ard, ard, life in the old days, little man'. Frank assumed this was why he'd personally never had any qualms selling drugs to the 'city types', maybe it would finish some of them off, the arrogant bastards, it was his way of paying them back for the old man's tough and uncompromising life. Frank had no intention of ending up like his grandfather, so self-promotion and a 'grab it while you can' attitude had been his mantra for years and up to now, it had served him well. Reminiscences of the past suddenly disappeared as his senses were overtaken by the aroma coming from a generous amount of 'Creed Aventus' as it gushed out of the bottle and into his large gnarled 'boxing' hands. He then proceeded to slap it onto his cheeks with enthusiasm and then gave himself a final slap for luck, it was just like going into the ring, he was now all psyched up and ready for action. Meanwhile Ross had returned home, he switched on a bare exposed light bulb to fight back against the winter gloom as it enveloped his dark and cold flat, the bulb's harsh light created grotesque shadows around the room and reflected in a cracked mirror that hung lopsided on the wall. Ross caught sight of himself, unshaven for days, hair un-combed, imagining that he looked better than he actually did and looking as though he had just woken up after being on an all-night 'bender'. He shook his head and thought, well Ross you can't look 'twenty-one' all your life and anyway tonight was to be the end of it all and he would then move on, that was his singular thought as the haggard but determined face in the mirror stared back at him. Outside in the street O'Shea twisted and turned in the cramped Fiesta trying to relieve a numb bottom. He turned the car mirror down and stuck out his tongue to view its pallor, it looked like the bottom of a budgies cage he thought and that's exactly how it tasted. He was tired of this 'stake out crap', he rubbed his eyes and thought he could do with a pint, he would give it a couple of hours then call his faithful foot soldier Danny to take over the night shift for him.

Frances walked tentatively into the bijou wine bar in Camden, formerly a working man's pub. Where many years ago dockers and labourers had jostled shoulder to shoulder on a Friday night after a hard weeks graft, now its clientele were jobbing actors, media types and 'B' list celebrities. She had asked Frank how she would recognise him, and he simply said you can't miss me 'I'll be the biggest bloke standing at the bar in a blue suit'. As she entered, some regular customers glanced her way, they recognised new faces and gave Frances a cursory once over in case it was someone of 'note' or a useful 'networking' opportunity, alas 'no' they decided, just a random stranger, they turned away and continued with their conversations. Frances hadn't been out like this on her own for years. She felt somewhat self-conscious and had deliberately turned up late to be certain 'he' would be there first. She hadn't decided exactly what to say but had settled on a story about a missing friend, which wasn't exactly untrue, but hoped it would be believable enough. As she moved towards the bar, with his back to her, stood a blue suited man who was a good four inches taller than everyone around him, that's got to be him thought Frances. Tall and broad shouldered with an American GI style haircut, he looked smart and in control. Frances was impressed, she then glanced at his shoes, she always thought, mistakenly, as it turned out, that you could judge peoples characters by their footwear and his Oxford Brogues didn't disappoint. For Frances there was something that seemed attractive about 'big' men, they seemed to command respect and she liked the thought of being in the company of someone who didn't get pushed around. Just as she was about to try an introduction, Frank turned around and looked straight at her. 'Got to be Frances, what can I get you to drink?' he said, smiling, he had a good set of teeth she thought, but his face although presentable, certainly showed the 'signs' of what she intuitively thought was years on the wrong end of a boxing glove.

Frances smiled at him, something she did subconsciously, and this was something John had always complained about, he used to say, 'no wonder you get weirdos coming on to you, smiling at complete strangers'. That always annoyed Frances, she couldn't help it, just wanted to be pleasant and always thought John was either jealous or just a miserable sod. Frances gratefully accepted a white wine and then he suggested sitting in a quiet corner where they could have their 'little chat' as he had described it on the phone. Frances was nervous but was trying not to show it, she had something up her sleeve, her 'Joker' and would wait for her opportunity to play it. She expected Frank to get straight down to business, but instead he did all the pleasantries you might expect from a casual acquaintance, not some private detective or thug, she still didn't know exactly what his line of business was yet. Frank asked her if she lived close by? Did she know the area? He even asked what she liked to do with her spare time. This was Frank just 'being Frank', he used his old psychological trick of softening people up and getting them to drop their guard, he was a master at it. He thought Frances was an alright 'bit of stuff' but maybe a bit too posh even for him'. She also wore a wedding ring, but 'so what, that meant nothing' he thought, so had his wife but that hadn't stopped her running off with some smarmy young estate agent. Who ended up with his beloved Audi TT being mercilessly trashed, courtesy of Frank and his baseball bat. It had been a senseless but hugely satisfying act of retribution, 'but that was all behind him now' and anyway, maybe this would be his 'lucky night'. Frances was barely halfway through her wine when the big man insisted on getting another drink in, she tried to insist on buying the round, but Frank was still old fashioned when it came to women and buying drinks, it was a male prerogative, that was how he saw it. As he returned from the bar, Frances now attempting to settle her nerves took a large gulp of wine and became bolder as she said 'so, Mr. Swift, what do you do?'. Frank just smiled and said 'mm, well, this and that, you could say, I suppose', he hesitated and looked thoughtful,' I'm a fixer of people's problems'. 'That sounds', she hesitated before continuing, 'vague but interesting', 'what sort of problems', she now smiled and laughed trying to take the edge off her pointed questions and making them casual rather than too inquisitive. Frank returned her smile, then took a 'big drink', and downed half of his previously full pint glass before replying, 'unpaid debts, people not behaving themselves, basically anything 'unpleasant', that 'nice' people don't want to be concerned with'. 'So come on' said Frank, 'now it's your turn, what does a 'good looking', Frances laughed feeling flattered, 'lady like you, want me to do for her then?' She hesitated and looked thoughtful, attempting to give her 'story' at least an air of verisimilitude, 'I want you, I mean, I would like you to find someone for me'. Frank now eased back in his chair as he said, 'Normally I ask people why they want someone found and what they intend to do to them, but you seem like a nice lady, so this time I won't', he said laughing. Frances could tell Frank was trying to weigh her up, somehow get inside her mind, but she saw this as 'the moment' and had made her mind up, she handed Frank an old picture of herself and Ross. Part of the photo had been cut off, the part that had shown John. As Frank looked at the picture, he wasn't so much interested in who was in the picture but 'who' or 'what' had been removed, that's where the intrigue lay for him. He looked at Frances 'well you're still a looker, so who's missing', he said while running his finger inquisitively down the edge of the cut off portion, 'oh just an ex, no one important', replied Frances without hesitation. She then smiled and pushed on, now scrutinising his face for any forthcoming sign of recognition as she played her 'Joker', 'his name is Ross Campbell', and immediately repeated the 'name' again now with emphasis on the 'Campbell'. She carefully studied his response like a tramp eagerly eyeing a discarded and half smoked smouldering cigarette. Frank didn't bat so much as an eyelid, but Frances was sure she sensed something in the way that he shuffled in his seat, and almost deliberately appeared to be disinterested whilst he looked at the photo and heard the name 'Campbell'. He wasn't the only amateur psychologist in the room she thought. Frank had been too long in the 'game' of extorting money, recovering debts, and making people 'sorry' for ever crossing his path to succumb to a sucker punch, furthermore he didn't believe in chance or coincidence. His mind similar to the very best of Sat Nav's now quickly recalculated his position as he thought, so why the old photo? What's your connection to Campbell'? What are you really after? He was intrigued and now knew for sure that this 'pretty bird' was playing some sort of game with him. He was enjoying the 'cat and mouse' intrigue of it all and decided to just 'play along' and not adopt his usual style of interrogation which consisted of a hand around the throat and slamming the person against the wall. 'So, what's the story?' said Frank, 'ex-husband? Boyfriend? 'No! Actually, he's my brother, I haven't seen him for nearly twenty years, and I need to find him,' she replied. Frank looked at the photo and thought to himself, if this is your brother whatever happened to a thing called 'family resemblance'. Her story was 'complete bollocks' he thought, but after-all, it was just a game. 'You were a brunette then, what happened? Frances laughed and said, 'being a blonde is more flattering after a certain age', 'no good for me' said Frank laughing as he rubbed his head in confirmation. 'So do you think you can help me' said Frances not wanting to prolong this meeting any longer than she had to. 'Depends, twenty years is a long time, how do you know he's even in London?' he replied. Frances had to think on her feet, 'I know it sounds ridiculous, but I can just sense it, you know when you just get a feeling about something?'. 'Well, it's your money, it'll cost five hundred a day plus expenses if that's worth a 'feeling' to you' replied Frank. The money wasn't a problem, but this gave Frances the opportunity she was looking for, 'I'll need to think it over, it's a lot more than I thought it would cost'. Frank was now one hundred percent sure that it was all a rouse, 'so your long-lost brother isn't even worth five hundred pounds a day' he thought. Playing the game and calling her bluff Frank said he would ask around as a favour and they could talk money later. This put Frances on the 'spot' because it would look odd if she said 'no' to this offer as well. She agreed somewhat reluctantly to leave the photo with Frank, he even asked her to put a contact number on the back. As she wrote her number, she struggled to stop her hand from shaking, even the alcohol couldn't mitigate her nerves, but thought she had done enough to convince him with her story. Frank now settled back into his chair looking at the photograph, Frances took another large gulp of wine and felt as though she now knew why John drank as he did. The wine was warm and calming as it slipped down and lubricated her dry nervous throat. Now a sense of euphoria arose within her, and aided by the sheer relief that this charade was nearly over, she pushed herself back into her seat and placed the nearly empty glass back on the table, convinced her deception had worked.

Chapter Fourteen
Vanta-Black

'A unique microstructure consisting of carbon
nanotubes, claimed to be World's darkest
manmade substance'

Deep Black

Ross stood outside his block of flats, he
looked up and then down the road. The
pavements were deserted of life and
daylight, it was late but not too late, but the time
wasn't relevant, as long as it was dark, he would be
able to complete his final campaign of destruction.
Taking a deep breath of air to clear his head and
focus his mind, the cold oxygen seemed to freeze
his nostrils then rushed down into his lungs and
coursed around his body like an additional dose of
adrenalin. Dressed as usual in his camouflage
jacket, courtesy of the long since gone Army and
Navy stall that used to frequent a local Saturday
market. He had his trusty haversack over his
shoulder, it contained everything he needed,
enough tins of black and silver paint to make his
mark, nothing flashy or particularly artistic this
time, no it was strictly a search and destroy
mission. There were five targets dotted around a
radius of approximately four miles, it would have
to be completed on foot. The cold air seemed to

numb his head, he could see the tiny diamonds of frost glittering on the roofs of parked cars as he peered up the street, to counteract the cold he pulled on his balaclava, this gave him warmth and focused his mind, this was his 'do or die' day. The idea of hammering the final nail into the coffin of his anger and burying this along with all his woes and then just disappearing had given him a new lease of life. One hundred yards up the street from where Ross was now standing, sat ex-Private Colm O'Shea in Frank's battered Fiesta Van, O'Shea made no attempt to hide this time, he was sick of the intrigue, and didn't care if this loser saw him.

Ross decided that although he felt cold, with his Balaclava pulled down over his face he looked suspicious and that could draw unwanted attention, so he rolled it up to form a hat instead. He had one last look up and down the street and saw nothing but the pale amber streetlights casting their glow across a 'litter' of haphazardly parked cars on both sides of the road. He set off with an earnest pace, his pains and troubles forgotten, head down against the biting cold wind he was on autopilot, the route he had decided on was pre-programmed in his head like software instructions on a silicon chip. It would take him the best part of three to four hours to get round his targets and that was without unwanted interference. O'Shea turned the ignition key in Frank's ageing Fiesta, it seemed to object almost as much as he did to being out on this cold winters night. The engine turned slowly 'over and over' without purpose, like a pensioner gasping for breath on a steep flight of stairs, it struggled and seemed incapable of movement. With O'Shea's patience rapidly disappearing and his frustration mounting, he was just about to slam his fist on the dashboard when the car suddenly burst into life. He quickly jumped on the accelerator and the car emitted a large toxic and ghostly cloud of thick diesel smoke. He followed Ross just as he had done the last few days and watched him as he disappeared down into the local subway, 'bollocks', shouted O'Shea, this now meant he would have to drive the long way round to catch up with his prey. As Ross entered the tunnel most of the subway lights were inoperative, mainly smashed, but two lights had survived and emitted a sickly pale white glow that barely illuminated the darkness. Daubed with mindless graffiti, devoid of any meaning or protest and without any artistic endeavour it offended Ross's eye, the floor was littered with beer cans and his feet crunched on broken glass. As he approached the halfway point of the tunnel, the 'danger zone, equidistant from escape at either end, a gang of six or seven youths entered from the far end, they were drinking and jokingly pushing each other around. When they saw Ross coming towards them, they started hooting and shouting at him. 'What's in the bag weirdo?, giz a look', Ross decided to try and ignore them, put his head down and keep on walking but they spread menacingly out across the tunnel to block his progress. Ross decided he had two had options, to confront them head on or turn and beat a retreat. He decided that he wasn't in a retreating mood and reckoned that if they thought he was some 'crazy loner' he could disperse them. Grabbing an empty wine bottle from the subway floor and holding it by the neck, he then smashed it against the wall and shouted his battle cry 'Come on then, you bastards', let's dance', he waved the broken bottle in front of him 'like a sword' as he approached them head on. Ross had always been told that a Glaswegian accent was enough to frighten most people and he now thought that teamed with a broken bottle represented the perfect combination to create 'absolute fear' and he was right, as the kids suddenly broke rank, some deciding to retreat and others running straight past him. Ross just laughed and shouted abuse at them as they dispersed, nobody was going to steal this final show down from him. As he strode triumphantly out of the tunnel, his adrenalin was in full flow, he hurled the broken bottle into the air like a 'grenade'. It seemed to almost float in slow motion, spiralling it's way upwards before crashing and shattering against some distant metal bins, narrowly missing a sleeping 'drunk' hidden in a nearby doorway. O'Shea was sat waiting for Ross to come out of the tunnel and had decided to call on the assistance again, of the younger and fitter 'tracker' in the shape of Danny. He'd given the kid some extra cash and had asked him to discreetly follow 'the Rat' and report back if anything unusual occurred. Ross strode away from the tunnel animated in both mind and body, now with his head up, determination raced through him as he powered his way to the first target. Following Ross turned out to be much easier than on previous occasions for Danny, this time he seemed to move in straight lines rather than in the convoluted and tortuous meanderings he'd previously employed.

Frances had spent an anxious ten minutes in the 'Ladies' debating her next move, something she hoped that would allow her to leave without it seeming too suspicious. As she returned to the table Frank had bought yet another round of drinks and Frances exhaled a deep sigh, she knew this wasn't going to be easy. She smiled and was just in the process of thanking him and about to attempt to make her excuses to leave, when suddenly his phone rang. Frank was enjoying himself, it had been a while since he had enjoyed female company as much as this, he considered ignoring the phone but then noticed it was 'cosh' calling, so felt compelled to answer. O'Shea described to Frank how the 'target' had appeared from outside his flat carrying a rucksack and dressed in 'fatigues' and that he had even pulled on a balaclava for what seemed like some sort of 'op'. Unusually for O'Shea, not the most loquacious of people, now vented his frustration through speech for a change, as he described the scene in such vivid detail, that Frank was in little doubt that this 'little scroat' was up to something. He told O'Shea to keep a close eye on 'the target' and when he appeared to be settled somewhere, Frank would join him and they could sort this little matter, once and for all. As Frank came off the phone, he glanced at Frances's long slim sun-tanned legs, and distracted momentarily thought to himself, 'you're a good-looking women', but any idea he might have had, to try and get Frances in the 'sack' would unfortunately now have to wait. 'Well, I'm afraid I'm going to have to end our little meeting for now, I've a problem to sort', Frank paused and with a change in his easy-going tone, said 'just some little tosser that won't behave himself, but it won't take long, can I drop you somewhere?'. To Frances's huge relief the meeting was over, politely declining his offer of a lift, saying she would make her own way home. As Frank stood up, he towered above her and offered his hand which Frances shook tentatively, it felt rough and gnarled, with knuckles disfigured from punching numerous adversaries both in and out the ring. As Frances turned and made her way out of the bar, she could only imagine what fate would await the poor soul on the receiving end of Frank's retribution, after his early departure from their meeting. Frances didn't have time to worry about anyone else, she was sure now that John had engaged Frank Swift's services and there was a connection with Ross, but exactly what that was, Frances didn't yet know.

As Frances got into the back of a taxi, the heater blew out a comforting and continuous flow of warm air, settling back into the seat, she gave directions for home. Meanwhile, Ross stood in the freezing cold night air watching his breath create plumes of mist as the heat from his lungs condensed, he now stood in the shadows, just across the road from his first target. The wind was cold and biting, he pulled his balaclava down over his face for protection from the weather and any CCTV cameras in the area, not that he really cared about being caught on camera, but it wasn't worth courting trouble unnecessarily. Now before him, across the road behind a wire fence lay target number one, not that big by John's usual standards, probably eight feet square and apart from the fencing, thankfully, it had no other protection. Ross was surprised at this, described by the press as an 'exciting' early example of John Noble's work, it was considered something of a collector's item allegedly worth in excess of a half of a million pounds. Ross had two choices, he could either go over the fence, which at seven or eight feet high wasn't too daunting a prospect. Or he could waste precious time cutting a hole near its base, that was small enough to gain entry. As he stood weighing up his limited options, he was being observed by Danny who had a reasonably good view of him, from a far less salubrious location, as he stood next to a line of filthy refuse bins, most of which were overflowing with detritus, the smell almost made him want to wretch. Danny had called 'in' as instructed on his mobile and given O'Shea, his current location. The young foot soldier had made his mind up, as soon as O'Shea showed up, he would get his money and run, he wasn't freezing his butt off anymore, not even for a hundred and fifty quid. He cupped his hands and held them to his mouth, he blew in some warm air to alleviate the cold and looked in Ross's direction. Suddenly, much to his amazement, without warning Ross lurched from the shadows and moving awkwardly   like a geriatric 'pole-vaulter attempting the high bar', he seemed to almost slide his body up the face of the wire fence. His clumsy attempt at clearing the fence unfortunately ended abruptly, when his scramble at the top saw him snag his jacket on one of the posts that held the fencing rigid. Caught like an unsuspecting fish on a hook, he was suspended just two tantalising feet above the ground, 'shit, shit' he said aloud as he now struggled to release himself. He twisted and yanked his body from side to side, straining every muscle in his back and shoulders but it was to no avail, he was stuck, and hanging like a prize Turkey in butchers Christmas window, in full view of the streetlights for all to see. He said to himself 'stay calm, think, think', he decided to attempt a downward jerking action with the full weight of his body. He lunged forward and jerked his rapidly tiring body up and down, up and down, nothing appeared to be happening then his jacket started to tear slowly at first and then without warning ripped fully apart sending him tumbling awkwardly down the other side of the fence.' Ross landed unceremoniously on his backside, he sat there for what seemed an eternity, shook his head and thought, 'what the hell was he doing', then he laughed to himself, 'daft old bugger', he said aloud. The cold of the night had now completely disappeared from Ross's body and was soon replaced by excitement seeking adrenalin. He quickly looked around to see if anyone had noticed his ungainly acrobatics, fortunately there wasn't a soul in sight, or so he thought. Scrambling to his feet, he found a corner into which the streetlights couldn't penetrate, and there he sat while trying to regain his composure. The fall from the fence had aggravated his already damaged leg and now the initial surge of adrenalin he had experienced was wearing off. The reality of pain combined with the intense cold brought him firmly back to reality. Danny's view of Ross's location was now impaired, but he knew he was in the fenced compound somewhere. He had passed on his location and the 'stone' was presumably on his way, he had stood motionless in the cold for so long and was now almost frozen to the spot, he had almost given up on him arriving before his body surrendered completely to the cold. No sooner had the thought of 'legging it' entered his numbed mind, when O'Shea lurched round the corner of the street, in his now, as far as Danny was concerned, trademark 'Noddy car'. Irritatingly he drove past him, even though the kid tried to wave him down. Danny saw him park further up the street and now saw his opportunity for an 'escape' as he jogged up the road. On reaching the car he attempted to open the passenger door, but it was locked, he wrapped his cold knuckles on the window to attract O'Shea's attention, who, glanced in Danny's direction but made no attempt to open the door. Frustrated Danny then banged on the window with his fist in frustration, this time O'Shea slowly lent over and opened the door. As Danny got in the car, the warmth of the heater blasted into his face, 'it's alright for some, bloody freezing out there man, why so long?' 'The big man' looked at him with silent contempt. He didn't appreciate people being smart with him, especially when he viewed them as nothing more than stupid kids. 'So where is he then?' barked O'Shea in a curt and unfriendly manner. 'In the compound just over there' said Danny pointing in the direction of where he had last seen Ross. He continued, 'He must be hiding in the shadows, he's mad, tried to scale an eight-foot bloody fence, but he's no cat, stupid sod got caught on the top of it, anyway I'm done in, can I have my money now, I'm bloody freezing'. 'I might still need you to follow on foot said' O'Shea, without thinking Danny retorted 'Fuck that', in an immediate response O'Shea grabbed him by the neck just under his chin and slammed his head against the car window. Danny attempted to spew forth a tirade of obscenities but the vice like grip stifled his words. 'No one swears at me, no one' said O'Shea, who eventually released his grip, but not before banging the kids head with some considerable force against the window for a second time. Shocked and dazed Danny fell silent, he thought about opening the door and doing a runner, but he was frozen with fear. O'Shea by now was sick of the whole affair, he wanted out as much as this stupid kid and in a knee jerk reaction, he took one hundred pounds out of his pocket and threw it at Danny and said, 'go on then, piss off'. 'The kid' looked at his miserly five twenty-pound notes with utter disbelief, he had been promised a hundred and fifty but decided that this was his best chance, do the sensible thing he thought, take the money, shut up and go. He got out of the car and slammed the door shut, calling O'Shea a 'twat' under his breath, and then proceeded to jog in the opposite direction to the compound, it had crossed his mind to shout Ross a warning and run off, but he wasn't that brave or stupid. The 'big man' had now moved his car to get a better view of the 'target' and was about to settle himself for a long wait, when he saw a figure move out of the shadows. Colm immediately recognised 'the Rat' in his fatigues, but rather than texting Frank he decided to wait it out and just observe. Ross had now regained his breath and composure, his leg hurt like hell but there was a job to be done and soon it would all be over. Standing back he looked at the image that was about to be defaced, although he thought of it more as 're-configuration', a 'make over' in modern DIY television parlance. He knew he should really stick to his plan and not get carried away and over do things, after all he had several other works to 'visit', but now that he was here, he had decided to savour the moment. The image was one of John's early ones, a protest directed towards the iniquity and unfairness of Thatcher's 'poll tax', he now undid the straps on his haversack and removed some cans of paint. He felt a slight pang of guilt, as he had been a staunch poll tax protester back in the day, but he knew this was no time for sentiment, that was all history, now this was a 'new form' of protest. O'Shea watched as Ross in wide sweeping movements with his arm, covered, to him what was one lot of graffiti with even more graffiti. In huge, tall black letters, Ross sprayed his tag 'SPYDER' across the image and finished it off with a web surrounding his tag. He could spray this tag all day long, it was now part of his soul, engrained and fixed in his psyche, performed with ease and confidence, like a soldier that could strip down and re-assemble his weapon blindfolded. Ross now carefully un-rolled the stencil of John Noble's face and placed it squarely in the centre of the web and proceeded to infill it with silver paint so it would stand out. Just like the ancient rule of 'Tincture', when Ross worked on the streets, he didn't paint dark on dark, similar to armorial crests of medieval times, it was all about standing out from the crowd. He stood back briefly to admire his work and being a perfectionist, he couldn't resist returning to the image and adding silver star like highlights to the letters of his tag. Lost in the moment he had forgotten that tonight's purpose was solely about getting the job done, it wasn't about 'art' anymore, he should have been moving swiftly from this target to the next as quickly as possible. Now realising his mistake, Ross hurriedly collected up his spray cans and put them into his haversack. He knew his body wouldn't be capable of scaling the fence again, so he decided to use his wire cutters at its base to facilitate his escape. O'Shea had watched with a begrudging admiration of Ross's prowess with a spray can, the letters, and graphics he'd created were accomplished with grace and skill, rounded, and flowing they weren't the usual ugly graffiti scrawl that he had seen on dis-used buildings around the area. O'Shea now decided to text Frank and tell him what the 'rat' was up to and asked him what he wanted to do. As Frank received the message on his phone, he was about two hundred yards behind Frances's Taxi as it sped her towards home. Frank had decided at the last moment to follow 'the posh bird' and see where she went, he didn't believe in coincidences and knew she wasn't telling him the full story. He wanted a bit of background information as he always liked to know as much, if not more than the person he had any dealings with. Ross was now crouched at the bottom of the wire fence, his hands ached with the cold and his knuckles seemed to crunch as he used his wire cutters to cut a hole in the fence that would be big enough to ease himself through. The job was harder than he expected, partly because of the intense cold and the wire mesh had an annoying plastic coating, it all added to his woes. He had to work the cutters backwards and forwards twisting and distorting the wire till it gave way, it seemed to take an eternity just to make a handful of simple cuts to create an 'L' shape opening to crawl through. If nothing else the effort seemed to warm Ross up and take his mind of the cold. O'Shea watched as he bent the flap of wire up out of the way and then saw him throw his haversack through the hole and then struggle to hold the flap of wire open to allow himself the opportunity to crawl through. With no reply yet from Frank, O'Shea decided to continue following in the car, hoping his 'prey' would just go home and he could just call it a night. Ross got to his feet and dusted himself down, collected up his haversack and then turned and took one more look at his handiwork and thought to himself 'one down five more to go', he then set off across the street in search of his next target. Just as Frank switched off his engine having seen Frances's' taxi's red taillights disappear up a long drive to a spectacular looking country house in Surrey. O'Shea had now started up the clapped-out Fiesta and began to follow Ross at a discreet distance. 'So, this is where she lives', Frank mused staring at the house and thought 'a looker with money, very nice', he was now even more intrigued and interested in his mystery client. He glanced at his phone and saw O'Shea's most recent garbled and not unusually succinct message 'the tosser is spraying graffiti, wot you want me to do?' Frank decided to ring Noble and tell him what was happening, little did he know he was actually outside John's house as he selected the number on his phone. As Frank sat in his BMW, John Noble was slumped half asleep and more than a little drunk in his chair, wine glass in hand, waiting for Frances to return home. Suddenly his 'special phone' rang and vibrated across the leather topped mahogany desk in front of him. Like a thief presented with the opportunity of an unattended purse, John snatched up the phone knowing it must be important, especially given it was late at night. Without any regard for the level or tone of his voice, a string of expletives rained from his mouth as Frank told him where Ross was and what he was doing, it was just as he had suspected. John's attention was consumed totally with his phone call to Frank, and he didn't hear Frances as she entered the house and was just passing his man cave door when she heard John say, 'I just want him stopped, I'm not asking you to kill him, just put a stop to it'. It was late, Frank couldn't be bothered himself so he told John that his associate would have a quiet word with him, O'Shea did everything quietly, including inflicting pain. John interjected, 'I don't want him to just have a quiet word, just stop him, don't you understand English, I mean, I don't want this bastard to even be able to hold a spray can again, just do what it takes, got it'. 'Hey, OK man, I get the picture, I'll sort it personally, this 'nobody' has really got under your skin, hasn't he?' said Frank probing for information. 'You've no idea, and it's none of your damn business' snapped John, as he took a large slug of red wine and attempted to stand up out of his chair but slumped unsuccessfully back down again. Frank was annoyed at John's condescending tone, but he kept his cool and thought you'll pay for that, 'hey you're the man, no problem, you can call the shots, but this will cost a lot more' replied Frank. 'I've said before, I don't care how much it costs, just sort it once and for all,' shouted John. 'Consider it done, I'll be in touch' said Frank, who didn't need telling twice, he then rang off abruptly, wanting to end the call before saying what he really thought. Frances stood motionless outside the door to Johns' room, listening intently, then as the phone conversation ended a deathly silence was shattered by the sound of breaking glass from inside as John shouted, 'that Bastard, I'll kill him'. John sat motionless after his outburst, he needed to unload his frustration and anger onto someone, but who? He couldn't tell Frances, no, but Hemmings would listen, after all he was paid enough, 'yes', he thought to himself as he muttered and nodded his head in confirmation to his own alcohol fuelled reasoning, Dave would have to listen, it was in his best interests as well. John scrolled through his contact list, selected Dave and then called. As John listened to the phone ringing, Dave was just removing his socks, that's all he was wearing as he stared at 'gallery assistant' Natalie, a twenty-five-year-old leggy economics graduate, who giggled as she bounced up and down on his recently acquired waterbed. Dave viewed his assistant as nothing more than an ornament for his gallery but unusually for him, as it turned out, he hugely underestimated her guile. A graduate and then an intern, she had struggled to secure a suitable and lasting position in the world of fine art. The opportunity with Dave and his prestigious contemporary gallery was something she was determined to play a significant role within and would use 'everything' in her power to get it. Dave wouldn't normally ignore a phone call, but as he looked at the caller information, when he saw it was John, he thought ', 'shit, not now, no way,' he stared at the bedside clock, it wasn't that late, but it was late enough. Without warning his entrepreneur brain took over, and against his better judgement he answered the call, 'two secs love' he uttered in Natalie's direction, who then flopped back on the bed and rolled from side to side to undulate the water filled mattress, the motion moved her body seductively slowly up and down. Dave looked at her and thought to himself 'you're a lucky sod, but you've earned all of this 'man' every bit of it'. Suddenly his thoughts of impending pleasure were interrupted by a garbled bomb of vitriol from John. 'Slow down mate' said Dave, 'just take your time'. John continued unabated 'that bastard has done it again', 'what?' 'Who are you talking about?' said Dave interrupting. 'Campbell, Ross bloody Campbell, who else would it be'. Not all this paranoid crap about Ross again thought Dave, but he just bit his lip and said in a begrudging and irritated way, 'What do you mean he's at it again?' John continued 'Hey look, I know you all think I'm paranoid, but he's destroying my work right now as we speak, I'm going to have him stopped once and for all'. 'Woh, woh, man, just stay calm', replied Dave. He'd heard John like this so many times before and knew he needed to diffuse the situation quickly, especially when John was not only drunk but angry. Frances now froze to the 'spot' on hearing John utter Ross's name and a chill ran through her. She strained to listen but only heard anything when he shouted, the mention of Ross had always made him react in this way. Frances moved closer to the door and as she did her handbag fell open and the contents cascaded onto the white marble hallway floor, it made a very slight, but she feared audible clattering sound and one metal topped lipstick seemed to roll in slow motion towards the door. Frances just stared as it seemed to gather momentum and hit the bottom of the door with a surprisingly loud tap, John 's voice now suddenly stopped. She panicked and had to think quickly, she slipped off her shoes snatched up the contents of her bag and crept carefully and quietly back to the front door. Her eyes narrowed instinctively as though this action would in itself quieten her turning the door catch and opening the front door from the inside and then pretending that she had just returned by slamming it loudly shut. John got a sudden start at hearing the front door shut, his mind focused on the broken glass lying all over the floor. In a fit of mounting rage, he had launched his wine glass and its contents at the wall. Now full of adrenalin he jumped up from his chair, 'thanks for nothing, I can tell you're not interested, I'll sort this myself'. Dave now attempted to halt John in his tracks, 'John, John, listen, listen, don't do anything stupid, he's a nobody, Campbell isn't worth it, let it go man'. 'It's too late, I've already put the wheels in motion' said John defiantly, he then ended the call without saying another word. Phone in hand like a smoking gun, John opened the study door and gazed into the dimly lit hallway. Dave just stared at his phone in disbelief 'stupid ignorant sod' he said out aloud, then tossed his phone onto the bedside chair and proceeded to fall over whilst attempting to remove his remaining sock. Passionately drunk and now firmly focused on Natalie, he laughed, and thought 'whatever, same old story' and assumed that John would just sleep off his 'drunken rant' in his usual manner. John stood in the doorway and stared at Frances, as she turned around, he saw the makeup she had worn for the clandestine meeting with Frank Swift. As her perfume drifted across the hall, he glimpsed a 'vision' from his past and knew why he had always lusted after her. Frances looked contemptuously at John, he was a mess, drunk and dishevelled, standing in his boxer shorts and stained T-shirt, whatever had she seen in him she thought and now couldn't even begin to imagine, but she knew to stay calm. 'Fancy a drink' said John, 'I couldn't, honestly, I...', now feigning a yawn 'I feel so tired,' said Frances. She restrained herself from her usual response of 'Don't you think you have had enough'. 'Go on have a drink, you used to be fun in the old days, let's have one together' he repeated. 'Yes, I was fun' said Frances and before she could stop herself, added 'and you didn't spend most of your time drinking your life into oblivion'. Before John could respond to Frances's unguarded comment, she attempted to quell his response by saying 'Look John I'm tired, I can't be bothered to argue, why don't you just come to bed'? I can't, I can't,' Frances now sensed a chink in John's normally stoic obstinacy as she said 'why not? Why can't you? Can I help? I want to help you'. She lied in an attempt to get to the truth, John now dropped his phone to the floor, pushed his hands through his hair and let out a loud frustrated sigh and said, 'I don't know its...', he stopped in mid-sentence. She knew it had something to do with Ross, but didn't want to ask him directly, was he about to open up, she waited and waited, he seemed to hesitate. He then shook his head and said, 'It's Dave asking for more fucking artwork, I'm sick of the pressure he's putting me under.' Frances knew John's world was imploding but it definitely wasn't Dave's fault, as usual he was lying to her, maybe she should speak to Dave, he would know what was going on, if anyone did. However, could she even trust him anymore? He wasn't the happy go lucky 'ducker and diver' she remembered from their squat days, he had become harder and shrewder, 'no' she would have to figure this out all on her own and the state John was in, knew she would have to act quickly, but how?

John now returned to his room and his bottle alone, finished off its contents and duly fell unconscious in his leather club chair, asleep with the empty bottle still gripped in his hand. Frances took a shower and decided to sleep in the spare room, a small room, one of the smallest in the house, and still not re-decorated, it had been her choice to leave it as it was. Frances knew it must have been a child's bedroom for the previous owners with its brightly painted walls and childlike fantasy murals of Unicorns and Fairies. The room had a warm comforting feel that always helped her to sleep contentedly, despite the problems that usually occupied her mind. Dave now lay alongside his most recent conquest, not only was she good at her job as his 'personal assistant' but was most definitely 'good' in bed as well. Things didn't get much better than this, and as he turned over and closed his eyes he thought 'you lucky bastard.' Having completed the start of his 'mission' Ross now crawled under the wire net fencing but struggled to stand up, it could have been the intense cold or being bent over he wasn't sure, but he swayed then staggered, felt disorientated, his mind seemed all at sea. He rested his back against the wire netting and took a large deep breath of freezing air that acted like a strong analgesic, it seemed to steady his thoughts and give some relief to his pain racked body. Now he had discomfort everywhere, from aching ribs to a throbbing knee, there seemed no end to the ailments, even his right shoulder seemed frozen in position. He was only in his early fifties but tonight felt like a geriatric. Leaning against the fence, he was unaware or simply didn't care anymore that he could easily be seen by passers bye. He lit a cigarette and took a long drag of nicotine fuelled smoke that raced around his system, it created a euphoric sense of determination for him again. He needed the impetus that this false stimulant gave him, he had a lot of work still to do, it had to be done and he was determined tonight would see an end to it all. He would then be able to clear out of London and take his long-awaited trip to Pont-Aven, maybe he would come back again, perhaps he wouldn't, it didn't matter, not a planner, he was a man of the moment, acting purely on impulse. This mantra had driven his whole life, usually it worked, sometimes it didn't but life had never seemed dull or predictable. He finished his cigarette and pushed his aching frame up from the wire fence that had provided an artificial crutch for his aches and pains. He looked around the street, it appeared desolate and abandoned, but he hadn't gone unnoticed as O'Shea observed his every move. Revitalised again he set off for target number two, it was just under half a mile away. Lurching away from the fence he threw his trusty haversack over his shoulder, pulled on his Balaclava, and set off tentatively across the road. As he walked down the street, the cars were parked nose to tail, he crossed the road, and passed in front of O'Shea who had momentarily taken his eye off 'the ball' while playing with his phone to relieve the boredom. As Ross passed the Fiesta he looked in and seemed to gaze at O'Shea, and as Sherlock Holmes would have said 'he looked but he did not observe' and 'the big man' went unnoticed. Ross's mind was now firmly focused on Postcode 'E1' the site of 'SPOOKZ' press and media celebrated artwork that now awaited its fate. Little did Ross know that cold and seemingly alone he was very much in the thoughts of Frances, who as she lay awake in her warm safe bed, thought about him and what John had said on the phone. Who had John been talking to? Was it Frank Swift? She prayed that it wasn't, although Swift was undoubtedly charismatic, she viewed him as an extremely dangerous adversary. Now the thought of Frank Swift somehow being connected in some way with Ross frightened Frances and made her question whether she still 'loved' or just 'cared' for him, she wasn't sure. Her mind was a mess, but she prayed that Ross, wherever he may be, was safe. Ross meandered backwards and forwards through cars and alleyways, tonight he didn't see the homeless lying-in makeshift beds of cardboard, his mind drove him towards the next target in an unrelenting almost robotic state of pre-determination. Colm struggled to keep up with Ross, one-way systems were no friend of the pursuer in a car, he was constantly having to divert and quickly go the long way round just to keep him in his sights, his frustration and anger to this seemingly pointless task pushed his miniscule level of patience to the limit and beyond. He noticed that Ross was struggling as he moved and was now a wounded Gazelle and O'Shea was the lion stalking him, as far as he was concerned tonight would have only one outcome and just like those countless nature programmes on TV, the Gazelle was doomed, it's fateful end was close at hand. Suddenly his mobile rang, the car swerved as he took one hand off the steering wheel to answer the phone. The Fiesta drifted momentarily and glanced the side of a parked vehicle and added yet another dent to the war-torn car before he manged to regain control. He placed the phone to his hear, it was Frank, 'Cosh, I want to meet up with you and sort this joker out', Frank continued without pausing for a reply, 'we'll lean on him enough to make him see sense, where are you now?'. 'I'm still following him' replied O'Shea, 'OK, when he reaches his destination, unless he's heading home, ring me and I'll meet you there' said Frank who then abruptly ended the call. O'Shea now breathed a sigh of relief, perhaps his job would be finished tonight after all. As Ross turned the corner of Coronation terrace, a row of run down and boarded up houses resembling a mouthful of decayed and missing teeth, lay behind temporary builders metal fences that stretched out in front of him. There was a pale orange glow from the streetlights that were, unusually for the neighbourhood not vandalised, they created useful shadows for covert activities and access into the site wouldn't be too much of a problem. Ross reckoned there would be some night watchmen, however they were usually too lazy to patrol on cold winter nights, so he assumed they would be in some warm little cabin on site, but that didn't really matter as he hoped to be in and out before they got off their 'lazy' fat arses. Ross now looked at the former workers terraced houses that had been conceived in the long-gone days of Victorian London, when the masses relentless daily toil fuelled a burgeoning British empire, now sadly derelict and beyond useful repair they were destined for demolition. Ross out of breath momentarily stopped to study these relics of the past. He imagined the life and times people had experienced in them. Visions of Armistice Day and VE celebrations flashed through his mind, and he could envisage the street parties that had followed to 'hail' the new dawn of peace in Europe. The cold seemed to disappear from his body as he imagined their jovial 'cockney banter' and could almost see the Union Jack bunting stretched and looping across the streets. There would have been rows of chairs and long tables festooned with homemade sandwiches, cakes, bottles of beer and lemonade for the children awaiting the return of their fathers. Now deathly quiet, all the memories and inhabitants had long since gone and their time capsule was about to disappear for good at the behest of the developers. They would create some impersonal and ludicrously expensive architect's dream for the 'young Professional' who's idea of community spirit rarely reached beyond the technological cul-de-sac that was Facebook.

Ross walked slowly up the street, he knew his next target was here somewhere but wasn't exactly sure where. There was plenty of amateur graffiti, and 'yes', it had its place but most of it was made up of mindless expletives without any purpose or meaning. There were no artistic protests against authority, it seemed as though the young had lost the will to fight anymore, no wonder 'the powers that be, walked all over us' he thought. As he surveyed the buildings, he saw a man appear from between some of the houses, overweight and barely able to walk, he looked like a paid by the hour security guard who must have been in his late sixties. The guard stopped momentarily, casually looked around and then went in the opposite direction to Ross, he definitely wasn't going to be an issue, and he thought, if he couldn't outrun him, well he might as well give up right now. As he dodged in and out of the shadows Ross was unaware that O'Shea was watching his every move and Frank was supposedly now on his way. Frustrated, Ross was just about to give up all hope of finding his target, he had looked at every pointless piece of graffiti on show, suddenly, providence smiled upon him. There it was, in all its glory, painted on a piece of Giraffe board, that had been nailed over a large broken window of a disused chapel, that proudly displayed on a large keystone above its arched entrance the inscription 'To the Glory of God MDCCCLXXXV'. The crumbling Gothic edifice presented an ironic backdrop for John Noble's contemporary street art. The image consisted of a desert landscape dotted with palm trees, that, instead of their own image cast shadows of oil wells, and in one of the trees sat a large vulture with the caricatured face of Ronald Reagan wearing a stars and stripes bandana. In its day, it had been a powerful indictment of US imperialism that Ross had very much agreed with. He like many others thought the Americans had involved themselves in far too many countries and backed one side against another disrupting and unbalancing many parts of the world, especially in the fragile Middle East. 'Peace' and 'stability' weren't something they were necessarily interested in, the endless availability of cheap oil came much higher on their agenda. There was no room for sentiment now, the image was currently behind Perspex, presumably awaiting its removal and transportation to some high street gallery or major auction house. However, they were going to be disappointed, it was soon to become yet another notch on Ross's belt of destruction. The temporary fencing was held in place by a series of black plastic tie wraps, Ross crouched down on the ground and started looking through his haversack and found his Stanley knife, it would make short shrift of the wraps. He simply slit the ties and moved two sections of the fence apart, so it was just wide enough to squeeze through, he then closed them back together in case the night watchmen noticed any irregularity in the line of the fence. As Ross stood looking at the image he was about to deface, down the street Frank pulled open the passenger door of the Fiesta and sat next to O'Shea. 'It's bloody freezing out there' said Frank as he rubbed his hands together, you alright then you fat bastard' said Frank laughing while at the same time playfully punching O'Shea on the arm, who just grunted disconsolately as he said, 'will be, when I can stop doing this crappy job'. Frank laughed at O'Shea's frustration and said, 'It's your lucky night, that's why I'm here, we'll sort this little 'Jock', when he comes back out'. Frank tossed a brown paper envelope into Cosh's lap, it contained one thousand pounds in grubby used notes, 'there's a little bonus for all your hard work,' he said. Meanwhile Ross began to feel a slight pang of guilt about what he was going to do, not because he was bothered about John Noble. 'No', it was more about street art and what it meant, as there weren't many proponents of 'real street art' anymore. The work was something of a classic of its genre, but at the end of the day it was on the street and that was where it belonged. Not on some loft apartment wall or posh gallery where its true meaning was lost and its value became one purely of a pecuniary nature, an investment and mere decorative adornment. The image was protected by an unusually heavy-duty type of plastic, Ross decided his best course of action was to loosen part of it at the top, and cheat as he saw it in his eyes, by pouring paint in behind the sheet. He searched in his trusty haversack and took out a hammer, he then rammed its claws firmly in behind the sheet and thrust the hammer up over, it took two hands and all the force he could muster to attempt to release the sheet from its moorings. Just as he thought it was moving, one of the claws snapped off and the hammer came loose having lost its leverage, 'shit' said Ross as his force upon the hammer was now redirected against him and pushed him backwards to the ground. A short sharp pain now shot through his head as it bounced off the hard unrelenting surface, temporarily numbing his senses. He quickly sat up and stared at the broken hammer, then in a fit of temper he jumped up and smashed the head of the hammer against the Perspex and a crazed pattern like a spiders web spread uncontrollably across it. Ross laughed ironically at the pattern it created, as he thought his tag was much easier to apply like this, however the artistic satisfaction wasn't as great. He now frantically searched in his bag and found his crowbar, this would do the trick he thought, he then thrust the splayed end of the top of the bar behind the sheet, this time it gave way and opened a gap wide enough to pour in the paint. By now O'Shea and Swift had left the questionable comfort of the tiny, cramped Fiesta and were standing in the shadows watching Ross as he struggled with the cover. 'What the hell is he up to' said Colm, 'beats me' said Frank, who shook his head and continued 'but he's obviously upsetting someone, and they are more than happy to pay good money to stop him, I don't get it, he's just destroying some shitty graffiti, he's almost doing a social service'. As they watched, Ross removed a pot of paint and poured it along the top edge of the cover' it ran down the inside like raindrops down a window, slowly at first but then picking up momentum as he increased the amount. The image slowly disfigured under a curtain of black paint that now descended like a veil, Ross poured just about every last drop out and then with a mix of euphoria and relief hurled the empty can over his shoulder. It spiralled through the air in what appeared to be slow motion and then crashed to the ground just centimetres from Frank's feet and a final splurge of paint then seemed to leap mischievously from the tin and splatter over Franks immaculate brown leather brogues. 'Bastard', Frank shouted without thinking, but Ross didn't hear his expletive, he was too busy spraying his spiders web and tag across the screen. He didn't bother to stand back and admire his handywork, this was nothing more than 'basic' graffiti in every sense of the word, he was almost ashamed to put his tag to it, but this wasn't the time for morals. He packed up his cans, fastened up his haversack and readied himself to escape to his next target. Ross took quick look around, there was no security in sight and as he moved from the shadows, the pale orange glow from the streetlights raised his spirits, 'Ex Tenebris Lux' he thought. Ross moved the fencing apart where he had originally made his entry and was closing the fence back together, when suddenly a movement that felt like a violent magnetic force took hold of him as he was suddenly grabbed by his haversack and yanked backwards and thrust against the fence. In front of him were Swift and O'Shea like two avenging angels, as quick as a flash Ross quipped 'I thought you two only hung around at the bottom of ladders'. 'I'm glad you have a sense of humour because you're going to need it smart arse,' said Frank. The 'big men' now stood either side of him, there was no escape, Ross hadn't appreciated the size of Swift and O'Shea, as the last time he had spent most of his time sprawled on the ground outside the Pink Flamingo. Ross wasn't small at five foot eleven" but Frank towered above him, and O'Shea's bulk made three of him. His heart was now pounding as his adrenalin raced around his system giving rise to his binary choice of 'fight or flight'. 'Flight' was out of the question and although he wasn't afraid of a scrap, he really didn't have the energy, desire, or stupidity to tackle his captors. Ross was in a tight corner, but his cheeky sense of humour was as ever undaunted as looking down at Franks feet he commented on the black paint 'What a pity, nice shoes mate, they look ruined'. Frank looking at Ross just shook his head as he said, 'what is it with idiots like you, they never learn their lesson, people give you advice, but you just ignore it, is it stupidity or recklessness? either way '*mate*' he emphasised the word 'mate'. Frank continued 'this is where it ends, I bet you're one of those nerdy loners that play computer games in sad little bedrooms, so in your language, its 'Game over', your money and your luck has just run out'. 'Me, a gamer, a nerd' Ross said as he laughed 'you haven't got a clue man, if you've got any qualifications which I doubt, they wouldn't be in psychology', Ross continued to laugh mockingly. Frank tutted and just shook his head again, he turned to O'Shea and said' you see, you try to be nice, and people just insult you, there's just no manners today'. Colm nodded his head in agreement, he'd had a belly full of following Ross about, he didn't speak much at the best of times and now he just wanted to get home to his bed. 'I'm surprised that someone like you '*mate'*, Ross now emphasised the word 'mate' as he looked at Frank, 'why let a parasite like Noble dictate to you and do his grubby little jobs for him'. At this Frank stepped forward and prodded Ross with his finger, 'nobody dictates to me, they want a service, they pay good money, I always deliver' retorted Frank. Ross then prodded Frank with his finger and said, 'don't fuckin do that to me'. 'See that Cosh' said Frank 'that's assault that is', he then raised his hand and drew it back as though he were going to slap Ross with the back of his hand. Ross instinctively tried to kick out, Frank moved 'swiftly' for a big man and deftly raised his shoe and stopped Ross's kick by placing it in front of his ankle. Ross immediately felt an agonising shooting pain on his shin as it collided with the sole of Frank's brogue, who now glared at Ross and tutted, he looked in O'Shea's direction and nodded to him. 'The big man' now stepped forward, his menacing figure now confronting and overshadowing Ross. Frank then stepped back and took out his mobile phone and started to video O'Shea squaring up to Ross. 'I've followed you, you little shit, all over town' shouted Colm, Ross replied laughing 'Well, that's what you get for being someone's Donkey isn't it?'. O'Shea immediately reacted by grabbing him around the throat and pinning him against the fence. Ross instinctively tried to lash out at O'Shea who released his grip and stood back, Ross slumped back onto the fence. He was on the ropes but had prepared himself for another onslaught when suddenly a menacing black Scorpion shot out from the dark, a huge fist now landed what Frank would describe as a 'corking right hand'. The crunching blow caught Ross fully on the side of his head, his legs buckled beneath him like warm candles, his lights went out as soon as the fist made contact and he collapsed uncontrollably to the ground, coming to 'rest' in a foetal position. As Ross fell to the ground Frank laughed as he had videoed the entire debacle on his phone. He then put his phone away and was just about to drag his hapless victim up from the ground and carry out his own retribution when he realised Ross wasn't moving, he appeared to be unconscious. Frank pushed open one of Ross's eyelids, there were no immediate signs of life, he had witnessed similar things in the ring during his boxing career and some of those fighters hadn't ever regained consciousness. 'Bloody hell' exclaimed Frank as he knelt beside the lifeless body, he grabbed Ross's wrist to feel for a pulse. He fumbled about searching for the 'pulsing' vein that he hoped would alleviate his worst fears, but there was nothing. He released his fingers and desperately tried again, suddenly he could feel a pulse, but it was weak, very weak, he was still alive but only just. 'Think, think' Frank said out loud, O'Shea just stood beside him motionless almost apologetic as he said, 'It was just a slap'. 'Some fuckin slap', 'we've got to make this look like ....' he hesitated,' a mugging, yes, a mugging that's it'. With this thought in mind, Frank went through Ross's jacket pockets, he pulled them inside out to show someone had rifled through them. He then ripped open Ross's jacket and shoved some small plastic packets of cocaine deep down into the hidden 'poachers' pocket, then he scattered some loose change around his limp and lifeless body. Frank reasoned that when the police found him, they would just think 'no hoper' junkie, got what he deserved. As Ross lay on the ground his brain disconnected itself from the 'present' and flashed with images of his childhood, he could see his late Grandfather smiling at him, holding out his hand. Ross attempted to reach for the outstretched arm, that offered help, but he couldn't quite reach it. Feeling calm and relaxed, the cold and dark of the night had now been replaced with a hot blinding white glow that Ross was now instinctively being drawn towards.

Chapter Fifteen
Metallic Gold

'Gold is completely inert to all known chemicals'.

Dark, Deep, Metallic Gold

John lay in a deep, almost coma like state on the sofa in his study, he had fallen asleep with his mind befuddled with drink, his dreams lately gave no sanctuary to calmer thoughts, he was confused and unsettled. In his current 'involuntary vision', there were many faces he recognised that stared at him but when he tried to acknowledge them, they just turned their heads dismissively away. Now feeling suffocated and mute, incapable of communication, he attempted to shout but nothing came out of his mouth. Suddenly a handful of people grew into a large jostling angry crowd, John looked above their heads and saw Ross, he was incensed at his presence and immediately made his way towards him. He pushed and shoved his way through the crowd but as soon as he got near Ross, when he looked again, he was just as far away, it didn't matter how hard he tried there seemed no way of reaching him. Still struggling, his arms became increasingly heavy, now unable to breathe, he was being crushed in a sea of people, hands touched his face and head, they were forcing him to the ground, he shouted in desperation, but his voice was lost among the noise of the crowd. Deafened and now lying on the ground, he feared being trampled underfoot and attempted save himself by flaying his arms about. Suddenly a crashing sound awoke John from his sleep as his arm swung out and knocked over a near full glass of wine on a side table next to where he lay. He was startled and disorientated, his mind still trapped in his dream, he looked around the room, but it was shrouded in darkness, even familiar objects draped in a black silhouette seemed unrecognisable. In desperation he groped the area immediately surrounding him, the warmth of the leather and the familiar feel of the buttons on his Chesterfield calmed him down, he breathed a huge sigh of relief, now, he was safe. As he regained his consciousness John was sweating profusely, he felt sick, his head was buzzing with a looming hangover. He looked around his room and as his eyes became accustomed to the dark, one by one the unfamiliar silhouettes slowly revealed themselves, but his dream was still very much in his mind, he knew you always seem to remember the bad dreams, the good one's just seemed to disappear. Frances was just across the hall in the kitchen getting a coffee and had heard the noise of breaking glass and was now knocking incessantly on the door, with growing frustration she rattled the handle, but it was locked. 'John, John, are you OK in there? What's going on?' she shouted, but no reply came, silence, now like the darkness within, had descended upon the locked room. Frances repeated her questions, she had a pretty good idea what was happening but had to ask, John suddenly barked out 'nothing, nothing, just fell asleep, that's all, knocked a glass off the table, I'm OK, just leave me alone, go back to bed'. Frances shook her head in frustration and disbelief, what had her life come too? Tired of trying to help, she was more than happy to leave him to it, as usual he was hung over and in a bad mood, this had become their usual morning ritual. John now sat in the dark with his head in his hands, nursing a throbbing hangover. Somewhat abruptly, his alcohol driven meditation was interrupted when his 'special' phone rang. He instinctively felt around the Chesterfield but couldn't find it. Frustrated he got up quickly, too quickly and his hangover started to pound in his head like a hammer beating a rhythmic pattern on an anvil. Moaning to himself he angrily pushed items aside on his desk, pulled at magazines and papers, but there was no sign of it, 'where's the bloody thing' he said aloud, finally he unearthed the phone by tracking it's muffled ring tone and found it secreted behind a cushion on the settee. He frantically pressed the green 'accept' button and just caught the caller, 'John mate its Frank, can you speak?' He pushed his hair back over his head and rubbed his eyes and yawned, as he lazily said 'yeah, yeah, what is it? 'Your little job is complete,' said

Frank. 'Campbell, so you 've had a word' said John, 'I did what you asked me to do, it didn't go exactly as I would have wanted, I had hoped we could just frighten him off, but well to put it bluntly he's an awkward little sod isn't he? Anyway, these things happen' replied Frank, with an almost inhuman level of indifference to the suffering he had caused. 'What do you mean? What happened?' replied John, 'well mm... 'Frank hesitated', Cosh slapped him, a little too hard'. At the mention of O'Shea's name, the image of Swifts' daunting side kick flashed chillingly through John's mind. 'So, what now' said John, 'well, it's like I say, he won't be bothering anyone for a while, we left him lying unconscious'. Frank continued, 'I've sent you a little 'vid' of it, you'll enjoy it 'he then laughed, 'It's not Oscar material and I didn't get Cosh's good side, the ugly bastard hasn't got one'. Suddenly John's hangover seemed to dissipate with the news of Ross and a feeling of smug satisfaction came over him, his nemesis was redundant, a spent force, he could move on now without thinking about him anymore. 'So, I won't be worrying about him for a while' said John, 'you might not be worrying about him full stop' said Frank laughing. As Frank ended the call, John stared at the phone in his hand, contemplating the good news as he saw it and without hesitation, he did a search on his phone for the message that contained the video. Like a man possessed he frantically scrolled through his latest messages but there was nothing from Frank. No sooner had he switched off the screen in disappointment when a pinging sound forewarned of an incoming message. He immediately opened his phone again and there it was, the 'video', the excitement was too much for John as he fumbled and nearly dropped his phone, he couldn't wait, and without a seconds delay he selected the video. It loaded slowly on his ageing phone, the image quality was poor, taken at night it was grainy and the voices were muffled but Campbells' guttural Scottish tones were unmistakable. Ross was wearing a balaclava so John couldn't see his face, he couldn't make out what was being said, but the scuffle and the ensuing blow that had rendered him unconscious and sent him to the ground captivated his now heightened senses. John easily recognised O'Shea's menacing bulk as the camera swung sideways and showed an un-repentant and grinning adversary, he was like a pit bull, a killing dog, he heard Frank call him off. Suddenly the video image swung downwards to the ground, the picture went black, and the video stopped 'dead'. John re-watched with a sense of awe, the emotions it engendered were reminiscent of those he had experienced on watching black and white footage of bombing campaigns taken during the second world war. When curtains of bombs rained down from the skies onto innocent people below, he now, like the pilots then, didn't feel personally responsible for the destruction and damage they caused thousands of feet below on the ground, somehow a second-hand account of Ross's attack was far less emotional. The video however made it seem very real and prescient, he felt no remorse or guilt at the sight of suffering, his twisted mind enjoyed this violent spectacle. Seventeen seconds, that's where the video timer stopped on the phone screen, that's all it had taken to end John's frustration and anger that had been raging within him for years. Was Ross dead or alive? He didn't care, his selfish and borderline psychotic mind relished every moment of those seventeen seconds of retribution.

John celebrated with a shower and a shave, which was unusual for him, as he often went for days unshaven, not because he was into 'designer stubble', 'no' he was just lazy and couldn't be bothered. He looked in the mirror and saw a 'new face' staring back at him, he even felt different, looked less troubled, a huge weight had been lifted from his shoulders. Now more like his old self, he splashed on his aftershave, it's aroma heightened his senses, now very much alive, stimulated, and invigorated, a zest for life had seemingly returned. He decided a trip into town and a visit to see Dave at the gallery was in order, he had even decided on a celebratory meal at one of London's top restaurants as a treat for Frances and himself. As he walked into the kitchen Frances was sat on a bar stool drinking a cup of coffee, she didn't see John at first, but could 'smell' him. Aftershave she thought, what s got into him, most days he would walk in and out of the kitchen like a half-dressed slob in the morning without even speaking. He stroked Frances's back with his hand as he passed, at his touch her whole body tensed and feeling of uncontrollable revulsion came over her, 'did he really think he could treat her like he had and that she would just roll over like some doe eyed puppy'. 'I thought we could go into town, get a nice meal, perhaps do a bit of shopping' said John expectantly. Frances wanted to ask what had happened to him, he seemed almost human, but now it was all too late, she wasn't interested any more. The mysterious 'goings on' in his study only a few hours ago had been the last straw, typical John she thought, everybody had to put up with his moods and behaviour and he thought life would just continue as normal. Frances had decided she couldn't do this any longer, 'Can't I'm busy today' she snapped, feeling rebuffed 'with what' John snapped back. He then put his hand on her shoulder, she brushed it off with hers. 'What's the matter with you? What do you want from me?' said John, 'just don't touch me' said Frances and then continued her offensive, 'you behave like a bear with a sore head most of the time and then you just expect everything to be OK, when it suits you, well it's not!'. Frances continued unabated, 'John Noble, the big unknown street artist worth a fortune, Dave puts up with your shit because he has to, but I'm sick of it'. John's temporary balloon of joy was now well and truly burst and hurtling around the room like a Moth fuelled by nitro methane. John now retaliated, 'Do you know what, I'm sick of you as well, moan, moan, moan, that's all I get, some women would give anything for what I've given you'. 'Given, given', Frances said angrily, 'you think it's all about money and possessions don't you, you're so sad, you really are'. She then jumped up and off her seat and thrust back the stool with such force that it toppled over and shot backwards across the kitchen floor, this physical display of emotion from a normally placid Frances even shocked John, he hadn't witnessed this level of anger before. Frances made no attempt to pick up the stool, she just stormed out of the kitchen without even looking at him. Shocked and angered by her attitude he retorted, 'Go on then fuck off you stupid cow', no sooner had he uttered the explosive rebuff then a part of him wished he hadn't, but he just couldn't stop himself. Frances had pushed him too far, what did she want? John's emotional threshold like a 'failed dam' was now well and truly breached and a torrent of negative thoughts flooded out, but he didn't care anymore, 'bollocks to it' he thought. He would go to town on his own, call in at the gallery, maybe Dave could introduce him to one of his litany of pretty 'assistants', yeah that would be alright, he thought, at least he might get more than an ill word and a sneer which was all that was on offer at home. Frances sat alone in her room teary eyed and shaking with a mixture of fear and anger as she heard the front door slam shut, 'good riddance' she thought as she sniffed and wiped her eyes. Things between them had been strained before but not like this, and now she couldn't help wondering, why the sudden change in his mood? The aftershave, the trip into town, it just wasn't like him. She had to begrudgingly admit to herself that there had been times when things weren't too bad, but was now past caring, there came a point when even the smallest glimmer of hope disappeared and all you were left with were doubts and a constant sinking feeling that seemed to engulf you in the presence of certain people. Frances decided she had to get out of this suffocating house in which she now felt trapped, she would go to the little café where the woman with the pink hair had made her feel so welcome and had talked 'to' her rather than 'at' her which John frequently did.

Less than an hour after their argument John entered Dave's gallery in Chelsea, by the front entrance, not by the back door as he usually did, feeling bullish and positive in a way that he hadn't felt for some time. Drawing himself up to his full height, he took a deep breath and surveyed the gallery, it was reasonably busy, and the usual suspects were there. He nodded a cursory acknowledgement to Simon who was giving his usual 'arty' spiel to a pair of 'thirty something professionals' who were standing back and showing great appreciation for what John would have described as one of his purely 'commercial' works. He despised people like this especially when they seemed to have plenty of money at an age when most people were just struggling their way through life beset with kids and a mortgage, but what the hell he thought, if they wanted to line his pockets who was he to complain. Instead of knocking, he decided to walk straight into Dave's office, and felt he had every right to, because 'he' was solely responsible for the gallery and its success. Opening the door unannounced he saw Dave in an embrace with Natalie, they both looked at John with an air of guilt and surprise. Unusually for John he felt their embarrassment and shut the door and stood outside. He could hear Dave castigating his 'assistant', 'I thought I told you to lock the bloody door'. John still feeling awkward, saw that Simon was free and gratefully accepted the opportunity to escape his current predicament as he walked towards him. Simon was unaware of John's role in the whole contemporary 'art' affair, Dave had simply described him as a sleeping shareholder, a 'mug' with money to invest. Simon smiled as John said 'Dave's a lucky sod isn't he, she's a bit of alright that assistant of his. Much to John's surprise 'he's an animal' retorted Simon, 'an ignorant bloody animal, she's young enough to be his daughter, they all are'. John was stunned into silence and was relieved when suddenly Dave came out of his office, closely followed by his assistant, 'It's OK, you can come in now John', he beckoned him over with his hand, as John turned and walked towards Dave, he heard Simon mutter under his breath 'Neanderthal'. 'I've finished my mm err... meeting' said Dave, then he just smiled and adjusted his tie. In the office Dave motioned for John to sit down and he opened the drinks cabinet and poured two generous Scotch's out. 'Sorry about just walking in before mate, I err...', Dave interrupted John 'it's OK, not a problem, stupid tart should have locked the door, you just can't get the staff these days' and then he just laughed. 'You're one lucky sod, she must be half your age and what a figure' said John, 'Just a few perks of the job' said Dave, 'has she got a friend then?' John asked, half joking. 'I could fix you up but what about Fran, I thought you two were inseparable' replied Dave. John laughed ironically and shook his head, 'I think you mean insufferable, I think she hates me as much as I 'did' Ross'. 'Dave looked quizzically at John as he said, did? So have you relented in your opinion of him', John was quick and eager to reply 'No! I do really mean 'did', there's been a bit of movement on that front, and everything is, as they say 'sorted'. This was exactly the kind of news Dave had been dreading, he hadn't seen John looking this confident and upbeat for some time and he found the prospect more than a little unsettling. 'So, what's happened?' said Dave, 'have you had it out with him', please tell me you haven't seen him, he could go to the press with it'. John hesitated before replying 'I doubt he'll be going anywhere soon. 'What exactly have you done', John shrugged his shoulders as he smugly said, 'well I haven't actually done anything myself, but I had some people of mine sort it', this made John feel big, as it sounded as though he were in control and calling all the shots. 'Hey just do me the courtesy of cutting all this bullshit 'people I know stuff', this is Dave you're talking to, not some street kid that's impressed with gangster talk, just be straight with me OK'. He continued, 'Just what have you done? What have you got us into', because as I said before we both have a lot to lose'. For once, in what seemed like years for John, he now kept his cool, 'It's OK Dave, we've nothing to worry about, these guys are pros'. Dave shook his head in utter disbelief, thinking to himself you haven't got a clue have you, 'That's all very well John but if the shit hits the fan and this gets in the papers, let alone the courts that's game over'. 'So, what exactly have you done to Ross then? Have you had him scared off?'. 'Well, it's a bit more than that' replied John.

Dave couldn't believe that after all he had said, John could be this pig headed and stupid. 'So come on then what's the score' Dave said as he leaned back in his chair and unusually for him poured himself another glass of scotch. 'Well, I sort of did what you suggested Dave, I decided to give Campbell a verbal warning, but he was so..., you know what I mean, a pain in the arse', 'yeah, you mean Ross just being 'Ross' replied Dave. John took a large mouthful of Scotch then continued, 'So I told these mm..', he hesitated while trying to find a suitable word to describe Swift and O'Shea, 'mm..., he laughed as he said, 'management consultants', 'big joke eh John, consultants, you mean thugs don't you,' countered Dave. John ignored the condemnation and continued 'I asked them to stop him one way or another', Dave interrupted, 'are you mad, what exactly do you mean one way or another'. 'You know Dave, John now nodding his head 'give him a bit of physical persuasion'. Dave stood up and slammed his glass down on the tablet, he couldn't believe John could be so stupid, and launched another verbal attack, 'you're mad, bloody mad, what the hell were you thinking, or did you even stop to think, so come on, what happened?'. John now took another large gulp of whisky before saying 'I don't know the full story, but they gave him a little slap that's all, and as far as I know he won't be troubling us', 'you mean, he won't be troubling you' Dave interjected. 'Alright then, me, yes me, me thinking about me for a change', John started to get annoyed and began to raise his voice, 'look I wanted him out of action, and I've got what I wanted, just accept it man, what are you worried about, you're sitting pretty, nice little gallery, totty on demand and plenty of cash'. 'Alright then John, so what are you saying, is he dead? John's voice quietened as he replied, 'no, they just said it went further than they expected, they left him', he now paused before finishing his sentence, 'lying unconscious'. Dave shook his head in utter disbelief as he said, 'for God's sake John, he used to be a friend to both of us', but before he could expand on his eulogy about Ross, John cut him off, 'it's my decision, its fixed, it's over and you know what, I wouldn't care if he were dead, he'll not be interfering in my life or my work again'. Dave sat back down in his seat and didn't say another word, John also sat in silence, their conversation just like Ross was seemingly now devoid of any meaningful life.

Val had just put on her blue nylon over jacket and was checking the level of the old metal hot water boiler. That had served thousands of loyal customers over the years and would hopefully 'churn' out a good hundred or so cups of tea during the coming day's business. No sooner had she replaced the lid, when the little bell above the door tinkled, here were her first customers of the day she thought. Without really looking she pronounced her usual cheery greeting and told the two men to take a seat and she would be with them in 'just a tick'. The two men who had entered the café were smartly dressed, the 'shirt and tie brigade', not the usual plumbers, painters and other trades that normally frequented the small and unassuming cafe. Instead of sitting down they came to the counter where Val was standing, 'Just take a seat' she repeated, thinking perhaps they hadn't heard her the first time. 'Thanks' said the taller of the two men, but we're actually here on official business', not the bloody council thought Val as she looked at the two men, what do they want me to do now, first she had to ask permission to paint the front of her shop, then they wouldn't let her put out a pavement advertising sign, what now? 'You know, you try and make an honest living and all 'your lot do' is make life difficult', what do the council want now '? said Val. 'We're not from the council' said the other man as he pulled from his inside pocket a Police ID card which he held up for her to see. Val was confused she hadn't reported anything, not even those kids that were always messing around outside the shop. 'I'm detective sergeant Peter Thompson and this is detective Geoff Bryant, we just want to ask you a few questions'. Val still taken aback, hesitated as she replied 'yeah, OK, why wouldn't it, I've got nothing to hide'. Sgt Thompson smiled and said 'pleased to hear it, mm Ms '? He was careful not to assume anything, 'it's Val to everyone that comes in here. 'So, Val, are you the owner of the', he then glanced around the café, 'Pink Flamingo then' said the detective, 'I am', she said somewhat defensively. He continued, 'nice little place you've got here, could we possibly sit somewhere quiet, we just need to ask you a few questions'. 'I can't, there's no other staff in at the moment to watch things' she replied. 'No problem, we'll do it here and try and make it as quick as possible, we can see you want to get on,' said Sgt Thompson. He then reached into his pocket and brought out a plastic bag that contained several items, he opened the bag and took out a small, crumpled business card and handed it to Val. 'Do you recognise this?' he said. Val looked at the card and although it was somewhat dog eared, immediately recognised the flowery script that she had chosen for her business card, it was from the first run, printed to advertise the cafe. 'Yes, it's one of my cards', and when Val turned the card over, scrawled in black pen was the message '*Paint Caff on Tuesday*'. She didn't recognise the handwriting, 'well they can't spell for one thing, but yes, it's definitely one of my cards' she repeated. The sergeant took the card back and said 'do you know a man by the name of Ross Campbell? ..., 'ah' nodding her head as she said it 'so, what's that daft lad been up to then' and laughed. Suddenly the expression on the faces of the two men said it all, she knew there was no need for them to say anything, it was a form of human Wi Fi, a message transmitted without physical connection, she had seen that look before many years ago when she had been told that her father had taken ill. Suddenly without warning Val's temperature went through the roof, she felt sick and lightheaded, her mind went blank and her legs without warning buckled. In desperation she grabbed for the counter, but her grip was ineffectual, and she started to sink towards the floor. The two detectives rushed around the other side of the counter and helped her to a chair, where she sat dazed but conscious. For once in her life Val was the one in need of a hot cup of sweet tea and there was no one to make it, 'I'm OK, I'm OK,' she said as the detectives fussed over her, 'just give me a couple of minutes to get myself together'. Eventually a feeling of calm settled upon Val, her body temperature had returned almost to normal, and the dizziness had subsided. 'Are you still well enough to talk? Would you like us to come back later?' the detective said. 'No! 'No, definitely not,' she replied, determined to know why they were here and what had happened to Ross. Val now impatient couldn't wait for the detectives to go round the houses explaining the who, what, where scenario, instead she simply asked them a single blunt and pointed question 'is Ross dead?' The officers looked at each other, hesitated and then said in unison 'no', then detective Bryant continued 'but he is in a bad way, currently in a coma'. Val shook her head, the dizziness started to return, she wanted to cry but no tears came, her head drooped, and she stared at the floor before eventually sitting upright again and saying, 'how did it happen?'

Nurses fussed around Ross, adjusting, and straightening his bed clothes for the morning visit of the consultants, he lay there oblivious to everything around him, motionless with his eyes closed, he was connected to a host tubes and pipes that even a time served plumber would consider a nightmare. Clipboards containing his personal records hung from the foot of the metal bed frame, all were marked 'confidential'. Then sweeping into the room like royalty came two senior consultants followed by some keen young 'Junior' doctors, they all stood in an ominous circle around Ross's bedside. The consultants were cold and aloof, they flicked through his patient records and conferred with each other via nods and facial expressions and said little in the way of conversation, they both knew this was a 'time' game. There would be innumerable tests to assess his neurological condition, followed by long periods of observation. Ross had left one world that was seemingly oblivious to his existence for another that was similarly anonymous. Only his inner world existed now and that could only be viewed by on-lookers in terms of electrical impulses peaking and falling on a never-ending array of small computer monitors that were wired up to his immobile body.

At the café Val's 'friendly' interrogation continued, 'Obviously we are not exactly sure what happened to Mr Campbell, that's why we're here', said detective Bryant. Val had now regained some sense of emotional and physical equilibrium as one of her young assistants was now at work and had made the 'much-needed cup of sweet tea'. Sipping her tea, she asked the detective again 'but what do you think happened to Ross?' 'We don't like to speculate' was his simple almost hackneyed reply. 'Oh, come on, if you want something from me and I assume that's why you're here, you owe me more than that, look at the state you've put me in, you can't just leave me in the dark you must have some idea,' she asked. The detective appeared unmoved by Val's plea, 'Initially we are just trying to locate family or friends of Ross', he used Ross's Christian name to add the 'personal' human touch. Val was now becoming frustrated and wanted to get their interview over with, 'as far as I know he has a sister, but they haven't been in touch with each other for years, he's from somewhere near Glasgow and I assume that's where his sister lives'.

Val continued, 'I don't know of any close friends, he kept things pretty much to himself'. 'How long have you known him for'? enquired the detective, 'three, maybe four years, he often comes in for his breakfast, sometimes he does odd jobs for me, and I give him a free meal or a cuppa in return'. 'Mm interesting, so he wasn't exactly flush in terms of money then' said the detective? The detectives now both looked at each other as their growing list of assumptions attempted to form some 'meaningful truth' from new facts and circumstantial evidence. Val broke the agonising silence as she said, 'come on, tell me, please tell me, what's happened'. 'We can't say too much but you've been straight with us, so ...', he then hesitated and looked again at the other detective for approval, who duly nodded in confirmation. 'Well... mm', the officer said as he leaned back against the counter, 'we initially thought he had been the victim of a mugging'. Val interjected 'Ross mugged, you must be joking he's got nothing and ...', 'quite' interrupted the detective, and then continued, 'we think he was attacked by a person or persons as yet unknown, who then arranged the scene of the crime to make it look like a mugging'. Val looked in disbelief as she said, 'but why would anyone want to do that to Ross, he didn't have enemies, everybody I know likes him'. 'Were you aware of the fact that Mr Campbell has a string of convictions for trespass and criminal damage going back years'. 'No' said Val, vehemently but surprised, now she was confused and thought to herself, what sort of things had Ross been mixed up in. Detective Bryant could see the look of confusion on her face, as he said, 'he was', then quickly corrected himself, 'I mean is, a ...' he then hesitated, they call themselves 'Street Artists' today, but back in my day as a young PC on the 'beat' they were just yobs with spray cans defacing neighbourhoods with their mindless scrawl'. Without consciously thinking, Val's mind, like a computer sorting a database of random facts, sub-consciously recalled the day in the cafe when Ross was cagey about something and had seemed animated about an article he'd read in the local free newspaper. Just like a paper trail in a forest her mind now gathered yet another imaginary clue as she further recalled how he had joked about appearing in the 'press' one day. Her mind raced with these thoughts, should she mention it now or just keep quiet, not wanting to cause Ross any more trouble, but conversely, she thought, maybe it could help find the people that had done this awful thing to him. Val remembered the day well, apart from it being her birthday, she recalled the image of Ross with blood on his hands, he'd been shocked and confused but then had eventually calmed down. However just when he had appeared to be OK, that newspaper he'd read had changed his mood again, he suddenly became angry and single minded, there was an air of fatalism about him when he'd expressed his thoughts. Val was now certain that something in that newspaper was the catalyst that had ignited this whole affair. In a snap decision, she decided to say nothing to the detectives and instead do a little investigating of her own. Her first task would be to get a copy of that newspaper he'd been reading, and knowing the date that shouldn't be too difficult she thought.

By the time Frances arrived at the Pink Flamingo the detectives and Val had left, the café was just about full, with only one spare table available next to the door that led to the toilets. Frances tutted, this was obviously always the last seat anyone would want she thought, but desperation made her settle herself there, she then looked earnestly around for the lady with pink hair. She didn't seem to be behind the counter and wasn't chatting to the customers, where was she? Frances pushed back her chair and stood up, its metal feet screeched on the hard floor, but the noise was drowned out by the chatter of the other customers, she moved to the counter where a young girl readied herself for yet another customer order. Frances asked the girl about the lady, who she presumed must be the owner, and the girl replied, 'oh you mean Val, she's had to go out, not sure how long she will be'. Frances was disappointed but told the girl that it wasn't important, although that wasn't strictly true as she was desperate to talk to someone and Val seemed a perfect choice, being a relative stranger, a good and sympathetic listener that didn't pre-judge you and left your anonymity intact. As Frances sat drinking her milky coffee, her mobile phone rang, she wasn't expecting a call and her immediate thought was it's John, but why? He wouldn't be apologising for their earlier confrontation, as it was always somebody else's fault, never his. She took out her phone, now resigned to speak to him and get it over with, but now looking at the number, didn't recognise the caller. Feeling lost in the café with no one to talk to, she decided on impulse to answer the call. The voice on the other end of the phone was deep and friendly, not recognising the voice she expected some sort of sales pitch to start, the caller then said, 'you don't know who I am do you?' Now pausing she said tentatively 'no', the man replied, 'it's Frank', 'Frank?' said Frances sounding confused. 'Yeah, Frank Swift, we met the other night', her mind instantly flashed back to the wine bar in Camden. Now caught unawares, this was her worst nightmare, with no time to fabricate a story, panic started to take hold of her thoughts, but she couldn't just hang up. 'Hi Frank' she said, now wishing it had been John after all, she had hoped that Frank wouldn't ring, even though he had pushed and pushed to get her number. 'I need to ask you a favour' he said. Frank was covering his back, he wanted an alibi for the evening of Ross's attack and had concocted what he thought was a believable story for Frances. He continued, 'I'm in an awkward position, when we had our little chat the other evening, my ex-wife's boyfriend's car was done over, it's not a pretty sight by all accounts. As usual the police always want to blame ex-partners, so I erm...', he hesitated, 'well I need an alibi'. Frank kept going, 'I say alibi, well that's a bit strong, just need someone to say where I was, that sort of thing, so the Police can't pin it on me, if anything comes of it'. Frances now relaxed a little as Frank continued, 'I left you about ten ish, 'was it that late?' replied Frances quizzically, as she knew that it wasn't and that he was lying but why? 'Do me a favour Fran would you, and say I left about eleven thirty if anyone asks, just so you know, I didn't turn his car over, but the Police like to clear things up quickly and I'm an easy target, former husband, ex-boxer and all that, will you do this for me, please'? His voice seemed softer now, somehow genuine. Frances was partly flattered but scared at the same time, she wasn't bothered if he had 'done the car over' as Frank put it, the boyfriend probably deserved it, anyway what harm could it do she thought? So, she agreed to Frank's request. He thanked her and seemed surprisingly grateful and in passing said, 'he hadn't had a chance to do any 'research' into her 'missing person' yet but would see what he could do'. As

Frank ended the call, he took his feet off the office desk and walked into his gym, 'Cosh' he shouted, but he couldn't be heard over the noise of the frantic exercise and shouting. Irritated that he had to walk the full length of the floor, where O'Shea was holding a punch bag while one of the young kids gave it a good 'going over'. 'Leave that a minute' he barked, 'and come into the office'. O'Shea followed behind Frank like a dog following it's master, he knew what it would be about, the 'loner' he had 'chinned' the night before. As they both sat down Frank tossed 'the big man' a can of beer, 'cheers, I'll drink it later' said O'Shea, 'get it open man, what's the matter with you' said Frank as he opened his can, O'Shea obediently followed. 'It's about last night Cosh, you should get yourself an alibi sorted, whether that 'nobody' wakes up or not, the police will still investigate', 'but no one saw us' replied O'Shea. 'You can't know that Cosh, there's CCTV around that area, in fact it's everywhere, you can't do anything these days, it's not like the good old days mate, when you're only problem was a grass'. 'Can't I just say I was having a drink with you', said O'Shea desperate to please his boss. 'Afraid not mate, I really do have an alibi of sorts, anyway the police wouldn't buy us having a drink together, it needs to be realistic, have a good think, is there anyone you can trust that isn't on the police radar'. 'Dunno really' replied O'Shea, he didn't even seem that bothered, he was either indifferent to the situation or too stupid to realise the enormity of the possible outcomes, but it's his funeral, if he doesn't sort something thought Frank. He wasn't going to let 'Cosh' screw things up for him though, and he was confident that whatever happened 'the big man' wouldn't grass him up, he wasn't that 'sort'.

Val had left her cafe some hours ago, and was sitting in yet another cafe, in a hospital. She was sipping a 'cup' of what could only very loosely be described as tea, it was a pale insipid looking liquid, devoid of any character or taste. Val thought if she served up this sort of 'dishwater' and asked two pounds for it, she would be out of business in no time. The detective had told Val to wait for him in the café and he would arrange to take her up to see Ross. She sat watching people come and go, porters pushed patients around in beds and wheelchairs, and she couldn't help but laugh at the irony of patients standing outside the hospital in pyjamas and dressing gowns desperate for a quick cigarette. It seemed incomprehensible that no matter how poorly they were, nothing, not even 'ill health' would stand in the way of their 'fix'. Val just shook her head and wondered why the NHS even bothered to try and help people when they wouldn't help themselves. Just as she became as comfortable as was possible on the hard and unrelenting wooden seats, a hand was placed on her shoulder, as she turned around there was one of the detectives, she had spoken to earlier that morning. The detective now introduced himself as Geoff and seemed quite friendly, more so than he had done during their first meeting at the café. 'Well, shall I take you to see Ross, he's in a special care ward and I should warn you before we go upstairs', he hesitated before continuing, 'be prepared, he's not a well man'. They walked to the lift that would take them to the second floor. As the doors opened an elderly lady was wheeled out on a bed, the elevator was almost full, and they had to squeeze in. Val wished they had taken the stairs as she hated being in confined spaces, especially lifts where everyone seemed to avoid eye contact and preferred looking at their shoes instead. On reaching their floor they followed the signs to the 'Intensive care unit', Geoff didn't know the entry code for the ward, so he rang the bell for one of the nurses. They seemed to wait ages for someone to press the release button on the other side of the door. As they entered, a nurse asked who it was they were visiting. The detective seemed to enjoy the power of flashing his warrant card and saying, 'official business, thanks, were here to see Ross Campbell', the nurse smiled and said 'he's in room... ', the detective interrupted 'that's OK, I know where he is'. Geoff then strode with an air of authority down the corridor with Val hurrying to keep up with him. She tried not to look around too much as she followed him, attempting to avoid too much suffering, but she just couldn't help looking into open doors and through the glass windows of the rooms. There were visitors sat at bedsides, some silently hoping for the 'best', some expecting the 'worst', while others were engaged in stilted conversations. Nurses came and went carrying out all their normal duties, changing beds, drawing curtains around patients while doctors waited sometimes impatiently to get on with their visits. Eventually they stopped outside a room marked 'No 14', here Geoff stopped and opened the door, he let Val go in ahead of him. Ross had bandaging around his head and one of his arms, he lay silent and motionless, he was surrounded by a host of bleeping machines that measured human 'existence' in terms of green and red coloured digital line graphs and bar charts. Val had prepared herself for what she might 'see' but as usual it bore little resemblance to reality. 'He won't know we're here but take a seat and just try talking as though he were OK, sometimes it helps' Geoff said, 'him or me' replied Val, 'both of you' he said, comfortingly.

Val pulled a blue plastic chair close to the bed, she looked intently at Ross and shook her head, how could someone normally so full of life now be so devoid of it? She held his hand, it felt warm and clammy, now, looking at him, what should she say? What could she say? It didn't really matter, you just had to say something, anything to break the agonising silence. 'You had better get well soon Ross', holding back her tears she continued, 'you still haven't finished the outside of my shop, half pink and half yellow, you artists, I don't know'. Val had read about people in comas and how they needed a 'spark' to ignite the fire of life that still smouldered within them. It could bring them back to the real world, not that Ross had ever seemed to be a fan of the 'real world' and Val wasn't sure she possessed the magic 'spark' that was needed. She just didn't know him well enough, hardly at all. While holding his hand, she thought, surely there must be someone out there who had the secret key, the 'spark' that would re-ignite his life and bring him back, but who were they?

John's earlier visit to the gallery had freaked Dave out, it took a lot to unsettle his calm and calculating mind, but John's dismissive and vindictive attitude towards Ross had done just that. Dave pondered his next move, he would help John as much as he could, but this wasn't philanthropy on his behalf, it was more about protecting the business. Dave debated how a scandal would affect things? It was difficult to know, he remembered someone had told him that any publicity was good publicity as long as they spelled your name correctly. Dave however wasn't convinced by this amusing 'glass half full' observation. When it came to John's tale of GBH, it would be a gamble either way. Dave had a considerable amount of cash tucked away in offshore accounts, and he didn't want the press investigating the 'gallery' that was tied inextricably to John Noble or some of Dave's other questionable business interests. He knew what the press were like, they didn't care who got hurt as long as the story sold papers, apologies were easy to print but character assassination remained like a permanent stain. He decided he needed an exit strategy that initially showed some support to John the 'Unknown artist' who wouldn't remain 'unknown' for very long if a murder story hit the newspapers. Philanthropy apart, the most important thing for him was an untouchable escape route. He could happily live abroad on his yacht and eventually buy a villa, he might even go back to selling luxury cars again, he now had more than enough money to underwrite a new business venture. 'Yes', he thought, he could see himself lounging in the sun buying and selling Rollers and Bentleys to people with more money than taste 'just his kind of punters'. Dave had already taken the precaution of contacting his 'legal man' Julian Tavistock, he always laughed to himself when the secretary answered the phone and said Tavistock, Tavistock, and Tavistock Lawyers, can I help you? Julian was the third generation of the 'Tavistock's', even though he was pushing fifty 'young Mr Julian' as he was known in the firm was the epitome of the legal fraternity. A privately educated Oxbridge man, he had an accent that was so 'glass like' it could cut you. Julian wasn't one of Dave's circle of pals, he was premiership material and Dave was Conference league. Dave couldn't stand his 'sort', confident, arrogant, and condescending, who thought the world and minions within it were seemingly created to provide them with a living and a good one at that. Dave had been introduced to Julian by a police contact, who'd told him, 'He might be a 'posh git' but he's a very 'good criminal lawyer'. Julian had rescued Dave from a few awkward situations, and he quickly discovered that 'young Mr Julian' was actually more than 'good', he was 'fucking brilliant' and with most things in life, you had to 'pay' if you wanted the best. Dave hadn't gone into too much detail but had sounded Julian out about 'a friend of a friend' scenario of paying a couple of goons to have a quiet word with someone and that things had got a little out of hand. Julian had said, that without obviously knowing all the facts it was impossible to give a decisive conclusion, the case would hinge on what he described as the 'intent' of the 'friend of a friend'. However, he warned Dave, that if found guilty of what he described as '... menaces', it would more than likely carry some form of shortish custodial sentence but if the 'plaintiff', he assumed that meant Ross', were to die then that sentence would be considerably longer. Dave worryingly decided he had heard enough, he didn't even tell Julian about John's list of misdemeanours and brushes with the law with respect to trespass, acts of vandalism and worse still his conviction for assault on a night watchman some years ago, all before his meteoric rise in the art world, albeit up to now 'a secret one'. Dave armed with Julian's candid legal conclusions sat and pondered his next move in his office. Over a large scotch he decided, he would try to head off any problems for John by engaging the services of Julian but ultimately not being a betting man, he would also stash away any remaining money for his 'rainy days' or as Dave saw it, his 'sunny day's in the South of France'.

Frank was standing outside his gym on the pavement getting a breath of fresh air away from all the exercise and frantic displays of pugilism, it got a bit stuffy and hot in the gym and the smell of sweat to even the most ardent of boxers had limited appeal. As he stood taking in a large deep breath, he noticed O'Shea half in and half out of the battered and battle-scarred Fiesta. With his legs outstretched and sticking out of the passenger side door like a huge beached Turtle, he appeared to be searching under the cars seats. O'Shea's huge hands moved from side to side, backwards and forwards under the seats like a minesweeper but he found it impossible to get into every nook and cranny, he groaned with impatience. 'Cosh, what the hell are you doing' said Frank, O'Shea got a start and hit his head on the steering wheel as he looked up in Frank's direction. He swore and then immediately tried to extricate his somewhat immobile frame from its current contorted position. On removing himself from the vehicle he said somewhat sheepishly 'I err... just lost some change the other night', just wanted to see if I could find it'. Change? Why? Thought Frank, what the hell does he want small change for, he was confused and somewhat unconvinced with O'Shea's unprovoked confession but what the hell he thought, and said, 'Do you need to borrow a few quid or something'. 'No, no, I'm good, it's just one of the coins had sentimental value, had it for years, it's an old half Crown, remember them Frank, the good old days, when money had a 'value' eh, my dad gave it to me'. Frank shook his head in disbelief, 'OK, I'll leave you to it then' he said still shaking his head and thinking 'daft sod' but then it was O'Shea he thought. As he walked away the 'big man' resumed his search, he was desperate and hadn't told Frank the whole truth about what he was really looking for. He was searching for his chunky eighteen carat gold Identity bracelet which he had lost on the night of the skirmish with Ross. O'Shea had a pretty good idea where the bracelet was, and 'hope' rather than 'reason' prompted his current actions. He searched the car thoroughly forcing his hands as far as they would 'go' in between and around the seat mechanisms, cut and abraded he had searched in vain. Certain this was where he'd last worn it, he previously hadn't been unduly worried but the thought that Frank had placed in his head about having a 'good alibi', suddenly pervaded his thoughts. O'Shea also knew there was an even bigger problem, the bracelet carried his initials and the Latin motto of his army regiment. He'd had it engraved many years ago in the forces, when he'd still been proud of his military associations, now he kept it purely for its bullion value, his 'pawnable' keepsake against hard times. O'Shea tried to ignore the nagging thought that the bracelet had come off his wrist when he had hit Ross, but somehow even though he tried very hard to convince himself it hadn't, somehow deep down he knew he was 'wrong'. He realised that he should probably tell Frank what had happened, but pride and stupidity overtook his reasoning, in the past he had buried his head in the sand and things had worked out for him, maybe, just maybe, he thought, they would again?

John was now sitting at a small Victorian wrought iron pub table in a cosy little 'boozer' down a cobbled side street in Soho. It had good memories for him, he used to bring Frances here years ago when 'things' had seemingly been alright between them. Now, everything seemed to have fallen apart, he looked at his glass and like his view of life, it was half empty. He had decided after his meeting with Dave that everyone had turned against him, but he didn't care anymore. John knew he had lost Frances, their marriage had been something of a struggle for years and was now well and truly over. 'Yes', in the beginning they had shared and enjoyed his somewhat unexpected and meteoric rise to anonymous 'fame' and the riches that had ensued. John had spent money without even thinking about it, having struggled penniless for years. The euphoria it had engendered had only lasted for a short time and in a strange way things seemed better between them when there was little or no money, but now he knew it was too late to go back. He felt pity for his own situation but there wasn't any left to share amongst the people he had spent most of his adult life with. Anger flared again within him and brought a 'cauldron of spite' to boiling point and it was about to spill over yet again. Ross was now redundant, a relic from his past and Frances was to all intense purposes lost to him. After several drinks, he'd made up his mind to leave Frances or more to the point throw her out, he would give her some cash, but was determined she wasn't going to get any part of 'his' house. John had jealously observed Dave's string of affairs with his staff over the years. He envied the hedonistic lifestyle, especially Dave's boorish level of indifference towards women which at present seemed especially attractive. John now brimming with alcoholic 'confidence' thought he had all the answers and the upper hand, but as usual he was misinformed by his own thoughts and flawed reasoning. As he sat there, his drink confidently in hand, planning how to dump his wife, he was, as usual well behind the current state of play.

Frances had returned home from the café, disappointed but still determined, John was out somewhere, she didn't know where and no longer cared. Sat alone in the house, with only her thoughts for company, she now preferred it this way. Her thoughts were like a vintage bottle of wine, clear and mature with the sediment of negativity at the bottom of the bottle, and she was now ready to decant the fine wine of her reasoning. Standing on a chair in the spare room she reached up and grabbed hold of her 'special suitcase', that contained all her most important belongings for a 'quick' and much longed for escape. She held the handle tight and with a sliding motion, as it was heavy, proceeded to dislodge it from the top of the wardrobe, its weight and Frances's deft movement guided it towards the bed, where it eventually settled. Normally anything that came down from the top of a wardrobe would be covered in dust, time's chronological reminder of under use, but this suitcase was regularly inspected and consequently dust free and ready for action. Frances un-locked the case and flipped open the chrome catches that made a comforting clicking sound. The case was a retro white leather 'job' from the 1950's with a stylish blue silk lining and pleated pockets in the lid which contained her passport, driving licence and a small but useful amount of cash. She then added some everyday clothing necessities to the already bulging contents and reckoned there was enough to last her at least a week or more. Frances closed the case and 'snapped' the catches shut with a flourish of positivity. Leaving the case on the bed she then went downstairs, John had left his 'man cave' open, Frances entered and quickly scanned the room looking for an ideal parting message. On John's desk sat the lugubrious looking *Martin Brothers* pottery comic bird, it appeared to look quizzically at her with its huge claws seemingly clamped to the desk. Picking it up slowly and deliberately, she knew exactly what was inside and with one swift movement like a shot putter, hurled it across the room where it collided with the Oak panelling. On impact it shattered immediately and then created an unstoppable chain reaction as it released a large 'atomic mushroom' cloud of white powder. Which then floated down seemingly in slow motion covering everything in its path with a fine white coating that looked just like an October 'fall of snow' that usually forewarned of a cold and unrelenting winter. 'Bastard' she shouted aloud, Frances revelled in the experience as it released so much pent-up tension, then without a second thought with her hand she brushed everything from John's desk onto the floor. Now almost on auto pilot she focused her impromptu 'therapy session' towards his special wine and whisky cabinet. The Georgian wine cabinet's wrought iron and gilded doors were now thrown open with 'enthusiastic anger' to reveal specially shaped racks for the display and eventual enjoyment of the fine bottled drinks within. One by one, she removed the bottles and then hurled them at the wooden panelling. Among the 'collection' were priceless bottles of rare Petrus wine and then her eye was caught by his pride and joy, a highly coveted 1972 single malt Brora, worth in excess of ten thousand pounds. As the bottles smashed the liquid ran in rivulets down the Oak panelling and glass littered the floor. Frances breathed in the release of bouquets, the pure scents of flowers, black-raspberries, currants, vanilla, and truffles, she then laughed at the thought of these pathetic descriptions John used to come out with after a visit to his vintners 'by invitation only' specialist wine tastings. What complete nonsense Frances thought as she stood there surveying her destruction, the room smelled of pure alcohol and she now detested it's sickly aroma, 'clean that fuckin mess up John you selfish prick' she thought. Now turning her back on his alcohol-soaked study and their life. she slammed the door shut and made her way back to the bedroom where the 'suitcase' was ready and waiting for the 'great escape'.

Chapter Sixteen
Sulphur Red Mercury

'Natural Mercuric Sulphide may have some
impurities'

Bright Scarlet to red Brown

Frank opened his office door and shouted over the incessant din for O'Shea, who was as usual leaning against a punch bag while someone else did all the hard work. Frank waved him over to his office and he duly came, 'grab a seat mate' he said and then tossed over a can of beer. 'What's this for?' said O'Shea, 'you're at the movies mate that's why' said Frank smiling. On a large wall mounted TV screen where they normally watched boxing promos and the 'big fights' was a still image from a currently paused video, 'what do you reckon to this then' said Frank, barely able to contain his laughter. He then pressed play and the theme to 'Rocky' with accompanying titles by his good self-rolled up the screen... *'Don't push me'*, starring *Colm 'Rocky' O'Shea*. As the two of them sat watching the short video of O'Shea battering Ross to the ground they laughed and laughed, Frank had put the video on a loop so the punch and Ross falling to the ground repeated endlessly. 'Corking punch that one Cosh, I could have been a champion with a right hook like that man,' said Frank. O'Shea laughed out loud at the sight of Ross going down and springing back up only to be knocked down again like an extra in a Buster Keaton comedy. Suddenly his laughter disappeared, and a sinking feeling descended upon him, as he noticed a flash of gold in the repeating video, to his horror there on his enormous wrist was the ID bracelet that he'd searched unsuccessfully for, earlier that day. There it was a 'beacon of guilt' for all the world to see. Fortunately for him, Frank hadn't noticed that O'Shea wasn't wearing his bracelet today as he normally did, but he now knew for certain where he had lost it and now his head was well and truly out of the sand.

John had returned home, his mind brimming with positivity provided primarily by alcohol, he was determined to move his life onwards and upwards. The decision was made, he would tell Frances that things were not working between them and that they needed a break from each other, this would be the first step towards them splitting up and separating for good. He walked into the kitchen, the central heating was off and there was an unwelcome chill throughout the house, he thought this strange because Frances had always, much to his annoyance complained constantly of feeling cold and the heating always seemed to be on, even on the mildest of days. Maybe she was upstairs he thought, so he half walked, then ran up the remaining steps, his mind made up, he just wanted to get the whole thing 'over and done' with. There was no sign of Frances in their bedroom, the bed was unmade, he couldn't be absolutely sure, but his sixth sense made him feel that the house was empty. He now started shouting Frances's name, his voice became louder and louder at the frustration of not being able to fulfil his plan. He stormed into the spare bedroom where she sometimes slept if they had been arguing, the bed was made but the wardrobe door was wide open and then he noticed the suitcase had gone from the top of the wardrobe. Frances was convinced that John never came into what she viewed as 'her' room, but he had seen the white retro suitcase before and had tried to open it, but it was always locked. It soon started to dawn upon John that maybe Frances had beaten him to it, and that she had left of her own accord. He should have been relieved at this thought but instead he felt a sense of despair and annoyance that he may have been robbed of the opportunity of saying his piece and for once having the upper hand. Running back downstairs, he was energised but annoyed, and needed another drink. He went straight into his office and immediately on opening the door the smell of alcohol flooded his senses. He stood motionless unable to move as he surveyed the trail of destruction that he immediately assumed Frances must had left behind. 'Bitch', he shouted aloud as he kicked the remains of his Martin Brothers jar across the floor. He couldn't believe that Frances could have done this, she knew how much his office meant to him, it was his sanctuary, the one place that had remained constant in his life and now it looked like a shipwreck. The despair he felt wasn't a consequence of Frances leaving him, it was more that she had stolen his thunder, just like Campbell had 'tried' to do. Was there no end to people messing with his life, he now felt unable to stop the inexorable tide of persecution that welled up within him. He slammed the office door shut and ran back up the stairs to their bedroom and started to ransack the drawers and cupboards in his search for a clue to her whereabouts. Something, anything, to give him an idea where she had gone. Now he'd almost forgotten he was going to end their relationship anyway. Drawers lay upturned on the floor, their contents, letters, perfume, jewellery scattered all over the bedroom floor. He pulled all her clothes out of the wardrobe and threw them about the room. Now turning his attention to the spare bedroom, he repeated his trail of uncontrollable destruction but still couldn't find any lead to her whereabouts. He thought about ringing her parents, she might have gone there, but they had always despised him and thought he wasn't their 'sort' and certainly not good enough for their 'precious' daughter. He didn't want to give them the satisfaction or the opportunity to tell him he deserved it, he could just hear her bloody posh mother gloating over his situation with a soliloquy of spite, 'we're glad, you've ruined her life, she should have left you years ago, Frances was always too good for you'.

John rushed downstairs, ran into the kitchen, and grabbed two bottles of Red, then went back to his man cave and sat at his desk in his favourite club chair. He surveyed the mess, just about everything was covered in cocaine and alcohol. Now out of the bottom drawer he took his 'emergency' ration of cigarettes. The smell of tobacco from a newly opened pack gave him great pleasure, from the ritual of undoing the cellophane wrapping, removing the silver paper covering, and then sniffing the uplifting and stimulating aroma of fresh tobacco. He slid out the first tightly packed 'pleasure stick', lit it and took a long slow drag. The sensation was triumphal, he proceeded to then pour himself a large glass of red wine, put his feet up on the desk, leaned back and shouted aloud, 'you know what, who gives a shit'. He was determined to calm down and take stock of the situation, the initial panic that had overtaken him had now subsided and the temporary stimulants of tobacco and alcohol raised his flagging confidence and obscured his previous feelings of anger and confusion.

Chapter Seventeen
Arsenic Orange

Orange, Hue Shift yellowish

A deadly cold silence was suddenly interrupted by the sound of a wine glass breaking as it fell to the floor. John awoke with a 'start', and then stared at his outstretched hand that had released the glass while he'd slept. As he looked around him and saw his office, the initial feeling of sleepy contentment rapidly dissipated. It was a cruel trick of 'the power of sleep', it alleviated negative conscious thoughts but on awakening reality consumed it's power in a blink. John surveyed his wreck of a room, it was a visual metaphor for his life and his state of mind, he reached for a half empty bottle on the desk in front of him. He raised it to his mouth and was just about to have a good long swig when instead he hurled the bottle from his hand, it crashed against the wall and then he watched a stream of blood red liquid cascade down the Oak panelling. He shouted 'no, no, no' while holding his head, then swept his hair back and gripped his head tightly again between his hands, almost trying to squeeze the pain and frustration from his mind. 'I've had enough, I've had enough, bastards they're all bastards', he shouted aloud, now teetering on the edge of a mental implosion of catastrophic proportions. His sudden and desperate cry of despair somehow drew him back from the brink and seemed to cause a positive synaptic chain reaction of nuclear proportions within his brain. Suddenly he had the solution, how stupid had he been, why not strike back in the only way he truly knew, after all he had been doing it all his life. He had always expressed himself through visual protest on the streets, why should his current predicament be any different as he reasoned with himself as both 'judge and jury'. John was sick of high street galleries creaming off their percentage and fawning over people with more money than sense, 'yes' it had been exciting at first, the artistic praise, the recognition albeit anonymous in the media and making huge amounts of money, but the 'street' had always been the 'authentic' canvas for his expression of opposition and justice. He would return to the 'street' one final time, 'yes' that was it, one final time, why had he been so blind to this before, there now seemed to be a light at the end of his dark tunnel of confusion, this could purge his mind of all the negative thoughts and frustrations that had plagued him. He needed the opportunity to let go, now convinced that everybody around him just didn't understand, they had their own agenda, and their desires came first, now it would be his turn. John roused himself and jumped to his feet, the movement was too sudden, and his body and mind swayed with the effects of alcohol and a newfound determination. He stumbled and fell hitting his face on the corner of the desk, then spat something from his mouth as he righted himself on the floor, he sat motionless with shock. Then as he moved his tongue around his mouth, something felt wrong, 'fuck' he shouted, as his tongue stumbled over the jagged remains of a tooth, he had lost the bottom half of one of his front teeth. However, his newfound resolve remained intact, he also had a permanent physical reminder of what had to be done, as every time he pushed his tongue against the shattered tooth, it became a motivator towards, rather than a detractor from his cause.

After dowsing his face with cold water in the kitchen, John pulled himself together and made his way to the garage where he kept a variety of items from his younger carefree days. Still feeling a little dizzy, with hands trembling, he fumbled with a bunch of keys but eventually managed to open a padlock to one of his cabinets. The lock swung free and fell to the ground, bizarrely, at the very moment the door opened, Frances was also opening a door to a small anonymous room in a not so respectable bed and breakfast, located near the Pink Flamingo Café. The room was cheap but certainly not cheerful, it would serve her purpose for now. As she stepped into the room, her nose was greeted by the musty smell of damp, probably emanating she thought from the well-worn heavily 'swirl patterned' green, brown, and gold coloured carpet. Like the room it had seen better days and it's once swirling deep cut patterned pile, now harboured the detritus of many hundreds of visitors shoes, but at least the bed looked clean at a cursory glance. Frances decided not to investigate the bed's cleanliness too closely 'what the eye didn't see ...' would have to be her mantra. She had been lucky to even find this accommodation, misleadingly described in the advert as a 'Bijou and delightful room' at short notice, even in this less than desirable part of London. She placed her white suitcase on the bed, its retro heritage fitted well with the décor, basic in its styling with an assortment of well-made but now tatty brown furniture items that complemented a look that would have been all the 'rage' in the early 1960's. The room didn't depress Frances too much even though she had left a picturesque Metro Land style architect designed residence for it, in a strange way it was reminiscent of her very first accommodation in London. That flat had allowed her to escape the confines of her parents suffocating control and had engendered a sense of freedom and a chance to express herself and develop her own personality without interference. Frances sank down onto the bed and breathed a huge sigh of relief, the last few hours on busy public transport had left her feeling tired but still empowered. Now she was free, free at last, this feeling was worth more than money, a new start, the unwanted baggage of her former life with John was now cast aside. She knew it wasn't going to be easy to start all over again but at least from this moment on, she was in control and could make the decisions about her own life, unfettered by Johns psychological problems and overbearing paranoia. As Frances searched through her suitcase and removed some items to be hung in the wardrobe, at home John was also pulling tools and miscellaneous gadgets out of a tightly packed cupboard. Each item he handled gave up its memory and attachment to him without any resistance. Momentarily he would hold each 'artifact' in his hand, and then wonder why he had kept it and then proceed to fling most of them across the garage and send them crashing to the floor. He knew exactly what he was looking for, like a man possessed, he searched for a white and gold vinyl Gola holdall from the late 1970's, it had always been his lucky talisman. The bag had accompanied him on many bombing campaigns and apart from some skirmishes with overzealous night watchmen, it had, unlike himself remained relatively unscathed. As is usual in these searches for mementoes of the past, the bag was right at the bottom of the cupboard and was the last item to give up its location, like a crab hiding in a rock pool from the eager beach combing schoolboy. As he unzipped the bag, it released a slightly damp but comforting nostalgic smell, inside were the remnants of its past use, two or three now empty and gasless tins of spray paint, wire cutters, a Stanley knife, and a carpenters thick almost 'log like' pencil for sketching complicated designs. Now the memories of past experiences and triumphs came rushing back to his mind, the bag represented his former freedom, a link to a past almost forgotten.

He emptied the old aerosol tins out of the bag and filled it up with his usual array of coloured sprays, black, silver and especially red because of its demonic associations. These cans like new recruits leaving 'basic training' had so far seen only the pampered warmth of his studio and not experienced the rawness of action on the streets. John had a good idea of the image he wanted to create, it was to be his 'swan song' so to speak, his final statement about Campbell, the full stop, the exclamation mark, his metaphorical grammatical 'strike' through. For the first time in years, he felt an unbridled sense of freedom and excitement, it was just like the old times with one major difference, never before had he driven to a 'target' in a one hundred-thousand-pound Range Rover. He threw his bag onto the pale cream leather passenger seat, slammed the door shut, turned the ignition key, the huge engine burst into life and throbbed with anticipation, John thrust his foot on the accelerator and revved the engine. Still under the influence of alcohol and drugs, if he were to be stopped on his journey, the Police would throw the proverbial 'book' at him, however this scenario didn't even enter his mind. John had tunnel vision, he was a man on a 'mission', and nothing was going stand in his way. As he sped out of his drive, a spray of gravel swirled from the rear tyres as they attempted to gain traction, his car slid violently sideways, and the back end crashed against one of the substantial brick-built piers that stood either side of the imposing entrance. The force dislodged one of his cherished sandstone lions that adorned the top of the pillars, it fell to the ground where the force of the impact detached the head from its body, it then rolled away unceremoniously, eventually coming to rest on the roadside with its eyes staring in the direction of the fast-disappearing car. John now forged ahead oblivious of the carnage, the red taillights glowed behind the Range Rover as it sped off, the exhaust fumes spiralled angrily out of the car and vaporised in the cold winter night air. He had always admired the array of dials and the orange glow of his dashboard, lit up at night just like an aircraft flight deck and detailing every function of the vehicle from sat nav location to current tyre pressures. The speedometer almost seemed to lag behind the pressure he placed on the accelerator as the car zoomed up to 140 kph, the acceleration was effortless and as he sat high above the road and other drivers, he couldn't help but feel superior. The early part of his journey consisted of mainly quiet country roads, but it wouldn't be as easy driving on the traffic congested streets of London, it would undoubtedly slow him down, that's if the Police didn't pull him over for speeding first.

As John entered central London he knew exactly where he wanted to be, no Sat Nav required, his mission was simple, to produce one final piece of street art, at the very location where Ross Campbell had been silenced some days before. There seemed to be an inevitability with John's choice of artistic retribution, he had always pushed boundaries and taken a gamble, this was to be another slap in the face for Ross, not only would he have created it, but it would be right under the nose of the authorities. His mind raced with a sick, almost psychotic level of pleasure at the thought of this, it seemed somehow like a natural ending, the final chapter, his work would finally be complete. For John it would signal the end to a nightmare that was unfortunately all of his own making, perhaps his life could have been different if only he had been man enough to recognise his shortcomings. John parked the Range Rover down a quiet side street but chose one that was a little more respectable looking than the location of his last foray into London, when two yobs had violated his 'pride and joy'. He was going to walk to the target, it would be just like old times dodging through alleyways to avoid unwanted attention and the Police. John was surprised at the swiftness at which he moved through the myriad of alleyways that formed London's hidden arterial pedestrian highway, used mainly by the lost, lonely, and desperate. John felt good, he had missed the adrenalin rush of a street mission, that feeling of excitement tinged with fear as you ducked and dived your way to a 'target'. Apart from the odd vagrant sleeping rough in the back alleys there were very few people about, not surprisingly he thought, as no one in their right mind would knowingly frequent these forgotten back streets after dark unless they wanted to score 'something' or mug someone. John made good progress to his intended location which was to be almost the exact spot that had witnessed Ross's brutal attack at the hands of Frank Swift and Colm O'Shea. Focused entirely upon his 'task' he was oblivious to the surroundings and the suffering around him, men, and women, but mostly men, lay asleep in contorted bundles of blankets while the 'lucky' ones zipped themselves into sleeping bags on filthy streets in fridge like temperatures. The 'lost' souls lay surrounded by their entire life's possessions in a variety of high street plastic shopping bags, not that Tesco or ASDA were likely to appreciate the advertising or marketing opportunity they provided. Literally 'a bag for life' which they laboriously moved day after day to their next temporary home on the street. John eventually stood sentry like, and positioned himself without knowing it, in the exact spot in which Ross had stood, motionless and hidden from passers-by in the shadows, he now surveyed the 'target'. The pale orange streetlights illuminated the row of boarded up buildings that had previously displayed the image that Ross had defaced. John shook his head and laughed at the thought of how Campbell had received 'his' deserved retribution for his wanton act of destruction. He looked at the space that had contained his defaced image, 'had' being the operative word. Dave, ever the entrepreneur, acting on an impulse arranged for the swift removal of the 'piece' for safe keeping to his gallery, where the additional graffiti from 'Ross's attack' had simply added to its value. Now in its place was a new piece of virgin board untouched by the evils of street graffiti, it proudly carried a 'Wadds' stencilled logo, the suppliers of the board. It acted not only as a barrier to illegal entry but was also and more importantly the street artists favourite canvas, and as far as John was concerned, like him, it was primed and ready for action. The details of the work he would create were emblazoned upon his mind, no need to sketch or write it down, he knew exactly 'what' he wanted and how it would be done. All he had to do was to gain entry and he reckoned that it would take him probably thirty to forty minutes to complete the image, barring unwanted interventions. The temporary fencing was the usual heavy mesh type with its feet set in concrete blocks, not even chained together only cable tied, it was easy for John to snip a couple of plastic ties and move the fencing apart to get in. On gaining entry he moved the fencing back into place, it was so simple he couldn't believe his luck as there were no signs of any security personnel around to hinder him. The board that would be graced with his first 'real' street work in years was small in comparison to his usual canvases, it was only about seven feet square and lay partly hidden in shadow, if John could have arranged the entire scene beforehand it couldn't have been any better. He started with his usual outline of the image in black, the details and colour would come later. The artwork wouldn't by John's standards be either political or artistically challenging. However, his unparalleled skill in the application of foreshortening gave his artwork a dramatic presence. It was a technique that brought the image to life and made the viewer very much part of the action, a feature he thought now sadly lacking in everyday generic street art. John now stood back to view his outline, it was the quiet before the storm, he took a large deep breath of cold air and then slowly exhaled, he stepped forward with a determined stride and began.

Sweeping motions and delicate curves appeared almost by magic as he started adding to his outlines, similar to a robot building a car, his arm swept backwards and forwards, up and down, stretching up on his toes to reach the top and then down on his haunches for the bottom, he moved with grace and purposefulness. With the image firmly fixed in his mind's eye, it soon took shape, he stopped briefly to catch his breath and as he looked at his nights handywork, thought to himself, bloody hell you're good, in fact your fuckin brilliant. There was no time to lose, not wanting to be interrupted, he had to work quickly, he'd always produced his best art when he worked with feeling and urgency, detached, and unfettered by negative thought, it was natural and wholly intuitive. Creativity flowed through his body and out of the spray can, there were no 'short circuits' no loose connections, just like electricity it came and went straight to ground without interruption. The outline depicted a large menacing figure with his back towards the viewer, he stood slightly side on and over his right shoulder the viewer could see a huge fist landing a blow on a balaclava covered face, the figure was falling backwards. For a 'static image' there was a huge sense of movement, the viewer could almost feel the enormity of the blow, the fluidity and movement were reminiscent of Francis Bacon's iconic and disturbing images. To the right of the figure on the ground was a haversack which bore the Pink Floyd multi-coloured iconic prism. John had caught a brief sight of the haversack on the video of Ross's attack but even if he hadn't seen it, somehow, he knew that 'stupid superstitious Campbell' would have taken it along for luck, he laughed at this, thinking how 'wrong' could Ross have been. The hand of the attacker was inscribed with a striking tattoo of a Scorpion, these personalising almost 'micro mosaic' touches were added via a small brush, this level of detail was unusual, but it had always been a trademark of John's work, this raised his street art to the level of the mural. Thirty minutes had flown by without him realising it, his mind focused and uninterrupted, the image was now almost complete, he added a title across the top of the image 'Art of Revenge' in flowing black, silver, and red letters. The red paint ran down and off the board like a rivulet of blood, he had been a little overzealous with the application of the paint, but it represented the climax of his work and now the deed was done. He stood back for the last time, and briefly considered adding his 'tag' but that was too obvious and dangerous. Although sweating and out of breath, the satisfaction and excitement 'of being on the street again' engendered a 'high' that he had rarely felt in recent years. He couldn't resist taking out his mobile phone to take a picture of his masterpiece and was just about to frame the image when without warning a hand grabbed the collar of his jacket from behind and yanked him violently backwards. Then a guttural booming Newcastle voice shouted, 'you cheeky bastard, that sod the other week made me look a right twat but you're not getting away with it'. John hit the ground with a thud, disorientated and winded, he didn't have time to gather his thoughts before receiving a series of targeted full-blown kicks to the side of his ribs and legs. His body winced and tightened with the pain as he shouted 'stop, stop' then the big dark figure said, 'you're not going anywhere' 'take it easy you don't want to kill him' said another voice, 'don't worry, I know what I'm doing, just go to the office and sort the coppers'. He could hardly breathe with the weight of his aggressor now kneeling down on him, John had assumed incorrectly that there was no security on the site. The watchman now shifted his weight slightly and rolled his 'captive' onto his side and then locked a grip around his shoulders and arm. John attempted to struggle free but found himself restrained by a vice like wrestling grip which he couldn't break. 'I 've got money', just let me go, I'll make it worth your while' said John, his words stifled by fear and exhaustion. 'No chance, last week I nearly got the sack, I need this job, you're going the journey'. By now the other night watchman, had returned and said the police had a car in the area, 'I had to tell them he kicked off and attacked you, otherwise I don't think they would have come'. 'No problem, mate, there's no CCTV here anyway, so it's our word against his'. When the Police arrived, John was on his feet although still somewhat unsteady with his arm firmly behind his back, he was still winded, shaken up and bruised from his experience at the hands of the overzealous security guard. 'Just let him go, we'll take it from here,' said a young PC. John saw the arrival of the Police as an opportunity but as usual his forthright approach and over confidence got the better of him. 'Thank God you're here, I thought these two thugs were going to kill me' John said, as he shrugged the night watchmen's arm away, 'the bastards'. 'Hey, hey' remonstrated the watchman as he moved in towards John again, the officer put his hand up, 'just leave this to us' he said. Now thinking he had some sort of Police protection John's troublesome confidence attempted a resurgence 'come on, let's get it over with, give me a caution for trespass', 'well actually sir', returning John's level of smug indifference, 'it's trespass, vandalism and assault and I think you'll be taking a trip with us down to the station'. 'Ah come on, assault you're joking these goons attacked me' retorted John, the policeman looked at the night watchmen and they just shook their heads and shrugged their shoulders before saying 'As I said on the phone officer, he punched me and kicked my mate, we were just doing our job, just like you lads'. 'You lying bastard' shouted John then he continued to rant, 'This is all complete crap and you're probably stupid enough to buy it'. He continued to dig himself into an even deeper hole when he 'questioned' the police officers suitability for their job role, referring to them as hapless plods', he had as usual when his hackles were raised, overreacted, and totally misjudged the situation. Unknown to John the young PC was near the end of his shift and probably, had he kept quiet, would have just cautioned him, and taken his details. However, John's condescending and now increasingly aggressive attitude combined with the Met's desire to increase the number of street arrests to impress senior officers, saw John duly apprehended but he avoided the indignity of hand cuffs by reluctantly agreeing to calm down. After a journey barely lasting ten minutes that seemed like a blur of blinding car head lights, he found himself at the local police station in one of the interview rooms. A pale-yellow central light hanging from a water-stained polystyrene suspended ceiling, illuminated a drab, and dated room with the ubiquitous grey metal filing cabinet, whose exterior was plastered with half peeling old white and coloured sticky labels that had been used to catalogue its changing contents over the years. There were no external windows to alleviate the creeping feeling of claustrophobia that started to engulf John. Now sitting on a small laminated wooden chair, flat and devoid of any shape that would allow for a reasonable level of comfort. He squirmed and moved around on its uncomfortable and unyielding hard surface in an attempt to avoid a 'numb bottom' as he waited for something to happen. There he remained without saying a word for what felt like an eternity and his enforced calmness was evaporating by the minute. Eventually two police detectives entered the room one male, the other female, John looked, and half smiled at the woman in her early thirties, she was attractive even in her basic Police uniform. With a cold dismissive stare, she ignored his attempt at a smile as they both sat down on chairs that seemed larger than John's and made him feel as though they were now looking down upon him. John reckoned this was some sort of amateur psychological 'bull shit' created to make him feel small and inferior, he pulled himself upright to regain some form of control. The two detectives didn't say anything they just looked at each other and flicked through the charge sheets that they placed on the table in front of them. Eventually the male detective introduced himself and his partner. John took no notice of their names, they were just faceless 'PC plods' as far as he was concerned. He didn't care, he viewed the whole thing as a pointless waste of taxpayers' money and just wanted to admit to their, as he saw it, trumped up charge of trespass and get on his way home. John as usual was too impatient for his own good as he barked, 'can we just get this over with, I'll admit to trespass, that's what you want isn't it?' The male detective shuffled the papers in front of him, ignoring Johns opening statement 'no, what we want is the truth and before we start this interview Mr Noble, I have to make you aware that it will be captured on an audio recording device'. The officer then switched on a small black machine on the desk in front of him and formally introduced himself and his colleague, he then stated the time and the commencement of an interview with 'Mr John Noble' and much to John's surprise and unease, his date of birth and current address. The officer continued without pausing for John to reply, 'you do not have to say anything, however, it may harm your defence if you do not mention when questioned something which you later rely on in court, anything you do say may be given in evidence'. 'Blah, Blah Blah, replied John, shaking his head at the same time, it had been many years since he'd heard this spiel, it was so 'old hat', he'd lost count of the times he'd been cautioned in his younger days. 'This is bloody ridiculous, I've said I'll admit to tress..' but before he could finish his sentence, the female officer said 'just calm down' and then her male colleague joined in , 'it's more serious than just trespass Mr Noble, we believe you assaulted the night watchmen' .'Bollocks', shouted John, 'they attacked me, morons the pair of them, look at that' as he pointed to a graze and bruise on the left hand side of his face. 'Why don't you just start at the beginning and tell us in your own words what happened,' said the male detective. John had been in this position before in his younger and poorer days and he knew the drill but now things were different in so much that he had money. 'Nah, I'm not saying anything else, I want representation, otherwise you'll just twist everything I say'. The detective just shook his head, 'if that's what you want, we can arrange...', 'Don't bother', interrupted John, 'I don't want some Mickey Mouse duty solicitor, I want my own people'. It was now getting late, and the detective should have been on his way home after a long shift, he pushed his chair back in exasperation, 'OK, no problem, Mr Noble, you're entitled to make a telephone call'. Now released from the claustrophobic interview room, John found himself standing in a shabby hallway whose insipid grey carpet had been given a much-needed injection of pattern and colour over the years from a mixture of tea and coffee stains. The female detective stood close by his side, he took a deep breath and suddenly became aware of an intoxicating perfume, freshly applied for her boyfriend, waiting outside to drive her home. 'Come on John, focus' he said to himself as he dialled Dave Hemmings mobile number. Dave's answerphone immediately kicked in and his ever confident 'tone' explained much to John's annoyance, 'that he was otherwise detained and that he couldn't remember her name for now, but he would get back to the caller as soon as possible'. 'Fucking great' said John aloud, as he proceeded to slam the receiver against the wall, he then left a garbled message demanding that Dave sort him something asap. John didn't go into too much detail, as he said, 'I'm in a spot of bother and need the services of a good lawyer', he turned to the female detective and asked for his current location, she duly provided the stations details for John to pass on, he finished his message with 'be quick mate, I want out of this shit hole'. Dave had heard his phone ring and didn't have the energy to interrupt the 'message' on hearing John's rant, instead he threw back the bed sheets and sat on the edge of his bed. He played back John's diatribe, and just shook his head in disbelief. Dave knew something like this was coming, it was just a matter of time and John's stupidity had not disappointed him. It was just after three o'clock in the morning and Dave felt like letting John suffer for ringing him at such an un-godly hour, but there was too much at risk not to take his request seriously. Even after coming off the phone, John continued his rant at everything around him including the female Police detective, it was late, she was tired and frustrated, and near the end of her shift, she just wanted to go home, and John was proving to be an unforeseen and annoying obstacle. 'We can't do anything, if you're not prepared to talk to us without your solicitor' she said, 'damn right I'm not' he replied, and as she ushered him back to the interview room, she had the feeling it was going to be a long, long night. John trudged down the hallway whinging and whining all the way back to the interview suite, the detective pushed John into the room and slammed the door on him. In the hall, alone and now temporarily free from his irritating presence she stood with her back to the door and banged head in frustration and said aloud 'God give me strength'. At that very moment one of the detectives that had interviewed Val at the Café walked past and on hearing her exclamation said 'surely it can't be that bad' laughing as he said it, but knowing it probably was at that time in the morning. 'God', she exclaimed again, 'you wouldn't believe it, we've got a fifty odd year-old bloke in there who lives in a two-million-pound mansion in Surrey, he was caught spraying bloody graffiti on a disused building site, what the hell is going on'. The detective at first was about to laugh and walk away, then his 'detectives' brain 'kicked in' and he asked the whereabouts of the building site in question. As she told him the location, he immediately became interested, in fact he became very interested, as detectives didn't believe in coincidences and the location now started a chain of possibilities for him. As John stood awkwardly in the interview room, Dave pulled on his boxer shorts, as it seemed somehow only fitting, given, he was about to ring his posh lawyer. He knew he was unlikely to get a reply, but he was in a bind, and couldn't go to see John himself, as their connection might arouse suspicion and the secret of Johns identity that had fuelled intrigue and public interest in the press over the years could become compromised. The phone rang and rang then went to answer phone, Dave rang off then immediately dialled again, it rang and rang and to his surprise this time Simon answered his phone. In his cut glass tones and sounding half asleep he said, 'David dear boy, what the fack do you want '. Dave always found it amusing how posh people said the word 'fuck' but somehow, they still managed to sound cultured and not in the least bit vulgar, uneducated, or common, 'why are you ringing me at whatever time in the morning this is'. Dave presented the basic facts he thought were required. However, Simon seemed uninterested, but he persisted with his immense powers of salesman like persuasion and when even that seemed to fail, he turned to 'old faithful'. It was amazing what the offer of large amounts of hard cash could do, even to someone you assumed had plenty of money, but Dave knew its universal power and was never disappointed with its magnet like force for cajolement. Simon eventually arrived at the Police station at 6:30 a.m. John was by now jaded, frustrated and generally being an even bigger 'pain in the arse'. As Simon strode confidently into the interview room, he was the perfect vision of establishment respectability, dressed in an immaculate Saville Row grey suit and sporting his striped dark and light blue old school tie. Simon introduced himself to the female detective, his persona oozed charm and confidence, standing a little over 6' 3" inches tall, he bore down on the diminutive detective. Simon smiled and asked to be left alone with his client to which the detective acquiesced with great pleasure as she was sick of listening to John's monotonous whinging. As the detective left the room John was straight off his chair, as usual he had no time for pleasantries and launched straight to the point 'I've been in this shit hole for nearly three hours, what's Dave been doing? I was expecting you an hour ago, I want out of here, I want to go home'. Unruffled Simon condescendingly replied, 'and It's a pleasure to meet you too John, let's just stay calm, just sit down, take a deep breath and tell me what happened and with a bit of good fortune, you'll be home before you know it'. Simon listened patiently as John presented him with a somewhat garbled description of the nights events. When he eventually stopped talking, Simon unfolded his arms and then pushed his chair back, leaned forward and placed his hands on his knees and looked directly at his client. 'Look John old chap, I spoke to one of the detectives before I came in to see you, I think if we conceded their charge of 'aggravated trespass' it would undoubtedly help our case, but it's the charge of assault on the security guards that's going to cause us a problem'. At this John kicked off yet again saying 'look at the state of me, pointing' again at his bruised face, 'they gave me a good kicking'. Simon knew he had to head off yet another rant for his own sanity. 'Let's just keep our cool John, leave me to have a word with them'. Simon then left the room and returned in what felt like an age to John, although he was away barely five minutes, 'good news dear boy, we're in luck, 'Mr Plod' say's you can go! '. Simon had spoken to the detectives on his arrival at the station and knew they were sick of the sight of John. Simon continued 'as luck would have it, I know the duty sergeant, he's in the same lodge, 'good egg' actually, anyway, they have agreed to a form of, what shall we call it, unofficial bail, but there is a possibility that they will pursue the aggravated trespass charges'. 'Then, I'm in the clear, a little slap on the wrist and a small fine', play their pathetic little game eh, bloody bureaucrats in blue', said John shaking his head in disbelief, he then rose to his feet. Simon looked at him as he said 'mmm, yes, I would concur with you on that point, however the assault charge on the security guard is a little more troublesome'. As John stood stretching his aching back and moaning at his level of discomfort, Simon as ever sat relaxed with his arms now folded having completed his goal. He then continued 'I've checked and there's no CCTV in that location, so it's basically going to be your word against theirs, but I'm not too concerned, and if these security guards have, and they usually do,' he then laughed to himself, 'any skeletons in the cupboard and this goes to court, I'll personally rattle their bones and hang them out to dry'. John just listened 'I think we are going to be OK John, dear boy, just go home, have a shower, relax and keep your head down, there's a good chap'. Condescending posh twat thought John, but for once he kept his mouth shut and did as he was advised.

Across town, Frances awoke to her first morning in the dreary B+B, but somehow the surroundings seemed superfluous. 'No' grand tiled hallway leading to a bespoke country kitchen or sweeping staircase and eight sumptuous bedrooms, but she was free, the shackles of a broken marriage now discarded, her mind was clear and focused. The die had been cast and the now rest of the day and more importantly her future life was her own, no more hoping that John wasn't hung over, or just in one of his unbearable moods or worse still both. Frances felt that a huge burden had been lifted from her shoulders but couldn't believe how long it had taken her to make this happen. As she lay on her back in bed staring up at the ceiling, a fly was trapped in a cobweb that stretched from a poorly painted Victorian plaster ceiling rose to the flex that protruded from it. As she watched it squirm, struggle and buzz frantically, with its life seemingly fading away, she jumped up, stood on the bed, and said, 'it's your lucky day too' and then proceeded to release it from the web, it instinctively flew straight for the window where the breaking morning light offered freedom and a new dawn. For the first time in what seemed like years, Frances actually looked forward to the day and felt a sense of growing excitement. Looking around the drab and lifeless room, it would do in the short term, but she knew it was time to push on and move her life forward. Her newfound freedom coursed through her veins like a 'drug rush', she decided to get ready and walk to the nearest Newsagent, get the local paper, and look for a better and more permanent place to stay.

Dave rang Simon as soon as he arrived at his gallery just after ten a.m., 'are we all sorted then Simon *old chap*', Simon laughed, duly noting his benefactors sarcasm before he replied, 'well that remains to be seen, David dear boy'. He hated being called *David*, only his mother had done that, but that's what 'Simon's circle' seemed to do, they always managed to make you feel somehow smaller than them and just that little bit inferior, was it intentional thought Dave? He was never quite sure. Dave lived by his lifelong mantra of

'Fake It, till you make it' he really didn't care about Simon and his condescending tones, after all he was the one with the pull, he'd got Simon out of bed at stupid o'clock in the morning to sort out John's mess. 'So, are we good then?' Dave repeated his question, Simon replied, 'chances are he will be charged with aggravated trespass but the charge of assault on the security guards remains in the balance, its essentially their word against his, but I think I may be able to swing it in your friends favour, if it does go all the way to court'. 'Sounds good to me Simon, I'll have a word with John, tell him to keep his nose clean eh, oh and thanks again for this morning, pop in the gallery next time you're in the area and I will sort out our little financial arrangement, I'll even treat you to my best Scotch you *posh git*. Simon roared with laughter at Dave's colourful turn of phrase, 'I'll hold you to that dear boy, now I must get on and you can continue to screw some poor unsuspecting punter'. 'They may be unsuspecting, but they are certainly not poor Simon' Dave replied. He was never lost for a retort and Simon appreciated his candour and street wise conviviality, but it was Dave's ready supply of cash that really tempted him and cemented their working relationship.

Frances found the local paper shop and bought a daily newspaper that seemed to contain a larger than average list of flats to rent. Where better to study the paper than that little café 'The Pink

Flamingo' with it's warm inviting atmosphere, rather than her stark and unwelcoming rented room, she thought. On her arrival at the cafe it was closed, odd she thought on reading the opening times on the door, which confirmed that it should have been open for business, but all was deathly quiet. Frances put her hand to the glass window to shield the street's reflections and peered in, looking for any signs of life. There were none, the tables had all been cleared and a lifeless dull grey pallor seemed to have consumed its normally friendly atmosphere. She felt an uncontrollable shiver run down her back and immediately wondered if the lady with the 'pink hair' was perhaps ill, or something even worse. This was the second occasion she had called at the café, and it had been closed. Frances hoped the lady was well, she had liked her the first time they'd talked and had felt a strange almost uncanny connection with her that you rarely experienced with a complete stranger. It was a type of magical 'bond' that somehow made you feel you had known them for years and immediately felt at ease in their company. Frances decided to grab a drink elsewhere and sit in the local park, it was a bright cold morning with dashes of blue sky that contained a 'winter sun' that could invigorate and give purposefulness to your thoughts and day. In the park Frances turned immediately to the rented accommodation section towards the back of the paper and ignored the rest of the news, that unknown to her contained an article that could change the direction of her entire life. There were numerous bed sits to rent, Frances had the money to take advantage of a more expensive flat in a better location than her current B+B but she was in a state of confusion, wanted a change but didn't want to commit herself to anything permanent. Her life for once had fluidity and could be channelled in any direction without having to consider anyone else. After thoughtful deliberation she decided to stay put in her present bedsit for now, she could leave at any time and liked the idea of being an autonomous 'free' roaming plant without any roots, but not a Triffid, 'no', definitely not a Triffid, she laughed out loud at the image now created in her head. Having decided to stay put for now, she closed and folded the paper in half, as she did so, a man came and sat beside her, invading her space without uttering a word. Frances felt an immediate compunction to move on, but good manners and not wanting to offend a complete stranger, instead she opened the paper at a random position and held it up as a form of both a physical and psychological barrier. Her eyes glanced at the pages without assimilating any information, she had been more than contented sat alone, now this man had disturbed her newfound karma. As she pondered her next move her eyes were somehow drawn to one particular heading '*Violent assault leaves man in coma*' but it wasn't the article that caught her attention, it was the photograph that accompanied it. The photo showed a group of young people, Frances now had to study the faces for a second time as she couldn't quite believe her eyes, because she was one of them. The impact of the image now flooded her memory with past recollections, her mind was drowning in an unstoppable tide of emotion. Shocked, she immediately drew the paper away from her face and was oblivious to everything around her including the stranger. Staring again at the photo, that although magnified and consequently slightly fuzzy, it undoubtedly showed Frances and a group of young people with eighties hair styles and clothes to match. One of the faces was circled, she knew immediately when and where this photo had been taken, it had been at the Camberwell Road squat in 1983. Ross's face was the one circled, and Frances stood on his right-hand side and John on his left, her heart both lifted and sank at the same time, they had been happy times, but their memory now tasted bittersweet. Still in a state of shock and now unaware of anything or anyone around her, she didn't notice the stranger rise to his feet and casually pick up her handbag and walk off. Frances's eyes rapidly scanned the article, she couldn't concentrate, and was now asking herself the question, why now? She kept thinking, why now? Her life had felt positive, but now she was presented with a new and more pressing challenge, and her 'new life' would have to go on hold. She now read the article intently, it detailed how Ross Campbell, an unemployed local man had been viscously attacked in the early hours of the morning and left unconscious. The date of the attack acted as a catalyst for her thoughts and reasoning, she remembered the date with ease. It had been the night on which she had met with Frank Swift at that wine bar in Camden, and the following day John's personality had undergone an almost cosmic like shift towards normality. He had been in an unusually good humoured and positive mood, that was totally out of character, so much so, that she could recall it without any effort. Frances continued to read, her hands gripping the paper as though it were a matter of life and death, in reality it was exactly that for Ross. The article carried no descriptions of the attackers, the Police thought the motive may have been robbery and they were appealing for anyone with information to ring the 'Helpline' number in the article. Her mind now started to slot her mental jigsaw of random ideas together, thoughts that had filled her mind for months, and they now created a disturbing image of John as some grotesque mastermind or worse still a perpetrator of a sickening violent act fuelled by jealousy and deceit. Frances now instinctively reached out for her handbag, she needed her phone and wanted to speak to someone, as her outstretched hand searched, instead of a soft leather bag which contained most of her belongings and more importantly her money, all she felt was a cold damp wooden planked seat. Instinctively she turned frantically around, it was gone, the bag was missing, now starting to panic, her eyes scanned the park like a searchlight looking for escaped prisoners, but the park was now empty, there was no one insight. She rose quickly and looked underneath and then around the bench, there was nothing, nothing, she felt an overwhelming sense of despair. Her desperation rapidly turned to anger, thoughts now focused on the stranger, the man who had sat down unannounced, had he taken the bag? Of course, he had, and if she hadn't been so unwilling to offend in the first place, it wouldn't have happened, she now cursed her middle-class sensibilities. Her head sank towards the ground, she rubbed her forehead with the fingers of her left hand and thought, 'How could she have been so stupid, what now? What on earth can I do? She repeated this question and damning judgement of herself over and over in her mind. As Frances sat alone in the park, her mind opened imaginary doors of possibilities but then closed and dismissed them almost immediately as impractical or downright ludicrous. She even briefly thought about going back to what had been her home with John but that was discarded in a flash, it had taken her years to break free and she wasn't going back. Her mind still raced with ideas, what about the lady that ran the café? No! There was no point as it was closed and devoid of life. Suddenly Dave Hemmings appeared in her thoughts, she didn't necessarily trust him, but he had always seemed fair and given her support with John through some of their rougher times, maybe just maybe he was a possible lifeline. She decided to go to the gallery and explain what had happened, after all Ross had been a friend of his as well, albeit years ago, maybe for old time's sake, surely, she thought, he would help, wouldn't he? Frances was desperate, it had to be worth a try, what had she to lose, there was no going back to John, that definitely wasn't an option. Frances walked the three miles or so across town, there was no choice as she didn't even have the cost of an Underground fare. Initially her journey seemed full of purposefulness as she strode earnestly with the newspaper which had read like a 'Victorian Penny dreadful', grasped firmly in her hand. That fateful story similar to a sudden earthquake had shaken her previously calm world apart, as she neared the gallery her resolve and confidence started to falter. What if Dave wasn't interested? Maybe he wouldn't care? Afterall he was John's friend, the 'golden child', the bringer of wealth, perhaps he would think she had got her just desserts? Maybe he would call John and tell him, and they would both laugh at her misfortune? As her mind suffocated any positive thoughts with a blanket of doubts, she knew it was too late to turn back, and now standing in front of the gallery, it was now or never. She stared at her reflection in the plate glass window, her hair was a mess, she looked bedraggled, hot, and uncomfortable. Where had the mornings positivity and confidence gone? That was life, like a surfer, one minute you were riding a high wave, then one tiny error could see you fall off the 'crest' and plunge hopelessly into the depths gasping for air and desperately trying to regain control. Frances had no handbag, hence no comb or makeup, in fact nothing, her life was in that stolen bag, she attempted to tidy her hair and make herself look a little less ruffled by using the window as a temporary mirror. She lost patience with herself and eventually gave up any idea of respectability and thought 'what the hell' and ignored her less than perfect image and walked into the gallery. Even at this relatively early hour of the morning there were customers viewing the current exhibits. Most of the works carried Johns 'SPOOKZ' tag, but oddly, she thought, not all of it seemed to be his usual style work, what was going on? Standing in an almost trance like state Frances didn't notice as Dave's 'personal assistant' approached and asked, 'if she could help?'. Tall, attractive, and of course young, Frances knew immediately it was one of Dave's 'personally' selected members of staff, she'd heard all about 'them' over the years from John, who stupidly had never attempted to hide his jealousy. Normal social pleasantries were jettisoned as Frances said, 'Yes, you probably can, I need to speak to Dave, its urgent'. The girl seemed surprised that this woman had asked for her boss by name, reticence and jealousy now crept inside her thoughts like a malevolent spirit into a seance, was this some dumped 'ex' about to cause a scene. Following Dave's recent directive to deflect anything away from him that could be a problem she said, 'I'm sorry, Dave', she immediately corrected herself, 'I mean Mr Hemmings is busy at the moment, maybe I can help'. Frances recognised a brush off when it came her way, but was now determined, 'look, I'm not after your job or Dave's bed, your welcome to it, but I need to see him now, just go and tell him, Frances needs to see him, do it, will you just do it'. Like a reprimanded 'naughty schoolgirl' the assistant was now shocked and stunned into silence by Frances's forthright manner, she opened her mouth to reply and not a single word dared to come out, she simply and robotically turned on her heels and walked away to Dave's office. Almost immediately Frances found herself sat in the cherry red leather club chair opposite Dave's desk, he had greeted her in his usual way, a hug, a smile, the usual comforting banter that put anyone within his company at ease. Frances's mind was doing overtime, there were as is usual in times of stress, more questions than answers. She suddenly blurted out 'I've lost the lot, it's been stolen, then there's this'. She held up and shook the newspaper that carried the article about Ross's attack, 'everything is a mess', then she almost started to cry but just managed to control herself. 'Fran, Fran, just take it easy, take your time' Dave said comfortingly. He rose from his chair and poured a small scotch which he placed in front of Frances on the desk. 'Just take a moment, I know you wouldn't normally drink whisky, even a particularly good one like this', at which he half laughed, 'go on just take a little drink to calm yourself'. Frances raised the glass to her lips without even replying and drank it all in one mouthful, she then proceeded to cough uncontrollably as the warm intoxicating liquid hit and burned at the back of her throat. Dave laughed again as he said, 'well that did the trick didn't it', attempting to lighten the mood, strangely after the coughing had subsided Frances did feel calmer and warmer, she smiled, her first since leaving the park. 'I'm sorry Dave but I didn't have anyone else to turn to', he knew that Frances had left John, but decided not to venture down that particularly tortuous path of guilt and blame. 'Just start at the beginning' said Dave, 'I've left John, but

I imagine you already know that, bet he couldn't keep that to himself'. Dave remained silent and just shook his head in mock disbelief. 'But I didn't come here to talk about John, look, someone's just stolen my bag in the park, it had everything in it, money, cards, my phone, the lot'. Dave poured Frances another scotch and then said, 'that's an easy problem to sort, I can easily give you some cash'. She immediately felt a huge sense of relief, what had seemed an almost insurmountable mountain of doubts an hour ago was simply and easily turned into a mole hill by Dave in seconds, his best friend 'Mr ready cash' was as ever the solution. 'Thanks, I'm so grateful' said Frances and then continued 'but this, what about this' now placing the newspaper article in front of Dave. He immediately scanned the article, speed reading it for key words and there they were, just like muggers waiting in a dark alley way, '*Ross Campbell, attack, left unconscious, motive robbery*' they sounded Dave's inner warning bells, but his face didn't show any trace of recognition or emotion. 'Well then' said Frances, 'well, surely there's got to be more than one Ross Campbell in the world' replied Dave sounding quizzical. 'Look at the photo, the photo, look at it' Frances's voice now raised, looking for confirmation of her thoughts. 'It's a bit fuzzy' he replied, 'it's me, Ross and John, I'm telling you', 'no, it can't be' said Dave feigning disbelief. 'It is, take a closer look' snapped Frances, 'are you sure?' said Dave quizzically, knowing full well that it was. 'Of course, I am, surely you must be able to recognise us all' said Frances her voice raised again with growing frustration. 'Be fair Fran, this must be over twenty years old' said Dave, 'more like thirty, it's from the Camberwell Road squat' replied Frances. Dave shook his head as he said, 'well if you say so, it must have been after I left'.

Dave now realised he had to show some interest, otherwise Frances would become suspicious, he now picked the paper up and read it intently. After finishing, he shook his head at the same time saying, 'I can't believe it, Ross of all people, surely he didn't have many enemies, everybody seemed to like him', 'apart from John that is' interjected Frances. Dave put the article down on his desk and looked at Frances. 'Come on, John wouldn't do anything like this, yes, we all know they had fallen out' he hesitated before saying 'over things', Frances interrupted again 'me, you mean me, don't you,'. 'Fran, Fran, it's no good going back into the past, what happened, happened, it was nobody's fault, that's just life, we all make mistakes'. Frances started to 'well up', her voice tightened, 'thing is Dave, I never stopped loving Ross, if it hadn't been for that stupid night when I was drunk and Ross and I argued over money and then...', she now hesitated before continuing, 'I slept with....,' but her words dried up, she couldn't

360

even bear to say John's name. Dave interrupted, 'that's gone Fran, don't follow a path that leads to regrets, think about the now, make it something you can change, that's where you should place your efforts'. 'I want to see him', replied Frances, Dave was confused as he said 'John?', 'No, not him, Ross, I want to see Ross, thing is, I want to help him, but I don't know where to start,' said Frances. 'Fran here, take this', Dave pulled an envelope from the drawer of his desk that contained at least two thousand pounds and passed it over, 'take this for now, till you get sorted', he continued, 'Leave this paper with me, I've got some contacts in the Met, I'll see what I can find out for you'. He was stalling, trying to slow things down, he needed time to take stock of the situation. Now his worst fears about John and his involvement in the attack were no longer on a distant horizon, 'no' they had arrived, it was a bumpy landing, and he feared worse was to come, it was time to consider his future and where he wanted to go next. 'You've been kind Dave, but she sensed his reluctance, 'I'll sort this myself, I feel I owe it to Ross', she then picked up the newspaper and held it firmly but carefully within her hand like a valuable artefact. Frances left the gallery with a renewed vigour, she had enough cash to get by, but more importantly was now determined to find Ross's whereabouts and do whatever she could for him. Her first port of call was a little phone shop to get herself 'connected' to the world again. After her new mobile was setup, she cancelled her credit cards then rang her stolen mobile number and much to her surprise, someone answered her call. A young kids voice grunted something inaudible down the phone, 'who is this?' said Frances. The voice remained silent, 'you've got my phone you creep and probably my bag, I just wanted you to know everything has been cancelled the cards, the phone, the lot', use the cash to buy yourself a conscience you sad little prick'.

Detective sergeant Jameson sat at his office desk, it was late afternoon and nearly time to go home, daydreaming he stared out of the one and only small grimy window that looked onto the waste ground across the road from the Police station. Piles of old and discarded red bricks created a temporary home for the remains of a long-lost summer as dead and dying spikes of Purple Willow Herb fought in vain against the cold winter wind and frost. The area was a scene of decay and neglect, but as he glanced at the disused and semi derelict buildings on the site, his eyes were drawn to the graffiti and images sprayed upon them. A kaleidoscope of thoughts and protests assaulted the senses, some were comical, some downright offensive. One slogan in particular brought a wry smile to his face, it was either a misspelling of Graffiti or the work of a 'street philosopher'

'*Gravity is not a crime*'. It suddenly dawned on Jameson they all had a catalyst, they focused the viewers mind on a 'message'. People, mostly kids he assumed, were speaking out in the only way they knew how. A detectives' job was a busy one with several cases on the go at once, and Ross's assault had temporarily gone to the back of his mind, however this graffiti suddenly dragged it back to the fore and gave him an idea. He now recalled the early morning chat with the female Police officer about the strange case of the wealthy bloke from Surrey picked up for aggravated trespass on the site of Ross Campbell's assault. Furthermore, she had described how he'd been spraying graffiti, Jameson now thought he should visit the site again and see it for himself. Fortunately, the site was on his way home, he decided to finish early, although he'd had a belly full of work 'today', once an idea entered his mind, his detective reasoning and desire to uncover the truth took over. He called it his 'sixth' sense and had to follow it through, as it had paid dividends in the past. So, after his shift, although he never officially felt as though the investigations stopped, as his mind was always churning over unsolved crimes. He decided to make the short journey to the building site. It was situated in a location that he wasn't that familiar with, but one thing he knew, it was an area you didn't visit after dark on your own. He parked his car and tentatively approached the site on foot, continually looking over his shoulder, he eventually stopped some ten feet away and stared through the wire fencing at the semi derelict buildings and graffiti. He didn't see this graffiti as the media now portrayed it, as though it were some form of art, to him it was just vandalism, however, he had to admit albeit begrudgingly that the image in front of him was striking and thought provoking. Now convinced that his reasoning in the office had been correct, the image was definitely there to convey the perpetrators 'message' and the clue to the attack must be contained somewhere in the image, but what was it? As he stood mulling over his thoughts, a workman dressed in paint spattered overalls, suddenly appeared, and stood in front of the image, he then took a drag on the cigarette that seemed to hang unaided from the corner of his mouth, the smoke magically escaped from his seemingly closed mouth. Now bending down he placed a tin of black paint on the ground, removed the lid, then filled up a paint tray. The detective was speechless as the workman using a roller began to paint over the image, within seconds more than a foot of it had disappeared into an abyss, a proverbial black hole. Detective Jameson shouted, 'woh, woh, stop, stop', as his only clue started to disappear before his eyes. The man just kept on painting out the image, the detective now had no choice, quickly he pulled the fencing apart, ran over and grabbed the back of the painter's overalls and yanked him backwards with some force. The man fell to the ground with a thud but still clutching his roller, the detective instinctively held out his left hand as if to say don't move then pulled out his warrant card with his right hand and held it firmly in the face of the painter now lying on his back. 'That's evidence 'said the detective, 'no its not, its bloody graffiti that's what it is' replied the workman. Jameson steadied himself and was now helping the painter to his feet at the same time saying, 'you can drop that roller now' as though it were an offensive weapon, 'It's OK, just leave it mate, I'll speak to your boss', he said. The bottom half of the image had now disappeared behind a curtain of black paint, but the significant part still remained. The detective now at close quarters stared intently at the image. Without doubt in his mind, it portrayed the attack on Ross Campbell and was a graphic display of brutality, with a huge menacing fist adorned with a Scorpion tattoo as its focal point. Without hesitation he took out his mobile phone and took several photos of the image, especially the tattoo. After smoothing over the incident with the site manager, he stood by the fencing and took one last 'long look' at the image. And as he did so, not only was the 'secret' to the attack there, but unbeknown to him another more obvious clue lay beneath his foot. Covered in leaves and hidden from view, he was standing on top of O'Shea's gold identity bracelet. He scrubbed his foot in the dirt and a tiny golden link appeared and then glinted in the fading light. However, it remained partially buried like part of a lost Saxon hoard of gold, waiting its opportunity to be discovered and reveal its story, he turned and went back to his car and the evidence lay undiscovered. His journey home was something of a blur as his mind focused on a mental image of the graffiti. He placed his worn but familiar key in the front door of his silent, lifeless flat, he lived alone and like most of the stereotypical TV detectives was divorced but unlike most of them he wasn't an alcoholic. When you lived for your work as he had always done, it took over your life, hence the failure of his marriage. Driven by the 'desire for truth', even before getting changed and grabbing a bite to eat he loaded the images from his phone onto his laptop. As they loaded, he showered, made a coffee, and then returned to check out their progress. Modern advancements in the most rudimentary of software allowed you to magnify to a greater level of detail and instinctively he zoomed immediately in on the hand in the image, he was sure the Scorpion tattoo held the secret but to 'who or what' he didn't yet know? The starting place now for any form of search was always the Internet, he typed in 'Scorpion' and as with all searches on the Web the amount of information it returned was colossal.

He quickly scanned the results, assimilating and rejecting it as he went. *'The Scorpion has come to represent unexpected death, it does not attack with any type of malice, but simply remains true to its nature'* Little did he know how accurate a description of Colm O'Shea this was. He continued his search, *A band from the 1970's, a member of the arachnid family*, 'Yeah, yeah' I know all this he thought, but where's the connection, what ties this together? He scanned image after image of Scorpions and related material, he then came upon *'the Scorpion Tank first manufactured in 1973 now discontinued'* ...., the information was overwhelming. However, experience had taught him to stay focused and not divert his search too much and be drowned in the abyss of unrelated facts and images, but he had the feeling it was going to be a long, long night.

Chapter Eighteen
Trapilo Blue

'Lake extract from the fruit of the Turnsole or
Heliotropum plant'

Red to Bluish Violet

Frances had returned to her B+B, fortunately for her, the landlord for a small 'fee' had provided a spare key, the original having been stolen along with her handbag. She was still clutching the newspaper article about Ross's attack and pondering her next move, should she go to the police and tell them about her suspicions? But would doing this make things better or worse? She didn't know, but surely had to do something. Dave had thrown her a lifeline, she had money and now could re-assemble her life yet again, but knew deep down that Dave couldn't be trusted, he wasn't a bad bloke, but he would instinctively always look after number 'one'. She sat for a while then decided to get out and breathe some fresh air but not in the local park again, 'no, definitely not' she thought, still smarting from her earlier stupidity, instead she would take a walk to the little café one more time and see if it was open. This time as Frances approached the café, the lights shone out like a beacon, the warm pale-yellow glow gave Frances a sense of wellbeing, of homeliness, why?

She didn't know, but somehow it drew her like a moth to a flame. Now standing at the door, a feeling of de ja Vue suddenly overtook her. Taped with great care to the glass, was the article about Ross's attack, neatly cut from the same paper she had been reading. The cuts followed the contours of the print and handwritten in thick black felt tipped pen was the message '*Does anyone have any info about my friend Ross, please ring...*' and alongside was a telephone number that she didn't recognise. Frances stood back and instinctively stared up at the shop hoarding that proudly displayed its recently painted title 'The Pink Flamingo Café' and alongside it like a close companion was the same telephone number. Now looking again at the article on the door, she pulled her copy of the article from her pocket and compared them, why? She knew they were identical, it was comfort and confirmation that someone else cared about Ross and wanted to help him. Now she didn't feel so helpless and alone anymore, she had a compatriot, and they could be inside the cafe at this very moment. Without hesitation Frances entered, there were a handful of customers scattered around, most sat on tables for two, engrossed in their own little world, isolated even in the smallest of café's. She immediately gravitated to a spare table in the window and moved the previous occupants empty cup and saucer to an adjacent table. Frances then carefully unfolded the article about Ross's attack and spread it on the empty table and smoothed it flat with her hand, now purposely placed where anyone passing or attending her table couldn't help but see it. She gazed out of the window, the last few hours had shattered her seemingly unbreakable newfound confidence. Mesmerised by passing cars and pedestrians outside in the street, she didn't hear the young girl standing by her side. 'What can I get you' the girl repeated in a louder voice, Frances was immediately shaken out of her trance, she couldn't think, autopilot took over as she ordered 'mm Latte and err... Ham sandwich, thanks'. She now noticed the girl looking inquisitively at the newspaper article on the table, but the girl said nothing and simply wrote down her order on a small, lined notepad and then disappeared off towards the counter. Frances started to read the article again but had scrutinised it so many times her mind was ahead of her eyes as she glanced across the text. Before Frances had time to look up two cups of coffee were placed on the table and there was Val, she smiled, didn't say a word, just pulled up a chair and sat alongside. Without warning emotion erupted within Frances and she started to sob as she said, 'it's just', 'it's just...' her words floated away on a stream of tears. 'I know, I know', said Val nodding while at the same time placing her arm around Frances to comfort her and what seemed like years of despair and frustration flowed out unstoppably. It was some time before either of them said a word, it was one of those rare moments when a strong emotional bond is forged, and words are somehow superfluous. Within an hour Frances had recounted the major elements from the last three decades of her life, her time with Ross, how they broke up, and now her failed marriage with John. Val sat and listened, she was good at that, being the owner of a café made you something of an amateur psychologist. People's problems were as much a part of your job 'Tea and Sympathy' she called it, a name Val had always fancied for the cafe but even for her, thought it was just a little too twee. They talked and talked, they had so much to say to each other, now they were the only ones that formed a link in the chain that could be Ross's lifeline. Val had recognised the young and pretty, hippily dressed girl pictured alongside Ross in the newspaper article. 'You develop a 'thing' about people and faces when you run a café', I should have been a copper, goodness knows my feet are big enough' said Val smiling and laughing for the first time. Frances was amazed that Val remembered her face, 'it wasn't just the photo', Val continued, 'the first day you came in, Ross had just gone, you must have just missed him, but there was something strange, a sort of aura. It's something you can't put into words, a definite link, a connection you can't explain, these things you just have to accept and believe that something exists beyond the level on which we communicate and interact daily'. 'God, that sounds so profound' Frances said, 'it's not meant too, I've always had what people call a 'sixth sense replied Val. She then continued, 'I remember when I was little, six or seven years old, I tried to tell my parents about my grandfather coming into my room and sitting at the bottom of my bed, even though he'd been dead for over two years, 'silly girl' they said, but I can recall that moment as if it were yesterday and I swear to this day it definitely happened'. Val now took a deep breath, she realised the 'time' was right, she put her hand on Frances's and told her about her recent visit to the hospital. Frances desperately wanted to see Ross and help in any way she could but they both desired two crucial things, him fit and well and to see 'justice' done. Frances gave Val her new mobile number and temporary address and they agreed to see each other again tomorrow but this time their meeting would be at the hospital.

Nearly twenty-four hours later, Frances had hardly slept the previous night, she had tossed and turned thinking about everything that had happened, but her biggest enemy was one of apprehension. Now standing in front of the hospital and looking up at the 1970's concrete façade, it had large undistinguished white metal framed windows, the curtains were drawn back, almost sentry like to attention, she felt a sense of foreboding and hoped her fatalistic preconceptions wouldn't be realised. Stepping off the pavement, her mind focused solely on the visit, an ambulance blasted its horn as she almost stepped into its path, frozen to the spot, her heart pounded, she felt like crying, 'come on Frances she said to herself, you can do this, you've got to do this for Ross.' Outside the main entrance people attempted in vain, to find a satisfactory seating position on uncomfortable concrete molded benches in the chilly winter air, others stood in their dressing gowns gasping on cigarettes, unable to kick the habit that was responsible for much of their ailments. As she stood in the large revolving door it magically swept round and deposited her on the inside, a sudden rush of sickly warm air and the smell of coffee from the café overwhelmed her senses. She anxiously scanned around looking for Val, then saw her in the corner of the café, on seeing Frances she immediately stood up, her tall, elegant frame topped with vivid pink hair was a beacon of friendly light in the fraught and fast-moving environment. People jostled past Frances as she stood motionless, it was visiting time, and everyone wanted to be the first in the queue for the wards that contained their nearest and dearest. They waved at each other, as Frances walked towards Val who then instinctively gave her a warm and re-assuring hug, something Frances's mother had

never done, she then sat down at the little table for
two, neatly tucked away in a quiet corner. They sat
and chatted while Val hurriedly finished off her
coffee before, they made their way towards the
lifts. Frances looked at the elevator and hesitated,
Ross was on the third floor and still in a kind of
intensive care, 'do you mind if we walk up the
stairs instead,' said Frances. 'Not at all' replied Val,
'it's just..., maybe it sounds stupid but somehow it
gives you more time to think, think about what to
say, how to react, oh I don't know, it's crazy, but I
don't know how to feel,' said Frances. 'It's OK'
said Val smiling, she then put her hand on
Frances's arm, 'you'll be fine, just take a deep
breath, it's going to be fine, you'll see.' As they
entered Ross's room, he lay silent and still, his eyes
closed to the world. Frances immediately froze
and just started to sob, unable to stop herself. She
wanted to, but emotions were unpredictable and
like a bolting horse you are unable to control its
wild nature, it would take you where it wanted but
eventually would run out of energy. Val put her
arm around Frances, and they settled on two hard
and uncomfortable blue plastic chairs, whose
intention she thought was to make visiting times as
short as possible, to allow the hospital staff to get
on with their duties. 'Come on, come on luvvy'
said Val in a quiet soft voice, 'look, he's calm and
in the best place, take his hand, talk to him, let him
hear your voice, the doctors told me anything

could bring him out of his coma, and even the most unexpected words or names from someone's past can bring them right back to life'. Frances stared at Ross, the square jaw line was still there, his hair although now a little grey had been combed but was somehow still wild just like his nature 'a free spirit', his face was thinner than she remembered but it was Ross, it was definitely the 'Ross' she had always known. She had missed him so much, tears started to well up inside her again, initially she fought the feeling but what did it matter, letting go she cried and laid the side of her head on his hand, it was warm and pulsed with life, thank God your alive she thought. Val looked on, she was pleased to know that here was someone else that cared as much as she did and undoubtedly a great deal more. Val sat and observed the tenderness that Frances displayed towards Ross, if Frances had been frightened at the thought of seeing him again and not knowing what to say, then she had been very much mistaken, now seeing them together, they looked as though they had never been apart. Frances talked and talked directly to Ross, sometimes coming close to his ear, and whispering. Every now and then she would turn and look at Val, seeking support and there was always a nod and smile to confirm she was doing the right thing. Val had told Frances that the doctors had no idea how long he would remain in a coma, it could be weeks, months or unbelievably years. Frances knew she had to focus on the 'now' give Ross all the support she could muster but knew the answer to helping him almost certainly lay in their past. There would be a key, possibly psychological, or even physical, that could awaken him from his current enforced state of cocoon like safety, his mind had shut down to protect him, somehow it had to be re-awakened. As Val and Frances came to the end of the visiting hours they walked towards the lift side by side,' I suppose you would rather go by the stairs' said Val pointing towards the stairwell, 'no, the lift will be just fine' replied Frances, her composure had returned along with a determination to see Ross well again and maybe just maybe she could play a part in his 're-birth'.

Frank sat in his office at the gym, now closed to the public, all was quiet, a punch bag swayed gently from side to side, untouched by a human hand, it moved with an 'unknown' energy. The ring was silent, the lights were turned off and a mysterious half-light shrouded the gym and familiar objects took on a new identities as only their silhouettes were visible. Frank had always liked this time of day, the afternoon shift was over, and it would be a couple of hours before anyone else came, then the Gym would spring back to life. It would welcome another series of kids who wanted to get rich just like their boxing heroes by beating the 'crap' out of someone. Most of them were misguided but who was Frank to deflate their dreams with tales of bent promoters, bungs taken for dives and cornermen that didn't always have a fighter's best interests at heart. Frank didn't mind time on his own, it allowed him to reflect on the vicissitudes of life without letting them destroy his appetite for fighting its challenges. There was nothing wrong with recollections from the past, 'yes', there were parts of it he would change, 'the loss of friends, his divorce, the failed title fights' but they all represented the fibres both good and bad that were woven together to form the material of his life. He felt comfortable embracing the past, but he'd always kept it tucked away in a little mental box to gaze at from time to time, and unlike some mentally weaker souls, he was always able to put the lid back on. Suddenly a gust of wind rattled the metal shutters on the gym windows and disturbed his momentary Karma, he found himself back in the 'now', however, his brief meditation had focused his mind and he knew where he wanted to 'go'. He had arranged an alibi for the time of Ross's attack but had not yet been paid for his trouble, he originally wanted two grand, now he thought perhaps 'five' was nearer the mark. The more he thought about that fateful night and the potential problems that could arise from his actions, he now concluded it had to be worth at least ten grand. He had decided to collect the money in person, and when Frank collected in person, there hadn't been a single occasion when he'd left empty handed.

As Frank readied himself to visit 'his client', John was presently lying half comatose and for all intense purpose's dead to the world in his man cave, a condition brought on through excessive alcohol and the consumption of some class 'A' stimulants. The Martins Brothers ceramic figure, what was left of it, had been working overtime, its head was 'off' and so was John's. Frank drove calmly and leisurely to his destination, in fact he quite fancied a place out in the 'sticks' away from the inner city 'grime and crime'. He could never quite work out how John had made his money, but was sure it wasn't drugs, as he knew most of the major players on the drugs circuit. John didn't seem particularly 'nerdy' either, so Frank deduced he hadn't made his money from Information technology. Maybe it came from the stock market, 'mmm he thought, yeah', he could be a 'barrow boy' trader made 'good' but realistically Frank couldn't see that either, anyway he thought, whatever John did, it was extremely profitable, and he wanted a piece of the action. As he neared John's country home its size and location was impressive. 'Lucky bastard he thought' thinking of his client, who he had supplied with quality 'gear' for parties on several occasions, but John had always insisted on them meeting some distance from his house. As Frank's BMW approached the twin sandstone piers that dominated the entrance to the driveway, a feeling of De ja Vue struck him like a well-timed 'right cross,' he knew he had been here before and it wasn't that long ago. It had been the night he'd followed that posh bird back to her lair, the 'looker' that wanted him to find 'the missing brother', well that had been her 'story'. The same mystery woman that had unwittingly provided him with an alibi for the night of the altercation with that 'loser' that John had wanted him to keep tabs on. He pulled his car round to the side of the house, the sound of his tyres crunching over the gravel immediately created a sense of well-being and wealth in his mind. Frank stepped out of his car and glanced about him and then walked his 'big walk', he had the unmistakable boxers roll, a commanding gentle sway of his body from side to side. He stopped outside the imposing porticoed entrance, turned and looked around again like a poacher hunting illicit game. There was silence, just what he wanted, not a soul and nothing to disturb him, he rang the doorbell, it amusingly played the first few chords from *'London's calling'* by the *Clash,* he laughed to himself, how right it was, he thought. He waited for a very 'long minute', but no one came, he rang the bell again, and again, still no reply, then he decided on the direct approach and hammered on the heavy oak double fronted doors with his large no-nonsense fist. He stood waiting yet again and still no one appeared, his patience was now wearing thin, he was in no mood to go home 'empty handed', there was a job to do, and it would be done. He looked around again, his eyes scanned the area beyond the large, manicured lawns and trees that formed the gardens, there didn't appear to be any near neighbours, no one to watch, no one to pry. He decided to circle the house like a big cat stalking its prey and eventually found an open downstairs window. How careless he thought, lifting the delicate and carefully crafted wrought iron window catch, and accepted the opportunity to climb in and gain what would be described as a 'lucky break' to a squatter who in their parlance described it as 'unforced entry.' As he stood in a darkened room, the curtains blew against him as the wind rushed in through the open window. A light shone underneath the door from an adjacent room, 'so there is someone in' he thought. Approaching the light, he slowly and silently turned the large brass handle and opened the door. It revealed an impressive, tiled hallway, which contained an elegant, wide, curved sweeping staircase that seemed gracious enough for an ascent to heaven. You couldn't fail to be impressed, he thought, this was a grand style of living far removed from his humble upbringing in East London. He hadn't seen the house before, having been kept at arm's length by John and treated like a mere trade's person, a 'supplier' of goods, albeit of a class 'A' variety. He looked around the hall, then a noise came from a room at the far end, something had fallen and broken, he couldn't be sure, but it sounded like glass. Years spent boxing and keeping jangling nerves under control as you entered the ring had taught him how to keep fear at bay and without thinking he instinctively moved towards the room where the noise had emanated. Frank tapped a friendly greeting on the door with the knuckle of his index finger, there was no reply, he then slowly pressed down the handle and cautiously eased the door open as it creaked on its large brass hinges. He quickly surveyed the room looking for any signs of life, the room was a stinking rubbish tip, there were empty takeaway cartons on the settee, jostling for space with numerous discarded wine bottles, unwanted clothes lay strewn across the floor. Frank's attention was then drawn to John, dead to the world and snoring away in his favorite leather chair. His head lay against the wing of the chair, his hand outstretched over the arm and a broken bottle lay in pieces on the stone hearth of the Adam style fireplace. Frank looked at the desolation around John and shook his head in disbelief and thought, 'man, what are you doing'. Frank had seen and personally experienced this kind of physical and mental desolation before, it was an uncomfortable flashback to when his wife had left him, and he'd gone off the rails. Without saying a word, he sat in the chair opposite and stared at the pathetic half shaven, wine-soaked slob in front of him. He had temporarily felt pity, but Frank was no social worker, he didn't want to be either, this visit was solely about money. Amateur psychology now over, he kicked the sole of Johns bare foot, who then momentarily flinched and mumbled something incomprehensible but remained very much asleep. Frank then proceeded to kick him a second time but this time with a greater level of force. The crushing pain of this blow suddenly invaded John's sleep, and he awoke with a start, shook his head, and opened his eyes, almost like a nightmare he immediately saw the colossal figure of Frank leaning forward and staring at him. John panicked and sprang to his feet, pushing his chair backwards as he did so. 'Who let you in? Shouted John, Frank calmly replied 'no one, you're all alone man'. 'Get out of my house, I don't need any of your cheap street shit'. 'I can see that' said Frank laughing, he then stood up and proceeded to pick up the remains of the ceramic Martin Brothers jar then slowly and deliberately dropped it onto the stone hearth where it shattered for the final time. 'Bastard', shouted John who proceeded to lunge forward and attempt to a throw a punch. Frank just swayed his body slowly almost balletically to avoid the assault and used John's own momentum to send him crashing to the ground. Frank just shook his head as he looked at the pathetic figure now sprawled on the floor half out of his mind on God knows what. 'Now that's no way to treat a friend and a guest, is it?' said Frank with a high level of sarcasm. John didn't say a word he just lay flat on his back groaning, his adversary now bent down and got hold of the neck of Johns sweatshirt and pulled him effortlessly up into a sitting position. John attempted to push Franks hand away but his vice like grip wasn't going anywhere. 'You owe me money and I only ask once,' said Frank. 'Is this why you're here, for two lousy grand'. 'It was two, but I want more, you have caused me a shed load of grief John me old mate', he emphasized the word 'mate', meaning that he was in fact was no 'mate' at all. 'No way, no way, more money for what? You're out of your tiny punch-drunk mind'. Without saying a word, Frank thrust John's head backwards, he yelled in pain, as his head collided with the cold hard stone fireplace. 'I didn't hear that, what did you say', said Frank, as he clashed John's head yet again, he then exclaimed' OK, OK, stop! You can have your lousy money'. Frank then dragged his hapless victim to his feet who then slowly made his way to a row of red leather books that sat proudly upon a large and impressive set of Georgian mahogany library shelves. The books had false covers and were simply pulled aside to reveal a small metal safe. John had trouble remembering the 'code' but a combination of fear and a desire to see the back of Frank his tormentor eventually brought it to the forefront of his mind. He opened the safe to reveal several bundles of cash, he pulled out a bundle and thrust it into 'the big man's chest, saying 'take it then, you cheating bastard'. Frank responded to John's characteristic and impulsive nature with a knee jerk reaction, as he slapped him across the head. Fortunately for John it was with an open hand but even so it carried a significant amount of force that would topple most people and he fell again, hitting his head on the shelves as he went down for a second time. John was now on the proverbial canvas and wouldn't be up by the end of the count, but Frank wasn't picking him up again. Frank pulled a further two bundles of cash from the safe and used one of them to slap John across the head. 'I'm having this as well, just for your 'lip' and this isn't the end of it, I know where you live now and you owe me big time, I'll be calling again'. Frank turned away, put the money in his inside pockets then straightened his jacket and strode coolly out of the room and left the house as though nothing had happened, it was all in a day's work for him. John somehow managed to raise his shattered and aching body to a sitting position, still stunned, his mind was too be-fuddled to totally comprehend quite what had just happened, but one thing was for sure, the gloves were now 'off' and there was nowhere to hide.

Chapter Nineteen
French Purple

'Preparation from the ink of the shellfish Murex
trunculis and Murex brandaris'

Reddish to Bluish Deep Purple

In a small pub, situated in Barking's backstreets, sat Colm O'Shea, he was just about to start his seventh pint. John Noble was down and seemingly out, but the 'big man' was very much on the up, he still had some of the cash that Frank had given him, and life seemed good but then it usually did after several large drinks. It was the next morning that his life returned to normal, and his prosaic everyday existence became reality once again. Colm was experiencing positive thoughts for once, he wasn't reflecting on what he usually saw as his wasted life. He had enjoyed his early days in the army, they had given him a sense of purpose, his home life hadn't been easy, and trouble somehow just seemed to follow him around. Being a huge physical force, his presence always attracted attention and the wrong 'sort' of people, it was a case of *Prid Quo Pro*. People had used him to get what they wanted, usually the recovery of 'bad debts' and in return he received much needed ready cash. He enjoyed the fact that people seemed to show him a form respect but in reality, it was just pure unadulterated fear. His notoriety gained over the years from pub brawls and acting as Frank Swifts hired 'muscle' also meant that as he got older every little punk who wanted to make a name for himself as a 'hardman' increasingly wanted to 'have a go'. 'They' wanted his crown, to be 'the man' who had taken on the colossus that was Colm O'Shea and won. Now there was little else in his life apart from his notoriety and that was about to catch up with him, but little did he realise that the very thing that had been his only positive influence in his earlier life would ultimately lead to his downfall.

As O'Shea drank, detective Jameson sat at his office desk where a small light illuminated a piece of A2 paper on which he'd written down all the facts of the case involving Ross Campbell. He created a visual map, a flowchart of brutality, words were circled or underlined, arrows connected lines with regard to the chronology of events. The names of all the major players known so far were there, Ross, the watchmen, the incidental facts, the location of the attack, the tattoo on the graffitied image, he even found himself doodling and drew a rather pathetic looking Scorpion. He stared at the cartoon like representation he had penned and then circled it furiously several times in frustration. At present there weren't any concrete facts, but he was convinced that the tattoo was the clue to the attack.

He studied and tried to make sense of all the links and incidental facts, but his mind kept coming back to the tattoo. He then sketched a rather comic looking tank and was laughing at his child like representation when suddenly it gave him an idea. 'Army', yes 'army', he said aloud, he'd arrested and interviewed a few ex-service personnel over the years and many of them sported tattoos of girlfriends and wives, random names, and football teams, but it wasn't uncommon for their regiment or unit to appear on them, the 'camaraderie of the ink' he called it. It was a tenuous connection, but most things were in detective work and when you were up a blind alley with nowhere to go you would happily follow any lead. Remembering all the search results that the internet had thrown up, he recalled the reference to the Scorpion tank, maybe this was it, 'a chance in a million', well several thousand he hoped? Opening his laptop, it was late, but he didn't want to take any of this home for a second time but begrudgingly knew it would remain in his mind whatever he did. Desperate to solve this case, he wanted to prevent it becoming yet another failed statistic 'an unsolved and forgotten crime'. Now loading up the internet by clicking the 'little red fox', in the search bar he hurriedly typed 'Scorpion tank' and a screen full of searches came back. 'Focus' he said to himself 'don't get lost in an array of pointless links and searches and find yourself wondering what you had been looking for in the first place. He found the myriad of facts fascinating but overwhelming, he found a specific 'Tank Corp', but they were not the only regiment to use tanks. The 'Scorpion' had been used in most of Britain's recent conflicts, the Falklands, Iran, Iraq, the list seemed almost endless, and his original clue now seemed more like 'one' in several million. Frustrated yet again, he pushed his chair back from his desk and stared at the laptop screen that now flooded the room with a bright blue light, that had grown in intensity as the darkness crept in from his one and only office window. He knew there was a link, but how much digging was it going to take, to unearth its secret, some ex-military personnel obviously had committed offences and had criminal records. However, he realised that his superiors were unlikely to allow him the time to carry out further investigations on a case that 'they' probably viewed as just another 'druggie' who'd got what he deserved. Police resources were stretched to the limit and each case depending on its column size in the newspapers would then be allocated a pro rata amount of 'time' and resources. Although this essentially unwritten Police guidance didn't form any kind of government policy, it was there but no one would admit to it. He rubbed his eyes as his frustration and tiredness seemed to be overwhelming. It was time to call it a day, maybe with a break, his synaptic gaps might generate yet another flash of ingenuity but for now the sparks had faded into the night. It was time to shut down his mind and laptop, he was onto something, and it was only a matter of time before the 'secret' would reveal itself.

As the world continued to revolve and people's lives moved on at a pace. Ross lay in his coma, cocooned from everyday life, senses dormant, his mind asleep, his brain functioned purely to maintain his life, interaction of any kind seemed impossible. Frances sat holding his hand as she had done every day while at his bedside. Somehow him just being there was enough, that they were 'together' again was all that seemed important. Questions and self -doubt continued to race through her mind as she looked at Ross lying motionless with his vital signs of life displayed on a series of monitors that flickered and annoyingly beeped. Frances tried to imagine what had happened to Ross over their years of separation, was he married? Did he have a family? Would he still care for her? She held his hand, this physical connection was a global symbol of affection, if there was someone else, they were seemingly unaware of his current predicament. Frances was his 'family' for the moment and that's what mattered. She tightened her grip and didn't care if there was someone else, she was here, they weren't, he was back, and Frances would savour this moment and the future would have to take care of itself. She then leant forward and whispered 'Ross I'm back' into his ear, and talked about anything that came into her mind, but always kept one eye firmly set on his face looking for the slightest flicker from his eyes or even better still a movement in his facial expression. The subject now centered on their visit to France, even though it had happened over twenty years ago, when they had walked hand in hand through the back streets of Montmartre. How they had laughed when Ross attempted his 'Pigeon' French and even though he couldn't speak the 'Lingo', somehow, he had managed to connect with the locals through the universal language of painting. His French contemporaries frequented the streets just as he did, they hawked their colorful tourist paintings for a few Francs even though many of them were talented painters but like most struggling artists they prostituted their talent to earn a 'crust'. Not a sign of recognition came from Ross's eyes or his face, but Frances knew she had to just keep reminiscing and presenting the past to him. In the hope that some detail no matter how small or seemingly insignificant, might just 'kick start' his memory and therefore begin his journey back to reality. Realistically she knew that this 'journey' may never happen, the doctors had described patients who had been in comas for years and that she should be prepared for the disappointment that he may never 'come back'. However, love really was blind, and Frances's mind wouldn't accept the worst scenarios, he was alive, things would get better, they had to, 'they' would have their day. Frances knew she had never fully come to terms with the end of her relationship with Ross and had tried to confront him with the facts at the time, but how do you tell someone you loved that you had just slept with their best friend. She felt uncomfortable even now talking about it to Ross but at least he couldn't just turn and walk away as he had done all those years ago. Frances now took the opportunity to say what had in the past been 'un-sayable', thoughts and regrets gathered into a 'private collection' were now whispered into his ear, 'things' she had wanted to say at the time, but back then Ross just wouldn't listen. It felt cathartic, releasing emotions and regrets that had grown with intensity over the years, some of the memories were still painful but at least here was the opportunity which she thought would never come again. However, there was no response to Frances's emotional outpouring, no reaction whatsoever, what would it take to bring him back? She thought. It was strange that the only person who knew the truth about that night more than twenty years ago was John and his lies had destroyed three people's lives and none of them had gained any sort of happiness, least of all John. Frances shuffled and then sat back on the uncomfortable plastic visitors chair and a sense of realism crept silently into her once positive thoughts, she stared longingly at Ross and knew things didn't look good. Fighting these tiny green shoots of negativity, with her hands in a prayer like clasp, she vowed to stand by him, 'he would get better, he had to get better' and she was going to do everything to make it happen.

O'Shea stood looking at himself in the mirror, he contorted his face like a championship gurner, he'd had a good night on the beer and unusually for him had overslept as it was well after 9 a.m. As he stuck his tongue out and examined it, last night's drink and a heavyweight kebab eaten on his way home had left an unpleasant looking coating on it and an even less desirable taste in his mouth. He rubbed and slapped his face with his hands in an attempt to put some colour back into the pale and tired ex squaddie that now stared back at him. Feeling his stubble with the back of his hand, a shave was required, he always shaved and washed every day, a throwback to his army routine he presumed. He found it therapeutic to shave as it seemed to not only remove his stubble but alleviated any lingering negative thoughts that sometimes entered his head on first waking in the morning, it made him feel alive. 'Yes', he thought, a good old fashioned 'wet shave' would set him up for the day. O'Shea was just rinsing the residue of shaving foam from his face when he heard a loud hammering noise at his front door. He looked at the small leatherette cased 1960's travel clock sitting on the narrow bathroom ledge, as usual it had stopped as he knew it wasn't three o'clock in the afternoon. Who the hell is this he thought, as he wiped his face on a towel, it couldn't be Frank as he normally called him on his mobile if he wanted something doing, in his line of business loud knocks on your door at unexpected hours of the day usually meant 'trouble'. He left the bathroom and walked the short distance to the front door and peered through his 'trusty peephole' a necessity for anyone in his line of work. The 'viewer' revealed a man with his back to the door, although somewhat contorted by the lens he appeared to be a tall reasonably well-dressed bloke in a suit. O'Shea didn't recognise him, but he knew that 'suits' normally meant trouble. He hesitated at first, but thought 'what the hell', then started to open the door with the 'confidence of ignorance'. There stood detective Jameson, who turned immediately to face the door on hearing several large bolts being drawn back. He had persevered at home with his narrow hunch the previous evening, trawling the Police databases for any ex-serviceman arrested in the locality in the last few years. O'Shea's name had shown up as a likely candidate, he'd been arrested after a major incident at a local pub when three people were hospitalised by an overzealous bouncer, 'one' Mr.

Colm O'Shea. It was a pure shot in the dark as Jameson was rapidly running out of ideas and time. The door opened about six inches, it was still on its safety chain, 'yeah what do you want?' 'Grunted O'Shea. Jameson immediately produced his warrant card and attempted to present it, to the small portion of Colm's face that was visible. Although Jameson couldn't see much, he could see enough to realise he was even scarier than his police mugshots. He now performed the formalities, 'I'm Detective Sergeant Jameson, Metropolitan Police, can I have a word Mr. O'Shea'. 'What about' snapped the big man with the door still six inches ajar, 'can we talk inside, if you don't mind sir, you probably don't want the neighbours to hear'. 'Fuck them, can't even speak English!' retorted O'Shea. 'Would you mind just opening the door, it'll only take a couple of minutes' said Jameson attempting to remain in control of his growing frustration. Colm shook his head and muttered something derogatory about 'coppers' and then released the chain and opened the door. He stood mountain like in the doorway and the detective now wished he had brought some backup with him. Jameson wasn't small, over six feet but the sheer bulk of this 'colossus' intimidated him, my God he thought to himself, as he looked at the enormous arms the size of legs. O'Shea had put on a large baggy sweatshirt before answering the door to fend off the early morning cold in his unheated flat, the volumous garment covered his arms and most of his hands, so there were no visual signs of any tattoos. This impromptu visit hadn't been sanctioned by Jameson's superiors, so he needed to be circumspect. He followed O'Shea into his living room and watched him slump down into a well-worn chair with grimy threadbare arms, making no attempt to clear a pile of old papers and clothes that littered the only other remaining seat. 'Do you mind if um...' said Jameson, as he motioned with his hand towards the only other chair in the room, 'whatever' came the reply from O'Shea. The detective dumped the contents from the seat onto the floor. Glancing around he assumed it was a furnished let, tatty, somewhat squalid and it needed something the media Lifestyle programs were fond of describing as a 'complete makeover'. However, Jameson couldn't quite imagine the flamboyant TV personality Laurence Llewelyn-Bowen giving O'Shea tips on interior décor. As the detective asked for some personal details, name, date of birth, all the usual starting points for his 'off the record' interview, he noticed an army regiment photograph on the wall. 'In the services were you' he said, 'might have been' replied O'Shea tersely, 'we can check you know,' said the detective forcefully. 'Well, that's your job isn't it', the detective could tell immediately that O'Shea to put it politely wasn't much of a 'conversationalist'. It was going to be like 'pulling teeth' but that was all part of the relentless fact-finding duties that made up the majority of his job. Jameson decided to push his luck 'we can make this easy here and now, or we can do it down at the station', his final remark was something of a bluff as the 'visit' was technically off the record. O'Shea didn't look at Jameson, but simply stared past him as he said, 'how about telling me why you're here?' Jameson ignored the request and continued to pursue his own general line of enquiry in an attempt to soften him up for a 'sucker' punch. He asked about O'Shea's past skirmishes with the law and enquired as to his current 'employment' status. Now without hesitation he attempted to land his 'sucker punch' by asking where O'Shea was on the night of the attack but didn't mention the incident. He just wanted to see and hear Colm's response, which came without thought or hesitation, 'down the 'Brickies', I'm always down there on Tuesday's and Wednesday's, in fact most nights, you can ask anyone, they all know me'. 'Mm, the *Bricklayer's Arms*, I know that mm..', Jameson hesitated before sarcastically saying 'hostelry'. He used the term 'hostelry' very loosely as it was one of the roughest pubs in the locality, it had lost its license on several occasions for drug dealing activities, as well as other anti-social and illegal practices. 'So why do you want to know where I was?' asked O'Shea. 'A man was brutally attacked near a building site on Jubilee Road that night,' said Jameson. He then paused before saying 'a Mr. Ross Campbell', he earnestly observed O'Shea's response. Not a flicker of recognition came, he was either very cool, innocent, or possibly didn't even know his victim's name. However, Jameson experienced 'the feeling' a detectives sixth sense, that he was onto something, and repeated Ross's name again. O'Shea shook his head, 'never heard of him', he barked, now seemingly irritated. Jameson sensed maybe, just maybe, he had touched a nerve, 'we're just following up some leads that's all and if you're alibi stacks up, you've nothing to fear, have you? 'I don't fear noffing', said O'Shea now looking the detective straight in the eye, his cold and unrelenting stare sent a shiver down Jameson's back. He'd dealt with some mean people in his job and this character was up there with the 'worst' of them. This coldness and total lack of empathy sounded warning bells, Jameson would take this further but now was not the time or the place. 'We'll leave it at that for the moment and if your alibi holds water, you're in the clear'. O'Shea just stared back at the detective and shrugged his shoulders dismissively, he was unmoved and made no attempt to hide the fact that he didn't care. The detective made his own way to the door and left the squalid flat, he then did his usual trick of sitting around the corner in his car to see what the suspects next move would be. He sat for over half an hour and was just about to call it a day, when he saw his 'target's bulky figure appear on the street. O'Shea looked furtively up and down the road, he then almost comically in Jameson's eyes, squeezed his over generous frame, 'the proverbial quart' into a pint-sized Ford Fiesta. It was going to be a long day thought Jameson as O'Shea tried repeatedly to start his car, the engine turned over and over but wouldn't fire up. Even from a distance Jameson could hear the car's battery struggling for life, suddenly against even the most impossible odds it started and then sent forth large cloud of filthy black diesel smoke, which would have sent shock waves through even the most casual of armchair climate protestors. O'Shea eventually pulled away narrowly missing a passing vehicle as he did so, Jameson now followed at a discreet distance, with the journey terminating some two miles away at 'Boxing Gym 2000'. Jameson knew of the gym, but more importantly knew of its proprietor and owner. One 'Mr. Frank Swift' who was well known in the area and his brief resume read something like 'ex-boxer and title contender, local Drug dealer and all-round villain' but admittedly a smart one at that. He had been on the Police radar for years, but he was 'Teflon' coated as nothing they tried to pin on him would ever stick. They had raided the gym on more than one occasion but had always failed to find any incriminating evidence.

Swift was clever, he used a series of anonymous and impressionable young kids 'known as runners in his trade' to do his deliveries and collections. Maybe O'Shea was one of his 'runners' but that was unlikely as they were usually just impressionable young kids that didn't ask questions.' No' he quickly dismissed this thought in favour of O'Shea as the provider of Swift's 'heavy work' the roughing's up, the intimidation, after all he was certainly more than well equipped for the task. Jameson decided he had done enough digging for now as he had unearthed a possible 'jewel' in the case with the connection to Frank Swift. Hopefully this association alone would lead his superiors to sanction extra resources and an official visit to the 'gym', but he definitely wouldn't be going back alone.

Dave sat in his office at the gallery drinking a very fine single malt as a reward for clinching a multi thousand-pound deal on one of John's newly conceived Triptych's that had only been on display for some two weeks. These new works were Dave's idea and were a diversion from SPOOKZ's usual street inspired art. This latest financial triumph combined with 'Simon's' his 'smart' Lawyers confidence in smoothing over John's transgression with the law promised a brighter future than even Dave could ever have imagined. The warm intoxicating nectar glided easily down his throat and engendered a feeling of superiority and well-being. Smug and self-satisfied, he only wished he had found such an easy way to make amazing sums of money out of items that had no intrinsic value, as they usually consisted of one hundred pounds worth of quality artists canvas or unbelievably at times a 'tenner's worth of chipboard and twenty quid's worth of paint. As he relaxed contentedly with glass in hand, his mobile phone vibrated across the desk, he casually picked it up with his left hand. Dave felt he was on a roll, maybe it was yet another sale? Then glancing at the caller information, John's name appeared, he shook his head with dismay and thought, 'bloody hell, what now, just when things were on the up'. He reluctantly pressed 'answer', it wasn't worth ignoring the call, because given John's present state of mind he would continue to ring till Dave answered. He smiled down the phone and attempted to counteract John's usual level negativity before it began, 'Hi mate, glad you rang, great news, just sold another painting'. John completely ignored Dave's ebullience and as usual dispensed with all the normal pleasantries, 'the bastard's been here in my house, my fucking house, demanding money'. 'Wo, wo, steady on John, who? What are you talking about?' Replied Dave in abject disbelief. 'One of those goons that did Campbell over is trying to blackmail me'. John then started to ramble incoherently, 'ten grand, took ten grand, hit me, my head is messed up, and he wants more'. Dave's positive mood disappeared in a flash, he sank his scotch in one mouthful, then slammed his empty glass on the desk, 'you bloody idiot' he thought 'you really have screwed everything up this time'. Dave knew someone had to keep it together, he clenched his fist to steel himself, 'Look, just stay calm and listen to me, I'll make a few enquiries and get back to you'. John appeared in no mood to listen, and continued unabated 'you don't understand, he hurts people for pleasure and now he's after me'. John swept his hair back and was shocked as he stared at the blood that appeared on his hand, it had been Frank Swift's calling card. 'Is he there now?' No reply came, 'look just stay calm, leave it with me and I'll sort something, are you listening to me John?', silence greeted his request. Dave now panicking continued trying to get John's attention 'John, John, talk to me', he repeated in desperation, 'for goodness sake man, talk to me' silence also greeted this request. Eventually after what seemed like an eternity John in a pathetic and distracted voice uttered a single solitary reply, 'OK'. Dave needed to act quickly and took this opportunity to say, 'just sit tight man, I'll be in touch', he then ended the call. Dave poured another big scotch immediately after coming off the phone, he had thought long and hard about his own situation and the on-going uncertainty surrounding John. He had already devised his own 'escape plan' and it included the very best bespoke pension portfolio money could buy. He'd made sure 'he' was in the clear, there was no connection between him and John's bungled attempt to silence Ross. His patience was exhausted, and he knew that you can only give people advice so many times and if they didn't take it on board you had to just let them sink without a trace into their very own egotistical quicksand. John had squandered his chances, a mixture of greed, vindictiveness and a flawed sense of personal superiority was about to destroy his very comfortable life, but Dave was determined that it wouldn't engulf his world as well. He was well prepared, having moved most of his cash abroad, his Battersea flat and the gallery were rented, he had always avoided the temptation during his life to lay down any roots. He had lived his life in a plant pot, not in the borders and avoided anything that would tie him down or make life difficult, he was a nomad and an opportunist and now it was time to move on. How much money do you really need? Dave thought, he knew you could never get enough but sometimes money really wasn't everything, especially if the alternative was 'lodging' free of charge at Her Majesty's pleasure. He had the best part of two million pounds sterling stashed abroad and if he wanted to, could conduct his business on-line and let one of his 'assistants' run the show in the UK, and he could hide in the background as an absentee puppeteer. 'Yes', he thought, this was a possibility but realistically he'd had enough, it was time for a change, everything had a lifespan and the gallery's was fading fast. Not a reckless gambler, he'd decided to quit while ahead and was convinced that he'd almost single-handedly created this amazing level of success and knew that John was too temperamental to ever have made it happen on his own. Dave didn't see himself as a rat deserting a sinking ship, 'no' he was more of a lucky rodent about to step onto a luxury yacht.

O'Shea stood in the gym and with little effort was steadying a punchbag, as one of the young boxing protegees pounded away as though his life depended upon it. He hadn't told Frank about the visit from the detective, he didn't want him on his back as well. O'Shea had convinced himself that his off the cuff alibi for the night of Ross's attack had been a master stroke, 'yes', he said to himself, it was all sorted and life was good. However, the only fly in his ointment of contentment was his missing ID bracelet. If found it tied him to the scene of the attack, but his concern focused more on the fact that it was worth the best part of two thousand pounds as it weighed a good two troy ounces. It was his 'keeper' his fall back in hard times, it had been in and out of the pawn brokers over the years and had saved his 'bacon' on many occasions. The thought of some little 'toe-rag' cashing it in for its scrap value in some back-street pawnshop, made him grimace and hold the punchbag with such force, that the kid punching it couldn't make much of an impact. As he stood by the bag, Frank approached and put his hand on O'Shea's shoulder, 'loosen up, give the kid a break, are you OK man?' Said Frank as he looked at 'the big man', who seemed unusually tense and focused, O'Shea said nothing but nodded an affirmative acknowledgement to Frank's question. Momentarily he had thought about mentioning his visit from the Police, but something held him back, he hoped it would all blow over and Frank need never know, anyway he thought, he'd been pretty smart with his alibi, which had been by design suitably vague. As Frank turned, he patted O'Shea on the back and started to make his way towards his office, when the detective that had questioned O'Shea earlier that day appeared in the doorway of the gym with a plain clothes officer and a PC. 'Afternoon ladies' said Frank and he laughed out loud, but O'Shea didn't join in, 'bloody hell' he said under his breath, having just convinced himself he had nothing to worry about and now here was his nemesis, detective Jameson as large as life. 'Somebody parked a shopping trolley on a yellow line eh' said Frank still laughing, Jameson responded, 'I'm pleased you have a sense of humour, Mr. Swift', giving special emphasis to the name 'Swift', 'feel free to continue, but have you noticed your associate Mr. O'Shea isn't laughing, maybe that's because he's just landed himself and possibly you in a spot of bother'. Frank looked immediately at O'Shea, who stone faced just shook his head, the detective continued, 'your alibi, for the night of Ross Campbell's attack, well there's a big problem with it, the 'Brick Layers' was actually shut for refurbishment, so you are going to have to think again aren't you'. Frank's face showed no emotion but inside he was seething, as he thought 'Cosh you stupid git, what have you done'. He had told O'Shea to get a good alibi sorted, Frank was a master of bluff, he hid his surprise behind a mask of bluster and humour and continued to laugh, 'hey Cosh maybe you had one too many somewhere else that night you silly sod'. 'Perhaps you can help him', Jameson said as he looked in Frank's direction, 'was he with you Mr. Swift? Because I would like to know where you were on the night in question as well'. 'I dunno, people come into your place of work, you try to be friendly and then they start accusing you of something or other, it's a bit of a cheek don't you reckon Cosh,' said Frank. He then straightened up his menacing 6' 5" frame and pretended to square up in a boxing stance to the detectives. They instinctively stood back to protect themselves and he just laughed, 'bunch of tossers, go on, get out of my fucking gym and if you want something come back with a warrant,' said Frank. By now a small crowd of wannabee boxers had surrounded the officers, feeling intimidated and outnumbered, they eventually left the gym but not empty handed. O'Shea had been their target the moment they had set foot inside and Frank, to buy himself sometime persuaded Colm to 'play their game' and he would sort 'something'. O'Shea's substantial frame was duly squeezed into the back of their squad car. As he sat alone in the rear of the car, the detective turned around from the front and used the time-honored technique of trying to make the suspect believe he was in trouble, and more importantly he was 'very much' on his own. 'Swift won't lift a finger to help you Colm', Jameson's training had taught him to use the Christian name of a suspect, it was supposedly psychologically friendlier, as though you were somehow on their side. O'Shea didn't say a word, he just kept staring out of the car window. Jameson jabbed again, 'he'll hang you out to dry, Swift doesn't have 'mates', he has 'gophers', and you are all expendable, just bear that in mind, think about helping yourself that's all I'm saying'. Meanwhile Frank had returned to his office and slammed the door shut, the general chatter and sound of exercise became a muffled backdrop to his immediate and troublesome thoughts. Not accustomed to drinking during the day, Frank without thinking took out a bottle of Scotch from the bottom drawer of his desk which was comically labelled 'medicinal supplies'. He sank down into his chair and emptied the contents of his teacup in one gulp and then re-filled it with whisky. Not a man for rashness, sitting back in his chair taking a measured drink, 'alibi' he thought, nodding to himself, must get my alibi sorted, it was the key to everything. O 'Shea had blown it, the police were onto him, Frank consoled himself insomuch that he'd advised him to get a watertight alibi, but the 'big sod' had either been too lazy or too daft, thought Frank. It was now O'Shea's problem, his funeral, but he was sure that 'the big man' would keep him out of it, he wouldn't grass, that definitely wasn't an issue. This thought calmed Frank's mind a little, but he realised he could have a major problem of his own as he recalled, the 'bird' Frances the 'looker', in the Camden Wine bar. She'd agreed to give him an alibi but when he'd followed her, she had gone to what he now knew to be John's house, with hindsight this been too much of a coincidence and he didn't believe in them. Frank decided he would have to take the gamble, it was an alibi of sorts, he had her name and a phone number, even if she had set him up surely someone in the pub that night would recollect the boxing giant, it would be up to the Police to check it out, it wasn't perfect but lies never are he thought.

O'Shea had arrived at the Police station, and his hefty twenty-three and a half stone was bearing down upon a barely adequate wooden chair. Generally   regarded   as   something   of   a complimentary phrase for overweight people, but he did 'carry his weight well', he didn't look fat just 'well made'. In the interview room were two detectives, one constable and the obligatory recording device. Colm grumbled 'haven't you got any decent chairs, I've only got one arse cheek on this bloody thing', pointing at the chair as he stood up to straighten his aching back. 'You're in a Police station not a hotel or hadn't you noticed, you'll just have to put up with it', at this O 'Shea grabbed the chair with one hand and flung it across the room like a matchstick. The PC immediately moved towards him and attempted a form of restraint. Without any apparent effort O'Shea thrust the PC against the wall, he had one hand round the officer's throat, the detectives both tried to pull his hand away, but he was an immovable object. Detective Jameson then grabbed hold of O'Shea's forearm with both of his hands as one wouldn't fit around, he unsuccessfully attempted to release the choking grip, the other officer now put his arms around Colm's tree trunk like neck but couldn't even pull his head back. The PC pinned against the wall was now turning a dangerous and uncomfortable purple colour and gasping for air whilst making a strange gurgling sound. As the detective continued to wrestle with O'Shea's arm, he tore off part of the cuff and sleeve and staring him in the face was a Scorpion tattoo. Momentarily distracted the detective was now 'very much back in the room' as 'the big man' like a wild animal had his prey and was throttling the very life out of him. The officer now 'gambled' and let go of his ineffectual grip on O'Shea's arm and ran to the hallway and shouted for extra assistance, eventually two tasers were used to bring their adversary 'down'. The PC released, slid down the wall in slow motion, and came to rest almost unconscious, although badly shocked and winded he would recover. O'Shea was now in paroxysms of pain, writhing on the floor like a harpooned Whale, lashing out with his arms and legs in every direction. Everyone just stood back and one of the officers shouted 'let the bastard suffer' they waited till the tasers had numbed their prey, his large frame may have contained plenty of adrenalin, but it could only last for so long. Eventually with the assistance of six of the biggest PC's the station could muster, O'Shea was pinned down and eventually carted off to the cells to cool down. The detective was a little closer to his prize now having seen the tattoo, but the chances of getting anything out of him in the short term seemed extremely remote, especially given his current state of immobility. 'What can you do with someone that doesn't appear to fear anyone or anything' Jameson thought, he was ninety nine percent certain O'Shea was his man or at least one of them but he still had his suspicions about Frank

Swift's involvement, there was a connection somewhere, he just had to find it?

Detective Jameson sat and thought about O'Shea, if he couldn't get anywhere with him at present where could he go next? He remembered talking to the female detective some days earlier, about a suspect that had created some 'street art' nearby the scene of the attack. He particularly remembered how frustrated she had been and how incongruous the man's actions had been as he seemed to have plenty of money and the idea of him daubing graffiti on a derelict building seemed to make no sense whatsoever. The 'Scorpion' was the key, the man in question would probably be charged with some minor offence of trespass but he could be the missing link, this would be his next port of call. He knew the female PC by sight and had spoken to her on a few occasions in the station and decided there was no time like the present. The canteen was always a good place to find fellow officers and detectives, maybe buy her a cup of coffee and see if she could help fill in some of the blanks in his investigation. He went immediately to the canteen and felt the need for a good strong drink after the time he'd just spent with O'Shea, but black coffee would have to do for now. It was standing room only in the cafeteria, it seemed to be full of PC's some just off duty and others waiting to go 'on', he scanned the café looking for the female detective but couldn't see any sign of her. He wandered up and down the rows of tables glancing around and acknowledging some fellow colleagues, but she definitely wasn't in the canteen. However, he thought, all was not lost but merely on hold, after O'Shea's uncontrollable display of aggression they would keep him in custody for at least twenty-four hours and he knew there would be another opportunity to interview him again tomorrow. As he turned and walked, he disconsolately shoved the swing doors open with his foot and there she was, his missing PC stood there right in front of him. However, unusually his first thought wasn't his case but the fact that she was now in civvies and that she looked very attractive, her uniform certainly understated her looks. Pull yourself together man, he thought, slightly tongue tied he cleared his throat smiled and said, 'off duty now', she returned his smile and just said 'I've had a belly full of today, but what's new'. 'Hey, m..', he hesitated on hearing and seeing her frustration, 'I emm, know you're on your way home, and you're dying to get away, but can you just spare me a couple of minutes'. She looked at her watch, her smile had now disappeared and reluctantly she nodded and said, 'five minutes OK, my boyfriend is picking me up'. Well, he thought, that sort of answered one of his unrelated fantasy questions, not that he'd seriously thought about asking her for a date. 'Do you want to grab a quick coffee' he said, 'I can't, honestly, I really haven't got time,' she replied. Jameson needed to act quickly, 'well can we just sit in there', pointing to the canteen, 'OK then, no problem but as I say...', but before she could finish her sentence, he acknowledged her desire to go home, so he pushed the door open and pointed to a couple of now empty chairs near the door. As they sat down Jameson glanced at PC Angela Harrison, she looked tired, her eyes told a story of a long and frustrating day, he felt guilty asking her to stay on even just a minute longer than her shift. Jameson got straight to the point, 'I just wanted to pick your brains about that guy you had in the other week in the early hours of the morning for questioning'. Angela laughed, 'You'll have to narrow it down a bit more than that' it's been a long, long day'. Jameson quickly corrected the vagueness of his question, 'Sorry, yeah, I mean the bloke that came in late on, arrested for   trespass and ...', before he finished his sentence she responded, 'what an arsehole he was, assaulted a security guard'. The memory of John flooded her tired mind with adrenalin, as she spoke with a renewed vigor 'bit of a mystery that one, lived at a good address in Surrey, plenty of money, randomly caught defacing a building with graffiti'. Jameson responded, 'yeah I went out and saw the remnants of what he had done', did you get much out of him? I mean about why he'd done it,' said Jameson. 'Not really, he spent most of the interview just ranting and raving and alleging that he was beaten up by the security guards'. She continued,' and to be fair, he was in a bit of a state, knocked about I mean, but it was the security guard's word against his and no CCTV, so who do you believe?' 'Putting the assault aside, any clue at all, why he did it? Any previous' said Jameson. Harrison nodded, 'Yeah, we checked his records, he had a litany of offences for trespassing and anti-social behavior, predominately graffiti related but most of it was years ago, nothing recent until this'. The PC continued, 'I was intrigued about his address and questioned him about his employment history and all he would say was, 'artist'. Jameson laughed wryly and said, 'some artist with an address like that'. Angela now yawned, a wide contorted yawn, not intentionally showing her frustration and fatigue, but Jameson could see she was shattered, he'd been there himself on many occasions. PC Harrison now pushed back her chair and stood up, and brought their brief chat to an abrupt end, however Jameson had what he desired, another promising lead to follow.

Chapter Twenty
Aluminium Powder

'Uncoated aluminium in powder form can be explosive, and can be ignited by nothing more than a physical shock'

Silvery metallic grey

F rances sat at Ross's bedside just as she had done, day after day, after day, he seemed lost to the world, she had tried everything that recalled their past together, in an attempt to coax him out of his coma. Her early positivity was beginning to wane, it didn't matter what she said, it seemed to have no effect whatsoever, not even a glimmer of acknowledgement came from those 'closed' cool blue eyes of his. She gripped his hand and thought to herself, maybe this was it, this was as good as it would ever be, they were back together but they would never be 'together'. The sadness she now felt welled up inside her and tears rolled down her cheeks, she wiped them away with her sleeve and thought to herself, 'don't be so selfish you stupid woman', at least your alive and well, pull yourself together and   focus on Ross, come on don't give up. She released her grip on his hand and took out her phone and scanned it for recent calls, there weren't any, why would there be? It was a new phone and number, she was totally 'disconnected' from her former life. Inadvertently Frances pressed the Internet icon and a series of news items, music, sport, and entertainment scrolled up the screen. As she glanced at the headlines it all seemed so pointless, so meaningless given her present situation. Then one particular news item 'vacuum like' consumed all of her thoughts, *Lou Reed celebrates landmark birthday with a one-off concert*. Tears came again as she thought about 'their' song *Perfect day*, she sobbed uncontrollably as the song's lyrics unlocked her mind and a tidal wave of memories surged uncontrollably out. Along with the tears came an idea, it was Frances's eureka moment, she searched frantically on her phone for the song, but couldn't find it, however there was a *YouTube* video of an earlier performance by Lou Reed. She just wanted the song, but a video would do just as well. She tried to plug the headphones into her phone, struggling to find the hole for them and fumbling with excitement she dropped the phone and the headphones onto the floor, they disappeared under Ross's bed. She cursed her carelessness and got down on her hands and knees, frantically searching for them. Eventually holding them again, she took a deep breath and sat back on her seat. This time, she methodically plugged the headphones into position, loaded the video and then suddenly hesitated as she thought, this is it, it was 'now or never', if this didn't work, what else she could do? She froze with the phone in her hand, as a feeling of excitement and fear gripped her, then tentatively she pressed 'play' and then placed one plug in Ross's ear and the other one in hers. The slow start of the song always made the hairs on the back of her neck 'tingle', then an uncontrollable and powerful wave of emotion swept right through her. She stared intently at Ross's face, waiting for a reaction but nothing came, she clutched his hand so tightly it turned white with the intensity of her grip. Oblivious to everything around her she shouted, 'come on, come on Ross' as the song played, but still nothing, nothing, no sign, or recognition. She released her grip and slumped back in her chair, her ear plug now stretched to its extreme pulled out, and she just stared disconsolately at the bed. Now, although she couldn't hear it, the song now reached its chorus '*it's such a perfect day, I'm glad I spent it with you*' and a tear rolled down Ross's cheek. Frances saw the watery tear, it represented the first raindrop from the storm that ends a drought, her spirits soared, she grabbed his hand and squeezed tightly again, 'come back, come back, Ross' she shouted ignoring everything around her. A nurse passing down the corridor came immediately into the room on hearing the shouting, 'look, look' Frances yelled to the nurse, while at the same time she touched the single warm teardrop on his face. As the song progressed almost every word seemed to create a tear, Ross's eyelids flickered with life, the song had stirred the smoldering embers of his soul.

Frances was quickly surrounded by a flurry of activity, people were checking computer screens and cable connections, touching and prodding Ross. She left the room while the staff checked his recent and somewhat unexpected neurological activity. Standing in the hallway just outside, she tingled with anticipation and excitement, the very thing that had seemed impossible only minutes ago was now an almost unbelievable reality. Frances was desperate to tell everyone the good news, but her choices were somewhat limited, she had left John, Dave was indifferent and self-centered. Frances had only one real friend, now the 'Pink Flamingo' sprang to the forefront of her mind. Val hadn't been to the hospital for some time and Frances presumed she just couldn't face seeing Ross in his current state. She called Val on her mobile, the phone rang and rang, come on just pick it up she begged, there was no reply, her heart sank, she was desperate to tell her new friend the good news. Ringing immediately again, the phone rang and rang, but there was no reply, only a deathly silence. Frances returned to Ross's room, it now took on a whole new atmosphere, it seemed alive, rather than in its former state of cocoon like silence, the activity had died down and there was just one nurse and a doctor at Ross's bedside.

Frances couldn't stop herself, she went straight to the doctor, 'It's a miracle isn't it' she said to him. The doctor smiled but his medical reserve, 'the doctors guarded enthusiasm' came to the fore as he said, 'things have a habit of changing without warning' but these are encouraging signs, a connection between his coma and the 'real' world has taken place'. The doctor continued, 'I don't want you to get too excited', Frances interrupted' 'but it is good, isn't it?' The doctor smiled and now looked directly at her, 'yes, it is but let's just take things slowly and keep prodding his memory eh, these are encouraging signs'. Frances nodded and looked thoughtfully at the doctor, her head dropped slightly, he was probably right, but there was now some hope and that was all that mattered, she could return to her rented room, anonymous and unloved as it was, but at least now she had something to cling onto. Frances stayed as long as she could at the hospital and then decided to return to her bedsit and take stock of the day's events, something she viewed as nothing short of a miracle. On opening the door to her digs, shadows were her only welcome, she quickly turned on the lights and a dim yellow glow attempted to brighten up the depressing room with its faded curtains and threadbare carpet, but it was to no avail, as Frances had to admit that it looked better with the light off. The room, however, was of no importance, she felt energized and excited as she took out some early photographs of her, John, and Ross, most of which catalogued happier times, but maybe, just maybe, happier times now lay ahead again.

Not more than two miles away Val sat alone in the café, the lights had been turned off and in the dim glow of the approaching evening, a pale streetlight shone across the brown melamine tabletops, she had shut the café early not long after ignoring a call, not knowing it was from Frances. It was a call that could have changed everything for Val. She sat alone as normal after shutting up the shop, but today was different, her life was in turmoil. Now torn between family loyalties and a moral dilemma, as a result of an emotional conversation with her sister-in-law had left her in an almost impossible situation. Val couldn't believe it, just when things had seemingly changed for the better, here she was again, as usual in a mess, her life had always felt like that. Just when it seemed that the light was breaking through the gloom, the storm clouds of emotional attachment were gathering on the horizon. 'Blood was thicker than water' that's what she had always been told since she was little, maybe it was but it didn't make the final decision any easier. Her sister-in-law Barbara had never been the same since her husband, Val's eldest brother, had passed away at the untimely age of just forty-five, and in many respects if it hadn't been for her support, Barbara would have 'ended' it all years ago as she just couldn't cope. Val had coaxed and persuaded her not to give in and keep going, convincing her that things would get better, and she needed to get through it all for her young son. As it turned out Barbara had survived the seemingly never-ending emotional turmoil of her bereavement, but the solution had resulted in an undying devotion to her son, who was now her sole reason for living. A 'spoilt brat' that's how Val saw him, he had always been in trouble even when his father was alive, he was just one of those kids that attracted the 'wrong crowd'. After years on the dole, he had found a job as a Night watchman or as they termed them nowadays 'security personnel' and his life had seemingly turned the corner to a brighter future. Being recently married and his new wife now pregnant. What seemed almost impossible to imagine had propelled him and especially his mother towards a halcyon future or that's how it had seemed. Barbara had told Val that her son had admitted to her that he had given some trespasser a 'good kicking' after catching him spraying graffiti on the walls at the building site which he had been patrolling. Val knew this was serious, as he had a record for assault and if convicted again, would undoubtedly go to prison. Her sister-in- law was almost inconsolable, the old ghosts of despair and doom from her past had returned and she couldn't bear to see Barbara destroyed yet again. Val shook her head as tears came freely and without hesitation, how could it be possible that her nephew had attacked one of her best friends, she had immediately assumed it must be Ross and why wouldn't it be, all the limited facts she had in her possession pointed to it. Val reasoned it couldn't just be a coincidence that Ross had been found unconscious outside the very site at which her nephew worked. In a sympathetic and tear choked voice she repeated to herself 'Ross, Ross' and thought how could this have happened, it was just her luck, her usual 'damn luck', 'why me, why me' she shouted aloud. What should she do? What could she do? She was damned if she helped her sister-in-law and damned if she didn't. Ross had up to now been just an innocent bystander and her friend, now he presented a danger and if he returned to consciousness and escaped the confines of his coma, how long would it be before the Police would find out about her nephew, then what would happen? Maybe Ross wouldn't fully recover after all and the secret of his attacker may remain hidden from justice, her mind now raced with ideas and possibilities. Why her? Why now? She kept asking herself the same self-pitying questions. Her nephew had been nothing but trouble since his father died, part of her wanted to let him sink without a trace into the quicksand of guilt and pay for what he had done to Ross. If her son was sent to prison, Val knew Barbara would pay a heavy, possibly even a fatal emotional price and did she deserve to suffer all over again. No! Thought Val, she didn't, but what could she do? Val closed her eyes which blocked out the dim lifeless pale light but unfortunately didn't relieve her negative thoughts, she couldn't let go of her anguish not even for a single second. Val knew she had to think of a solution but who's side should she take? Who had most to lose? And more importantly would she be able to live with her chosen course of action? If life had taught Val anything, she knew that crying wouldn't fix the problem, now wiping the tears from her face in a defiant gesture with the back of her hand, which she then stared at, who did these wrinkled and worn old hands belong to. Val had known for years that when you didn't look in the mirror, life almost felt unchanged, but she had now viewed the irrefutable evidence that time had indeed marched on, it would be a long soul-searching night.

Frances awoke to a brighter morning than she had known for years, the sun was struggling to sneak between the chink in her bedroom curtains. Gleefully she allowed its presence into the room by throwing them back with such energetic enthusiasm that it disturbed and sent forth a shower of dust particles that glimmered jewel like in the early morning light. The view that greeted her was a dull and bleak looking block of red brick 1960's council flats with washing lines strung haphazardly between concrete balconies. However, today she didn't see their prosaic and uniform utility or downtrodden inhabitants, today they could be the most desirable art deco flats in London for all she cared. Frances had re-kindled her boundless enthusiasm for life, an energy, she thought had escaped from her body years ago, but it was back with a vengeance, and it felt good. She would get ready and even put on some makeup today. Then pay a visit to the shops and get some items for herself but also as a treat for Ross, now convinced he was coming back to her and that they would both celebrate together sometime soon.

Val had attempted to sleep the previous evening, but it had been impossible, the night was not only long but psychologically unbearable. She hadn't returned home last night, just couldn't motivate herself to move from the café. Instead, she had slept in her father's old armchair that was still in the back of the shop and had been since the early 1970's. The chair was a *Parker Knoll*, she had always thought it a funny name when younger, the thought raised a nostalgic half-smile on her face remembering how her mother always thought it was 'posh' as it had cost seven pounds three shillings and sixpence when new. She gazed at the thin polished wooden arms and faded upholstery, her father's presence was somehow in that chair, that's what she always thought when looking at it. Val stroked the smooth wooden arms, it always gave her a feeling of warmth and sense of comfort when things were difficult.

She had decided what to do, and had explored every possible avenue in her mind, most of which led to dead ends because it always came back to the same basic question 'Ross' or her 'nephew', and although she didn't care about the 'nephew' it was Barbara she was thinking of. With her mind befuddled and confused with tiredness, she had convinced herself that Ross, given the limited information she possessed, had been assaulted by her nephew and was now in a deep, seemingly inescapable coma, and was to all intense purposes already 'dead to the world'. Her memory now only recalled the images from those first few days in hospital, seeing Ross asleep and hearing the doctors saying, 'he may never wake up again', but that was days ago, she had to see for herself again. Val had to get to the hospital as soon as the visiting hours allowed, but as usual there was a problem, what if Frances was already there. She now remembered speaking to one of the nurses, Julie, she was sure that was her name, a young nurse straight from university, who had told Val to visit almost at any time. It was a long shot, but she had to take it, maybe it would be her one and only chance. Val would spend the rest of her morning just clock watching, she didn't have any of her usual zest for opening the café, let alone being polite with an ever-increasing hoard of 'young professionals' that came to her café. This new type of 'customer' somehow thought it 'cool' to frequent what had at one time been a poor but thriving area for the working-class Londoner. 'Stuff them' she thought, let them go to some High Street plastic café instead and buy a 'larteh' for 'stupid' money. Then spend three hours drinking it, while commandeering one of their tables for a change. As she sat, the room was silent save for the old *Westminster* clock ticking in the background, clunk clonk, clunk clonk, its monotony of accuracy was almost deafening in the small back room. Val had previously liked the clock, it had been her grandmothers but now it seemed like a ticking bomb counting down the seconds of her life.

Across town, little more than a mile away Frances was hitting the shops, she had the cash that Dave had given her, and was looking to spend. It was strange but pleasing, similar to when you first meet someone and want to buy them a special gift, a present that says, 'I really like you'. She found herself in a small old-fashioned chemist and scanned the shelves, 'mm... aftershave' she thought to herself, then stopped and realised that it had been nearly twenty years since she had bought Ross a bottle. She looked intently at the well-stocked shelves of toiletries and there it was *Cool water,* she picked the sample bottle up and sprayed a small amount on the inside of her wrist, its aroma instantly bringing back memories of their earlier years together. She smiled, picked up a box and was just about to make her way to the till when she suddenly thought to herself, 'what are you doing?'. You're still married to the man who Ross despised, what makes you think he would even want you back after all these years apart. She hesitated, clutching the aftershave, a woman behind the counter was watching her like a hawk, she glanced in her direction and the assistant just stared, making her feel like a shop lifter. 'Cheeky bitch' thought Frances, 'do I look that hard up, that I would steal a budget bottle like this'. The incident focused her mind again, her hand gripped the bottle tightly and she thought, well even if he doesn't want me back, I owe it to Ross, to be there and help him pull through, and after that 'then we will just have to see'. The official hospital visiting time was still some one and a half hours away, so Frances decided there was plenty of time to enjoy her shopping, something she hadn't done for a very long time. John had always manipulated and watched her every move whenever they went out, now she was in control and this 'freedom' represented a breath of fresh air, in what had become a stifling and suffocating 'existence' with John.

Val was now ready, well as ready as she would ever be, she had decided what to do and had to be at the hospital before Frances, otherwise what she intended to do would be impossible. Normally she would just take the bus, the 'twenty-seven' stopped just after the hospital, but today impatience drove her actions, she made her mind up and just wanted to get there and put an end to her torment. A torment that had begun the instant she had received the phone call from her sister-in-law the day before, although it felt much longer ago than that. She rang for a taxi, it would be there in ten minutes. Staring at the clock again, she knew that 'it' would all be over on her return, then she would see that damn '*Westminster*' clock again. It was a supposedly inanimate object but somehow it was strangely 'alive' and seemed to stare back at her from the mantlepiece, its 'tick' disapproving and judgmental. Before there was any more time for contemplation, a car horn tooted outside the café, the taxi was there, her stomach was churning with fear, her hands felt cold and clammy, her head was spinning with thoughts. 'Come on pull yourself together' she said aloud, then picked up her bag, opened the door and went to turn over the café sign but it already said 'CLOSED'. She pulled the door to, the lock snapped shut, it was an ominous 'sound' that seemed somehow final, but I will come back, surely, I will, won't I? She thought. Val knew things would never feel the same after today. Sitting in the back of the Taxi, the driver turned and said, 'morning love, hospital, is it?' Then he did his usual 'weather forecast' spiel followed by his latest diatribe on politics. Val nodded politely but made no attempt to engage with him, it was against her nature, normally she would be leading the conversation but today the pedestrians and the cars just flashed by as their drivers were swallowed up by a raging torrent of city traffic. The cab pulled up outside the hospital, the fare came to eleven pounds, she handed the cabbie a twenty-pound note, said 'thanks' without looking, got out and went straight into the building without even waiting for any change. The cabbie got out and shouted after her 'your change love', but she just walked on with a determined almost robotic stride, he just shook his head, got back in, and thought it must be his 'luck day' and drove off. Val was on autopilot, just as she had been throughout the journey, her mind was focused on finding a lift and the correct floor, her jangling nerves had receded but not gone completely. The physical actions of 'doing something' rather than just 'sitting and thinking' produced adrenalin, a human's natural source of power in times of great need. Val stepped out of the lift and looked through the 'crossword patterned' reinforced glass panes of the locked ward doors and could see straight up the hallway. She pressed the entry button and waited for someone on the other side to release the doors, it seemed like an eternity before anyone even noticed her presence. People looked in her direction but simply didn't seem to see her, ignoring her now frustrated attempts to enter by pressing the buzzer, eventually a passing anonymous hand appeared and pressed the release button, Val then stepped through into 'another world'. She was greeted by the usual array of abandoned trollies lying against the walls, nurses were coming and going, blue uniforms, brown uniforms, white uniforms, everyone graded in a supposedly equality driven world. The nurses went about their duties purposely not making eye contact with strangers, they had enough to do without additional questions from visitors. Val stood watching a large formidable looking woman in a brown uniform, who eventually approached and asked her 'what she wanted', it was a curt question to which Val replied, 'I've come to see Ross, sorry, I mean Mr. Campbell, I think he's in room 312', she attempted a smile, but it had no impact upon the granite faced member of staff. 'It's not visiting time yet for another hour' the woman tersely replied, 'I know but I err...', Val hesitated not knowing what to say, then to her relief, the young nurse that had said she could come almost anytime then approached. The nurse seemed senior to the woman in the brown uniform, she smiled and walked with her down the corridor in the direction of Ross's room. His door was closed, so she peered through the small viewing pane and could see him lying motionless on the bed, still in his enforced coma. 'Is it alright if I go in and just sit with him' said Val, 'of course, of course' replied the nurse, while at the same time reassuringly touching Val's arm and smiling, 'I'll just go in first and check everything is OK'. Val watched the nurse checking the tubes and cables attached to Ross, she couldn't be sure but strangely there now seemed far fewer than on her first visit. The nurse beckoned her into the room, and she sat beside his bed, 'I'll leave you to it' said the nurse, closing the door behind her as she left. Val looked around the sterile cream coloured room, there were no pictures, in fact 'nothing' to intrude upon its anonymity, its singularity of purpose. On the bedside cabinet was an array of unopened packets of tissues, sweets and a small, creased picture of Frances propped against a box, she looked so young, slim with long blonde hair, and barely out of her teens. Val looked at Ross lying with his eyes shut to the world, then again at the small insignificant photo, it struck a chord within her, here was a girl wanting to be part of his future, Frances could be the catalyst for a positive new beginning for him. Val's conscious, previously suppressed suddenly assumed prominence in her thoughts, could she really take this opportunity away from him? Standing up quietly and being careful to stop the feet of the chair screeching on the floor, she searched the room and found a spare pillow in a cupboard on the other side of his bed. She sat back on her chair with the pillow in her hands, it felt smooth and crisp as she stroked it, 'a pillow, a pillow' she thought, seemingly harmless but it could be a murder weapon, not brutal but soft and 'suffocating'. She looked at Ross then at the pillow, she had spent hours rehearsing and preparing herself for this moment and 'here' it was, 'here' she was. Now crying and thinking, could she really do this to a good friend, just to save her useless, selfish, troublesome nephew that had never done a good turn for anyone in his life. Now gripping the pillow, she thought 'yes', and besides Ross might never wake up again, maybe her actions would save him further suffering, then her conscious fought back, 'no, no' this is wrong, surely, he deserves a 'chance' unlike her waster of a nephew. Voices now befuddled her mind, she was drowning in words, 'the doctors saying he may never recover', 'her sister saying she couldn't go on', her mind was spinning but the moment was here, it was 'now or never', her heart was pounding, and her mind almost paralysed with confusion. She stared one final time at Ross, he lay still and serene, there were no visible signs of life, his eyes were closed to the world. Sobbing, she tried to convince herself yet again, 'I'm not taking a life, its already gone', now standing over Ross with the pillow in her hands, she froze. Val just couldn't do it and the pillow fell from her grasp, she cried uncontrollably at the hopelessness of the situation. Still sobbing, she touched his hand, then without warning Ross's eyelids blinked open and then closed with the speed of a camera shutter. Val eagerly leaned forward and touched Ross's face, he's alive, thank God, you're alive, it was a miracle, her prayers had been answered and they were both reprieved. Val now felt she had the strength to get her sister-in-law through whatever happened. She had done it before and even if the nephew was sent to prison, they could cope, they would have to 'survive' that's what life was all about. Still crying but now they were tears of joy, she picked up the pillow and pressed it to her own face and was suffocated by emotion. Suddenly she felt an arm around her, it was Frances, who bent down and hugged her. She didn't say anything at first but just held and comforted Val and then after what seemed like an age, Frances lowered the pillow down and away from Val's face. 'Hey, come on, Ross has come back to us, it's going to be OK, come on, please stop crying,' she said. 'I know, I know', replied Val, as she gratefully squeezed Frances's warm and comforting hand. To the outside world Val was desperate to see her friend well again and free of his coma, but unseen she had climbed out of an emotional chasm filled with guilt and her tears weren't just for Ross, there were just as much for herself. As she sat, still gripping Frances's fingers another hand touched both of theirs, they froze initially and stared at Ross, his eyes were now fully open, he was looking at both of them, they both excitedly held on to his tenuous return to life.

Frances without thinking bent down hugged and kissed him, Val gently touched Frances's shoulder, then stood back as she said, 'I think we had better call a nurse'. After almost half an hour of waiting in a nearby day room, they were allowed back in to see Ross, and although he was still lying down, his eyes were now open. They both sat at his bedside, he turned his head to look at them, Frances spoke first, Ross looked quizzically and smiled but didn't reply, he looked tired and confused. The doctor had told Val and Frances not to spend too long at his bedside, but the initial signs were promising even though he was disorientated and had no re-collection about what had happened to him or indeed why he was in hospital. 'My God' Val thought to herself, he couldn't remember a thing about his near fatal attack. Life was strange, maybe things do happen for an 'unknown' reason, as she could so easily have destroyed her life, Ross's and everyone connected to him, and it wouldn't have made the slightest difference. She felt an immense sense of relief but would always have to 'live' with the thought of what she might have done but was also determined to make it up to him in any way possible. Val could see that Frances and Ross needed time on their own, after all they had a lot to catch up on and the best way to help now was to leave them together.

Val relaxed for the first time in almost fourteen hours as she stepped out of the hospital, the smell of disinfectant started to fade as she walked out of the large revolving doors. The cold fresh winter air and the noise of the traffic was a welcome relief from the claustrophobic confines of the hospital. Inhaling a large breath of fresh air, it cleared and soothed her previously troubled mind, she felt focused and emboldened. She knew from past experience that you can only descend so far into the depths of despair before you have to climb towards the light, or you would be consumed by darkness. No isolation within a taxi was required for Val now, she rejoined 'real life' and boarded the number Twenty-Seven for the cafe, smiling again and even talking to an old woman on her journey home, who recalled her experiences as a clippie during the war, Val loved people, and a good old natter, that's how her life had always been. On arriving back, she stood and looked at the cafe which only the previous day she had considered selling, 'yes' unbelievably she now thought 'selling' what had been her family's literal 'bread and butter' for over seventy years, but not now, 'no', 'not now' she determinedly said to herself. On opening the front door, she was struck immediately by the silence that almost hurt her ears. Val needed to get going again, wanted to fill the café with lively chatter, smile again and bring some happiness to the lonely less fortunate souls that frequented her café. She walked through the shop and stood in the backroom where the previous night she had been on the edge of a psychological precipice, the '*Westminster*' ticked away with its usual ominous almost condemning tone, it consumed her attention in the silent room. 'That clock, that bloody clock' she thought, 'it watches and listens and almost seems to judge me', but not anymore. It may have been her grandmother's pride and joy, but she now hated its very existence. Taking three long strides to the mantel piece, she picked the clock up unceremoniously and it clanged with objection. Val then walked to the bin, pressed the pedal with her foot, the lid sprang open to attention and in it went face first, the lid closed slowly like a giant marine Clam consuming its prey and she felt a weight had immediately been lifted from her shoulders. Next, she threw the curtains open wide and sunlight gleefully painted the entire room a golden yellow, it brought warmth again to the cafe but more importantly to her life.

O'Shea had spent an uncomfortable two nights in the local police station and detective Jameson's superintendent had said they would have to release him without any 'hard' evidence, the police detention had all been based on Jameson's hunch and now that just wasn't enough. To make things worse there was also the chance that O'Shea would make a 'claim' against the Police for the use of the tasers as it could be argued that it had been an unnecessary use of force. The detective was dejected and felt that all his efforts seemed to have been for nothing. Sat at his desk he looked at O'Shea's belongings that were lying in front of him, they struggled to find a space amongst the stack of case files and empty coffee cups that cluttered his desk. The belongings were sealed into a zipped plastic bag tagged with O'Shea's name and date of birth. He opened the bag and tipped the contents onto his overcrowded desk, there was a roll of banknotes, he guessed about four to five hundred pounds, some small change and a lighter that had a coloured enamel image of the elusive and mysterious 'Scorpion'. Jameson handled the smooth chrome lighter, rolling it around in his hand, he stared at the image, that 'bloody creature' he thought, and knew it was the clue to the case, but it seemingly wasn't going to reveal itself. The other items included a state-of-the-art mobile phone, that seemed an expensive and somewhat incongruous piece of high-tech kit for one of Swifts foot soldiers. He viewed O'Shea as a rough and ready character, the detective didn't have him down as some sort of technology junkie, his interest was spiked yet again as he instinctively pressed the phones 'ON' button. The phones screen sprang to life and a topless girl looked back at him and a password prompt appeared across her ample bare chest. The detective shook his head 'bloody passwords, everyone's life seemed to be ruled by passwords these days' and he thought 'well that's it, yet another dead end', if he couldn't get into the phone, he knew his superiors were unlikely to spend time having it hacked. He was just about to put O'Shea's possessions back in the bag when he thought, what the hell 'and he typed in 'Scorpion' as the password, a message appeared *Password must consist of letters and numbers.* He shook his head in frustration, he laughed to himself and said 'think of a number, any number' he needed some magic but where would the inspiration come from. He sat back in his chair holding the phone and was just about to throw it back onto the desk, like the 'towel of submission' into a boxing ring, when he noticed O'Shea's DOB on the plastic bag. It was a long shot, he typed 'Scorpion1961', a momentary lapse, then a small icon whirred on the screen, he was just about to punch the air thinking he had 'cracked the code' but nothing happened apart from an audible taunting laugh 'Huh,Huh,Huh', if his day wasn't bad enough now even the 'bloody' phone was laughing at him .Undeterred he now typed in O'Shea's Army number on the end of 'Scorpion', then the number on its own, the phone laughed again at him 'Huh,Huh,Huh'. Jameson now knew this was a pointless waste of time, there was the proverbial 'needle in a haystack', but this was a needle in ten haystacks. Having been beaten by the phone and his own growing frustration, he threw it and watched as it spiraled almost in slow motion through the air towards a nearby desk. It landed awkwardly on its corner, the impact sprang the back off the phone and then a small neatly folded piece of paper popped out. He jumped up and grabbed the 'origami like' object and unfolded it to reveal the best thing that had happened to him all day, a single magical word written in blue biro 'tinbellies61', it appeared that O'Shea couldn't always remember his own password. Now Jameson would have the last laugh, he quickly reassembled the phone, typed in the password, no laughter came this time just a voice saying 'wotcha big fella', Jameson shouted aloud 'get in'. He didn't waste a second, the first port of call for him were the text messages, there were only a few, he scanned them quickly but there was nothing incriminating. He then looked in the 'media 'folder where he found a handful of videos off 'YouTube' which were mainly vintage boxing 'matches' or probably better named 'mismatches' as the few he viewed were all over within seconds of the start of the fight. He pushed his chair back from his desk stretched out his legs and exhaled a huge sigh of resignation, there's nothing here he thought, reconciled to defeat, they would just have to let him go. Four random videos were all O'Shea had on his phone, he had viewed three of them and thought he may as well see the last one, unlike the others it was an un-named video roughly twenty seconds long. Probably porn he thought, did he really want to know what the twisted mind of O'Shea liked? Curiosity then gained the better of him and instinctively he clicked on 'play'. The video was dark and grainy, probably shot at night, it seemed to be people arguing but poor-quality sound, muffled by wind noise made the voices indistinct but just audible enough. Looking intently, he saw two dark figures, Jameson almost squinted trying to make them out, he leaned forward watching with a renewed interest, the phone firmly held between his hands, he couldn't be certain, but one of the characters could be the massive 'bulk of a man' that was O'Shea. As the video progressed the 'cameraman' had stood back to gain a better shot, he then stared with utter disbelief as he watched 'the big man' land an almighty right-hand punch to the head of someone wearing a balaclava, the blow wouldn't have been out of place in the previous boxing videos he had seen. The force sent the balaclava wearing victim to the ground where the camera and the victim stayed motionless. A voice was then heard saying 'for fuck's sake Cosh', it was Swift's gruff, gravely unmistakable cockney accent, a little muffled but it was definitely him. Jameson immediately stood up and punched the air as he held the phone aloft with his left hand and shouted 'yes!' The few officers in the far corner of the room looked disapprovingly in his direction, one pointing to a phone he was currently using, 'sorry' Jameson said sheepishly but the moment was euphoric. Now it was all just a matter of time, O'Shea wouldn't be released after all and more importantly, he would soon be joined by his boss, the untouchable, well untouchable up to now, Mr. Frank Swift.

Chapter Twenty-One
Pozzuolana Red Earth

'Highly hydraulic Volcanic pumice from Umbria'

Light Bluish

It was now three days since Ross had awoken from his coma, he was sitting up in bed, Frances had been to see him without fail for every visiting hour available. Although he couldn't recall anything about the night of his attack, his earlier memories were intact. In fact, it was just like old times seeing Frances again, yes, there was the pain of their past break up, but he had, in his mind, forgiven her years ago. Should he tell her about his feelings for her now, then thought, what was the point, because as far as he knew, she was lost to him both geographically and matrimonially. Ross's negativity was, he soon discovered unjustified, as Frances said 'sorry' yet again, for what had happened between them and explained how painful her marriage had been over the years. Ross wasn't surprised, he knew what John was like and ultimately his greed had forced Ross into a final showdown where 'SPOOKZ's artwork became for him the physical embodiment of their historical rift and current confrontation. Ross still couldn't remember all the details of the night of his attack, the police had been to see and interview him, but he'd told them very little. He'd thought their questions were somewhat strange and couldn't make much sense of them. They had talked about a 'Scorpion tattoo' and some ex-squaddie who Ross thought could possibly have been one of the two thugs that had attacked him outside Val's café. That memory was as clear as a bell, the sight of 'O'Shea' not that he knew his name, had stuck in his mind, similar to that of seeing a rat on a beautiful summer's day. But quite how he'd come to be lying in the hospital was still something of a blank, a jumbled and incomplete jigsaw of memories that didn't quite fit together. The desperation and anger he'd felt before the near fatal incident that the Police kept asking him about had left his mind and soul, his body had used his amnesia to create a sense of wellbeing for him. As far as he was concerned, he had gone to sleep and woken up with the one thing he had always wanted, Frances, and now nothing else mattered. Now his feud with John was extinguished, just like a candle's flame caught in a draft, at first flickering, gasping for oxygen, then suddenly snuffed out by a gust of wind and now the aroma of candle wax and the drifting trail of smoke, represented the fading and lost memories that had initially fueled his anger. His mind was calm, but his body ached with the 'pain' of enforced inactivity, he struggled to pull himself up in his bed, the effort seemed out of all proportion to the meagre achievement of sitting almost upright. He asked a passing nurse if she could get him a mirror, the long-lost vanity of trying to look good for someone had returned to his life, he was eagerly waiting for today's visit from Frances. Just before he looked into the mirror, he imagined seeing his swarthy chiseled features but what greeted him didn't match his mind's eye, gaunt and much thinner than he could possibly remember, he shook his head in disbelief and thought who was this wreck of a 'stranger' staring back at him. Why would anyone, let alone Frances be interested in this, he almost felt like crying and wished he had never asked for that 'damn' mirror, but he knew it didn't lie, and the truth hurt. He disconsolately dropped the mirror down onto the bed clothes and pushed his open fingers through his hair, brushing his long fringe towards the back of his head. Before he had time to contemplate his less than what he considered attractive exterior, she was there at his bedside kissing him and holding his hand, the softness and warmth of Frances's long elegant fingers caressed Ross's palm and his feelings of inadequacy and desperation simply seemed to vanish. It had been many years since Ross had felt that 'thing', that indescribable 'thing' that people talked about, but no one seemed to quite understand called 'love'. Whatever it was, 'love' made everything feel alright even when it wasn't, it engendered an indescribable feeling of comfort and stimulation when someone 'special' connected with you in a way that was both physical and psychological.

For the first time in years Ross found himself in a 'good place', but it was confidence born from ignorance, he was recovering slowly from his attack, but the doctors hadn't mentioned anything to him yet, but there were worries with regard to his memory retention and recollection of facts. In a strange way O'Shea down at the Police station was suffering from a similar affliction. Sitting in the interview room once again, a detective now repeated yesterday's questions about the night of the attack. He just shook his head and said, 'how many times I gotta say it, you stupid or something? I was in the Pub'. 'I hear what you're saying but we can prove you weren't', replied the detective, 'you've got nothing on me, and we both know it' snapped back 'O'Shea. The detective had given him one last chance to come clean with him, 'OK then' the detective thought, if that's the way you want it. He then placed 'the' mobile phone on the table in front of them both, 'recognise that', he said defiantly. At which O'Shea shook his head and said 'dunno, why should I'. 'It's your phone, we took it from you when we brought you in' said the detective raising his voice and beginning to lose patience, without thinking O'Shea then replied 'yeah, OK it looks like mine, so what'. The detective then proceeded to attach the phone via a cable to a large TV screen in the corner of the room. Jameson then took over from the other detective and proceeded to switch the phone on, a mirror image of the phone's screen suddenly appeared on the forty-two-inch TV, then up came the buxom girl and the password protected prompt. Colm sat with a conceited grin, considering himself 'safe' as he saw the password protected warning, he laughed and said, 'just like you two', looking in the detective's direction 'a pair of big tits eh'. O'Shea's uncharacteristic level of confidence and humour was ill conceived, as his smile and smugness were immediately wiped from his face as Jameson proceeded to type in the correct password and gain access to the phone. He then navigated to the videos he had watched earlier, 'some good boxing matches on here but there's one in particular you might enjoy' said the detective as he loaded the late-night confrontation with Ross. Its quality didn't transfer too well to the 'big screen', but it was more than obvious what was happening. O'Shea watched with ambivalence but when he heard Frank call him by name, he just shook his head and looked down to the floor. 'Yes, it was a 'corking right hand', you nearly killed him,' said the detective. O'Shea now raised his head as he said, 'that little scroat, he's garbage, a junkie, why the fuck do you care about people like that, haven't you got anything better to do'. 'I'll take that as a confession then' said Jameson, 'yeah

I gave him a slap, so what' replied O'Shea aggressively. 'He's been in intensive care for nearly three weeks now, that's why we care, we want to stop 'your boss' letting his goons, that's means you, loose on the streets', said Jameson. O'Shea remained silent, the detective continued sensing victory, 'we know its Swift on there, you may as well admit it, why protect him, is it fear? O'Shea let out a deep laugh and shook his head as he said, 'people like you wouldn't understand' .The detective had read O'Shea's army record and knew all about his involvement in a smuggling racket, 'so are you going to keep quiet, just like you did in the army, get dumped on all over again, while the brains behind it all, like that officer in your regiment who walked away without even a slap on the wrist'. Jameson continued unabated, 'you're a mug Colm, a prize mug, your boss will drop you like a stone when he gets wind of this, but if you give us Swift, we can help you, there's a deal in this for you'. The army reference brought forth past and very painful memories for O'Shea, a significant nerve had been struck, as he replied, 'what sort of deal?'. Jameson had placed a hook in the water with a large amount of bait and 'the big man' was almost ready to snatch it. 'I can't promise you anything specific, but it will be mentioned in court that you were 'very cooperative', that's the best I can do'. O'Shea now looked at Jameson earnestly and replied, 'but how can I trust you?',

'you'll just have to take my word Colm, anyway what have you got to lose? O'Shea wasn't really a gambling man but recognised better than even odds, he had nothing to lose, whatever happened he would be 'sent down', he knew that. Now the memories of his 'misery' in solitary confinement in the army and his silence at the time came flooding back, his loyalty had counted for nothing in the end. His 'honour' amongst thieves had seen him drummed ignominiously out of his regiment and he alone had carried the 'can'. 'Yes', looking back he had been a mug, why do it again now, he thought, 'Ok then, what you wanna know', said O'Shea, with an air of resolve and resignation.

Within hours of O'Shea's capitulation, they had picked up Frank Swift from his gym, he was his usual confident self, always raised to his full height, he loved the feeling of superiority it gave him. Jameson would now have the pleasure of seeing Swift's face when they presented their evidence. As 'Big Frank' sat down in the interview room, Jameson looked at 'the ex-boxer' who was smiling, arrogant and seemingly in control, 'you smug bastard, I'll wipe that look off your face' he thought, but he would enjoy the cat and mouse game that would lead up to it. 'So come on then, let's have it, let's have your latest 'Hans Christian Anderson stuff, sorry I mean unfounded allegations don't I' said Frank laughing. 'All in good time' replied Jameson, pausing, and then eventually continuing, 'you know, life's funny isn't it, there you were, big title fight in Vegas, you must have done all right, money wise I mean, so how did you end up running some back street gym and flogging 'street shit' to no hopers and minor celebrities'. Frank just laughed and shook his head, as he countered, 'they're serious allegations officer, whatever your name is', he as usual appeared suitably unruffled. He sat back in the chair and just stared the detective straight in the eye 'it's all a bit 'old hat' isn't it, I've heard all this crap before, you've got nothing on me, I run a respectable business that offers kids a chance to be something'. 'Yeah, drug runners apparently', jibed Jameson. Frank simply smiled before saying, 'what would you know about real life, you're a plod, a shiney arsed nobody'. Swift continued, 'I've travelled the world, fought some big names, at least I'm a somebody', 'was Frank, was' interjected Jameson, 'now you're a nobody, just a two-bit drug dealer'. He was determined to try and rattle or at least get some sort of reaction from Swift, that was his usual interview technique, he saw it as a challenge, interrogation was all about unsettling the individual, tipping the equilibrium but Swift seemed too experienced to fall for it. Frank just shook his head and laughed, 'you're wasting my time, you've got nothing on me, and you know it, you're just fishing and unfortunately for you there's nothing to catch'. Condescendingly and mirroring Swifts insouciance Jameson tried another tack, 'OK then Frank, let's start again, where were you on the night of September 13ᵗʰ. Frank parried the question 'that' was weeks ago, how do you expect me to remember some sort of random date like that' he replied. The detective then came off the ropes and jabbed at Swift, 'all that boxing affected your long-term memory, eh, eh' he goaded, this time Frank didn't laugh, the sparring temporarily ceased, and he responded with a big right hand as he said, 'fuck you, you've got nothing on me'. The detective had connected with his target, Frank had lost his cool, now Jameson stepped up the pace with some well-directed body shots. 'The night of the 13ᵗʰ where were you?', 'I don't remember' said Frank, 'well, let me jog your memory, Mr. Ross Campbell was brutally attacked and left unconscious on that night, ring any bells'? Swift now attempted to regain his composure, metaphorically he stepped back from his opponents jabs and started sparring again, 'No, can't say that it does , I wouldn't be involved in some street brawl, all my fighting was in the ring' , the detective jabbed again , 'no I suppose you wouldn't, you'd just get one of your thugs to do it for you', his jab was followed by a looping right hand as he said 'someone like Colm O'Shea perhaps ?' The detective stared intently at Swift as O'Shea's name left his lips. Not a flicker came from Franks face, he just leaned back, and the blow didn't even make contact, 'he was good, the detective had to admit that, very good in fact'. Jameson continued jabbing, 'interesting character O'Shea isn't he, does he frighten you'? Frank smiled and shook his head slowly from side to side as he said, 'no one frightens me', 'well he isn't frightened of you either Frank, that could be a problem for you'. Thoughts now rushed through Frank's mind, Cosh wouldn't, would he? He wouldn't grass, grass on a mate, he tried to convince himself, but knew when the pressure was on, sometimes people do throw in the towel for an easy time and some sort of deal. Frank ignored the negativity now growing in his mind and counter attacked again with a thundering right hand of his own, it was he thought his killer blow, this would end the detective's growing bravado. 'What night did you say it was again,' said Frank. The detective repeated 'the 13th', 'not the date, what day was it' snapped Frank, 'Thursday' replied Jameson. 'Just remembered, I was on a date', said Frank. 'Really' said the detective and with sarcasm added, 'who was this lucky lady then'. 'Frances, but don't ask me her last name, I never ask their last names' said Frank laughing, 'convenient that, some random bit of skirt eh,' said Jameson. Frank continued 'That's not very nice is it, this was a classy bird', he then reeled off her mobile number, 'ring it, ask her, nice bit of stuff actually, well out of your league sonny'. Jameson took the blow squarely on the chin, his legs buckled with the big man's latest revelation, Swift seemed too self-assured, too confident for it not to be true. Now Frank was off the ropes and picking his shots from the centre of the ring. Jameson couldn't think, he needed a breather, he sounded the bell for the end of round one and left the room to stand in the corridor just outside the interview room. Now ringing the mobile number Swift had given him, he expected some chatty Essex female to answer the phone but there was no signal, no tone, no voice, in fact 'nothing'. Standing perplexed with his phone held down by his side he pondered his next move. He had Swift's dubious alibi that depended on some anonymous mobile number and was certain the backroom tekkies could trace its owner, he was certain it was a lie, but now he had to prove it. They could hold Swift for twenty-four hours if required, 'yes', he thought, I'll let him spend a few hours in a grotty cell, the stark change of environment and psychological deprivation sometimes paid dividends? Jameson left Swift to stew for nearly three hours in solitary, that's how long it had taken the tekkies to get the information he needed. Frances, full name Mrs. Frances Noble, resident of a good address in Surrey's stockbroker belt. She was it seemed in Franks parlance definitely a 'posh bird' and not short of a few bob. What if any, was her connection to Frank Swift, maybe she was a bored housewife with a lack lustre accountant husband, who liked a bit of rough, he'd seen that scenario before. The mobile phone company had provided the Police with the new number that she was now using. He rang the number from his desk phone, a slightly surprised atonic and confident girly voice answered, the detective said, 'Is that Mrs. Frances Noble', her voice hesitated as she replied tentatively 'mm yes, who's this?', 'Hi there, this is Detective Sergeant Jameson from the Metropolitan Police, would it be OK if I asked you a few questions'. Frances immediately panicked and said 'Is it John? What has he done?', 'John?' quizzed the detective, she hesitated and repeated the name again, 'John, my' she hesitated before saying, 'husband', 'no its nothing to do with your husband, it concerns someone who has given your name as an alibi for them'. 'Alibi, for what? Said Frances sounding confused. 'I can't say too much about the case' said Jameson, 'but it concerns a Mr. Frank Swift, who claims that he was', he hesitated, as an unpleasant image of Swift and this woman in the throes of some sordid liaison flashed through his mind, he quickly cleared his thoughts, and continued, 'he claims that he was out with you on Thursday evening, the 13th of September'. Frances froze on hearing Swifts name, she now recollected his call asking for her help, not long after John had gone off the rails. Did she tell the truth or simply deny it all, she hesitated, had anyone seen them together at the wine bar, did they have CCTV footage? Frances had never been a gambler, but things recently had started to go in her favour, she didn't want any more problems and decided to take a chance. 'Never heard of him, who is he?' She replied confidently, 'are you absolutely certain, just take your time' said Jameson, sensing more cracks appearing in Swift's defence. 'Yes, I'm certain, I'm a happily married woman' said Frances, she laughed to herself at the thought of her lies, but it suited her purpose, her voice now becoming defensive. She knew that Swift was mixed up with John in some way, to her they were both bad news and didn't owe either of them any form of loyalty whatsoever. Frances continued the pretense, 'I have never cheated on my husband', Jameson interjected, 'I wasn't suggesting that you mm ..., but before he could finish his sentence Frances cut in, 'anyway, who is this man? What has he done?' Jameson realised the conversation was now over, he had what he wanted. 'I'm sorry Mrs. Noble, I can't disclose any facts of the case, but I appreciate your time, if I need to contact you again can I get you on this number'. Frances simply said 'yes' and sighed with relief that he hadn't probed too deeply into her denial of Swift's alibi.

Jameson now felt he had the upper hand, and deliberately hadn't questioned the voracity of Mrs. Noble's reply, was she telling the truth? He wasn't certain. The phone call over he tried to imagine what she was like, she sounded about fifty, quite posh, why would this woman have been interested in a thug like Swift? Her absolute rebuttal of Swift's claims were a veritable concerto to his ears, he didn't have him yet, but sensed the end of the fight was looming, and it was Swift's turn to be back on the ropes. He immediately brought him back into the interview room, he seemed surprisingly unruffled, his daunting man mountain sized frame sat once again facing Jameson. Swift still sported a supercilious grin, and the irritating air of confidence and indifference that Jameson detested. Frank didn't waste a second, taking great pleasure as he said, 'so can I go now'. The detective pushed his chair back and smiled, he was going to enjoy this, 'well mmm...' he said and then paused, letting Swift think he had won before saying 'I've found your mystery lady, but you have a problem'. Jameson continued without pausing, Mrs. Frances Noble denies all knowledge of ever having met you'. The 'blow' rocked Swift, 'Noble' the name echoed in his head and suggested something he'd never been able to accept 'a coincidence'. Noble had started this whole affair and this woman with the same surname, could it be it his wife? Had he been set up by the pair of them? Sitting motionless, his mind raced with ideas as he silently contemplated his next move. Swift sat bolt upright and clenched one of his enormous fists and then rubbed his other hand over the top of it as he stared menacingly at the detective. The evil stare went straight to Jameson's core, it was frightening and psychologically disturbing and not for the first time did he feel uncomfortable in Swift's presence. 'I want to see my solicitor', said Swift, he then relaxed and sat back in his chair and folded his arms. He decided if found guilty, he wouldn't drop John into the mix, as he doubted there would be a 'deal to be had' in handing him over to the Police.   Noble was a 'nothing', 'a nobody', at worst Frank reckoned Noble would probably get a 'suspended sentence'. Swift decided it would be better to keep his 'Joker' out of the mix and perhaps organise the collection of a regular 'pay off' from him if he was 'sent down' and then continue to screw him for cash when he got out. 'Blackmail' was a dirty word, but it could also be a profitable one. Swift had seen Noble in his lair, he was a coward, 'yes', he had money and apparently lots of it, but no stomach for trouble and would represent an easy target for Frank in the future.

Later the following day Jameson decided to visit his 'key' witness Ross. The hospital had informed him that their patient was making 'good progress', and if possible, Jameson wanted his side of the story about the attack. The detective disliked visiting the hospital, the very smell of disinfectant made him almost wretch. He hated the never-ending round of washing hands, pressing buzzers to gain entry, the sight of so many unfortunate people, he wanted in and out as quickly as possible. As he walked down the corridor a tall, robust, and formidable looking nurse stopped him 'dead' in his tracks as she forcefully asked, 'do you want something' paused, then added 'it's not visiting hours yet, and we are rather busy'. On showing her his warrant card, his 'talisman' immediately softened her manner, with authority he now said, 'I'm here on official business, I've come to see Ross Campbell'. 'It's your lucky day, he's awake but still in his room' she said. As he approached the room, he popped his head around the door and there was his target sitting on the edge of a bed while an attractive looking woman in her mid to late forties helped him to put on some slippers, without saying a word he watched them intently. They were laughing as she struggled, 'you've got two left feet' she said, 'I don't even want them on, old man's things 'slippers' Ross replied laughing. He seemed to be enjoying the attention and fuss, it was obviously something he wasn't accustomed to. As Jameson entered the room, he announced his presence 'Hi Ross, I'm detective Jameson from the Metropolitan Police' he then flashed his warrant card as confirmation. Frances froze immediately on hearing his name, was it a coincidence? Possibly, but now panicking she just wanted to get out of the room. Jameson looking at Ross continued, 'I've been here before to see you, but you were...,' he hesitated, 'out of it' replied Ross, 'mm, yeah that about covers it' said the detective half smiling. Some elements of the attack had returned to Ross's memory, but he had kept the details to himself, he'd had dealings with the Police before and knew it was best to always say as little as possible and never 'offer' information unnecessarily. Why was this detective here? What had he done? They were Ross's first thoughts, that's what always sprang to his mind when the Police came calling. Ross was feeling more like his old self, still weak in body but his mind definitely felt sharper, and he was confident that the 'coma' could be used as a 'cover' for almost any eventuality, if he thought it necessary. 'I just wanted to ask you a couple of questions about the night we found you unconscious, that's if you feel up to it' said Jameson. Frances stood up, frowned and looked at Ross as she said, 'you still look tired, I think it's too much for you'. He responded with something akin to his old fervor, 'I'm not too bad, anyway what's a few questions, I'm OK honestly' Ross said whilst nodding assuredly and looking at Frances. 'I would appreciate your cooperation, it won't take long,' replied Jameson. Frances grasped her opportunity to escape, 'I'll go and get myself a cup of coffee and leave you to it' she said. Now turning away from Ross and looking at the detective, 'there's no need to go' said Jameson, he then probed 'Miss....? Frances ignored his question and replied, 'no, I don't mind, I think it's probably easier'. She kissed Ross on the cheek and promptly left the room. 'Girlfriend?' asked the detective, 'well' said Ross nodding, 'yes I think you could say that', 'I didn't catch her name' said Jameson, always gathering snippets of information. 'It's Fran, we go back along way' replied Ross, with the detectives mind firmly focused on gathering information to put Swift away, for once the name didn't immediately activate Jameson's radar like grasp and association of seemingly un-related facts. He pulled up one of the plastic stacking chairs and sat opposite Ross and then took out his notebook. 'Let's start at the beginning shall we', we found you lying unconscious outside a building site on Jubilee Road at 3.00 a.m., what were you doing there at that time of night?'. Ross's mind skipped immediately back to the night in question, the image of his breath escaping into the cold evening air came to his mind, he recalled the anticipation and anger that he had felt that night. 'I was on my way home' said Ross, Jameson was certainly in no mood for anymore bullshit, he'd had a rough time with Swift and any patience he might have had was well and truly exhausted. 'Come on Ross, that site isn't anywhere near your flat, was it about drugs? Were you running errands for Frank Swift? You don't need to be frightened, you can tell me, we've got Swift in custody,' said Jameson. 'Drugs' said Ross defensively, his momentary lightheartedness disappeared in a flash, 'drugs, why would it be about drugs? Never touched any of that stuff in my life'. 'OK then Ross', Jameson's tone changed radically from his initial friendly albeit official air. He wanted Swift and wasn't going to let some 'junkie' stand in his way, as he said, 'we found Cocaine on you in small 'dealer' sized plastic packets'. Jameson sat back and waited for a response, 'no way, I'm no fuckin dealer' retorted Ross. 'Come on Campbell, just level with me, it's all in the report and doesn't have to be a big deal for you or us, but we need to know who supplied it,' re-affirmed Jameson. 'Don't know what you're on about, I don't touch drugs' repeated an increasingly frustrated Ross. 'OK, OK then, so tell me why you were there at that time of night' replied Jameson. Ross fell silent, Jameson continued as he sensed cracks appearing in Ross's responses, 'look, we know all about your past brushes with the law, trespass, acts of vandalism, you've been at it for thirty years, come on, just tell me the truth'. Ross looked down at the floor, he was confused, if he had drugs on him someone must have 'planted' them, he immediately thought of the Police, 'bastards' he thought, they never change but why would they have done it? He was determined to stand his ground and repeated his earlier answer, 'I've already told you, on my way home'. Jameson now tried another tack, 'look, I'm trying to help you, someone carried out a vicious attack, you were lucky to survive, we want to put these people inside, come on, were you dealing for Swift and got caught up in a rival gang's area?' Ross just shook his head, and thought that nothing 'changes', now he seemed to be the 'accused' and no longer the 'victim'. 'Look Ross, we could turn a blind eye to the drugs we found on you, it's the people who supplied them and did this to you that we want'. Jameson was determined to get Frank Swift, and 'everyone' was expendable if they stood in his way. He continued pushing for the truth as he saw it, 'come on Ross, we have information about the people who we believe did this to you, we just need some corroborating evidence to clinch it, let's put aside why you were there and concentrate for now on what happened'. Ross could still see in flashbacks the looming figures of the two men that attacked him, he remembered them from the café when they had almost toppled him from his ladders. He knew that the people who attacked him would have contacts, he also knew how they worked, you didn't give evidence on these sort of people, they never go away, and would make you pay one way or another if you 'grassed'. 'I can't remember', said Ross feigning amnesia, now falling silent he looked at Jameson before continuing,' Look I remember being there, it was cold, so bloody cold, next thing I was here in hospital, in the warm, the incident is a complete blank'. Jameson shook his head in frustration, not believing a word Ross had said, he couldn't prove it, but he knew this character was either lying or more likely frightened. Jameson continued, 'you must remember something, how many people attacked you? There must be something, something you can tell us. Ross shook his head again in denial as he said, 'I've told you, I was on my way home, I can't remember anything else', he then put his head in his hands, if this feigned display of desperation didn't work then nothing would he thought. 'Are you OK? Just take your time,' said Jameson, who was now convinced Campbell was holding back the truth. 'I'm tired, I just can't remember, what's wrong with me' said Ross, his voice muffled as it fought to escape from behind his hands. He remained bent over with his face partially hidden, 'I need some time, more time, I just can't think,' he said. The nurse that had stopped Jameson on his arrival in the ward now hovered in the doorway, she'd heard their conversation and now came to Ross's rescue, 'I think that's enough for today, don't you officer'. Jameson held his hand up towards the nurse without even having the courtesy to look at her, 'OK, OK, we'll leave it here for now, I'll be back in a day or two and we can continue with this', said Jameson, who then rose to his feet and put his notebook in his inside pocket, he was frustrated, he wanted Swift, and wasn't going to let this lying 'no hoper' stand in his way.

As Frances walked back down the corridor towards Ross's room, she saw the detective coming towards her. She panicked again, turned away from Jameson and as a distraction stopped a nurse and asked her where she could get a glass of water from, to her relief the detective walked silently past. Frances entered Ross's room, without saying a word, she could see his mood had changed, the lighthearted contentment she'd experienced with him just moments earlier had vanished, he sat on the end of the bed staring blankly towards the window. Frances looked at him and said, 'what's wrong?', 'he shook his head slowly from side to side, as he said 'same old shit, nothing changes'. Frances put her hand on his shoulder while saying, 'come on, please tell me, what's happened'. 'Nothing, nothing' Ross said in a defiant tone, 'come on' Frances said, now almost begging, 'please tell me, I need to know, I want to know, don't shut me out again'. Ross had spent so long on his own, he was used to withdrawing and bottling his feelings up. 'I'm sorry' he said and turned and looked at Frances,' it's nothing you've done, that copper that was here, he was asking questions about the attack, he said, they found drugs in my coat, I've never been involved with drugs, you know that'. Frances looked at him, and suddenly felt guilty as a negative thought flashed through her mind, 'maybe he was on drugs now, after all she hadn't seen him for years'. She fought the negativity her mind had generated, 'pull yourself together' she thought, 'No!' Ross wouldn't do anything like that, she had to support him, because without unequivocal trust there would be no future for them. Ross continued, 'I think they're using me as an excuse to put the people 'away' that attacked me'. Frances interrupted, 'but you don't know who did it?' she hesitated, bent down and looked him straight in the eye, and with a more forceful tone said,' do you? Ross remained silent, Frances shook her head, 'you do, don't you, why don't you want to tell them'? 'I can't, I just can't, the bastards that did this to me, make people disappear'. He continued without pausing, 'I want to start again Fran and not be looking over my shoulder all the time, what sort of life would that be, I need to leave all of this behind me'. Ross then attempted to stand up, but his weak legs could barely even support his thin pain wracked frame, he managed to stand momentarily but then collapsed back helpless onto the bed. 'Fuck' he said choking back tears, 'it doesn't matter what I do, there's no escape for people like me, is there? Burnt out street punk, a nobody, a junkie, that's what that copper thinks'. Frances got hold of Ross's hand and squeezed it tightly, saying, 'you're a good man Ross, you can do anything, you just need to believe in yourself'. Still looking frustrated and dejected, Frances put her arm round him and said, 'there is a way we can escape, we can just go', we've got no ties'. 'Go! But go where?' said Ross, Frances looked directly into his eyes, kissed him, then said 'abroad, somewhere, anywhere, does it really matter, let's just go, there's nothing keeping us here'. She continued sensing this was the moment, 'I told you about John and me, the failed marriage, it's all over, it was before it even started, let's just go, go and start again, please, please let's do it'. Ross looked at Frances, everything he ever wanted was right here beside him, and now her tenderness and loyalty had touched his soul. 'But do you think we can really do it?', 'I mean just leave all this behind' said Ross, 'why not, we have each other, what else matters, no-one knows anything for sure, it's the promise and chance of something that's makes trying worthwhile' replied Frances. 'God, you make it sound so simple, can it be that easy? said Ross with tears appearing in his eyes again. Frances was just about to embrace him when a doctor and a nurse came suddenly and unannounced into the room. The doctor looked at them both and said, 'we need to do some tests, check everything is OK', he smiled at Frances and said, 'you can wait outside, it shouldn't take long'. Frances hesitated and said, 'I'll.... err', she then paused, 'come back later, there's something I need to do', now kissing Ross, she whispered in his ear, 'I've got a plan'.

Chapter Twenty-Two
Chrome Orange

'Said to be lightfast but may darken by
atmospheric Sulphates'

Bright intense Yellow through to reddish Orange

Frances's attention was solely focused on 'their' escape plan, she walked out of the hospital almost in a trance and stepped out into the cold winter air. Her ideas were still something of a jigsaw of possibilities that didn't yet fit comfortably together. Unfettered and fresh cold air, now, druglike, rushed into and around her body, her mind raced with anticipation. Top of her list, although she didn't want it to be, was to return to her former marital home one more time and recover some of the authentic jewellery she had forgotten in her initial rush to get out and away from John. It wasn't for wearing, it was all to be sold to raise cash for the escape fund. Knowing she hadn't possessed the confidence to have done this a week ago, now emboldened, she felt able to confront John, that's if he were sober enough to talk. She would take a taxi and would hopefully be in and out in a flash and would just ask the driver to wait, it wouldn't be cheap, probably eighty pounds each way, but it had to be done even though she knew every single penny was vital. The taxi journey was a blur, she gazed out of the window and saw nothing but her internal thoughts. As the taxi neared the house, she asked the driver to stop in a layby some two hundred yards away, saying, 'I won't be long' and hoped she wouldn't. Her ideal scenario would be an empty house where she could just get in, take the jewellery, and make her escape like a 'first rate' burglar. As Frances stood between the large imposing pillars at the entrance to the drive, she noticed that one of the lions that usually stood proudly on top was missing, it was strange and she wondered if it was an omen, but there was no time for such apocryphal semantics. A small piece of her was excited but the bigger part was terrified at not knowing what to expect inside. Staring at the house she had once called her 'home', memories, some good but mainly painful ones flashed through her mind, but it had to be done, there was no turning back. Moving tentatively down the gravel drive she scanned the house and grounds looking for any signs of life. On approaching the front of the house, she saw John's white Range Rover parked awkwardly with the rear wheels on the drive and the front wheels partly buried in a neighboring flower bed. Her heart sank, as 'he' would undoubtedly be in, she didn't want to admit it to herself, but this was her worst fear. She wasn't frightened of John, 'yes', he had a temper but had never hit her, but he was irascible and indignant, in a nutshell, a consummate all round 'pain in the arse'. Frances fumbled in her purse and took out the front door key then pushed it into the lock as quietly as possible, the large wooden entrance door was prone to swelling and jamming in damp weather. A firm push would be required to get it open, it was impossible to do it silently, she narrowed her eyes while pushing against the formidable oak paneled door, in the vain attempt that this action could possibly decrease the noise. She gingerly stepped inside but didn't close the door for fear of creating even more noise, leaving it temporarily on its latch. Now standing motionless she listened intently for any signs of life, instinctively her eyes were drawn to John's study, perhaps he was in there 'out of his mind' as usual or just sleeping off another hangover, either way that scenario would make her task a lot easier. The jewellery was upstairs, hidden in the bottom of her wardrobe, as she crept silently towards the stairs, a noise came from the kitchen, it sounded like a cupboard closing. She realised it was no good and would have to face her nemesis, turning away from the stairs she moved back towards the noise. The kitchen door was ajar, she tentatively pushed it open with her foot and was just about to say 'heavy night was it' but there was no sign of John just an attractive young female. Partly clad in one of his shirts, she sat cross legged on a bar stool eating toast. Frances gawped open-mouthed in shock and amazement, it was Natalie, Dave's 'assistant' from the gallery, sitting in 'her' kitchen looking like she owned the place. It was the age-old scenario that you thought you knew exactly what you would find, she expected John hungover and unshaven, with dirty unwashed plates filling the sink and take-away cartons strewn around. However, life always had the habit of distorting the vision you expected. Frances was initially speechless as Natalie turned and looked her up and down with an indignant stare. With her mouth half full of toast, she fought for control of her words as she said, 'John's upstairs, he said 'you' would turn up sooner or later', she then continued with her breakfast and turned away. Frances thought you 'cheeky cow' and in her mind she was running over to Natalie and dragging her off the bar stool by her hair and throwing her out of the front door, but being pragmatic, she realised this unexpected 'presence' could make things so much easier. She turned without saying a word and made her way across the hall and started climbing the stairs totally oblivious to the clattering sound her shoes made. She made her way to 'their' former bedroom, the door was wide open, she was about to walk straight in, then hesitated and put her head around the door to see if John was there. There was no sign but then she heard him, singing in the shower, if you could call it that, she thought. It suited her purpose though, now deftly moving towards her wardrobe she opened the door and pushed her hand underneath a pile of neatly folder jumpers and felt around expecting to find her 'hidden' jewellery box. Her hand swept across the smooth pine drawer base but there was nothing, she couldn't feel a thing, confused she tried again, but there was nothing, nothing. In desperation she pulled out the jumpers and threw them on the floor and then started to search all the other drawers. Now facing away from the en-suite bathroom she was unaware of John's presence behind her, as he said 'well, well', she turned around and there he was standing with a towel wrapped around his generous midriff, while water dripped from him onto the carpet. 'They've gone, I knew you would come back for them', he said smugly, 'I want them, they're mine,' shouted Frances. 'Yours, yours, hell as like they are, I bought you those and just remember you walked out, I've taken them back, they're mine now'. Frances retaliated 'You really are a sad little man aren't you, trying to impress that 'vacuous' piece of skirt downstairs are you'. 'Oh, you've met Nat, have you! Actually, she's got a double first in Economics and Business management, your just jealous, and what's more she's got twenty good years on you, no on second thoughts, make that twenty-five'. 'Stuff you, she's still a tart, I hope she takes you to the cleaners, do you share her with Dave, is she the gallery's new bike! It didn't take

469

you long did it,' snapped Frances. She stood looking at John and all she saw was a flabby 'washed-up' waste of space and then thought about what he had done to Ross all those years ago, supposedly his best friend. 'Does Dave know about 'Natty' then', she said sarcastically, 'You mean Mr. forty percent, the thieving bastard, he's gone, run off with his stash of my hard work' barked John. Frances was shocked and surprised to hear that Dave had gone, she could hardly believe it, 'but why? She asked, 'couldn't take the pressure could he, he's all mouth, just a puppet salesman' replied John. Frances knew this was all nonsense, this was just John feeling sorry for himself, as usual if anything untoward happened in his life it was always someone else's fault. She knew exactly what Dave was like, he had the confidence and determination that John could only ever dream about. If he had gone, and John, for once in his life, was telling the truth, then something catastrophic was looming, because Dave was always one step ahead of the game. Now Frances didn't care what happened to John and returned to her main reason for entering the 'Lion's den' as she saw it, 'I want my jewellery'. 'I haven't got it' snapped John', 'John don't mess me about its mine, just give it to me and I'll be gone' Frances said, now almost pleading. John simply shook his head and said, 'no way, forget it, it's not going to happen'. Frances began to lose her temper and self-control as she shouted 'Ross and I need...' she stopped in mid-sentence, but it was too late. John shook his head and laughed ironically 'that loser, that fucking loser, I might have known it, you just couldn't stay away from him could you, they should have finished him off'. 'What do you mean! Who should have finished him off, what are you talking about'? yelled Frances. She rushed forward and tried to slap John across the face, but he was too quick and simply pushed her aside with little effort. Now holding back tears with her growing anger, she shouted 'you know what happened to Ross don't you, you selfish bastard, twenty years on and you still can't let go of your jealousy and bitterness'. She continued unabated 'You got me, you got what you wanted, it was my fault remember not Ross's, that night, that bloody night, I wished so many times that it had never happened'. John had a smug expression and laughed, before saying, nodding as he did so, 'if only you knew', and continued to laugh. Frances was confused, what did he mean, why was this so funny to him, before she could reply John started again, 'You walked out on me remember, I didn't ask you to leave, you left me, so don't expect anything, you're lucky your clothes are still here, I was going to throw them out, go on, take them and get out'. 'Stuff the clothes, anyway you chose most of them, probably suit that tart downstairs, I just want my jewellery' Frances said again, 'it's mine, just give it to me'. 'Don't you listen' shouted John, 'I told you, it's gone, and if you thought I would give you anything to help you with 'lover boy' you must think I'm stupid, he tried to mess with me and my work and now he's paid the price, you're on your own now 'love', he exaggerated the word 'love'. Just as Frances was about to have another 'go', Natalie entered the room, pushed past her, and stood beside John, she stroked his arm with her hand, as she said, 'are you OK love'. 'Yeah, just fine', and staring at Frances, he added defiantly 'I think we're finished, don't you'? Frances suddenly felt an additional surge of anger, she was a volcano ready to erupt, the sight of them together was more than she could bear and without even thinking, turned around, picked up an alarm clock from the bedside table and threw it at John. He attempted to parry it away, but it caught him on the side of the head and instantly drew blood. 'Bitch, you stupid fuckin bitch', he shouted while wiping the freshly drawn blood away with the back of his hand. He immediately lunged forward raising his hand intending to strike Frances. Natalie quickly stepped in front of him barring his path, while saying, 'it's not worth it John, look at her, she's pathetic'. With Natalie's seemingly genuine support he stepped back, 'You're so right' he said, now with his hand stemming the flow of blood from his wound he shouted, 'go on, get out, before I throw you out'.

Frances turned and walked out of the bedroom without saying another word. She descended the stairs with haste and made directly for the front door and was just about to step outside when she caught sight of John's gleaming wristwatch on the hall table. The watch shone like a beacon in the dimly lit hallway, a limited-edition Rolex, she remembered how obsessed he'd been with it and had talked about nothing else when he first bought it. Worth at least thirty thousand pounds, it was enough to start a new life, she stared at it and hesitated momentarily, then snatched it up and slammed the front door and made her way back to the waiting taxi. Frances sat in the back of the taxi, her heart was still racing and powering adrenalin around her body. Opening her hand, she stared at the gleaming eighteen carat gold Rolex and admired its measured sweeping second hand with its calmness and perfection. It seemed to both mesmerise and soothe her, but unfortunately couldn't erase her middle-class sensibilities about theft. Frances thought about how low she had sunk, this is what John had reduced her to, had she taken it out of spite? Or was it purely for the money? In truth she knew it was a mixture of both. She stared again at the watch and shook her head, just as she had done when he'd bought it, the incongruity that such a small item could be worth so much money, it's value represented the cost of a small, terraced house in some of the poorer parts of the UK, it was consumerism gone mad but for now it could supply a precious 'lifeline' for herself and Ross. On her return to London, she paid the taxi driver for her 'little' round trip which had cost more than she had imagined, nearly two hundred 'escape fund' pounds. Now counting the remaining cash that Dave had given her, she had a little over seven hundred pounds left and knew that wouldn't last long and decided to sell the precious timepiece before John realised it was missing. Frances knew that most of the pawn brokers and secondhand jewelers had CCTV so decided to do her best to change her appearance before visiting any of them. She tied up her hair put on some dark glasses but when she saw herself reflection in a shop window decided it made her look even more suspicious not less, she laughed, and a nervous uncomfortable crazy sound came out that seemed to mock her and what she was doing. Taking a deep breath, she undid her hair and let it cascade down again and removed the sunglasses, at least now she thought, I don't look like a criminal. She would just take her chance, what was there to lose, now it really felt like all or nothing. Frances had seen a small backstreet pawnbroker about two streets from her B and B accommodation. It was probably her best chance as it offered anonymity drawn from location and size. She walked the short distance to the shop and looked from across the road at its shabby facade, with paint peeling almost artistically from an old grey and gold hand painted sign that proudly proclaimed, 'T.J. O'Rourke and sons, Purveyors of Fine Quality Jewellery Est. 1910'. After her brief period of calm, her heart started pounding again, her mouth felt dry, she stepped forward and off the pavement then back onto it, 'I can't do this' she thought and stood motionless. Putting her hand in her coat pocket she immediately felt the watch and then thought about Ross in the hospital and John now shacked up with 'Natty', and her resolve returned, she stepped off the pavement again and walked without hesitation towards the shop. To prepare herself, she pretended to be looking in the window at some of the items 'for sale' but was actually trying to see who was behind the shop counter, and hoped it was someone old and kindly that wouldn't ask too many questions, but unfortunately, she couldn't see the proprietor. It was no good, she just had to do it, and pushed open the door. An electric buzzer sounded immediately as she entered the shop. She stood in front of a glass topped counter that contained a wide assortment of expensive but ostentatious gold jewellery, there were large knuckle duster sized 'keeper' rings and enormous looped necklaces which were an ideal choice of 'investment' for the 'street entrepreneur' with more than his fair share of 'rainy days'. Suddenly, a man in his early thirties came from behind a red velvet curtain at the back of the shop, he was tall, well dressed and had the now omnipresent 'designer stubble' for his age group. 'Hello' he said cheerfully, 'anything catch your eye?' Hi, mm.., no, not really, don't get me wrong you've got some nice things...', lied Frances, she hesitated before continuing 'actually I err... want to sell something', she then placed the watch on the counter. The man nodded at the sight of the watch 'Nice, very nice' he exclaimed, 'do you mind if I..' he motioned to pick it up. Frances, her mouth still dry with fear, just nodded her agreement. The young man picked it up and immediately tried it on his wrist, Frances thought how rude and presumptuous but didn't comment. 'Expensive looking watch, but is it real?' he said, Frances was speechless, the man could sense that his joke had missed the mark as he quickly said, 'only joking, no offence intended but I will have to take the back off and check it, there's a lot of good fakes about'. He meticulously placed a velvet covered board on the counter and proceeded to use a small clamp like device to remove the Rolex's back plate. Then, seemingly oblivious to Frances's presence he stopped talking and carefully scrutinised the watch with his jewellers' loop, now clamped to his eye like a limpet. Eventually after what seemed like an eternity, he placed the watch on the counter and replaced the back, nodded, and said, 'seems OK, how much do you want for it?'. Frances without hesitation replied, 'as much as I can get', the man smiled wryly and then responded with his 'get out clause' to offer as little as possible, 'have you got its original box and papers'. Frances's heart sank, the hammer blow of reality now struck home, she shook her head, 'then you're looking at nine grand,' he said. 'Nine, nine', Frances repeated with incredulity now flooding her mind, and then said, 'but it cost more than four times that'. The man sensing her desperation drove home his advantage, 'OK then, fifteen if you bring the box and papers and I will also need a verifiable name and address'. He looked knowingly at Frances as he added this small but devastating and crucial caveat. Next came his sucker punch as he said, 'look I tell you what, you're a nice lady, I'll stretch it to, ten, cash, without any details required'. He knew that people only sold watches and jewellery of this quality when they were desperate and had limited or no other options. The buyer always had the upper hand, that was how he ran a successful business, he placed his immaculate manicured hands on the counter either side of the watch, and looked at Frances, waiting for a response. She needed more and wasn't going to give in easily, and replied 'twelve, I'll take twelve', he looked at her and then shook his head 'tell you what, eleven and that's my final offer, take it or leave it', he then lifted the watch off the protective velvet cloth and placed it on the glass topped counter. Frances had no choice, she knew that, and unfortunately for her, he did as well, she really wanted to tell him to 'get stuffed' and walk out but couldn't. 'OK then', I'll take it, said Frances reluctantly, smugly, he smiled and immediately put the watch onto his wrist and looked proudly at its sweeping seconds hand and stylish face, Christmas had come early.

Frances walked out of the jewellers' with a 'wad' of used banknotes in her coat pocket, they had a grubby and slightly seedy feel to them. She was surprised at how large a parcel of used twenty-pound notes could be, keeping her hand in the coat pocket, she resolved to herself that no one was going to steal from her again. Feeling confident and now on a 'roll', without hesitation she resolved to complete the next part of her plan. In the hospital Ross had asked Frances to get him some clothes and items that he needed from his flat, the most important being his beloved talisman the vintage 'Nikon'. He had given Frances the key to the padlock that the council had fitted to his broken front door. It was strange but the flat was only a short walk from where she was currently staying, two people, whose lives had been intertwined for years were no more than a stone's throw apart and neither of them knew, now fate had brought them together. Frances couldn't decide whether to go via her B+B, maybe get changed and hide the money, but she was excited, her adrenalin was racing and on a high, 'no' she thought, 'I'll go now and get it over with'. She had Ross's address scribbled on a small scrap of paper and had a rough idea where it was and would follow her own inbuilt sat nav. Which consisted of a hazy collection of street names and locations recalled from her younger days spent in London. After walking purposefully at first, she soon became lost and disorientated. Standing and gazing at 'towering' blocks of 1960's grey, anonymous concrete council flats, no doubt they had been a developers and architects dream in their day she thought, but now they represented the epitome of social despair and urban decay. Confused, she looked at the scribbled address again, she was sure it was the right area, but which block was it? Her head spun and swam with confusion as she turned through a full three hundred and sixty degrees, all the 'dinosaur' like flats looked the same. Suddenly a lifeline appeared in the form of a slightly stooped old woman dressed in a head scarf, she wore a tatty long winter coat and was dragging a dilapidated shopping trolley behind her, which had one wonky wheel that squeaked on every rotation as she approached. Without hesitation, desperation prompted her to ask the old woman for help. Frances said 'hello, I wonder if you can help me?' The woman stopped and said something she didn't understand, in what she took to be an Eastern European language, possibly Polish, but wasn't sure. The lady looked friendly enough and smiled but looked confused, to overcome their language barrier, Frances in desperation showed her the address on the small, crumpled piece of paper. The lady's smile instantly disappeared, as she pointed with a crooked arthritic index finger to the further most block of flats and said, 'ten tam' (that one there). She then placed her hand on Frances's arm and said 'uważajcie, źli ludzie' (take care, bad people). Frances had no idea what the woman had said but simply smiled, thanked her, and set off with a renewed vigor. As she approached the block of flats, Frances suddenly became aware that there were fewer and fewer people about, she began to feel somewhat isolated and vulnerable. Now feeling the money in her coat pocket, she realised the magnitude of her foolishness. The area looked like the aftermath of a conflict, 'the remnants of a warzone' she thought', with boarded up windows, abandoned furniture, graffiti daubed across walls and rubbish piled high alongside overflowing bins. She started to panic, 'come on get a grip, just go in, get what you want and get out,' she said aloud, trying to overcome her growing fear. Frances knew it wouldn't be safe carrying 'ten pounds' in this area, never mind 'thousands' but it was too late to turn back, it had to be done and the sooner the better. The flats had a main entrance and a lift, that was of course given her current luck, marked 'OUT

OF ORDER' scrawled in 'council-fix-it-later old-style font'. She studied the flat numbers on a grubby and graffitied sign in an attempt to locate Ross's flat, he was number 317, so she assumed it was a trip to the third floor.

A random collection of empty beer cans and litter on the concrete staircases laid a trail towards Ross's flat. As she ascended the stairs an aroma of stale urine and cooking conjoined to create a sickening testament to a grim working-class existence for the residents. Unseen children shouted and screeched as she passed door after door while staring at their numbers hoping that the next one would Ross's flat, but 'no' it was always further on. She couldn't believe that Ross lived here and now recalled some of the squats they had shared many, many years ago, they had been far from palatial, but somehow, she couldn't remember being bothered about their surroundings when they were younger, now she felt appalled at the squalor that surrounded her. On approaching the end of the corridor where Ross's flat had to be, a gang of youths joking and jostling each other, stood blocking the walkway, as she drew closer, they stopped talking and just stared at her, she was terrified and gripped the money tightly in her pocket. Frances knew that she couldn't turn back, and it was important not to show fear, her progress came to a halt as they stood in her way, 'can I get past please' she said. 'What's a posh bird like you doing here, looking for a bit of rough' said one of the youths', the others just laughed and jeered loudly. 'I'm visiting a friend' said Frances, another youth then imitated her voice as he said, 'Oh, I'm visiting a friend don't you know'. Without thinking Frances had a surge of bravado and to her own amazement said, 'just fuck off you little turd' and pushed the youth aside, his friends now laughed and taunted him and ignored Frances as she walked on, her burst of anger and bluster had paid dividends, but her heart was pounding all the same. She located the flat's front door, but there was no need for a key, as the door had been kicked open and the padlock lay twisted and broken on the floor at her feet. She pushed the door tentatively open with the toe of her shoe and as it scraped across the detritus on the floor, it eventually revealed what could only be described as a bomb site. The walls were scrawled with obscenities whose misspelling amply demonstrated a failing educational system. Furniture lay overturned, books were strewn across the floor and with additional pieces of broken crockery and glass it made a colorful if tragic mosaic of pointless destruction. Above all else, Ross had wanted his camera, which for safety he had hidden, she knew where to look but its hiding place, behind a small dirty wall grate had been discovered and mercilessly been ripped from its fastenings. As she moved about the flat her feet crunched on broken glass, she stared around the room with total dismay, anything of any value had been stolen or trashed. Frances bent down and picked up a book about Andy Warhol which lay discarded on the floor. She flicked through its pages, studying the iconic 'pop art' images of Campbell's soup tins, now cast aside like an old shoe. The book had little value in the current neighborhood, but the 'soup' definitely would have, she laughed to herself at the thought. It had been a pointless mission, the flat was completely ransacked, the Nikon had gone, along with anything of even the slightest value. Just as she was about to leave, her eye caught sight of a broken CD cover lying face down on the floor, she picked it up and turned it over and read its title aloud '*Lou Reed Transformer*', she prized it open. The CD was missing but inside was a faded Polaroid photograph of her, Ross, John, and Dave, she stared with shock and amazement that he had kept this, after all these years. The hairs now stood up on the back of her neck, an uncanny feeling swept without warning through her soul, looking at that photo and seeing them all smiling and having fun she almost wanted to return to 'that' past. They all looked so young and happy, Frances was almost moved to tears as she recalled those carefree days when nothing seemed to matter, when worries and problems were the possessions of the old. She turned the photo over and scrawled on the back were the words 'Fran and Ross Xmas 1985', she shook her head and almost felt like crying, but held back the tears as she thought 'we're back together now, that's what matters'. 'Never look back you might trip up' something her grandmother always used to say now flashed through her mind, and she nodded in agreement with its simple wisdom. She smiled to herself, placed the photo back in the CD cover and threw it onto the floor, deciding to leave the past where it belonged. With her mind focused and her conscience clear, she walked out of the flat and back along the landing, she pushed past the gang of youths still in the corridor, without even a tinge of fear. On her way back to her B+B she bought Ross some new clothes and shoes from a work wear shop, the only clothing establishment that was open, not particularly stylish but they would do for now and she reckoned that Ross would see the funny side of it. Now on entering her dreary rented room, and hoping this would be for the last time, she dropped the clothes on the bed and collapsed down next to them both mentally and physically exhausted. She had wrestled with her next decision all the way back from Ross's ransacked flat, but her experience of seeing John with his new woman and his usual level of conceit had pushed her frustration and resolve to the limits. Now taking out her mobile phone she searched for the telephone number of the detective who'd asked about Frank Swift's alibi. Frances now knew that John had been involved with Ross's attack in some way, although probably not physically, but she was convinced he must have orchestrated it in some way and that he should 'suffer' for what he had done. Frances didn't want to speak to the detective directly but hoped that if she rang, maybe just maybe, there would be an answer phone on which an anonymous message could be left. She couldn't use her mobile, as they would be able to trace her phone number, so decided to use the rather grubby looking payphone in the hallway across from her room and then it wouldn't matter if they traced the call, she and Ross would be long gone. The day had taken its toll on Frances and as she sat on a thread bare but comfortable armchair, having returned from making her call, for once it seemed things had gone her way. There had been an answer phone and she had left a short message for the detective, linking John with Ross's attack, hopefully they would follow it up, and give John an uncomfortable time. The thought gave her a 'not inconsiderable' amount of pleasure when she reflected about how she had been mis-treated by him over the years. Furthermore, there was the new woman, the young and attractive Natalie, not that she was jealous of her, it was more that John seemed to have moved his life on quickly and relatively painlessly. Sat with her head in her hands, the euphoria she had felt earlier in the day had been diluted by an exhausting afternoon of mental and physical vicissitudes. Frances knew she had to remain focused, and even though Ross didn't know it yet, they would have to leave tomorrow. Especially if he wanted to avoid being dragged through an awkward investigation into his attack, that could end up with him having to give evidence in court, something she now knew he dreaded for several reasons.

Chapter Twenty-Three
Freemans White

'Analysis of some brands of Lead White are in
fact Adulterated by Lead Sulphate and Calcium'

Greyish to White

Early next morning in Surrey, it was a bright
almost warm winters day, John stood
outside his residence with an air of
conceited confidence in his country tweeds, and
his new 'assistant' looked vivacious even in her
casual jeans and T-shirt. John stared longingly at
her while she was unaware of his gaze and thought
'you lucky sod, she's gorgeous', it made him feel
like a 'thirty-year-old' again, the world was
seemingly at his feet. He oozed confidence and it
felt good, they were preparing to leave for the
gallery, it would be their first day together. He
intended stay in the background as usual and
Natalie would manage the 'front of house' duties,
she would also have her own assistant to carry out
the more mundane admin tasks. As he stood on
the front steps of his small estate, he inhaled a large
amount of country air, it carried the slightest hint
of manure, but it smelt good, it was the earthy
promise of nature. He jingled the keys to his
gleaming white Range Rover, now back from the
paint shop, as he waited for Natalie. She offered

John a new future, gone were the feelings of guilt that had consumed his relationship with Frances, he suddenly felt free to do as he wished without blame or condemnation. As he contemplated the prospect of his newfound good fortune, a metallic grey saloon pulled into the country lane adjacent to his house, then drove aggressively up his drive, hurling gravel and dust into the air as it accelerated towards him. Suddenly it came to an abrupt halt but not before it skidded several feet on the shifting gravel, it stopped just in time with inches to spare, in front of the Range Rover which blocked its path. John stared at the car and attempted to see who was driving, he instinctively shuffled backwards to his front door preparing for a quick escape, the previous grueling and humiliating episode at the hands of Frank Swift flashed through his mind. His head still ached at times as a result of being levelled against his stone fireplace some days earlier. He had one hand on the front door and was just about to step inside and slam it shut when two men simultaneously stepped out of the car, he breathed a sigh of relief on seeing them, it wasn't Swift, his heart calmed and reverted to a normal beat. The two men approached John and one of them said 'Mr. Noble', Mr. John Noble'. John still feeling slightly uneasy and still in two minds whether to dive behind the safety of his front door then said, 'who wants to know, what do you want?' 'We're the Police Mr. Noble', they were now standing in front of John and showing him their warrant cards. Feeling more at ease, he relaxed into his now familiar belligerent stance both physically and psychologically, 'about bloody time' he said, 'that Rolex watch cost me nearly forty grand'. 'Watch?' said the detective sounding and looking confused, John responded facetiously 'yes, you know the thing you put on your wrist to tell the time, I reported stolen, bloody hell, no wonder nothing works in this country anymore'. The detectives looked at each other and shook their heads, 'no, we're here on a different matter, it concerns the violent assault on Mr. Ross Campbell'. Natalie stepped out of the house and appeared from behind John, she had changed into her gallery attire, an elegant black evening style dress and both the detectives' eyes were instantly drawn to her striking presence,' is everything alright John' she said. John was shocked at the mention of Ross's name, he hesitated as he said, 'yeah, things are fine, just give me five minutes Nat', he then motioned for her to go back in the house. John refused to answer any of the detectives' questions, 'where was he on the night of the attack? No comment, 'how long was it since he had seen Ross?' No comment, question after question received the same tedious reply. Eventually, tired and frustrated at John's seemingly unbreakable resolve to remain silent. The detectives gave up and told him if he didn't cooperate, there would be no alternative to a trip down to the station, where they would continue with a full-blown interview, they hoped this tactic might break John's stubbornness. It didn't, he remained unperturbed, he had been 'here' before and Simon, Dave's smart Lawyer had sorted everything for him, and he expected the same scenario again. John was duly taken to the station for further questioning, the Police car passed Frances's taxi going in the opposite direction to the hospital as they neared central London. Just like planets orbiting in the solar system they formed part of a larger whole but never collided or connected, oblivious to each other's presence. Frances stood by the side of the road as her taxi drove off, now with all her possessions by her side, a white retro suitcase and a hold-all containing amongst other things some clothes for Ross. She stared up at the towering edifice of the hospital, foreboding, grey and anonymous and like most people she appreciated hospitals and what they could offer, even though they carried hope and despair in equal measures. Frances had it all worked out, a military plan that Ross's grandfather would have been proud of. Its culmination would be their escape to a small cottage on the south coast that had been used as a holiday home for years by her family since childhood. Now almost robotic in movement, her mind so focussed it was almost pre-programmed as she made her way in through reception, up the stairs and then directly to Ross's ward without even stopping to think. One of the many ancillary staff that worked tirelessly and seemed to cope with any emergency opened the door for her and smiled. Frances said 'hello' and moved directly down the corridor to Ross's room, she walked straight in and was just about to excitedly unveil her escape plan to him. However, she was now confronted with an empty room and bed, there was no sign of Ross. The items that Frances had brought him previously had all been removed from the bedside cabinet. She started to panic, where had he gone? Had the Police been again? She turned abruptly to leave the room and as she did, a tall, grey-haired man in his seventies dressed in a hospital gown stood in front of her blocking the doorway. She smiled but he didn't return her greeting, grim faced he menacingly said, 'where the hell have you been, you stupid girl'. Speechless, she seemed frozen to the spot unable to move or talk. She now started to panic as the man advanced towards her and spoke again. 'You should have been here hours ago, we know what you're up to, what your little game is, the Police are onto you'. Frances stepped back but the man moved closer again, she now spoke 'I need to get out, please just let me ......' but before she could even finish her sentence, he grabbed hold of one of her bags and looked inside and said, 'stolen, all stolen, I knew it, you'll get locked up this time my girl'. Frances's mind went into melt down as thoughts raced through her head, how, how did they find out? Then like a light illuminating and giving shape to a dark mysterious room, she thought it must have been that stupid vengeful call to the police from the B+B. She cursed her stupidity and now knew why Ross wasn't here and it was all her 'fault' yet again. Just as Frances's whole universe seemed to be disappearing into a black hole of unimagined despair, a passing nurse appeared behind the old man and then squeezed past him and into the room, she then spoke 'come on George, let this lovely lady get on, it's time for your pills'. Frances stared at the nurse, who could see the fear on her face, she then smiled and said, 'It's OK, he's just confused but wouldn't hurt you, thinks you're his daughter, come on George' she repeated now leading him away by the arm. The nurse guided the man out of the room and then gave Frances the ultimate reprieve when she said, 'Ross has been moved to an all-male general ward at the end of the corridor, just turn right out of here and walk all the way to the end, it's the last one on the left, you can't miss it'. Frances stood motionless outside the empty room and watched as the nurse led the man away, she dropped her bags to the floor and rested the back of her head against the wall and breathed a huge sigh of relief. Her heart was still racing, she needed to calm herself, now closing her eyes she stood in complete silence. In less than a minute with a renewed determination she moved again with haste down the corridor to locate the men's ward. Tentatively she looked through the room's glass viewing pane, it was full, some men were asleep in bed, others sat on chairs, and then there was a solitary figure stood alone and silhouetted against one of the external windows. He was looking out at a low milky white autumnal sun struggling to be seen in an increasingly grey leaden sky. Frances recognised him immediately, it was Ross and even though he had lost weight, he stood tall with his awkward right foot turned slightly in over, it was unmistakably 'her' Ross. His arms were outstretched upwards, holding either side of the window surround, he looked like some sort of renaissance figure in an ecclesiastical oil painting. She approached and gently touched his shoulder, as he turned round, tears were running down his face, he looked like a frightened and caged animal. He put his arms around her and sobbed on her shoulder, 'it's OK, it's OK' Frances said comfortingly, she kissed him, 'were going Ross, were getting away today, today'.

The train rumbled slowly out of inner London towards the outskirts, it eased past derelict buildings covered with graffiti, while a multitude of anonymous blocks of run-down council flats dominated the skyline. People were crammed in cheek by jowl to support a city infrastructure that offered them little reward in return for their labour. As the train picked up speed the fleeting images became indistinct and the reminders of a past that Ross wanted to leave behind morphed into obscurity. For the first time in years, he felt calm but strangely excited at the same time, he recalled the feeling as a child on a train, the smell of diesel in the train station, the never ending announcements of arrivals and departures, that feeling of a new beginning as you placed your bags up on the luggage rack and settled into your seat, the window seat if you were really lucky. He held Frances's hand tightly, he felt a sense of well-being that had been missing from his life for longer than he could remember. Once underway their escape plan had worked without fault, it had started with a trip to the day room in the hospital, where Ross had put on the new clothes that Frances had brought. He then put his dressing gown back over his clothes and Frances had wheeled him in a chair to have a 'ciggy' with all the other 'patients' that were desperate for a 'smoke' at the front entrance of the hospital. Once outside, he simply stood up and put his arm across Frances's shoulders for support. Chameleon like they blended seamlessly among the myriad of visitors who entered and left the hospital and were soon carried away into the maelstrom of everyday life that surrounded them. Ross was somewhat disorientated, but just being with Frances and now escaping the confines of the hospital and hopefully his past, he felt as though life was now beginning to 'smile' at him. He felt an inner peace and contentment, akin to something he'd felt many years ago. When as a boy he had walked through country lanes on a daily basis back from the local school to the warmth and safety of his grandparent's whitewashed cottage on the West coast of Scotland. As the train sped through verdant green countryside, the past melted away like a discarded ice cream on a hot summers' day, they were both now well and truly on their way. Their initial destination would be Frances's parent's little used holiday cottage, which lay only a few miles from Bournemouth but more importantly was only a stone's throw from the English Channel. Here they would stay for short while and use the time to get their heads 'together' before taking a boat to France to start their new long-awaited life as a couple.

As Ross and Frances guided their lives towards a brighter future, John's was about to take a new direction and not one he could ever have imagined. He was now sitting with Simon, his 'smart' lawyer. 'Tarzan' John mockingly called him, he was clean shaven, tall, blonde, and distinguished looking, he had brushed back wavy hair and represented everything John detested about the middle classes. Simon was the sort of person he'd often seen at launch parties for his many art exhibitions, their middle-class confidence oozed forth and they always spoke in relaxed and measured tones. Their speech never seemed hurried or inconsequential, somehow, 'they' had a way of making people feel inferior without actually having to try too hard. Sporting what John presumed would be an old school or university tie and immaculately dressed in a navy-blue pinstripe suit, he had to admit, albeit grudgingly to himself but not to 'Tarzan', that he definitely looked the part. John thought that if he was impressed surely this would impact upon the hapless detectives that had brought him in for questioning. Simon shook hands with John and they both sat down in the interview room where the detectives had left them alone for their 'confidential' client chat. At least on this occasion John also felt he looked the part in his tweeds and felt reasonably confident that he would be out of this grubby local 'nick' in no time and reckoned if he paid this 'toff' now sat opposite him, enough money, things would be just fine. 'Well, here we are again' said Simon as he glanced around the room,' and then continued 'not exactly the Ritz is it, but its good to see you again John, albeit I imagine we both wished it were somewhere else eh, yes, the environment could be a great deal more convivial'. He then hesitated before continuing, 'and you look somewhat different to the last time we met'. Simon now cast his mind back to John's garb of grungy student, when he'd been arrested for aggravated trespass, 'to be fair though, you had been doing a little night shift work hadn't you', Simon laughed at his little quip, his client didn't. 'You, smug, arrogant bastard, thought John but he needed this posh git on his side, so for once he just bit his tongue and said nothing. Simon opened his briefcase, the clasps clicked confidently and then echoed in the sparsely furnished interview room. He now spoke earnestly, 'I'll not waste anytime John, I imagine you're desperate to get out of here', really meaning that he was. He took out some papers, shuffled them confidently before placing them on the table. 'John, we have plenty of time but what I want to do, first and foremost is to get you out of here'. He continued, not allowing John time to speak, 'I made some brief notes last time I was called in by Dave and I'll run through them, tell me if they are incorrect in any way and add to them if you so wish'. John nodded and said, 'OK let's just get on with it eh', his usual curt manner and impatience returned, 'as you wish' replied Simon, as he eased back his chair and put his hands behind his head. He then stared at the water-stained ceiling tiles and down the walls with their peeling and blistered paint and finally his eyes ended their journey with the coffee-stained grubby carpet, he took a deep breath and thought 'what a toilet, get me out of here' then he spoke. 'So! The last time they had you in this esteemed portal of crime and punishment, they were talking about a minor act of vandalism and trespass, I don't see this as too much of an issue'. John who'd been staring down at the floor lifted his head and said somewhat contritely, 'well, thing is, now they're trying to link me with an attack on some no-hoper that had been vandalising some of my street art'. 'Do you know this ...', Simon's atonic and cultured voice made it seem almost comical as he said 'nooohoeperr'? 'Yes, you could say we have history, he's called Campbell', said John, Simon laughed as he interrupted, 'can't he afford a Christian name then, 'John nodded, and stone faced said, 'Ross', Ross Campbell'. Simon duly noted the name with his fountain pen, its scratching sound was comfortingly official but also irritating to Johns ears. John continued, 'he used to be...', then hesitated before saying, 'a sort of a mate, many years ago, but we fell out over some 'tart' and things turned sour, well you know how it is with women'. 'Indeed, I do, the dangerous femme fatale' said Simon nodding in agreement, 'yes, indeed John dear boy, women can be the bane of a man's simple existence'. John thought 'yeah' that's another way of putting it', as he continued, 'well anyway, I haven't seen Campbell for years and apparently he was 'done over' in the early hours of the morning a few weeks back and they think I had something to do with it'. Simon responded directly and unequivocally 'and did you'? John was taken aback with his frankness and direct question, 'look the more I know, the more I can help you' said Simon, sensing his clients unease, he now stared directly at John, who now hesitated. Could he really trust this person that lived on a completely different planet to himself, on the other hand he needed his help, and he was a top-notch lawyer. 'Well, mmm', John hesitated in mid-sentence, 'I err, may have asked some people to keep an eye on him and maybe, I mean just maybe, they could have given him', he hesitated again before saying 'a little slap'. John continued apprehensively, 'What could I do, Campbell was ruining some valuable street art worth tens of thousands and well you can't just sit back and take it can you'. Simon continued to listen and said nothing until John had finished. 'Tens of thousands you say, yes of course' Simon responded sarcastically, not believing a word of it. John sensing Simon's sarcasm and disbelief sat up straight and with pride said' SPOOKZ, man, that's me' you must have seen my work on TV and in the papers, I'm the unknown artist'. Now 'the penny' or more aptly in Simon's case 'the sovereign' dropped as he looked intently at John and responded. 'Yes of course, of course, it all makes sense, I've read about your exploits in the media, your name is synonymous with graffiti', he quickly corrected himself, 'I mean street art'. He continued, 'I still can't believe it, Dave Hemmings the crafty so and so, he didn't say a thing about you'. Simon pushed back his chair, put his hands behind his head and crossed his ankles as he stretched his legs out from under the table, he couldn't believe it, and sat in a stunned silence. 'Dave and I didn't tell anyone, we couldn't, my anonymity is everything, if the press got wind of this, well, I'd be finished, the 'unknown artist' is an enigma, and it has to stay that way, you get that, don't you' said John firmly. Simon nodded his agreement 'sure, sure thing, Mr. Spookz' said Simon laughing as he did so, 'sorry but I just had to say your name'. He continued, 'Dave even persuaded me to buy one of your, I mean Mr. 'SPOOKZ's works less than a year ago, twenty thousand pounds, a sure-fire bet of an investment he told me'. He irritatingly for John, laughed again, 'I thought I was mad at the time', twenty thousand, Dave you crafty old dog'. John feeling a sense of growing esteem interrupted, 'and he was right, it's probably worth at least double, if not more than that now'. Simon moved towards the table again speaking as he did so, 'OK, OK, John, I appreciate your candidness, but let's concentrate on our current problem, is there anything to link you to', he hesitated and then in a sarcastic tone said 'this mmm... gentleman, Mr. Campbell'. 'Nothing that I know of, I mean, it's not like 'I' did it, is it', said John. Simon in a cautious tone replied, 'no but you must appreciate that if you 'were' and I'm

500

confident it won't get that far, 'were' say charged with inciting this attack, it would be a serious crime, carrying the possibility of a custodial sentence'. John shook his head at his lawyers hypothetical outcome as he said, 'they've got nothing on me'. Simon responded, 'but there is the question of trespass and the vandalism charge'. John sat upright before replying, 'so what, that's nothing is it? I've been done for this sort of stuff loads of times in the past and just got off with nothing more than a slap on the wrist'. 'Things have changed John the authorities now take a take a dim view of recidivism these days', 'what's that in English' replied John, 'constant re-offenders,' said Simon. John just nodded at Simon's response, and remained silent as Simon spoke 'look, they will want to speak to us soon, I think we should be prepared to answer some of their questions and possibly depending on how things go, perhaps admit to the trespass and minor vandalism charge, give Mr. Plod a little carrot of success eh, lets...'. John interrupted Simon, 'that wasn't vandalism, that was art, worth a small fortune, well it would be if I had added my tag to it'. 'Tag, yes, well of course, mmm... quite', said Simon, not really understanding what a 'tag' was, but now knowing John's artistic identity, he was in no doubt as to the value of his 'art' and also his capability to pay an even larger legal fee. Simon with his arms confidently folded, smiled and said, 'I 've got a good feeling about this, yes! Let's admit to 'minor' trespass and let them call it vandalism if it makes the Plods happy'. He continued, 'I'm pretty sure we'll get off with a caution, and as you say, if they don't have any evidence linking you to the attack, I can't see it going any further'. Simon was now in full 'legal flow', 'If you are unsure about any of the questions during the interview, just stay silent and look at me and I will answer for you, but whatever you do, please don't lose your composure'. John nodded and said, 'yeah OK, no problem', Simon smiled and hoped John would indeed do as he asked but had his doubts, having witnessed his clients unpredictable volatility at first hand during their previous Police interview.

John felt confident and his usual bullish and overzealous nature was right near the 'surface' swirling like a dangerous current in a seemingly calm and easy flowing river. With their client chat over two detectives now entered the room. A female detective that John recognised from the last time he was interviewed, and a male detective, who was one of the men that had picked him up from his home earlier that day. The detectives sat down and opened a file in front of them then politely introduced themselves. The female detective instantly recognised the 'type' of lawyer Noble had engaged, 'a twenty-four-carat smart arse', she had seen this condescending barrister type on numerous occasions. She knew he would be as smooth and as slippery as ice and disliked everything about 'his sort'. Right down to the little middle-class idioms they employed, 'sticky wicket', 'straight bat old boy', 'a good egg', basically she saw him as a condescending and irritating 'twat'. Simon's overly confident and measured tone as he introduced himself immediately reinforced the detectives' initial observations and prejudice. However, she was now 'fired up' and ready for him and his rich client, 'let the 'game' begin' she thought. The 'first round' was amiable enough, as they asked the usual preliminaries name, address, and when John stated his address, the female detective delved as she responded, 'mmm ... expensive area, you must be doing very well Mr. Noble and just what is it you do?' She couldn't understand how someone could be picked up for defacing a derelict building in the early hours of the morning but live in such a 'well heeled' area, and as with most of the 'crime' that came across their desks, she now suspected his activities and wealth could be linked to drugs. John sat back in his chair, smiled, and said, 'this and that', 'any particular type, of this and that' the detective replied. 'I'm an artist, OK', John said with his voice slightly raised, Simon glanced John's way, as if to say 'stay calm, this is all part of their little game'. 'Could you elaborate a little more on that for us Mr. Noble, 'you say an artist, what kind of artist' probed the detective. Simon interrupted

'I don't think my client's occupation is particularly relevant', Simon sensed John's obvious discomfort and now was fully aware of the need to maintain his anonymity as an artist. 'On the contrary...' the male detective replied and was immediately interrupted by Simon, who decided to take the lead, 'with respect detective, my client is more than willing to cooperate, but I think your current line of questioning is somewhat pointless, my client has stated his occupation, can we please move on'. Simon looked at his watch to reinforce his view of the irrelevance of their current line of questioning and to further suggest this could all be tied up sooner rather than later. The detective now responded, 'OK then Mr. Noble, can you account for your movements on the night of the thirteenth of September, when a Mr. Ross Campbell was brutally attacked and left unconscious'. John looked in Simon's direction, who nodded his approval to answer, 'I was at home, I always am on a Thursday' replied John, 'funny that, I didn't say what day it was, you must have a very good memory for dates, can anyone corroborate this' the detective replied. 'Shit', John thought, how could he have been so stupid, he could feel panic rising within, confused, unsettled, and without thinking, he responded, 'yes, my, my ...' he hesitated but it was too late to stop, he had to continue, 'my wife was with me!' 'All night? Responded the detective, 'yes! All night, just ask her' barked John. 'You can rest assured that we will check everything, Mr. Noble, we always do', said the detective, sensing John's rising level of unease. Simon felt the need to try and re-dress the balance of the interview as he interjected, 'I think we all agree that my client has answered all your questions and pending your confirmation of the facts, I'm sure you have lots of important issues to attend to, how about we tie this all up and then we can all get on, what do you say'. The detectives looked at each other, then completely ignoring Simon's plea, the male detective said, 'have you..., 'he paused for dramatic effect, 'Mr. Noble, ever had any dealings with a Mr. Frank Swift?' The question shook John and went to his very core, he froze and looked at Simon, who could instantly tell from years at the 'bar' that this was a very unexpected and unwelcome question. Simon very subtly shook his head and John simply said, 'no comment'. Like a dog with a cornered rat, the detectives sensed the beginnings of a kill, disguising surprise was a skill and John hadn't practiced that particular form of 'art' adequately enough. Simon also now felt a little uneasy, his 'bet noir' was not being told everything by his client, but he knew that you had to expect 'the unexpected'. Simon thought this random 'name' was perhaps a stab in the dark by the Police, but he was wrong as the detective returned with a second wave of attack. 'Colm O'Shea, ever heard of this man Mr. Noble', John looked in Simons' direction for the second time in what he saw as a worryingly short space of time. However, Simon 's face was 'Swan' like, calm and collected on the surface but behind the mask his mind raced with thoughts, mainly misgivings about being ill informed, he subtly shifted his eyes and gave a minute shake of his head which said nothing but everything at the same time. John took his cue from Simon yet again, 'never heard of him' said John, however in his mind was the nightmarish vision of the Buffalo like proportions of the menacing O'Shea. Simon could sense that both he and his client were batting on a 'sticky wicket' and knew there were more 'bouncers' coming their way. The line of questioning was too directed, too well informed, it was leading his client somewhere he really didn't want to be, on his way back to the 'pavilion'. Simon now countered with a bold attacking move and stepped out of his 'crease' and confronted the intimidating bowling as he confidently gathered up his 'legal' papers and said, 'well then, is that all? 'He paused and said 'my client has given you some forthright answers, I think we are finished here, unless you intend to press some charges'. Simon knew if they didn't respond positively to this ultimatum, they could expect a very uncomfortable innings. The detective simply ignored this second request and returned to the subject of O'Shea, 'Mr. Noble you say that you have never heard of Colm O'Shea, would it surprise you to hear that he has been charged with the assault on Ross Campbell'. The atmosphere was tense, Simon knew there was a 'Googley' coming, and he was feeling powerless to determine which way it would 'turn'. John on the other hand had a second wind of confidence and arrogance probably gained from the Cocaine he had taken prior to being arrested at his house. Without thinking he launched into an attack of his own, not just stepping out of his 'crease' but moving halfway down the wicket, 'why are you still hassling me over this? I've done nothing wrong, apart from minor bloody trespass which we went through last time'. John continued his rant 'what about me, where are my rights, what about that goon of a night watchmen that kicked the crap out of me', he continued unabated,' what have you done about that? It's me that should be pressing charges, look you've got nothing on me, and as my 'brief' says, just stop wasting everybody's time'. After his outburst John stood up forcibly and thrust his chair backwards, its metal feet scraping and screeching across the floor, he ended his rant with, 'I'm going, I've had enough of all this crap'. Simon also stood up hurriedly in an attempt to calm John down and he said, 'as you can see officer, my client is rightly and understandably frustrated, John, please take your seat again'. He acceded to Simons request and reluctantly slumped back onto his chair, 'now, is there anything else officer? Said Simon authoratively'. Having seen John's explosive reaction to his questions, the detective knew he was onto something, and like the most tenacious of Jack Russell's, he had hold of the Rats' neck and wasn't going to let go. The detective now leaned forward as he said, 'OK then Mr. Noble, lets return to the night you were arrested for trespass and vandalism, why exactly where you there?'. 'Not this shit again' snapped John, Simon immediately looked in John's direction and shook his head, 'No comment!' barked John. The detective continued, 'can I refresh your memory then, you were caught spraying graffiti', John interrupted 'art you imbecile, its street art'. The detective laughed wryly before continuing 'whatever you say Mr. Noble, to you it's art, to me it's just mindless scrawl, can you recall the subject matter of the graffiti, sorry I mean art' he said sarcastically, 'it was pretty unusual wasn't it ?',John replied immediately, 'I dunno, how am I supposed to remember every bit of *art* I create', he now emphasised the word 'art' in retaliation to the detectives jibe , then just laughed as he shook his head. The detective was un-perturbed and continued, 'The graffiti had a title, didn't it?', 'no idea, what you're on about' snapped John. 'Let me refresh your memory then, it was '*Art of Revenge*', that's what you sprayed above it', do you remember now?' John initially sat in silence then shook his head and said, 'no comment'. The detective continued his probing, 'your 'art' depicted someone being assaulted and the hand of the assailant which is the focal point of your image carried a very distinctive tattoo, do you remember that then?' The questions were growing in intensity and John, feeling under increasing pressure sat in silence, he couldn't think, his body temperature had started to rise to an uncomfortable level. He felt lightheaded, the feeling became unbearable, needing help, in desperation he looked in Simon's direction like a floundering puppet whose arms and legs had suddenly become detached from the cords that gave them support and he was crashing earthwards. Before Simon could utter a word the hammer blow came, 'I'll refresh your memory shall I, it was a Scorpion tattoo, that's pretty unusual and distinctive, isn't it? I mean quite a random choice, don't you agree Mr. Noble, what made you choose that?'. John shrugged his shoulders and felt as though he were on his own as he said, 'so what, a tattoo's, a tattoo isn't it, artists license that's all'. The detective tightened his grip on his Rat, 'Well not quite, here's the problem for us, Colm O'Shea, Mr. Campbells' assailant also has a prominent tattoo and guess what it is?' John remained silent again, 'go on, just have a wild stab in the dark' said the detective sarcastically', no reply came, 'well, shall I put you out of your misery, it's a Scorpion, major coincidence that, don't you think?'. Simon could see John's middle stump cartwheeling out of the ground, comprehensively clean bowled, however John was a little slower at picking up the delivery. 'Either this is the most amazing coincidence Mr. Noble, a one in a million, if you were a betting man I'd say, my point is, you know who attacked Mr. Campbell and furthermore we believe you instigated that attack'. John without thinking allowed years of anger and vitriol to overtake him as blurted out 'so what, he's a nothing, a nobody, a waste of space'. The detective responded by slamming his hand on the table as he said, 'don't you realise, he could have died, and what's more...'. Simon hurriedly interrupted, 'I need to speak to my client alone'. 'There'll be plenty of time for that', after we have charged your *client* said the detective, who now felt a supreme sense of smugness at having ensnared John Noble and sent his smart-arse lawyer back to the Pavilion for a 'duck'.

Chapter Twenty-Four
Painting by numbers

Six months later ....

Frances handed yet another satisfied customer a carefully wrapped, framed photograph entitled, *The Harbour at Pont-Aven*. In the image sunlight glinted and swirled on the water like electricity, the brightly summer-coloured sails of the yachts bellowed with nature's energy, it captured the very essence of the idyllic French village. The girl smiled and handed over thirty Euros which Frances duly placed in the till, the girl then turned and left the small but intriguing gallery that nestled in a cobbled street just off the harbour, that proudly displayed a range of photographs and paintings by Ross Campbell. Frances could just see a glimpse of Ross, who stood to the left of the shop doorway as the customer left. He had put on weight, looked calm and 'free' and was a man at ease with life, an image that couldn't have been further removed from the gaunt and troubled soul Frances had seen months before in the hospital after his attack. As usual he was spraying yet another 'tag', but this time it wasn't on some peeling plaster wall of a disused building site or railway arch in the dead of night, 'no' they were now for tourists to take away, their very own bespoke 'tag' at a bargain price of fifty Euros, this was the first time Ross had ever made money from his art. He still didn't particularly care about money, but he appreciated its importance in funding a new lifestyle for them in their own little gallery. As Frances closed the shop door behind her, she stood outside and could just smell the refreshing and invigorating sea air. Standing proudly behind Ross as he spray painted on his easel, a constant stream of curious tourists stopped to watch him, some just admiring the skill and fluidity with which he created a 'tag', others looking for a souvenir to take home with them. She put her hand proudly on Ross's shoulder, he immediately turned around, spray can in hand and smiled, the aroma of coffee and freshly baked bread from local café's filled the air. Ross's smile said it all, he couldn't believe his luck, for once he had everything he could possibly have dreamed of, in fact he had more, he had Frances, someone he had often thought was lost to him forever. Ross and Frances had spent a nervous two weeks in hiding at her parents' small cottage near Bournemouth. A chance meeting with a local fisherman had ended in a deal costing them five hundred pounds each, which had seen them make a short anonymous sea crossing in his small fishing boat to France. It had always been Ross's dream to end up in an artist's colony and this combined with Frances's flair for business meant the gallery with its bijou one bedroomed flat above seemed to be made for them and their new life together. Ross hadn't attended the trial or given any evidence, he had eventually been contacted by the French police but by the time they had found him the trial in England had been completed in his absence. All ties with their old lives seemed disconnected, they still communicated with Val who seemed settled and contented with her 'café life' again. They had invited her for a holiday to see their new lives, as they both felt that they owed her a huge debt of gratitude, but strangely, they thought she hadn't taken them up on their offer.

As Ross and Frances stood in the warm afternoon sun, they contemplated shutting the gallery earlier than usual and going for a walk down to a little bistro for a drink. Meanwhile John Noble back in England was preparing for a very different kind of afternoon. John had received a twelve-month prison sentence for his part in Ross's attack and his 'brief' had advised him to be cooperative with the prison authorities and volunteer for any 'Prison activities'. Simon thought any seemingly selfless acts of goodwill could possibly help reduce his sentence by a good few months. During his trial the papers had exposed John's true identity, with his background now known he had been asked by the prison Governor to help fellow inmates by organising and leading a 'beginners art class'. John stood in the makeshift art room, which had formally been an admin office, no longer used it had peeling blue gloss paint on the upper part of the wall and a forest green on the lower, a rudimentary suspended polystyrene ceiling with rusty water stains completed the picture, it provided an environment not wholly suited to the pursuit of the finer arts. John asked one of the staff if the class was still on, as no one had turned up yet, the officer simply shrugged his shoulders and said nothing. John felt more than a little nervous about the prospect of teaching a room full of prisoners but as Simon had said 'be purposeful and show willing dear boy, it will pay dividends, and may even reduce your sentence'. Useless posh 'tosser' John had thought at the time, however Simon was convinced he'd got his client a good deal with his sentence, but as usual John was unconvinced. The officer now spoke to John, 'depends, it's a numbers game, sort of 'painting by numbers' you could say', the guard laughed at his little quip, then continued, 'you need a minimum of fifteen to start it, then if they drop out which they normally do, it doesn't matter just so long as you start with fifteen'. John moved to the front of the room, an array of mis-matched desks and chairs were scattered about. On one desk lay a rudimentary selection of brushes and tubes of paint, some of which already had half their life squeezed out of them, they now lay awaiting their 'final' fate. As John waited, one by one a somewhat eclectic range of prisoners entered, he nodded to each of them in turn and some returned his acknowledgement. He recognised some of the faces but not many, it was a large prison and you kept 'yourself' very much to yourself, to avoid any unnecessary interest or trouble. John anxiously counted the men as they entered the room, it was slow to start but gradually gained in numbers, eventually rising to fourteen, 'just one more needed' he dreaded the thought. The men talked amongst themselves as John waited and hoped that the required number wouldn't be reached, and he could be spared his teaching ordeal. He had his last 50p in life's virtual slot machine and the reels of destiny were spinning. His eyes were fixed on the entrance to the room, then just as it seemed that the starting quota wouldn't be met, the reels stopped one by one, Cherry, Bell, then a Lemon, he was out of luck! Now an enormous figure of a man, partly in shadow, stood in the doorway with his arms outstretched and his hands resting on the upper parts of the frame. John initially gave the prisoner a contemptuous glare before the fifteenth attendee stepped into the room. His glare rapidly turned into a look of horror as the prisoner stared straight back at him with a wry smile. John's up to now 'easy ride' in prison was just about to become 'very bumpy' as his fifteenth student was no other than 'the big man' AKA Frank Swift.

Printed in Great Britain
by Amazon

27327742R00293